Romantic Suspense

Danger. Passion. Drama.

Tracking The Truth
Dana Mentink

Rocky Mountain Survival
Jane M. Choate

MILLS & BOON

Dana Mentink is a nationally bestselling author. She has been honored to win two Carol Awards, a HOLT Medallion and an RT Reviewers' Choice Best Book Award. She's authored more than thirty novels to date for Love Inspired Suspense and Harlequin Heartwarming. Dana loves feedback from her readers. Contact her at danamentink.com.

Visit the Author Profile page
at millsandboon.com.au.

Tracking The Truth
Dana Mentink

MILLS & BOON

TRACKING THE TRUTH
© 2024 by Dana Mentink
Philippine Copyright 2024
Australian Copyright 2024
New Zealand Copyright 2024

First Published 2023
First Australian Paperback Edition 2024
ISBN 978 1 038 90575 8

ROCKY MOUNTAIN SURVIVAL
© 2024 by Jane M. Choate
Philippine Copyright 2024
Australian Copyright 2024
New Zealand Copyright 2024

First Published 2024
First Australian Paperback Edition 2024
ISBN 978 1 038 90575 8

MIX
Paper | Supporting
responsible forestry
FSC® C001695
www.fsc.org

Published by
Harlequin Mills & Boon
An imprint of Harlequin Enterprises (Australia) Pty Limited
(ABN 47 001 180 918), a subsidiary of HarperCollins
Publishers Australia Pty Limited
(ABN 36 009 913 517)
Level 19, 201 Elizabeth Street
SYDNEY NSW 2000 AUSTRALIA

Cover art used by arrangement with Harlequin Books S.A.. All rights reserved.

Printed and bound in Australia by McPherson's Printing Group

If ye then be risen with Christ, seek those things which are above, where Christ sitteth on the right hand of God. Set your affection on things above, not on things on the earth. For ye are dead, and your life is hid with Christ in God.

—*Colossians* 3:1–3

DEDICATION

To Susan S., a woman of God who encouraged so many.
You will be missed.

Chapter One

Roman Wolfe lay on his back in the tall grass, cloaked by darkness, invisible. Even the sliver of moon was cooperating, playing peekaboo behind the clouds. He used a special remote to trigger his car to unlock, put his finger to his lips and whistled once, a piercing signal that sliced the winter night in this northernmost fringe of California, a stone's throw from the Oregon border.

It's all up to you now, Wally. Don't let me down.

The lake water rippled, counterpoint to his thoughts. He'd left the two-year-old black-and-tan bloodhound in his car a mile away. Now it was up to the headstrong Wally to let himself out of the vehicle and do his thing. No sweat on the first part. Wally had mastered opening the car door his first day with Roman. After that, the dog had proved difficult to train, but he'd chalked that up to the ownership transition.

Wally's first adopter was swept up in the excitement and prestige of possessing a bloodhound, without considering the steep challenges of the breed. No blessing is free, his uncle Jax used to say. He dismissed that thought immediately.

He breathed in the frigid air, recalling his days as a navy master-at-arms, patrolling the base in the wee hours with various dog companions. Those days were full, planned, monotonous sometimes, but always purposeful. His seven months as a civilian had been an adjustment when he'd come home to Whisper Valley, a skip and jump from Oregon's Crater Lake. Home? *Yes. How long before you finally believe it?* He forced away the uncertainty he'd probably never outgrow.

Home is the people who chose you. He'd been an unofficial part of the Wolfe clan since he was a sixteen-year-old runaway. Beth Wolfe had officially adopted him when he'd returned home on leave on his birthday at age twenty-two. It was still surreal. He'd blubbered like a baby. How many people actually got adopted as adults? Plenty more, if Beth Wolfe had her way.

"You're a Wolfe now," she'd said with tears in her eyes.

Part of the pack. Now he and his adopted

siblings all worked for the fledgling Security Hounds investigation business, Beth's dream. He'd made it his dream too.

He cocked his ear at a sound. Wally? No, surely not yet. It was coming from the direction of the lake. A motorboat at this hour? He could check the time but he didn't want to give Wally any help by way of a light. Not that it would matter since Wally was scent-driven, basically a nose with a dog attached. Still it had to be closing in on midnight. Roman had chosen the ridiculous hour so there would be no possibility of interruption from a fisherman or hiker and no danger if the dog went wandering instead of completing his training exercise.

The nearest road was a mile away, which was important since Wally, like all their other bloodhounds at Security Hounds, had *zero* street sense. Put an interesting odor in front of that dog and he'd scamper across a six-lane highway without a backward glance. Typical bloodhound, except for the fact that Wally was proving to be much less interested in doing his job than his canine counterparts. Each one of Roman's four Wolfe siblings was teamed with a highly trained bloodhound, which they deployed when needed in the course of their detective duties.

But Wally? It was looking like he was going to be assigned to the couch to nap and nowhere else if he didn't start shaping up.

The quiet washed over him again, along with the chill. The January temps in this untraveled section of Whisper Valley were generally enough to discourage casual outdoorsmen, but there were diehards, like himself and his brother Garrett, who might be out and about at such an odd hour. He breathed deeply of the pure night air. Whisper Valley was a phenomenal place to raise and train champion bloodhounds…and to headquarter an exclusive investigations business. And an excellent place to call home, if he could only make his heart accept it.

He mentally ticked away the moments while listening for the odd boat noise, which he couldn't dismiss from his mind. Someone night fishing? In January? With a motorboat? Maybe it was his navy training that made his instincts prickle. That and the fact that they'd already seen a lot of weird stuff in their inaugural year in the investigations biz.

He batted a flying insect away from his buzz-cut hair.

Why don't you let it grow out? his sister Stephanie always suggested.

He'd told her he liked the low-maintenance cut, but it was an evasion. He buzzed it because it was red and he'd been constantly teased in school, in his half dozen foster homes, at work, until the moment the military had shaved it off for him, like they'd detached him from his less than stellar past. *Thank you, Navy.*

Pain stabbed at him, but it was not the pain of leaving the military six months prior. He'd been ready to start a new challenge. It was the pain of betrayal from the man who'd pointed him to the service, after whom he'd modeled his life, the one who'd made him believe in himself again: Theo Duncan. Theo, who'd confessed to shooting and gravely wounding an unarmed man.

The invisible knife gouged his gut again. God had shown Roman one more time that he had no reason to trust any man alive and no woman either, for that matter, except Beth Wolfe and her other four children.

A splash...louder now. A fish? Trout could get to be a pretty hefty size, which could account for such a noise. He sat up and checked his precision watch. Wally should have found him by now. Another failed mission. Why would this dog not do the job for which he was born and bred?

His phone vibrated.

"Well?" Stephanie said.

"Wally's a dud. He only finds when he feels like it."

"Wally is sensitive. He's had a rocky start. Besides, you offended him by making such a big fuss about breakfast yesterday."

"He literally snatched the scrambled eggs and hashbrowns off my plate in the space of thirty seconds. He'd been planning the whole theft, waiting for me to turn around to get the ketchup from the fridge." Roman realized he sounded ridiculous.

"At least he left you the fried tomatoes."

"Good thing he doesn't like tomatoes or I wouldn't have gotten those either." There was still no sign of the gangly hound galumphing through the grass. He wouldn't admit it, but he was beginning to worry. He checked the GPS tracker affixed to the dog's collar. "Unbelievable. He's still sitting there in the car. He hasn't even budged."

Stephanie's guffaw was so loud he had to hold the phone away from his ear. "I cannot wait to tell everyone about this."

By dawn, Stephanie would have told the rest of his siblings. Chase, Garrett, Kara and even Beth would be enjoying his failure. He couldn't help but smile. They were the only people he'd ever allowed to laugh at him, which gave him permission to laugh at himself. "I need to go back before he decides to try to drive the car himself."

"Might be a better driver than you."

"Funny. We'll talk later about assigning me a different dog."

"Don't think so, bro."

He forced back the frustration. "I can't work on cases unless I have a reliable dog."

"Wally can't get enough of you. He wouldn't survive the breakup and he's already lost one owner. Besides, we have a big event to prep for, remember? Not the time for changes." She disconnected.

Roman brushed a wet leaf from his ski cap and took a step. Now he heard distinctly the whine of a motorboat in the still air. Maybe a muttered oath? As if the person was struggling with the engine? Rising hairs tickled the back of his neck. He considered. Mind his business and hustle back to Wally? Or satisfy his curiosity and check out the lake?

One more glance at the GPS assured him

that Wally wasn't going anywhere. He might as well indulge in a little field trip. He shouldered his pack. The night was dry, at least. A recent rain had softened the ground so he avoided a spot of mud as he jogged toward the water, an easy path that ended in a stop at the bluff where he could get a vantage point. The lake was fed by river water that traveled from Oregon's Upper Klamath Lake and pooled and glimmered below, deep and still.

Until he caught the gleam of a boat bobbing on the surface.

From his backpack, he fished out a pair of night-vision binoculars.

He almost dropped them in shock as a woman leaped from the bow of the boat.

No, not leaped, his brain corrected. She'd been thrown.

And he'd gotten a millisecond glimpse of her hands outstretched, bound by a thick strip of tape.

Roman grabbed his pack and took off at a dead run.

Cold slammed Emery Duncan like a collapsing brick wall. Seconds ticked by. As she swam into consciousness, she struggled to process the screaming messages from her body. Her senses were fogged, thick and slow. At first the only thing her brain could interpret was intense discomfort, of being frozen an inch at a time, a presence all around her, thick as her fear, like being swallowed in a wet gulp. *You're in the water.* Panic choked her as she struggled to figure out which way led to the surface. Why couldn't she see? Move her arms? Her lips were held shut. Terror spurred her to jerk and thrash. A breath, that was the only thing she was fighting for, one single breath. She writhed like an eel.

Her head broke the surface and she tried to gulp in some air, realizing that her mouth was sealed with duct tape. Water burned her nose as she inhaled. Her feet and hands were also bound tightly together. Helpless, she tried to stay afloat. Still she could see nothing. Now she understood her eyes were covered by a soggy piece of material. She reached her tethered hands to try to shove the blindfold aside. It was too tight and she only succeeded in crumpling it enough that she could detect the barest sliver of darkness. Again she was sinking, the water lapping her chin and edging closer to her nose.

Was she in a pool? No, the water was far too

cold and she caught the fetid smell of vegetation. How had she gotten here? Slowly her brain provided a spark of memory. She'd been thrown from a boat only a moment before the engine had sputtered off. It must still be close by.

As she fought down the panic, she could detect no sound of the motor over her thrumming heartbeat and the wind-rippled water, only a muffled clank as the captain tried to restart the craft. A new level of fear threatened to overwhelm her. As soon as her attacker got the boat working again...

God, please... She didn't want to die, her life silently pushed out by the water filling her lungs, swamping her senses. Again, she struggled to float away from the vessel, her bound hands and feet working against her. Her father had told her many times about the navy training he'd done as a much younger man. *Slow is smooth, smooth is fast*, she could almost hear him say.

Immediately she stopped thrashing and eased onto her back. Floating, more or less. If she could figure out which way to shore... Ripples of wind driven water broke over her face. The strong smell of wet earth made her nostrils flair. Left, she decided. Solid land lay in that direction. If she wriggled and dolphin-kicked, she might make it.

No, she *would* make it. Theo Duncan didn't raise a quitter, no matter his own tarnished legacy. After pulling a breath through her nose, she oriented herself toward what she believed was the edge of the pond or lake. It was a matter of making slow progress while her attacker was busy with the boat, resting when she needed to, as long as it took to get herself to a depth where she could stand. She wasn't going to die, not now, not this way, with so many unresolved issues in her life. Not with Ian depending on her. Was that a motor sound?

One awkward kick sent her floating along. Another kick and she was getting some momentum.

You got this, Emery. Whoever had thrown her in would have to jump in himself to get to her. As long as she kept moving away she might make it.

Then she felt movement near her. She froze.

Splash. Not a rodent or fish. The two-footed kind of animal.

Someone was coming for her, closer and closer. Though she hadn't detected anyone leaping from the boat, it must be the person who'd dumped her in the water, who wanted her dead. Or an accomplice. Her scream was trapped behind her taped lips.

Desperately she tried to shove herself farther toward land, but a splash of water broke over her, burning her eyes and nose, leaving her momentarily unable to breathe. There was no option to keep it slow when she was going to be caught so she thrashed for all she was worth to get away from her pursuer.

The effort was futile, but she fought on until she felt hands pulling at her. She struck out, but her wrists were captured in a large calloused palm. Only one more chance left. She stopped wriggling, let him get close, and then slammed her head forward as hard as she could. Her move hit the mark, and in spite of her own pain, she rejoiced when she heard a male grunt. She was released.

The celebration lasted only a moment. Then he was reaching for her again, tearing at the blindfold. A man's face appeared, indistinct in the cloud-filtered moonlight, and so close. Where had he come from? The boat? She tried to thrash away.

"Shhh," the man said. "Guy's still out there but he's having motor trouble. Hold still, would you? You almost broke my nose. I'm trying to help."

Help her? She scanned frantically. She was in a lake or maybe a pond, quiet and overgrown. No nearby cars, no civilization. What were the chances this stranger just happened to be in the area when someone was doing their best to kill her? She reared back as he reached for her.

"I'm a good guy, mostly." The whisper was deep and commanding. It felt as if she'd heard it before. "I'm going to untape your mouth if you'll let me."

Let him? What choice did she have? She remained taut as wire while he peeled the tape away from her lips. It left them raw and torn.

"Stay still. I'll tow you to shore."

"Untape my hands first." At least she could defend herself from him…or anyone else.

"I have a knife in my backpack and I can cut you loose on shore. You're getting close to hypothermic. Priority one is getting out of the water before the guy gets his motorboat back in action."

She wanted to resist, to insist that *he* do as *she* wanted, but she was so cold it felt as if her heart might not continue to beat. *Who are you?* All she could make out was a set of wide shoulders, close-cropped hair and heavy brows crimped with concentration or maybe suspicion. At the moment it didn't matter who he was. This man was all that stood between her and certain drowning.

Still her nerves hopped like frogs in springtime. "He tried to kill me."

"Float on your back. We'll move faster."

On her back? She knew she had to trust this man but it was difficult to put herself in such a vulnerable position. "I..."

They both jerked as a motor sputtered to life.

She tried again to yank her wrists free of the tape but it held fast.

Helpless was her first feeling.

Terror was the second.

Chapter Two

Roman twisted to track the shadow of the motorboat speeding across the water. The searchlight fixed to the bow blinded him. He swam between the woman and the oncoming boat. Bound as she was hand and foot, she wouldn't be able to escape to shore, even with Roman's interference. He had to take a chance.

"Stop!" he shouted. Maybe the guy would back off if he knew his victim wasn't alone anymore.

The harsh light almost blinded him, but he snagged a quick glance at the woman who was mercifully still treading water. Seconds ticked by and the vessel churned forward, engine obscenely loud. It did not slow.

He heard her scream for help. Waste of breath. There would be no one anywhere close. No option but one. Time to play offense. He'd been doing that since he was a kid. The boat was close enough now he could almost make out the silhouette of the person standing at the wheel. Close-fitting hat, jacket, face swallowed up by darkness. A mask? Gloves on the hands?

A moment longer...

The boat continued to plow straight at them.

When the vessel was only a few feet away, Roman surged to the side and grabbed the starboard gunnel. His weight hauled the boat low, jerking but not slowing it. He yanked with all his strength and got one leg over the side. One more hoist and he'd be aboard and the moment after that he'd take control of the situation, pull the kill switch cord, stop the boat, deal with the driver.

Too aggressive, he heard Theo, his former mentor, say. *That's what gets you into trouble.* Yeah, well Theo should have followed his own advice. The boat swerved as the driver twisted the wheel. The sudden motion bucked Roman back and he grappled for hold. The aggressor swung out a hand, curled around a sharp blade.

He deflected the blow away from his face, but the blade nicked his forearm. The cold delayed the pain and Roman didn't lose his grip on the side. His weight caused the vessel to veer off course in a wobbling orbit. At least he'd bought the woman more time.

Grabbing at his attacker, he got a handful of jacket and pulled. The knife skittered loose and he heard it clatter to the boat's keel. The attacker came up with an oar and smashed it down a second after Roman pulled his fingers away. The sound clanged through the night, the oar impacting metal instead of flesh and bone.

He regrouped and tried again to heave himself over. This time the oar caught him in the throat.

Gagging, he toppled backward with a splash.

"Look out," he heard the woman shout, but he was struggling for breath, trying not to inhale the water while keeping himself afloat. The driver cranked the throttle, spun the wheel and bore down on him. He was out of options. He'd have to hope he was fast enough to get out of the way and try to reboard in spite of his bleeding arm and labored breathing. Chances were slim to none. He hoped the woman would at least make it to shallower water, maybe hide in the rushes, or scream for all she was worth. Fury bit him like a viper.

There was a mighty splash from the direction of the shore. His pulse roared in his ears mingling with the sound of...barking? Incredulous, he saw Wally churning through the water, enormous ears flapping like sails, moving with all the ferocity of a charging rhino.

"Wally, retreat." He didn't want Wally running into the attacker's knife or getting his skull cracked open by an oar. But his words were drowned out by the barking.

Wally foamed the water as he careened straight for the boat. His big front paws made contact with the stern. He heaved his unwieldy body upward. The dog was actually attempting to climb aboard. Roman commanded him again to desist but there was a high-pitched protest from the throttle as the driver put the boat into Reverse. Wally was shaken loose and fell back into the swirling lake. He barked at a deafening volume until the boat vanished from sight.

After one final earsplitting howl, Wally spiraled around and swam for Roman. He flopped his big paws on Roman's shoulders, swabbing him all over with a sloppy pink tongue. "Easy there, Walls." Roman was still breathing hard. His knife wound was leaking blood into the water. He was relieved to see over Wally's flank that the woman had managed to get her wrists free somehow, her expression mirroring his own incredulity.

"You done good, boy." Roman hugged the hundred-thirty-pound baby. Wally whined and tried to stick his egg-sized nose in Roman's ear, but Roman eased him aside. "Reward time for you later, I promise. We got a situation to deal with right now, big fella." Wally managed to get in one more massive lick under Roman's chin.

They swam to the woman who was shivering violently. Wally shoved his saggy face in hers.

"You're a hero dog." Her voice was high and shaky.

Wally shook his ears as if to agree.

She eyed Roman's torn sleeve, flesh gleaming white in the gloom. "You're cut."

Her voice sounded so familiar. Odd. "Minor. Got to get out of here before boat guy comes back. Someone wants you dead. Know why that is?" Not the time for interrogation, he chided himself.

When she didn't reply, he extended his un-injured elbow toward her, but Wally inserted himself right next to her. She held onto his harness and the dog immediately paddled toward the bank, easily towing the woman in his wake. Roman could only shake his head.

"So you won't follow a scent like you're 'sposed to but you'll carry out a full-blown water rescue operation?" he muttered. Wally sailed along without hesitation, his long tail like a rudder. Bloodhound bodies were not built for aquatic pursuits, but Wally didn't seem to know that.

With one last look around for any sign of the motorboat, Roman swam along behind them trying to let his uninjured arm do the lion's share of the work. The woman let go of Wally's harness as the water shallowed out. She hopped over the mud onto semi solid ground and fell to her knees. He slogged out after her and they were both treated to a sprinkle bath as Wally shook the moisture from his coat.

Roman's arm began to sting and he noted the blood was trickling from the wound. That could wait. He eased close to the woman, careful not to spook her. She was picking at the tape that encircled her ankles. He fished a penknife from his backpack and cut through the restraints before he pulled out a silver emergency blanket and offered it to her. Trying to keep his cell phone dry, he dialed his sister and continued to watch for signs of the returning boat.

"No signal. Must be in a dead spot. Can you

make it to my car? It's about a mile from here. I'll keep trying to call as we go."

Her teeth chattered. "I can make it."

"Injured? Bleeding at all?"

She shook her head. "No."

"Who are you?"

"Emily," she said after a moment of hesitation. "Emily Bancroft."

The name wasn't familiar. Why did she remind him of someone? He pulled a roll of bandages from his pack and awkwardly tried to apply one to his arm. He was about to use his teeth to help rip the packaging when she reached out and did it for him. Her fingers were trembling, but long and elegant, and she knew exactly what to do.

"Medical training?" he asked.

"Traveling nurse, but before that my father taught me the basics."

Nurse. Her father. That's when the pieces slid into place. The familiar voice, slender fingers, determination to do it herself. He stood there, out-and-out staring. She must have realized something was wrong because she gathered the blanket tighter around herself. "What is it?"

"I know you by another name."

She cocked her head, a fleeting sliver of

moonlight gilding her heart-shaped face. Her eyes were dark silver but he knew in the daylight they were blue-green. Last time he'd seen those eyes, six months before, they had been unrecognizable, filled with the same disbelief and anguish he'd felt.

"I'm Roman Wolfe." The moment lingered long and taut between them. *Your father was my hero*, his heart added, *until he confessed to attempted murder*. The comment was unnecessary. She knew exactly who he was. They would always be tethered together in the time before both their worlds had tilted.

"You're..." She pulled the blanket tighter. The words dried up.

What was there to say? He felt the yank of guilt in the wake of a fresh stab of betrayal. Her father had wrecked him and he'd about-faced for his own sanity. He'd had no other choice. Not a day had gone by that he hadn't wondered about Emery. Now, here she was like someone who'd stepped out of a dream. "Why are you using a fake name?" He stopped himself. "Never mind. We should get to my car." He hoisted the pack. Wally clambered to his feet and set off down the trail.

After a long moment that made him wonder if she would follow, she hurried after the dog.

Emery Duncan's dad confessed to shooting a man. Now she was going by Emily Bancroft.

Did it have anything to do with why someone had tried to kill her?

Emery settled into the seat of Roman's pristine old Bronco, Wally lolling in the back. She recalled their first meeting, her fifteen-year-old self watching Roman arrive in town, the sixteen-year-old red-haired rebel who worked on the Wolfes' ranch where her father helped out sometimes. Her dad mentored Roman, helped him sign up for the Navy when he was of age. Privately she'd grieved when Roman had enlisted and they'd lost contact.

And she hadn't seen him again.

Until two days after her father confessed to shooting local businessman Mason Taylor at the Taylor estate, where Emery's sister, Diane, lay crumpled on the lower floor after plummeting from the balcony above.

Theo Duncan's confession was concise. He'd hated Mason's brother, Lincoln Taylor, he said, detested him for the way he'd treated his daughter Diane when she'd shown up with a baby. Diane had been in a relationship with the married Lincoln Taylor. Hilary, Lincoln's wife at the time, was nothing but scathing toward Diane also. Emery understood. Her sister rarely considered the consequences of her destructive actions.

But it was her father who'd confessed to plotting to kill Lincoln and nearly murdering Mason instead. Diane had tried to stop him and she'd fallen. Mason had survived, though he couldn't remember the actual shooting.

Her dad's confession.

The arrest.

Diane unresponsive in a hospital bed.

Diane's three-month-old son, Ian, in the arms of a social worker.

It was all a painful, horrifying blur. One day had bled into the next until the September afternoon Emery had found herself fumbling to unlock the door of the cabin in Whisper Valley where she and Diane had grown up with their father after their parents' divorce. Her fingers refused to cooperate. The keys fell. She'd turned to see Roman Wolfe watching her as she retrieved them. He'd approached in that lanky lope of his that always made her think he belonged on horseback or the heaving deck of a ship. She hadn't even known he was stateside. His civilian clothes confused her.

Emery.

Even before he'd spoken, the question had shone on his face, intense as the beacon on a lighthouse. *"Is it true?"*

She'd known what he meant. *Is it true that your father shot Mason in cold blood?*

No, she'd wanted to say, to shout, to scream. The truth stood between them like a poisonous snake ready to strike.

I read in the paper he…confessed, Roman had said finally.

I don't care what you read. Dad couldn't have done it. Her heart yearned to hear him say he didn't believe it either, that the evidence couldn't be true, that he, like she, stood by Theo Duncan no matter what.

But Roman's expression had shattered, the hurt showing almost as profound as her own.

Almost.

Roman had lost a mentor, a father figure.

She'd lost…everything. She could still hear the rattle of the door after she'd let herself in and slammed it shut against him. Had he knocked, she might have let him in. But he hadn't. And that was that.

Her aching limbs brought her back to the present and she couldn't control the shivering. He cranked the heat.

"The hospital is an hour-plus from here, but Beth is…"

"A nurse, I know." She knew Beth Wolfe, his adoptive mom and a retired air force flight nurse and they'd chatted about the profession. "No hospital necessary."

He didn't look at her. "All right. I'll take you to the ranch."

"I don't need—" She stopped. But what did she need? Her temples throbbed and her thoughts were hazy.

"We'll call the cops as soon as we get there."

She groaned inwardly. The police had done nothing to help uncover the truth about her father. They took him at his word. He'd confessed, after all. What kind of help would they offer her? She wanted to believe he'd been protecting Diane with his confession. Had to be.

He shot a glance at her dark bob, which had been natural blond when he'd last seen her. "You dyed your hair and you're using an alias. What happened?"

A call to his phone delayed her answer. "Steph." He gave her a quick rundown of the situation. "My ETA is twenty." His look slid sideways to her. "She's declining medical transport."

Talking about her as if she were some random accident victim, someone to be dealt with and off-loaded. She was going to insert a remark but fatigue pulled her back against the seat.

When he finally ended the call, he cranked the heat up one more notch. "Police are sending a unit to the lake and then to the ranch."

She wasn't at all sure she had the self-control to keep her temper in check if they started asking about her father. She gritted her teeth to keep them from chattering as they drove. Roman finally pulled the Bronco up the long gravel drive of the Security Hounds ranch.

Before he could help her out, she hopped free, grateful that, though her legs were stiff and her wrists burned from where they'd been bound, she was no longer shivering. The wide front door opened and Beth Wolfe led them inside. Her short blond hair showed streaks of gray, but at sixty, she emanated grace and style in her soft slacks and flowy knit top. There was something hitched about her shoulders though, as if she were experiencing pain. Steph nodded to them, a phone pressed to her ear and a one-minute finger raised. Roman grabbed a cloth and began to towel off the big bloodhound.

Beth led her to a guest bedroom done in soft greens with oil paintings of Crater Lake on the walls. She gestured to a pair of women's sweats laid out on the bed. "Probably too big since I'm taller, but dry. Are you sure you don't need an ambulance?"

"Yes." Emery spoke a little too forcefully. "I'm an RN."

"I know." Beth cocked her head. "Your father was extremely proud of that."

Her father... She shrank back to the days after his arrest, the looks she got in town, the whispers, the sheer shock of it. Beth had come—in between the reporters who hounded her— walked right past her father's precious geranium patch and knocked on the door. To offer support? She'd been the only one. And Emery had cowered there behind the curtain, face puffed with crying, silent, until Beth had gone away.

Beth left now, without a word, and Emery put on the dry clothes, bundling her own into a soggy ball and leaving them in a discreet corner of the bathroom floor where she could retrieve them later. Why had she let Roman bring her here? But what choice did she have? *Talk to the police, get it over with, figure out your next steps.*

Voices filtered from the living room where Emery joined them. A fire blazed in the hearth and she resisted the urge to sidle up to it. Beth handed her a steaming cup of coffee and gestured her to the sofa. Roman was changed too, into a soft pair of denim jeans and a long-sleeved tee the same cocoa brown as his eyes. His nose was swollen from her head-butting but hopefully not broken.

Then came the questions, delivered politely, from Stephanie, Beth, Roman and Garrett who'd taken up positions in the cozy room.

How had she come to be in that boat?

Who had subdued her and how had they accomplished it?

She heaved out a breath and faced them, putting into words the frightening truth. "I don't remember."

Stephanie quirked a perfectly shaped brow. Her twin brother, Garrett, mirrored the expression. Unnerving.

Garrett poured himself coffee. "You were going by a different name? May I ask why?"

She heaved out a breath. "It's complicated. Can we stick to this evening's events?"

Their collected frowns communicated their perplexity, but there was nothing she could do except say it again. "I don't remember how I got to that lake, or who tied me up and threw me in."

Or why...

And that was the worst part of all.

Why had someone wanted to drown her?

And what was she supposed to do about it?

Chapter Three

Roman used all his will not to flat-out gape at Emery. She had no memory of almost being killed? "If you have a head injury, you should be in the hospital."

She ignored him, rolling the mug between her palms without drinking from it. She was thinner than he remembered, the mischievous quality that had fascinated him, missing. The fine blond hair she'd worn long to her shoulder blades was now blunt cut at her jawline, chestnut brown. The blue-green of those eyes though—a melding of spring grass with the cornflower of summer skies—hadn't changed. He forced his gaze away and focused on what she'd revealed.

Steph brushed a palm over Cleo, her highly efficient liver-and-tan bloodhound. He knew she was buying time to process, like he was.

"What is the last thing you *do* remember?" she said.

"I bought chocolate milk just before 11:00 p.m. At a gas station. It was called the Mighty something or other. I made a phone call."

Garrett was already typing in the information on his laptop. "Must be the Mighty Mart. Twelve point two miles south of here."

"Who did you call?" Roman demanded.

She blinked. "A family friend."

"Who?" he pressed. Too heavy-handed.

Her lips thinned and Beth inclined her head slightly, indicating he was pushing too hard, too fast. But why not? She'd be dead if he'd been a few moments later and Wally hadn't decided to show up. He bit back his remark.

"I finished the milk and I was on my way to Whisper Valley. I heard a car behind me and then…" She blinked. "I woke up being tossed into the lake."

Roman repeated the question. "But why were you on your way to town? You moved away, right?"

He saw her throat convulse as she swallowed. "It's not important."

"Yes, it is."

Her left eyebrow quirked at his tone. "Isn't that for the police to decide?"

A world of challenge in that sentence. Why were they badgering her for information? She wanted to know. Beth got to the particulars before he did.

"Apologies, I thought maybe Roman would have told you. Our new business here on the ranch is an exclusive investigative agency we started a year ago called Security Hounds. You were away then, so you likely didn't know."

"I thought you rescued dogs."

"We do, and we retrain them for tracking and trailing, but we keep a team of them here permanently. They help us find people, or things, or answers." She waved a hand at her children. "This pack has skills, as much stubbornness and curiosity as the dogs. It was a natural fit. So we can help you, you see."

"You won't want to." Her voice was hard and brittle like glass long exposed to the harsh elements. "My dad is in custody awaiting trial for the attempted murder of Mason Taylor as you all know." Her gaze swept the room. "His military buddies have all deserted him too."

Roman's stomach contracted to a fist. He hadn't deserted Theo. Other way around. Not the time to say so. "Doesn't mean we can't help you."

"Not saying you can't. Saying you won't want to." The accusation screwed his stomach tighter.

He hadn't reached out to help her before, not since that day she'd slammed the door. He'd slammed one too, on the man whom he'd trusted with everything, a man who'd burned them both. Theo didn't deserve their help, but Emery shouldn't suffer any more because of her father.

"Your father was—" Beth stopped "—is a friend. He was there for me and the kids when my husband died. He's a good man, deep down. I won't be convinced otherwise. I know your sister was injured the night of the shooting too. How is she?"

"Alive, unresponsive in a long-term care facility. Has been since that night."

Beth added softly, "And the baby?"

Roman's head jerked up. There was a baby? Why hadn't he known that?

"My nephew, Ian. He's nine months old now. I've got custody. Fortunately, a friend is watching him so he wasn't in the car when…" Her hands trembled.

Emery was caring for her sister's baby? As if her life hadn't turned upside down enough.

Emery examined each person in the room but her gaze came to rest on him. "Like I said, I can't remember anything after the chocolate milk and the car behind me except for the question of why I was on my way here. That part I do know."

Silently he willed her to finish.

She lifted her chin, almost in defiance. "Since Dad went to jail…he's refused to see me, talk to me, and hasn't even answered one single letter or call." Her voice wobbled.

He can't face you.

"He had a heart attack a week ago and was transferred to the prison hospital and then to county. I'm told…" She cleared her throat. "He roused briefly, scribbled a message and asked the hospital orderly to pass it to me. He's been unconscious ever since."

Roman's mouth went dry.

She folded her hands in her lap, palms pressed together. "The message said, *go home, Ree Ree.*" Her mouth trembled once and then she steeled her expression. "That's where I was going. Home, to his cabin."

She was returning home because of her father's mysterious command, and while en route, someone had tried to drown her. He scanned the faces of his siblings and his mother. He knew what they were thinking, what Emery needed.

Roman's stomach contracted. He believed that God brought him to situations so he could help. But this one...with her, when he had tried so hard to put Theo's horror behind him? He realized his family was looking at him now, waiting for him to take the lead, or turn away. They knew his pain and they wouldn't add to it by making the decision without his consent. That's what family did...what it was supposed to do, strange as it still felt.

He pulled in a deep breath. "Emery, I think you're going to need help recovering the missing hours."

She shook him off. "The cops..."

"Will investigate the incident, but there's a bigger problem at play here."

"What's that?"

"Someone didn't want you to go home."

The light drained from her eyes. "Do you think it has something to do with my father's message?"

"I don't know, but that's what we do here at

Security Hounds. We get answers." *We.* It felt so good.

She wasn't going to find the truth by herself, or from the police, he sensed. And if the mess wasn't sorted out soon, the would-be killer might get another chance at finishing what they'd started. He could be cool and professional if it meant he could offer protection. That's what he'd spent his whole career as a navy master-at-arms doing, anyway.

Emery was simply another person that needed help.

But would she accept it?

Looking at her troubled expression, he wasn't sure what her answer would be.

Finally she pulled in a breath. "No, thank you. I appreciate your offer but I am going to stay at a hotel until the police find my car. All I need is a ride, if it isn't too inconvenient."

You're dismissed, soldier.

He was going to argue when he caught Beth's expression. Instead, teeth clenched, he nodded. "I'll drive you."

Save for the small hotel that was closed due to a problem with the plumbing, there was only one lodge close to Whisper Valley, twenty minutes from town. The police reported they wouldn't be able to interview Emery for several hours so she'd left her contact information. No sense loitering around the ranch if she didn't have to.

Roman's insistence on driving her left her uneasy. What were they supposed to talk about?

"You sure you want to stay at the Lodge?" he asked.

"Why wouldn't I?"

"It's owned by Hilary now, Lincoln's ex."

Emery's stomach dropped but she kept her tone level. "Not much choice. Hopefully she won't recognize me." She shifted, eager to change the subject. "So you're a detective now?"

He shrugged. "More of a manager, I think. I'm still learning the detective end of things. Working on boosting the business any way I can. Beth's scheduled for some long overdue back surgery and I want to be up to speed on how everything works before that happens." His voice warmed. "We've got a big publicity event coming up. It's actually…" He trailed off, suddenly uneasy.

She wondered why but before she could ask, she caught the elegant silhouette of the Taylor home against the black sky. Her memories sucked her six months into the past.

Her sister Diane's text... I was all wrong. Need help.

After her initial annoyance and suspicion, she'd messaged her sister. No reply. From a home health visit she was finishing up near Whisper Valley, she'd phoned her father.

Don't call the cops yet, he'd said. *She doesn't need another blot on her record. Not now.*

Not since she'd shown up in town with a baby. Typical Diane. Moving from one train-wreck to another, only now there was a baby involved in the mess. Typical Dad, trying to correct the damage. What if she'd moved faster? Not let her own difficulties with her sister delay her decision-making? Would things have turned out differently that night?

A touch on her hand startled her.

Roman's mouth had softened slightly. "Bad memories?"

"Yes." And before she could stop herself, the words were tumbling out as she noticed a light on in the Taylors' upper story. "I've tried so many times to imagine what happened that night. It's hard to put into words."

His tone was cold. "I understand why you wouldn't want to talk about it."

He understood? Not likely. Part of her didn't want to share further, but she also felt an almost ferocious desire to force him to face what she had, to hear him say the facts couldn't possibly be what they seemed. "The Taylors' security guard found Diane on the ground floor. My dad was next to her with a gun in his hand and Mason upstairs bleeding from a gunshot wound." She jerked a glance at him. "I know what it looks like, what you think, what everybody thinks, but my dad didn't charge in there intending to kill anyone."

"I've read his statement. He was angry at Lincoln for refusing a paternity test, calling Diane names when she threatened to take him to court. He said Diane's gun was at his cabin. When she texted you, requesting help, he took it, planning to threaten Lincoln into accepting the baby. He didn't realize he was confronting Mason, not Lincoln, because it was dark and they look alike. Diane tried to stop him but he shot Mason and she staggered back and toppled over the balcony rail."

"I know that's what he said," she snapped. "But it couldn't have happened like that."

"Why not? His fingerprints were on the gun."

"Yes, his, but not hers. That doesn't seem odd to you? It was Diane's gun, but her prints weren't on it? She carried that gun when she went on night walks, but Dad said she'd left it at his place when she'd visited earlier in the week. That's strange to me since she walked almost every evening."

Roman shrugged. "Lincoln said he was out for a drive. Arrived back to find the cops all over and his brother shot."

She couldn't hold back. "Convenient that he wasn't there when it happened, isn't it?"

"Cops—"

"Roman, my dad must have confessed to protect Diane. I'm sure of it. That's the only conclusion that makes sense."

"So you're saying he lied, then? Diane did it?"

She swallowed and ducked her chin. "He's always tried to help. I know my father and so did you, once upon a time. He mentored you."

Roman fixed his dark gaze out the front windshield. "My bad for trusting him."

The comment cut an angry path to her heart. *Her* bad for thinking this calloused person was the sensitive young man she remembered. With burning eyes, she stared at the Taylor house.

Did the events of that night have something to do with her near drowning? Couldn't have.

The newer structure on the property was sleek and substantial—the showroom for the Taylors' classic car collection. There was a banner erected along the fence line with dates advertising some sort of show. A dark silhouette behind a curtain caught her attention. Was someone tracking them as they drove by?

Her imagination, had to be, but the goose bumps remained.

The terrain became more hilly and thick with trees and another fifteen minutes brought them to the inn. The old property had changed hands many times during her childhood years. She hadn't realized Lincoln's ex-wife was the most recent owner.

Since Roman was dead silent, she had plenty of time to observe the upgrades. The rustic building had been renamed The Inn at the Pines. New outdoor lighting picked up the elegant flagstone drive, a freshly paved parking lot, a new roof gilded by the moon. The cabins sprinkled throughout the property had been similarly glamorized from what was revealed by the artful landscape illumination. She prayed there was a vacancy, determined not to complain about the cost, though her bank account was recently depleted with the purchase of diapers and baby clothes. Every day she checked the mail with baited breath, praying the insurance company would inform her they were paying for all of her sister's care. Fat chance.

She intended to thank Roman in the car and check in herself, but he was already out, walking to open the door for her. In a flash, she'd done it herself. She didn't want anything from Roman, especially some sort of forced gallantry. Roman left Wally in the back seat.

A stately woman in a blazer and silk blouse greeted them, large brown eyes taking in every detail, it seemed to Emery. Hilary, her nametag proclaimed. Emery was face to face with the woman who had just cause to despise Diane.

Her mouth went dry. "I'd like a room please."

"Of course." Her gaze drifted to Roman. "For one?"

"Yes."

"Name?"

"Emily Bancroft."

"All right. We have one cabin available. Fortuitous since there's a car show this weekend and our visitor count is higher than usual." She chatted on about the amenities. Emery felt she could hardly keep on her feet.

"Paying with a card?"

"Cash." She always carried bills since her cards were under her real name. Settling into life as Emily Bancroft felt as if she could give Ian and herself a fresh start. Especially here, so near Whisper Valley, she wanted no one to know who she was, for Ian's sake. Ian... She experienced the customary mixture of anxiety and warmth that came whenever she thought of her nephew.

Thankfully she had emergency cash in her pocket, since her wallet was likely still in her car somewhere. Would it be enough to cover the room cost? Hilary tapped her blunt-cut nails on the gleaming countertop. "There's something very familiar about you."

Probably Hilary remembered her from the newspaper articles plastered everywhere after the shooting. *Beloved townsperson shot by local resident.* They'd included a family picture of Theo, herself and Diane. There was also a strong resemblance between the sisters. Emery fingered her hair, edging back a few inches. "I've got that kind of face."

"Are you sure I don't know you? Maybe from

the car showroom? My ex-husband, Lincoln, runs it with his brother, Mason. People travel from all over to see those cars."

"I…" Her words trailed off and she could think of nothing to add.

"Emily just arrived in town," Roman said smoothly. He flashed that charming smile. "But you know me." He introduced himself.

"Oh, Roman. Didn't recognize you with your hat pulled down over your forehead." She smiled. "Your brother I'd identify in a heartbeat."

"Yes, Chase is a gearhead. He'd go the Taylors' showroom every day if he had the time."

Hilary returned the smile. "Of course. I think by this point I've met all your siblings and mother during our planning meetings."

What planning meetings?

"Yes, ma'am." He offered a friendly smile before he turned to Emery. "There's a coffee station in the corner there. I know you could use a cup after your long trip, right?" He turned back to Hilary. "She's exhausted."

Grateful for the save, Emery scurried to the dimly lit corner to pour coffee. Hilary took the cue and prepared the room key. "Go ahead and settle in. We'll take care of payment in the morning. I'm headed to bed now, but my night clerk can assist you with anything." Hilary's smooth brow crimped. "No luggage?"

Only the luggage that's in my missing car.

"Traveling light." She quickly strode out into the chilly night. Roman caught up with her.

He walked her along the flagstone path and up to a rustic chic cabin, then waited while she unlocked the door. The interior was bright and elegant, a small bedroom opening off a suite area, all done in creams with charming woodland scenes hanging on the walls.

He stood like a dark cliff, hands jammed into his pockets. "You sure you're okay staying here? Matter of time before it comes to Hilary who you are."

"I'll be here only for the night. I've still got my secret identity in place." Her smile was brighter than she felt.

"I…"

"Roman, I appreciate what you did for me. You…" She gulped. "You and Wally saved my life. I can't—" *and I won't* "—ask you for any more."

After a long pause, he turned and left. When the door closed behind him, she immediately latched it. The large rear sliding doors looked out on a swath of crowded pines, impenetrable shadows. She pulled the vertical blinds closed and turned on the lamps on the fireplace mantle. Cozy and safe.

Since she had no suitcase to unpack, she drank the rest of the decaf and decided on another shower. No doubt she was paying a hefty sum for the cabin, she might as well get her money's worth.

After checking once more to be sure the doors and windows were locked, she treated herself to the hottest shower she could stand and pulled on Beth's borrowed clothing. Tomorrow.

By then the police would probably have located her car. She'd load up, return to her central California apartment and stay there with Ian. Try to forget she'd ever come back to Whisper Valley.

Her father's command played in her mind.

Go home.

Well, she wouldn't. And he wouldn't want her to if he knew how close she'd come to dying.

Not just dying, being murdered.

She desperately wished she dared call again to check on Ian. It was after 1:00 a.m. so that would be just plain inconsiderate. In the morning, she told herself. Picturing his little double chin made her smile. Every moment with him was still an exercise in terror and joy, but the past few weeks the joy had been winning out.

She'd folded the covers to climb into bed when a squeak made her freeze, sheets gripped in her fingers. The old logs expanding in the moist air?

That was it, no doubt.

Another squeak. Her pulse raced.

What if it wasn't the expansion of wood, but the noise of a footstep on the slatted porch? Barefoot, she glided as silently as she could, muffling a cry when she struck her shin on the edge of a chair.

Now she could hear nothing but the soft whir of the cabin heater and her own harsh breathing. Easing to the front window, she hooked a finger around the drape and peered outside. Quiet and still, a slice of forest punctuated by the soft glow of the office windows in the distance. She could not see another cabin from this viewpoint.

Isolated.

But there was no one there and the door was still firmly locked.

Relieved, she let the curtain fall back into

place. She decided to leave the lamps lit in the living area. Like Ian's choo choo train night-light, she thought. Comforting, that was all.

And why not turn on the light on the back porch? It wouldn't disturb anyone else. She padded to the slider and flicked on the light.

A dark shadow was caught in the glow.

Masked, one gloved hand raised to the door handle.

Emery screamed.

Chapter Four

At the scream, Wally threw up his snout and howled, vibrating the Bronco's windows. Roman was out and running across the parking lot with the dog right behind before the sound died away. *Emery. Had to be.* He stumbled on a rock and almost went down.

He sprinted along the flagstones and straight up to her cabin door, whamming a fist on the wood.

"Emery, it's Roman." He reached for the knob when she threw it open, pale and trembling. Wally didn't wait for an invite. He bolted inside, jowls flapping and rose up on his hind legs to paw her stomach.

"Down, Wally."

The dog ignored him, as usual.

"I saw someone…" she panted, one hand on the dog, and pointed to the rear slider.

He immediately ran outside, phone flashlight activated. No one was there. To be sure, he whistled for Wally who actually obeyed and joined him. Wally's black nose went immediately to the ground, wafting up great gusts, but without a specific scent article, the bloodhound would be pinballing from one aroma to the next with no target. Roman figured he'd at least bark and alert if there was a stranger in the proximity, but Wally seemed perfectly content to nose around the grass and up to the shrubby border where the lawn met the trees. There was no one hiding, of that he was fairly certain. Wally was a trainwreck in some ways but he generally knew when there was a stranger about. A distant engine noise told him how the peeping Tom had gotten away.

Roman hooked a finger through Wally's collar and guided him back to the cabin. He didn't want him to disappear into the forest and be forced to choose between chasing his dog or staying with Emery. They rejoined her in the cabin and she added what she could.

"I don't know if it was a man or woman. I couldn't see the face. But I saw a gloved hand raised as if..."

"They were going to try to open the sliding door?"

She gave one sharp nod.

He considered, thoughts rolling through his mind. Who? And why? The same two questions looming since they'd barely survived the lake.

A knock made her jump. Roman looked through the peephole and opened the door. Hilary's eyes were wide as she took in Roman and the dog he was restraining from slobbering on her.

"What's going on?"

"Possible intruder." To preempt her next question he added, "I was pulling up here to give something to Emily and I heard her scream."

Hilary's delicate brow arched. "I heard a scream too but I wasn't sure where it came from." She looked at Emery. "Tell me."

Emery repeated her story.

Hilary's brows furrowed. "You were mistaken. No one would be skulking around here. It's a quiet area. You were probably mistaken."

"I wasn't," Emery said quietly. "I'm going to call the police."

Her frown deepened. "Is that truly necessary? It'll upset the guests."

Roman stared. Was she kidding? "You've already got an upset guest."

Her lips thinned. "All right. I'll call. They're not quick on response time around here but I imagine they'll get to us when they can. In the meantime…"

"I'll stay here." Roman got the words out before he thought it through. Both women stared at him but he kept his gaze on Hilary in case Emery was about to countermand his bold pronouncement. "On the couch. Your office sign said pets are allowed, right? I'll pay whatever the fee is."

"Well, small pets, sure, but your dog is sizeable and…"

Slobbery was no doubt her next word. "If he damages anything, I'll pay. I'm sure you want your guests to feel safe?" A challenge rang in Roman's tone and Hilary didn't miss it.

She straightened. "Please call the front desk if you need anything. I'm off for the night but my assistant can help you. Of course, when the police arrive, she'll wake me."

Roman slid a look to her feet as she walked out. Walking shoes, jeans, as if she'd been out walking instead of headed to bed. Might Emery's prowler have been the nosy innkeeper checking on her new guest? But why would she?

When Hilary had gone, he locked the

door. Jaw set he turned around to find Emery crouched, giving Wally a tummy scratch.

"You're going to spoil him."

"Why did you come back?"

The weight of her stare made him uneasy. He freed the object from his pocket. "Brought you an extra cell phone we had at the ranch until you get yours back. The Security Hounds phone number is programmed in. And mine." His was the first on the list as a matter of fact.

"Thank you."

He expected her to take him to task for inserting himself into her situation. But she continued to focus on Wally, rubbing him down until his eyes rolled in their fleshy orbits.

"For staying here too. It's only a couple of hours until morning or the cops arrive, but it's an imposition."

"No big deal." He felt relieved that she didn't seem inclined to want to fight him. If she'd argued, it would have been a long night with Wally jammed in the Bronco, keeping watch from the parking lot.

The fireplace lamps lent a soft sheen to her hair, which tossed him back to his teen years, landing on a bright spot in a tumultuous ordeal. He didn't recall much about the mother who'd remanded him into the foster care system at age five. Two years he'd remained in the system until his uncle Jax returned from working overseas and took him in. At Jax's place he'd thought he'd finally found a home with his fun-loving, impetuous uncle. The memories turned sour when Jax remarried and everything fell apart for Roman. At sixteen, he'd walked out, landing at Wolfe Ranch where Theo Duncan volunteered. Dark times, pulsing with anger and hurt.

But there was Emery. He remembered watching her and her father standing over a rescued litter of roly-poly bloodhounds. The puppies were adorable, but he was mesmerized by Emery and Theo, their easy relationship, the love they obviously shared. When he left Jax's and he'd shown up at the ranch, Beth had offered him that kind of love, and Theo had too.

His thoughts soured with echoed snippets. Theo's voice...

If a man can't control his fists, he's not a man.

Holding a grudge is like drinking rat poison and waiting for the rat to die.

All of that meant precisely nothing now that Theo had gunned a man down in a fit of anger and unforgiveness. No matter what Emery said, the facts didn't lie. Her father was in jail for attempted murder, where he belonged, but he'd left a lot of wreckage behind for Emery.

Go home, Ree Ree.

What was Theo playing at? Roping her in again after flat-out ignoring her? That thought tormented him as she said good-night and closed herself in the bedroom. He lay on the couch, comfortable enough until Wally heaved himself up too.

"There's no room for you, dog."

Happily unconcerned, Wally settled his bulk over Roman's shins and started snoring in short order. Roman texted Stephanie since she was a complete insomniac and told her what had happened. She texted back.

Emery needs Security Hounds.

She did. And if she'd agree to the help, Stephanie or Garrett could be point person on the case. Roman was squarely focused on the event he had to be sure was a success, the Cars For K-9s show at the Taylor estate. Security Hounds was struggling financially and he desperately needed to prove to Beth that business was picking up or she'd never stop working long enough to have her back surgery. Her pain was a solid punch to his middle and he wasn't sure how much longer she could take it.

What would Emery think if she knew of his partnership with the Taylors?

His jaw tightened. Why should it matter, anyway? Theo'd confessed and left them all to deal with the fallout as best they could. Case closed.

He tried to put the thoughts away and lull himself to sleep.

After what felt like only a momentary rest, Emery was up, dressed and headed for the small coffeepot in the room when she found Wally and Roman entering through the front door. Roman held two mugs of coffee, one of which he offered her. She was glad to see his head-butted nose looked much less swollen in the clear light of morning.

"Got it from the lobby. There was a blueberry muffin too but Wally snatched it from my hand while I was trying to hang onto the coffee. Fortunately Hilary didn't see that little stunt."

Wally wagged his tail at Emery as if he were being lauded by his owner. She giggled.

"Cops called," Roman said. "They can't get an officer here until later but they asked you to meet them at Wolfe Ranch to answer a few questions."

"I want to get back to my apartment and Ian." She sighed and sipped the coffee while Wally sniffed her pant leg. "But I guess I need to give them whatever info I can before I leave."

"Wally and I checked the area this morning. Stayed far enough away not to mess up any footprints, but I don't think there are any. The flagstone butts right up to the patio."

"Hilary thinks I was imagining it."

He didn't reply to that. Did he believe the same thing?

"We can go anytime, Ree. I settled up for your room so you wouldn't have to do a face-to-face," Roman said.

Her cheeks flamed both at what he'd done and his use of her nickname. "Oh, wow. I'll pay you back, whatever it was." Her thoughts raced. How, exactly? She'd had to curtail her work hours for Ian's sake. Her sister's medical bills were mounting and there was a mortgage payment on her father's cabin due, which she had no idea how to pay. Prickles danced up and down her spine.

"Ready to go?"

"More than ready."

They drove back to Whisper Valley and she again found her gaze on the Taylor estate and car showroom. "Why would Hilary take over an inn so close to the Taylor estate after divorcing Lincoln? My sister said it wasn't exactly a friendly parting." Lincoln had been unfaithful to Hilary with more than one woman and Diane was the latest in a string. It made Emery cringe that her sister had been involved in ruining a marriage. How had Hilary felt about Diane's arrival with a baby in tow when the ink on her divorce papers wasn't yet dry?

"The car showroom attracted visitors but there was no place close for them to stay. Hilary and Lincoln made some sort of business arrangement for her to renovate and run the inn so the visiting car enthusiasts would have lodging. You'd be surprised how far car aficionados are willing to travel to take a look at the Taylors' collection." He shook his head. "My brother Chase is a total car nut. That guy would crawl in an engine and live there if he could. Cars are just a way to get from A to B in my view, but he'd probably slug me in the shoulder if he heard me say that."

She slanted a look at him.

"What?"

"It's just…nice to hear you talk about family."

He kept his gaze fixed front. "The Wolfes have been incredible. Better than blood. That's why I'm dedicated to helping Security Hounds succeed." His fingers tightened on the steering wheel and she knew what he was thinking. He'd considered her father family at one time too. The tight line of his jaw communicated what his silence didn't.

I need to get out of here, away from him, back to Ian. Her fingers clenched into a fist. A little while longer, after the questioning, and she'd be gone. The drive seemed endless, though it was less than half an hour, but they eventually arrived back at Wolfe Ranch. Wally trotted off to join two other hounds in digging holes in the large fenced yard.

Officer Dell Hagerty of the Whisper Valley Police Department was already seated in the living room. Emery's head pounded and her body ached from her earlier contortions in the river as she repeated the story, exasperation mounting. "I still can't remember how I got from my car to being dumped in the lake."

Hagerty's suspicion was obvious and irritating. "What I want to know is why would your father tell you to go home?"

"I don't know. I'm sure he wouldn't have if he knew it might have put me in harm's way."

The quirk to his lip increased her ire. What he didn't say was clear. *Your dad confessed to attempted murder. His trustworthiness is nil.* Officer Hagerty had been part of the police team that had investigated, but they'd taken Theo's confession at face value. "My dad took the blame to spare my sister, like I said back then. I'm sure of it."

"So your sister did it and he was covering? Why would she shoot anyone?"

"I don't know. I thought she and Lincoln were amicable at least." Her last text was confusing, out of the blue. "It could have been an accident." The untenable position she was in... defending her father meant blaming her sister. "Or maybe someone else was involved."

Now they were all looking at her with pity. One gun. One set of prints. One man shot. Precisely two suspects. Her sister or her father. And one big fat confession. Her father couldn't have gunned down Mason Taylor. Her sister's volatile temperament made her guilt much more likely, but Emery didn't want to believe that either. According to their father, she'd changed, or tried to, since she'd had Ian. There had to be some missing piece.

The police had been no help in finding different answers because they hadn't wanted to. Case closed. She blinked back to the present, to the suspicious cop staring at her.

"Your father asked you to come back to his cabin, but didn't tell you why, and on the way you were attacked and dumped in the lake, but you can't remember by whom or how?"

Her cheeks were molten. "Yes, Officer. That's about the size of it."

Hagerty looked at Roman. "Do you have anything to shed light on this? Did you get a look at this boat operator?"

This boat operator. As if she were making it up.

Roman crossed his hands over his stomach. "No, but I can tell you someone was bent on killing Emery and then me for getting in the way. What she said is true, every syllable of it."

She didn't know why Roman was vehement in his defense of her, but in that moment she felt a surge of gratitude.

"And someone was prowling your room at The Inn at the Pines?"

She nodded miserably and let Roman fill in the details.

"She checked in as Emily Bancroft," Roman said, startling Emery. She hadn't remembered they didn't know her alias.

Hagerty's brow hitched. "Why are you using a fake name?"

Her anger bubbled up. "My car windows were smashed in twice after my father's arrest and someone painted *Diane's a tramp* on the side of Dad's cabin. Can you blame me? We're living in the Central Valley now, but it's not that far away that the hatred can't reach us."

Hagerty said nothing.

"I was given custody of my nephew. He's a baby. I didn't want any problems to follow us."

Hagerty nodded. "Fair. I've got two kids and I can understand that." The officer asked a few more questions before he excused himself. "I haven't found your vehicle yet. I'll call you if I locate it after I check out the inn. Where will you be staying?"

"I'm going home to my apartment. Both Dad and Diane are in a hospital an hour from here so I'll check on them on my way back. I'll rent a car." With what money? She had a maxed-out credit card and only a borrowed phone. Plus, she owed Roman for her short stay at the inn.

Hagerty shook his head. "Would you mind

staying until I can check the inn in case I need you to point anything out to me? Might take a couple hours since there's only one other officer on duty today besides me."

Her heart sank but she nodded as Hagerty left.

Beth stood. "You can stay here, Emery. For the day or however long it takes. We've got plenty of room. Too much as a matter of fact. Chase is working a case out of the area this week and Roman decided to live in his trailer near the kennels instead of a bedroom in the house so we have a spare."

"Says we make too much noise." Stephanie rolled her eyes.

Roman shrugged. "I like to be close to the dogs, but yes, you're noisy. And your country music drives me bonkers."

Emery was at a loss. "I appreciate it, but I should…" Should what? Her backpack with her clothes was in the car, which she couldn't find, along with her wallet. Renting a vehicle would be expensive and she'd need her license. What exactly was she going to do? Wait there awkwardly on their front porch until the police did or did not find her car? Go back to the expensive inn she couldn't afford?

There was nobody she could call on, except Gino, Diane's old friend, who'd arrived in her life just in time, and he was on baby duty hours away at her apartment. No friends had stuck with her after what had happened. She was entirely alone. The weight of it was crushing.

"Please." Beth patted Emery's knee. "Stay for a while, at least. You look exhausted."

Exhausted didn't begin to cover it. Her mind was numb, body battered, spirit troubled. "I, uh, thank you. You're very kind."

Beth walked her down the hall where she fetched her another set of clothes. "In case you need a change. Here's a bedroom where you can rest or get away from the chaos that is my ranch. Between the dogs and the people, it's rarely quiet."

After thanking Beth again, she felt desperate to talk to Gino, to make sure Ian was all right. She called with the phone Roman had given her but there was no answer. Why wasn't Gino home? Her pulse thudded harder. *He's just taking Ian out for a walk and doesn't hear his phone is all*. She left a message adding that she'd been in an accident the previous day. The bed beckoned but she didn't want to allow herself to be too comfortable. *Not staying. Only visiting.* She settled on pacing away a half hour, wishing she had Ian in her arms. Maybe a drink of water might fill the empty spot.

She heard voices in the living room. Padding softly out, she found Stephanie and Roman deep in conversation. Roman caught sight of her when Wally trundled over to give her a good sniffing as if they hadn't just spent several hours together. She scrubbed the dark patches on his tawny sides.

"Um, hi. I wondered if I could, um, have a drink of water." She felt silly, childlike.

Roman immediately went to the kitchen and returned with a glass. His fingers brushed hers and she felt it to her toes. Nerves.

Stephanie fixed dark eyes on her. "I'm not one to sugarcoat anything so I'll say it out straight. I don't have great hope that Hagerty's going to find much evidence to help here. And your prowler at the inn is likely the same person who tried to drown you."

She groaned. "This has to be a bad dream."

Stephanie perched on the arm of the sofa, unapologetic. "Sorry to be a downer, but there's plenty of wildland around here and Hagerty's got a lot on his plate now that there's another potential crime scene to investigate. Totally your choice to decline the services of Security Hounds and frankly we've got other irons in the fire, but you're making a mistake to go it alone."

"Won't be my first one." Her need to flee was almost overwhelming.

Roman gazed through the window. "Let's give Wally a crack at it."

Stephanie yanked a look at Roman, eyebrows lifted to meet her dark bangs. "Wally the breakfast-snatcher? He didn't even deign to find you last night."

"Until it mattered," Roman said.

Needles of ice pricked Emery's skin. The dog had come through with everything he had. If it weren't for Wally, Emery would be dead and perhaps Roman too.

Stephanie shrugged. "Your sweat equity, not mine. Why don't you take a half a day to work it and if Wally turns up nothing, Cleo and I will take over."

Roman's wide shoulders hunched. "It's Emery's call."

Stephanie rose. "Okay. I'm going to do some background for another case. Let me know if you need me and Cleo." She left.

The silence unrolled between them. The room was suddenly very small.

Roman shifted uncomfortably. "Emery, I know what you told Hagerty, but do you have any idea why your dad would have sent you that message?"

"No."

"No guesses? Hunches?"

"No. I don't understand anything involving my father."

"I don't either."

His bitterness was like a living creature and it awakened a surge of smothering shame. This was why she could not accept his help. Because deep down she knew that she was partially responsible for what her father had done and if that guilt was exposed, especially to Roman, she would not survive it. She'd abandoned her father, left him to deal with Diane alone because she was sick to death of it all. What's more, she was secretly relieved that he'd responded to her sister's frantic text, which had let Emery off the hook.

Right now, there was only one tiny thread keeping her heart intact, the faintest hope that somehow, someway, her father would reveal another side of the story, one where he wasn't murderous, and Diane wasn't either. A third party…someone…anyone. But Roman would think that was self-delusion. More than likely he was correct. She shook the hair from her face. "I'm leaving as soon as I can. I appreciate the offer, but I'll figure this out on my own."

"How?"

"One day at a time, like I've been doing for six months."

He didn't flinch, didn't look away this time. "You need Security Hounds," he said quietly.

"I don't need anyone." *Just herself, and God.* She remained silent, wishing she could disappear into the floor, out of this house, the town. Roman had once been the center of her teeny-bopper crush. Now he was a stranger who reviled her father, like everyone else in Whisper Valley. His brown eyes searched hers fleetingly. She kept her chin up, mouth firm. He headed to the front door.

Roman wanted to give Wally a crack at finding her car.

To him, it was a case, one she was sure he didn't even want.

To her…she remembered the terror of waking up bound, gagged and drowning.

To her, it was life and death.

Her death.

And if she were gone…who would be there for Ian?

She felt again the frigid water closing over her.

"Wait," she blurted.

He jerked around. "You change your mind?"

"Maybe it wouldn't hurt to let Wally look. I have to stay in town for a few hours anyway."

He smiled and her stomach tingled. He was older now, his face tanned, worn and more angular, but the smile was the same one she'd briefly lived for as a teenager. She looked away. No time for silliness.

"Great. I'll get Wally harnessed."

She tracked his wide shoulders as he departed. A couple of hours, that was all. What could happen in that time?

A shudder rippled her spine.

Plenty.

Chapter Five

Roman's mind reeled as he drove. Why had he volunteered, anyway? He certainly didn't want to involve himself in her case. But something in his gut told him his breakfast-swiping dog could find the car. Locate the vehicle. That was all.

"Wally's in training to trail people but maybe we can do some reverse engineering." He pulled to a stop at the lake where he'd found Emery and unloaded the dog, clipping the long lead to his harness. "All right, boy. Let's see if we can make this work."

While Wally nosed around, Roman scoured the ground for something the perpetrator might have dropped near the boat launch. "If we can find a scent article, Wally could theoretically lead us back to the place where you were abducted, providing we've got one attacker here and not two working together." He realized that Emery had stopped several paces behind him, hugging herself.

"Are you cold? I've got an extra jacket in the vehicle."

She shook her head and he saw the gleam of tears. "It's...hard to be back here."

It took a moment to sink in. Mental head slap. He was clueless. Of course, it would be difficult for her to relive being abducted, dumped in the water and left to drown. It was a wonder she'd held it together at all after that trauma. He edged closer. "I'm sorry. I should've thought about your feelings coming back here."

She flashed a shaky smile. "Gonna buy me an ice cream to make me feel better?"

He grinned. "You remember that?"

"Do I recall the time you found me sobbing after Diane ruined my dress the day before the freshman dance? Yes, I do. You got this absolutely terrified look on your face and offered to buy me ice cream if only I would stop crying."

He shrugged. "I'm still prone to panic when a woman is in tears." At least she appeared a bit more relaxed now. "But I never did make good on that ice-cream offer, did I?" And why hadn't he? Because the gap between her sixteen and his then seventeen was huge. Because he was so uncertain, living in a borrowed place with a borrowed family after his split with Uncle Jax. Because she was so incredibly gorgeous then, and now, he realized with a start. "I'll make good on that ice cream soon."

"Sure." She'd heard the offer for what it was—hollow. She moved away from him, hopping over the mucky areas of the bank.

She doesn't want anything from you. That's good. Too messy. "The police have photographed and gone over the area so we probably won't—"

She cut him off. "Look."

Caught in the reeds, barely visible in the tangle, was an oar, no doubt the same one with which the would-be killer had tried to take his head off. "It must have floated to shore and gotten hung up here." He took a photo and pulled out a rubber glove, snagging the oar between two fingertips and raising it just enough to both leave it in place for the cops and allow Wally access.

"Now we've got something. Time to shine, Wall." At Roman's whistle, Wally splashed torso deep into the sludge and inhaled a snootful, nostrils quivering. After a flap of his massive ears, he set off along a muddy track away from the lake.

Emery hustled after them. "The water didn't weaken the scent?"

"Not enough to throw Wally off. It's not a question of can he find the trail, it's a question of does he want to." Roman sighed. "I worked with German shepherds in the Navy and once they understood who was the boss, they were amazingly disciplined. Not so much with bloodhounds, at least this one. He tends to decide which scents he's interested in following."

"Headstrong, imagine that."

Was that a message for him? He bristled until he recognized it was the truth, whether or not he wanted to admit it. Headstrong, quick to offend; he'd read similar on his military evaluations. Both were qualities he'd tried to work on through prayer. Mixed results thus far. The praying had tapered off and pretty much vanished since Theo's confession. Theo, the man who talked incessantly about God and love and grace and forgiveness. Hypocrite.

Stomach sour, Roman let out the leash and Wally pranced along, stopping, sniffing, circling, moving on and off the path. "He's pretty green, but if he can't turn up anything, I'll get Cleo and Stephanie out here."

Wally stopped dead, turned, and stared at Roman.

Emery giggled. "It almost looks like he's offended you're discussing his replacement."

"Sometimes I think he's a better mind reader than a tracker."

With an indignant swing of his ears, Wally bounded around a turn, pushing through a patch of tall grass overhung with bare-limbed trees. Roman held a branch to the side until Emery passed beneath.

Wally took them to a marshy area where a rickety pier protruded into the water.

"Might be where your abductor put you in the boat. This is a public dock. Anyone could have access. Could be the person noticed someone else's boat tied up here and decided to use it."

She didn't answer and they scurried to keep up with Wally as he trotted away from the dock, into the tall grass.

"We're doubling back toward the highway." In two more minutes, Wally had drawn them near the shoulder of the paved road. The dog stopped and zeroed in on the ground, sitting and looking at Roman for a moment.

"I might have been driving this road," Emery mused. "It's the best route into Whisper Valley." Before she had a chance to add to her comment, Wally was off again, nearly tangling Roman in the long leash.

"He's got something." He jogged now to keep up as Wally charged on. They emerged at the edge of a ravine, cloaked by tangled shrubs. Wally barked incessantly. Roman pumped a fist as they spotted the rear bumper of her Honda jutting from the foliage and two sets of tire tracks. Emery gasped.

"The abductor ran you off the road here. Took you to the dock and launched the boat. Afterward he returned to his own car and left yours here."

When she ran to open the door, he stopped her. "Cops need to photograph. I'll have Steph contact Hagerty now." His mind spun as he dashed off the text. "It looks as though they sideswiped you to force you off the road."

She nodded her head slowly. "I have a fleeting memory of clutching the wheel. That's it."

"Likely you hit your head. The attacker dragged you from the car unconscious and..." *sensitivity, remember?* "...uh, and then you know the rest of it."

There was not much left of the other vehicle's tire tracks except for the deep gouge in the wet earth. Emery craned her neck. "My phone and wallet must be in there somewhere. A small overnight bag too."

Roman set about photographing the car and scene as best he could without mucking up any evidence. He itched to present the findings to Security Hounds. With their combined resources and talents, it would simply be a matter of time before they'd uncover the perpetrator. Pride swelled inside him. Pride for a pack of exceptional people of which he'd become a part. Had to be a product of God's grace and nothing else.

They sat on a fallen tree trunk and he rewarded Wally with a treat. The dog snarfed it in a nanosecond and stared at him intently.

"He wants more?" she asked.

He offered another treat. Wally let it fall to the ground, untouched, and fixed his surly gaze on Roman. He sighed. "No, uh, there's a particular toy he wants, but I'm trying to get him weaned off it."

"Why? I remember when I visited the ranch with Dad, they rewarded with toys sometimes."

"Bad optics." Wally continued to glare at

him. He glared back. "You're a bloodhound, and your breed's origins go back a thousand years. Your findings are considered admissible in a court of law. You can't go around whining for that kind of toy. Where's your dignity? Your self-respect?" He offered a sturdy rubber KONG. "How about this one? The rest of the dogs love these things." Wally was unmoved. He stamped one fat paw into the ground.

Emery cocked her head at Wally. "Aww. He did a great job finding the car. Besides, if you don't give it to him, he won't want to do the next job you assign."

Hello, defeat. Next stop humiliation. "Fine. Here's your Binky, you overgrown infant." Cheeks warm, Roman fished the pacifier out of his backpack. Wally brightened with a joyful yowl and snatched the pacifier, scooting off to drop it on the ground and lick every centimeter of the pink plastic.

Emery gaped. "You're kidding. His reward is a baby pacifier?"

"Unfortunately. His previous owner said his son's kept going missing until he found Wally's stash under the sofa. All ten of them. He doesn't chew them for some reason so I don't worry he'll swallow the pieces, just licks and licks and gathers them like they're a brood of chicks and he's the mother hen. It's the weirdest dog behavior I've ever seen and if my siblings found out they'd never let me hear the end of it."

Emery exploded with a peal of giggles that had him laughing too. Her hair had come loose from the clip, swirling around her face in the unruly mass he remembered from long ago. He felt the desire to reach up and tuck a strand behind her ear.

Whoa. He stood and held out his palm to the dog. "All right, buddy. Bring it."

The dog curled his body tighter around his prize and turned his back to Roman.

"You're interrupting quality Binky time." Emery's cheeks were pink from laughter. She wiped her eyes.

"Wally, I said bring it."

The dog's head swiveled and it was another three seconds before Roman heard it too. A car. Hagerty rolled off the road toward their grassy hideaway and stopped. He got out.

"So you found it. Good work," he said. "I was nearby so I'd like to think I'd have tracked it down eventually."

Roman stood and snagged an anxious glance at Wally, but Emery somehow moved into position to block Hagerty's view of the dog and his toy. Had she done that on purpose, knowing Roman would be mortified if the cop found out?

They filled Hagerty in about the oar while he photographed the car from every angle. Opening the door with gloves, he videotaped the interior, removing her wallet and phone, which he bagged.

He heard Emery sigh and found himself empathizing. How long would it take before she got her wallet back? And with a baby to care for? He considered for the first time that she might be struggling to provide for her sudden charge. Paying for care while she did her job as a traveling nurse must cost a mint.

"We'll have to hang on to your vehicle for a bit," Hagerty said.

She gave one firm nod. Roman admired her strength. Always had.

Hagerty pocketed his phone. "I'll have the car towed and analyzed at the lab. Not going to lie. It'll take a couple of weeks at the minimum. At least you can start the insurance process, maybe get a rental."

Expensive. Her frown deepened.

Wally barked.

"What's the matter with him?"

A car appeared through the deep grass, bumping and jouncing.

The sunlight on the windows was blinding. The tall grass bent in both directions as the car plowed right for them.

Emery snagged Wally's leash, uncertain. Sensations spun through her, the swish of the grass parting under the tires, a glint of glass, the flash of silver chrome. It seemed unreal that they might be crushed now, while she'd been focused on the quickest and cheapest way to get home to Ian.

The vehicle punched toward them like a metal fist.

Fear made her sluggish. Which way to run? She tried to dart to the side. *Too late.*

Roman dove at her, snagged her around the middle, hurtling the three of them to one side. They tumbled in a tangle of elbows, knees and paws. Wally yelped as he skidded onto his back, ungainly legs paddling the air. A millisecond later Hagerty dove onto the ground next to them. Through the fringe of grass she saw the car slam to a stop near the police cruiser. Wheels dug into the mud as the driver changed course, yanked the vehicle back toward the road. With a squeal of tires, it retreated.

Roman was on his feet, slipping on the damp ground as he scrambled.

Wally barked and leaped upright and though she tried to hold on to his leash, he yanked it clean out of her fingers and took off after Roman. She got up at the same time as Hagerty and they ran, following Roman's path through the wall of grass, up the slight slope to the road.

Her fuzziness morphed into fear. Roman and Wally would be no match for a murderous driver. Frantic breaths clawed their way out of her mouth and her heart rate soared.

Hagerty panted as he came to a stop. A moment later she did too at the sight of Roman and Wally staring at the empty road in the direction the car had escaped.

Relief, both strange and comforting, flowed through her. No way they could have caught up. Silly to imagine Roman and Wally might have been in danger.

Roman swiped at the dirt on his forehead. "You okay, Emery?"

"Fine, now that my heart's started beating again. One minute we were talking and the next…" She breathed out, analyzing. "It seemed as though the driver was surprised to see a police car. Was that your take also?"

Roman nodded. "Whoever it was had to be responsible for your crash, or an accomplice, because they knew exactly where to look. It's not visible from the road."

"And the fact that they took off like a spooked horse," Hagerty added.

The most telling behavior of all. "Innocent people don't flee an accident scene?"

Hagerty reached for his handheld radio. "Correct."

Roman huffed out a breath. "I couldn't even get a partial plate number. You?"

Hagerty shook his head. "No, and my car camera won't have anything since it was facing the other way. Might have been a Mercedes, black paint."

She'd thought Mercedes too, but that was about as much as she'd been able to notice.

"Could be," Roman said. "By the time I caught up, they were nearly around the turn."

"What about that?" Emery pointed.

Hagerty looked at his body cam as if he'd forgotten about it. "Might have gotten a glimpse before I hit the dirt." He flicked a clump of soil off the lens.

"A glimpse could be enough." Roman brushed the dirt from his clothes. "Can you forward the footage to Security Hounds?"

"No. That's property of the police."

Emery saw Roman's jaw firm, shoulders gone military straight as he prepared for battle.

"One look is all I'm asking. A screen shot is fine. You said yourself it will take weeks to go over Emery's car and now you've got an almost hit-and-run on your hands."

Was Roman pushing too hard? Finesse was not in his repertoire, at least from what she remembered.

And then he surprised her by shoving his hands in his pockets. "I'd really appreciate your help on this, Officer. Garrett would be the point person on this case and he's an ex-cop. He wouldn't ace you out."

Emery had to stop herself from staring.

Roman's unexpected humility did the trick.

"I guess maybe we could do that," Hagerty said.

Roman exhaled. "You have my word that if we find anything helpful, you will be our first call."

Hagerty sniffed. "We'd better be."

Roman took Wally's leash. They left Hagerty

at his vehicle, talking into his radio. Wally scampered to the rutted mud and snagged his pacifier, grudgingly handing it over to Roman.

Back in Roman's Bronco, Emery tried to rub the grass marks from her pants. She'd always detested stains. They reminded her she'd worn her sister's hand-me-downs since she was six years old and their parents divorced. Their mom had moved to Europe, found a new way of life and a new man. Denise went through life skidding from one mess to the next, and Emery and her father had been the cleanup team. Until she'd had enough.

I'm not doing it, Dad. No more and you shouldn't either. Diane is a grown woman and now she's shown up with a baby that she figures we should support. I can't do it. I won't do it. I've got my nursing career, my own apartment and I'm not coming to the rescue. Not this time.

I understand, honey. I really do. We'll talk soon.

But soon never came. If only she'd known what would happen barely two weeks later. Diane would move into Lincoln Taylor's guesthouse, insisting he was the father of her child. Lincoln allowed her to stay but refused a paternity test. More drama from which Emery was happy to be well out of. Diane called their dad with a rosy report of Lincoln's warming to his son. It seemed as though her sister might actually be putting things back together...until that strange text.

Emery tried to put the past from her mind. The present was messy enough. Her morning call to the hospital had indicated no improvement for her sister, and she hadn't been able to reach anyone who could update her on her father's condition.

Too much for me to handle, Lord.

But somehow she had to. Ian needed her. And God would help her deliver.

She snagged a sideways glance at Roman. "That was...nice the way you asked for Hagerty's cooperation."

He shrugged. "Learned a thing or two about dealing with people in the military. And like Theo used to say..." He trailed off and gripped the wheel, a vein in his jaw jumping.

She finished softly, "Patience wins over force."

He didn't look at her. *Done talking.* Never wanted to even think about all the love her father had showered on him. Her spirit filled with bitterness and anger.

"He would have chosen to believe in you, no matter what the facts said," she muttered.

His quick glance showed the mocha of his

eyes had darkened. "I know you want to acknowledge only the best in him, Ree, but in my experience, facts win out every time."

Roman might have learned a bit about patience, but his flinty unforgiving nature hadn't softened one iota. He wouldn't extend any grace to her father. "You're not stuck on facts, you're hung up on the disappointment because of all the people that hurt you in your life. Your mother, Jax and my father." She saw him flinch as her arrow plunged deep. Shame licked at her but she shook it off. The silence thickened until it nearly swallowed her up. She forced some deep breaths and kept her thoughts to herself as they returned to the ranch.

Chapter Six

Beth met them at the door. "Surprise visitor here to see you, Emery."

Her nerves prickled. Did she have the fortitude for any more surprises?

But a familiar cry had her running toward the living room.

Gino's ruddy face broke into a smile when he saw her, the light gleaming on his prematurely bald head encircled by a wispy fringe of hair. Ian was tucked against his chest. "There you are."

She hurried and wrapped them both in a hug before she took her nephew. "This is Gino Kavanaugh," she said by way of introduction, "and this is Ian." She savored the warm heft of the baby. "And how's my big boy?" Ian offered a gummy smile and grabbed for her hair. She twirled him until he gave up a belly laugh and she buzzed a raspberry onto his cheek. The lurch in her heart told her that despite her anger at her sister, love had found a way in. A chill rippled her spine. Love wasn't enough to keep him safe. What if he'd been in the back seat of her car the day before?

Thanks, God, for keeping Ian away from the danger.

Her mouth went dry as she realized her predicament. Now, Ian wasn't away. He was right here in Whisper Valley where she'd been nearly drowned, run over and stalked in her hotel room.

Cradling Ian to her shoulder, she allowed Beth to gesture them into chairs. Stephanie and Garrett joined in, their identical body types and coloring startling. Wally galumphed over to Emery and nosed the baby's socked foot, brows crinkling. "Gino and Diane went to school together. They've known each other since fifth grade. He's been a good friend, a lifesaver, in fact."

He shrugged and scratched at his sandy mustache. "Diane looked me up after Ian was born. Asked me to help and I said yes, of course. That's me, a yes man all the way, especially where Diane is concerned." He blushed. "Have a passel of nieces and nephews so I'm familiar with baby care. Diane and Ian lived with me for a few months before she decided to confront Lincoln." He bobbed his knee. "After Diane's accident, I figured I could help Emery with Ian since I work online. Doesn't matter where from, as long as there's a wireless connection. I rented a unit in Emery's complex and became good old Uncle Gino."

Emery smiled at him. "Without Gino, I don't know how I would have managed and that's the truth."

"How wonderful," Beth said. "A gift from God."

She wanted to agree wholeheartedly but her nerves were bow-taut. "But what are you doing here now?"

Gino shrugged. "I was worried. You called me from some number I didn't know, all you said was you'd had an accident. I called back repeatedly, but I couldn't get you."

"I called from the cell Roman loaned me." She'd told him her temporary location, but not many details.

She'd earned his recrimination, realizing she hadn't checked the messages on the cell Roman had given her. A seasoned mother would do better, not a mommy impersonator such as herself. Waves of guilt swept over her at her own negligence. "I'm sorry. Things have been…unsettled. I should have told you more in my message."

His glasses magnified his eyes in an owlish fashion. "What happened to you, Emery…" He darted a look around the room. "I mean, Emily?"

"It's okay, Gino. They know my real name. No keeping secrets from the Wolfes, since they've known me since I was a kid." She took a deep breath and told him in as succinct a manner as possible about her harrowing return to town.

His skin drained of color. "Who's after you?"

"That's what the cops are trying to figure out," Roman said. "How did you get to Whisper Valley, Gino?"

Roman's question startled her. Why was he asking?

Under the mustache, Gino's lip crimped. "I took the bus."

"Why?" she asked. "Didn't you want to drive?"

"My car wouldn't start and I was getting more and more worried. I packed up Ian in his car seat and got on the bus and then took a taxi from the station to here."

She patted Ian's back when he fussed. Beth was at her side in a moment, all the dogs watching. "Let me walk him. I should remember how to lull him. The twins were terrible sleepers."

"That was Garrett's fault," Stephanie said. "He kept me awake."

Garrett twirled a pencil. "Okay, I'll own that, but all the rest of the trouble we got into during our formative years is on your shoulders."

Stephanie's smile was impish. "Probably."

Gratefully Emery handed her the wriggling baby. Beth began to walk in gentle loops, bobbing him up and down and patting his diapered bottom. She limped a little, her jaw tight, but her smile was beatific.

Gino still fingered his mustache, nervous.

She didn't want to ask in front of the Wolfe family, but she forged ahead. "What aren't you telling me?"

His gaze darted around the room. After a long pause, he spoke. "Last week I had this feeling that someone was following me while I was out walking Ian."

She gasped. "Why didn't you tell me?"

"I was afraid it was paranoia. I've been an insurance investigator for twenty years so you get to be distrustful." He shot her an accusing glance. "Maybe I'm right to be paranoid. I mean, you're living with an alias, so…"

Roman leaned forward. "Did you see who it was following you? A man? Woman?"

Gino shook his head. "Might have been a rental. I noticed it when I stopped to adjust Ian's blanket. Then when I got coffee on our way back, I saw the same vehicle again outside the shop."

Garrett watched as his sister jotted notes on her iPad. They weren't on the case officially, but he was secretly happy to see her acting as if they were.

"Make? Model?" Stephanie asked. Beth listened intently as she continued to joggle Ian.

He shrugged. "Compact. Dark, four-door."

Roman frowned. "You didn't notice the license plate? A partial?"

Gino scowled. "No, I'm not a detective, clearly, just a nanny. My insurance duties are mostly online sleuthing. I'm not the Dick Tracy–type."

"It might be nothing." Emery saw the collective Wolfe family frowns. It wasn't nothing. It was terrifying, the world spinning uncertainly around her, clouded with danger. The question that was foremost in her mind every single morning since the shooting presented itself again.

What should I do? The question had assumed even more heft since she was now responsible for a child. Most often in these moments she descended toward panic until she remembered her father's "top-three" list.

If there's too much, Ree Ree, pick the top three things you have to do for that day. Three is easy, right?

First, go back home.

Care for Ian.

Book more nursing jobs to keep them afloat.

The rest…rent a car, continue to visit her sister and father, etc., etc. would all happen eventually.

"You should—" Roman started.

"No." Her temper snapped to life in that one tiny syllable. She tried to clamp down on the rising emotion. "I'm sorry, but do you know how often I've heard that from people in the last six months? Cops, lawyers, social workers, nurses have all said, you should do this or that… and then they vanish and it's me left do it all. I'm only one person." She cringed at the desperation ringing in her own words. *Deep breath, Emery.* "I know you mean well, all of you. I ap-

preciate what you've done for me and I'll continue to cooperate with Hagerty as best I can,
but I'm taking Ian home. Time for another bus
ride, sweetie." She held out her hands for the
baby, proud that they did not shake. There were
no friends here in Whisper Valley. Only people
who hated what her father had done, thought
her sister a tramp, and the Wolfe family who
pitied her. She didn't need that.

"Actually," Gino said. "Um, can I talk to
you privately?"

Her gut clenched.

Beth laid her cheek on the top of Ian's head.
"I'll greedily accept a few more minutes with
this cutie. Who knows when I'll have a grand-
baby to hold?"

Stephanie rolled her eyes.

"Don't look at me," Garrett said. "I just killed
my last surviving houseplant."

With a feeling of dread, Emery followed
Gino to the porch. She could feel the weight
of Roman's gaze as she left.

"Whatever you're going to tell me is more
bad news, isn't it?" she said the moment the
door closed behind them.

"I really hate to give you this." He pulled an

envelope from his pocket. "And you know I'm going to help you however I can."

The return address was a bank and the sticker on the envelope read *Forward* to her apartment address. The low-grade worry hitched into full-blown fear. "What is this, Gino?"

His lips puffed as he blew out a breath. "It's a letter of default for your father's cabin. It was forwarded to your apartment when you put in the request with the post office."

A request that she'd finally handled much later than she should have, but she blamed that on Ian's arrival and all the other bombs that had detonated after her father's arrest and her sister's injury.

"It showed up in your mailbox yesterday right after you left, along with these." He handed over several more. "I opened them. You told me to handle anything important anytime you were away nursing or whatever. The short story is the bank is foreclosing. Your dad hasn't been making payments on the place."

Foreclosing. Missing payments. "But…he's in jail. How could he possibly have been keeping up with his finances? I knew there was a payment due at the end of the month but…"

Gino looked at a spot over her head. "The

problem didn't start with his incarceration. It seems he's been delinquent before, repeatedly. They sent a thirty-day notice last year and he managed to pay that and stave off action, but not this time." Finally his gaze traveled to her face. "I did some digging, used some channels I shouldn't have and, um, he'd taken out a second mortgage as well. To cover...expenses. Likely the same reason he worked as a handyman on this ranch, I think. His military pension wasn't enough to cover it."

Her heart plummeted to her shoes. *Expenses.* He'd helped pay for her nursing school and though she'd repaid every last nickel, it had taken her a year to do so. Had that contributed to his insolvency? And her sister's stint in a rehab facility had cost tens of thousands. Likely Diane hadn't come near to repaying it, if she'd even tried at all. Her father had bankrupted himself for them. Is that why he had told her to go home?

"I'm so sorry," Gino said.

Her heart boomed in her chest. "But there must be some way to stop it... If I repay...?" *With what?* She was barely surviving. Tears blurred the writing on the envelope. "A leniency schedule?"

He shook his head.

"So there's nothing I can do?" she whispered.

"The cabin is lost, I'm afraid. If I had the money, I'd pay it off in a flash."

"I know you would." Pulling in breaths through her nose, she tried to stave off hyperventilation. Her father would be crushed to lose his cabin *paradise* as he called Whisper Valley. He'd rather sell off all his possessions than let go of his home. Then again, what did she know of him, this man who refused even to see her when he'd been remanded to jail? That hurt most of all. Perhaps deep down he blamed her for giving up on Diane.

Gino put a hand on her forearm. "There's... not much time."

She blinked. "Time?"

He nodded. "The foreclosure begins a week from today."

One week? Of course. Why not? No sense prolonging the agony.

"Somebody will need to pack up his belongings," he added gently.

And that would fall to her too, of course. Along with a baby and everything else. Her head swam and she felt like screaming.

He offered a faint smile. "I brought my laptop along so I could stay and help you with packing and the baby. Like I said, have Wi-Fi, will travel." He sighed. "Sorry, not the time to joke."

"I couldn't ask for a better friend. I appreciate it." She barely managed the statement around the lump in her throat. She caught a flicker of emotion that he quickly concealed. "Is there something else?"

"No, nothing. I'll...go in and get Ian ready to drive to the cabin. Give you a minute, okay?" He patted her back. "I'm real sorry to have to tell you. Your dad would never have wanted you to deal with all this alone."

He let himself back inside.

A dark cloud ballooned in her stomach. Her top three had just changed. Again.

Care for Ian.

Pack up her father's belongings.

Maybe book a local nursing job to pay for a rental car back home at the end of the week.

She wondered how she'd explain to the Wolfes and Roman that her father was a deadbeat in addition to a would-be murderer.

Roman wouldn't be surprised.

In those brown eyes, she'd see the self-righteous glint and the hurt underneath.

His thoughts were clear as a winter sky. *Never should have trusted him. He wasn't the man I thought he was.*

Despair weighed her down as she forced her feet back into the Wolfes' den.

Roman kept urging Wally out from underfoot as he hauled a bag of supplies his mother had packed to the Bronco.

He kept his jaws clamped shut to prevent him voicing to Emery the thoughts rocking his brain. *Your father bankrupted himself? And now that's your problem too?*

But Emery could barely get the words out and even a thick-skulled guy like himself could see she was near her breaking point as she climbed into his vehicle, strapping Ian into the car seat Gino had brought with him.

Beth stood in the doorway, face pained, having been unable to convince Emery to stay at the ranch. She waved and he saw her wince under the bright smile.

That tiny tell ratcheted his muscles. Beth desperately needed surgery for the back condition that caused her unending pain. She'd steadfastly refused the procedure due to the cost and length of recovery *until Security Hounds lands on all four paws*, as she put it.

His jaw clenched. They would be set, if the Cars for K-9s event went off as he'd planned it.

Their fledgling detective work was too sporadic and there wasn't a huge market for bloodhound pups so they'd curtailed their breeding program. They needed to snag a search and rescue contract with the county and he knew just the way to make that happen.

He drove to a quiet sloping road through the pine trees. Ian gurgled from the back seat and Gino played some sort of game with his toes. Emery stared grim-faced out the front window. Wally sat backward on the front seat between Roman and Emery, staring at the baby action going on in the rear, thumping Roman's shoulder with his eagerly wagging tail.

"Don't drool on the kid, Walls."

Gino chuckled. "I'm diverting the saliva slinging."

Roman wasn't sure how he felt about Gino. Something about the man plucked a distrustful chord, but Roman didn't trust much of anybody. Gino the friendly baby helper would have no reason to lie about his reasons for showing up. Would he? No use talking to Emery about it, or anything else. She was mute, every muscle strained.

He'd found some flattened cardboard boxes from their bulk shipment of dog food and rolls of packaging tape, the only way he could think to assist. His anger at Theo threatened to explode like the volcano that had erupted twelve thousand years before to form Crater Lake.

Theo had shot someone and gotten himself jailed, and he'd left a mess behind that was flowing over onto his daughter. He deserved nothing. Emery should leave town and let the bank send people to dump his belongings at the nearest auction house. The twenty miles of road did nothing to mellow his anger. They bumped along an uneven graveled path until they came to a wood-sided cabin with overgrown shrubs crowding the curtained front windows.

As soon as he put it in Park, she was out, striding to the door of the cabin as Gino extracted the baby. Wally hovered at Gino's side, his big nose sniffing at the wriggling bundle. "Hang onto him," Gino said, suddenly thrusting the baby at Roman. "I have to get the car seat loose. We'll have to rent a car at some point when we're done packing."

Startled, Roman gathered Ian close. Too

close? Not close enough? It seemed like the baby's limbs were all wobbly and not working together. He'd never actually held a baby, he realized in that moment. Not a human one, only the newly born puppies he'd tended after he'd returned stateside. But dogs were born with eyes and ears sealed shut, balls of chubby helplessness. Ian craned his little head in Roman's direction, an old man's frown crinkling his feathery brows. Was Roman grabbing him too tightly? Loosening his grip could result in him dropping the tiny human who'd flung out a fist to bat at Roman's baseball cap.

"Whatcha need, baby boy?" *Baby boy.* The nickname he'd both loved and despised, bestowed on him by his uncle Jax. For a moment he could only stare into Ian's small perfect face, buffeted by the flood of memories.

I haven't stopped loving you, baby boy, but there's room in my life for a wife and more kids, Roman. You're gonna be seventeen soon. Can't you understand that?

There's no room in mine, he'd wanted to shout, his adolescent rage spilling into oaths, slammed doors, a hastily packed bag. *You replaced me, gave me up for someone else.*

Uncle Jax had tried to talk, repeatedly reach-

ing out over the years, including a text only the
week before Emery's attack at the river.

Hey, baby boy. Just thinking about you.

He hadn't replied, though he'd ached to.
Every time he thought of Uncle Jax his heart
was filled with a mixture of shame, sadness,
disappointment and regret. He wasn't seventeen anymore, hadn't been for a decade, so why
wouldn't he reach out to his uncle?

A bird hurtled from the thick trees with a
raucous cry and Roman reflexively clutched
Ian closer. The bird was probably startled by
a fox or feral cat. Wally's nose quivered as he
tracked the bird. Roman felt uneasy. Theo's
cabin was remote, too far away from help if
Emery needed it.

The late afternoon sun sank behind the distant hills. Wind rattled the branches. Gino
was still wrestling with the car seat so Roman
walked Ian to the cabin, whistling to Wally to
follow. He found Emery inside, standing in the
middle of a small living room on a braided rag
rug. She was frowning at the lumpy sofa and
the bookshelves crowded with detective fiction.
There was a scent of pipe tobacco and Emery
had already opened the small kitchen window

to air it out. Theo and his pipe. The ache of it cycled through him, as he was sure it did with Emery.

Wally plowed in, awash in an avalanche of new scents to experience.

"I…uh… Here," he said, handing Emery the baby. "He feels like he might be cold, but I'm not sure how he's supposed to feel so…" His babbling dried up.

She gathered Ian close, much less awkwardly than he had, kissing him absentmindedly on the forehead and murmuring something he didn't catch. That tender tableau hitched his breathing.

What are you here for anyway, Roman? She doesn't enjoy your company and the feeling is mutual.

She surveyed the stuffed bookshelves and the kitchen with ancient cupboards no doubt crammed with things. Her sigh was weary, resigned. "This is going to take weeks."

"I'll help." Had he really said that? Now? With everything he had to do for the Cars for K-9s event? What would Emery think if she knew he was a temporary partner with the Taylors?

He straightened. What was wrong with that? They were the victims, not the perpetrators.

She quirked a brow at him, probably trying to figure out how to decline his offer.

"I... I mean..."

Gino's arrival saved them both. "I'll put this in one of the bedrooms." There was a small insulated bag slung over his shoulder. "Brought along a few prepared bottles and his snacks, some diapers and clothes too."

Ian decided at that moment to cry. Wally jerked away from his sniffing and let out a blast of a bark, which made the baby cry louder. Roman quieted the canine. The dog settled into a low-grade whine as the baby continued to fuss.

"He needs a nap." Emery's exasperation was clear as she looked around.

Gino finally entered with the car seat. "We can put him down on your dad's bed until we get a porta crib. Watch him to be sure he doesn't roll off and roll up some towels as a bumper. Can you get me a clean diaper and I'll change him first?"

Emery pulled one from a bag Beth had provided.

Roman felt envious of their efficient partnership. He eyed the bookshelves, every inch crammed. "I'll fill some boxes."

Emery shoved the hair away from her face. "This is going to take weeks, especially with a baby."

Gino's mouth thinned. "We can do it. We've been handling everything for six months, just the two of us."

Roman cocked his chin. "That mean you can't tolerate a little assistance?"

"Not from someone who despises Theo."

He gaped. Not what he'd expected. He was rallying a response when Emery gestured to Gino. "Why don't you take Ian into the bedroom? Maybe he'll nap for you. You're the baby whisperer."

Gino didn't look at Roman as he accepted the whimpering child and left the room.

Emery turned and fished her credit card out of her pocket. At least Hagerty had been able to return it with her wallet. "I'm sorry to ask, but is there any way you could get us a portable crib?"

"It's not a great idea to stay up here alone after what happened to you."

"I don't have a choice. There's no one else to take care of my dad's belongings."

No one else to clean up the mess her father had left behind. No one to care for Ian but her and Gino. She should stay at the ranch. But he could not say the words because her lips were trembling and there was a sheen in her eyes of tears she did not want to shed, not in front of him.

He closed his mouth, gesturing away her credit card. "I know where I can borrow one." *She needs you to get a crib. She doesn't want your help.* Enough said. "I'll bring the boxes in before I go get it." He flipped the light switch, relieved that the power worked. At least that bill was paid up. For how long?

He'd nearly reached the porch when he heard an engine, a car winding along the lonely road. No other houses out this way and the road did not connect to any other major thoroughfares.

His stomach tightened.

Who would be driving to Theo's cabin? And why?

Chapter Seven

"A visitor. I'll see what they want, okay?" He hustled out with Wally in tow and closed the door behind him. His gut churned. Someone had learned she'd come to town? Ready to spew more hatred at her and her sister's child for what had happened?

It was a Mercedes, black. Three people got out. Innkeeper Hilary, her ex-husband, Lincoln, and his brother, Mason. Here? Why would they come to Theo's place? What could they want?

He managed a friendly smile. *They are your business partners, remember?*

Hilary zipped her sleek jacket and reached into the car for a cardboard box while Lincoln, dark-haired, lean and muscular, stared at the cabin. Mason took the box from Hilary. He was shorter than his brother, his frame stockier. When he stepped toward Roman, he subtly lurched, favoring one leg. They'd only spoken on the phone so Roman was unaware the damage from the bullet hadn't fully resolved. Would it be an injury that would impact him the rest of his life?

"Roman," Hilary said, surprised. "I didn't expect to see you here. We were planning on leaving this box on the porch since we didn't know where else to send it."

Wally stood on hind legs, front paws balanced against Roman's hip to sniff the carton as it passed into Roman's arms. "I was bringing up some packing boxes." He paused, figuring he had to add some sort of explanation. "Place is being sold."

Lincoln cocked his head. "Selling?" He raised a brow. "Nah. Not Theo. He seemed like the type that would live out in sticks until his last day. Let me guess. Foreclosure?"

Roman shrugged, feeling a swell of irritation. "Not my business." Nor Lincoln's.

Lincoln's expression was calculating. "Diane said he was struggling financially."

Roman hid his surprise that Diane had shared that fact with Lincoln but clearly not with Emery. Then again, there had been serious friction between the sisters.

Lincoln leaned against the car, arms folded

over his muscled chest. A gym rat, obviously. He should try filling holes and running bloodhounds all day. Better than any workout.

Hilary shook her head. "That explains why she showed up insisting you support her and the baby. The daddy pipeline was drying up."

Lincoln frowned. "Maybe she was telling the truth about Ian. Maybe he is mine."

Hilary's expression was as cold as her words. "More likely she was lying. As you'd expect from someone who took up with a married man."

A dark flush crept up his neck. "We were having problems, Hilary. Divorcing, remember? We were waiting on lawyers."

She glared. "You never could wait for anything, could you?"

Roman would gladly have been anywhere else but in the middle of this family drama.

Mason shifted. "Uh, this doesn't seem like the right time to hash all this out. Lincoln can take a paternity test down the road if he wants to."

Lincoln shoved a hand through his hair. "I was considering it but I hadn't had time to make the decision when she…"

Hilary interrupted. "You made it clear you

never wanted children, not when we were married. I don't see why you'd want one now."

"Think of how I felt. Diane and I were getting things worked out." Lincoln shook his head. "I come home from a drive to find Mason shot, Diane unconscious and her dad being arrested."

Hilary grimaced at him. "Yes, and her father intended to kill you, don't forget, and got your poor brother instead. It was astonishing that Mason didn't bleed to death."

"Right," Mason said. "Talk about being in the wrong place at the wrong time. I was reaching for the light switch and kablam—a shot comes out of nowhere and down I go."

Roman remembered Mason's account of the shooting. He'd been upstairs, heard a noise and walked to the balcony, where he'd been shot without even being able to identify who'd done it. He'd passed out, then roused to find medics treating his gunshot wound and cops swarming the house. If only he'd been able to provide an eyewitness account to clear things up.

What things? The case was open and shut, wasn't it?

Lincoln's gaze clouded. "I don't know why Diane would have told her father things were bad between us, or why he'd bring a gun to the house."

"You did decline the paternity test," Mason said. "Maybe it set him off."

"Yeah, but I wasn't done mulling it over. No cause for him to become violent like that."

Hilary sniffed. "You should consider yourself fortunate. *You* didn't get hurt." She patted Mason. "Theo probably saved you from a woman trying to use her baby to trick you into a marriage, Lincoln."

"Please, you two," Mason said. "When Diane recovers…" His words trailed off.

If she recovers…

Mason held up his hands. "Anyway, sorry for airing out the family laundry. Dad's rolling over in his grave, no doubt. He'd talk your ear off about cars, but never personal stuff."

Lincoln's cheeks flushed and he didn't meet his brother's eye. "Right. Roman has things to do and so do we, so let's leave him to it."

Roman nodded. "Yeah. I need to get these inside."

Mason quirked a brow. "I'm surprised you'd be packing up Theo's place. Didn't know you had a connection to the Duncan family."

He shifted, reluctant to share but unwilling

to lie. "Theo Duncan was a friend for a while." Before Hilary could ask the question that appeared to be forming, he added, "What's in this box?"

"Baby stuff. Diane left them at Lincoln's house." Hilary shrugged. "Outfits and some toys and bottles."

"How is she?" Lincoln said. "Diane, I mean."

"I don't know details. Still hospitalized," Roman said.

"What a tragedy," Mason said. "Hopefully not for too much longer."

"Why do you care?" Hilary demanded. "She and her father are the reason you're in pain and walking with a limp now."

Mason sighed. "Come on, Hil. Diane's father's in jail. And hasn't she been punished enough? She's got a baby and all, and honestly she was a good mother, from what I could see. That's why we brought these things back here." He pointed to the box in Roman's arms and caressed Wally with his free palm. Wally snuffled at him. "Didn't seem right to donate them. Figured maybe someone would come and pick them up and deliver them to Emery. We saw her in court that one time. We figured she'd get temporary custody, at least. Is that what happened?"

Roman took a breath. How much of Emery's business was it all right to share?

He was saved from answering when the door opened and Emery stepped out. The look of shock on the faces of the three visitors was textbook.

Hilary gaped. "Wait a minute. Now I recognize you. You look like your sister, even with the change of hair color."

Emery wrapped her arms around her middle. "Yes," she said after a moment's hesitation.

"You might have used your real name when you checked into my inn."

Emery stared at Hilary. "Would you, if you were me? After everything that happened in this town?"

Hilary didn't answer.

"They brought some of the baby's things," Roman said.

Emery's posture was rigid with discomfort. "Thank you."

"How's... I mean, how is he? The baby?" Lincoln asked.

Emery cocked her head. "I'm not sure why

you'd want to know, since you refused a paternity test, from what Dad told me."

Hilary's eyes narrowed. "We're talking about the same dad that shot Mason, right? Champion father material."

Emery's cheeks flamed. Roman put a hand on her forearm. This was turning into a disaster.

Lincoln was already edging back toward the car. "Okay. We'll be at the ranch to talk details tomorrow, Roman. The weekend is coming fast."

Emery shot him a look.

He felt his cheeks burn. "Yes. I'll be at the ranch at ten. We'll go over the info."

Mason smiled. "This is going to be the most amazing event ever to hit Whisper Valley. It's our chance to shine. Right, Lincoln?"

Lincoln acknowledged the remark with a shrug. Mason's smile dimmed. Hilary touched his arm. "Your brother's excited too but overwhelmed. Don't worry. He'll be at his best when the clients arrive." She turned to Roman, ignoring Emery completely. "We'll be ready. There's a lot riding on it."

Didn't he know it. Roman called Wally away from sniffing Lincoln's Mercedes.

After a deep breath, he walked inside behind Emery, sliding the box onto the table.

She jerked the window closed, locked it and pulled the curtains. "That was awkward, but inevitable, I suppose. I was bound to run into them in town. I guess the cat's out of the bag now. I won't need my alias. Emery Duncan, the youngest of the no-good family, has come back to Whisper Valley."

"Most folks won't think that."

She shook her head. "It's exactly what they'll think." After a beat, she added, "So you're partnering with the Taylor family? What's that about?"

"I should have said something sooner." He told her about the car show, wondering if he sounded defensive. Why should he? "I'm hoping to land a contract with the local police departments and county to provide tracking services to supplement our detective work," he explained. The idea had been born out of a missing persons case with which they'd assisted. Stephanie and Cleo had tracked a child who'd wandered away in a storm. The child's parents donated a small sum to Security Hounds and begged the police department to bring on a bloodhound instead of having to call for one. "After many conversations with Hagerty, myself and the police department, I worked up a

plan with the Taylors for a Cars for K-9s benefit. The dogs will be on site for some demonstrations to wow the crowd."

"A win-win situation for both parties." Her
posture was stiff.

"The Taylors are donating ten percent of
their take. If the event brings in enough money,
the county will offer a contract with an agency
for search and rescue."

"Security Hounds, of course?"

"We'd be the perfect choice. No other bloodhound training facilities around. I can prove
their abilities with the demonstrations we've
planned for the weekend event at the Taylor
estate."

His mind latched on to all the small details
that needed to be tended to before the first Cars
for K-9s event kicked off at the ranch. It would
be followed by a second demonstration on Sunday culminating in a reception at the Taylor
showroom. Plenty of audience participation.
Roman intended for Security Hounds to have
a presence in every aspect. It had to work, since
he'd blown up the budget with advertising, re-
vamping the dogs' travel trailer and even gotten the family matching shirts and caps, much
to their dismay.

"We're going to be the group law enforcement looks for when there's a fugitive, a lost child or pet, et cetera," he'd told them.

Steph was on board and Garrett was amenable, but Chase had doubts about extending themselves in what would be a 24/7, 365 day a year availability. Kara remained quiet, as per usual.

"We can't be all things to all people. Detectives, dog rescuers, et cetera," Chase had said.

"Steph, Garrett and I can handle the search and rescue aspect and we'll come together when there's a case that requires it," he'd insisted. "You and Kara can be floaters to pitch in whenever you can."

The project was in limbo until Beth stepped in. "I say we go for it, but without the county's buy in, we'll be dead in the water before we even start."

Dead in the water... Roman realized he'd been lost in his own jumbled thoughts as Emery watched him quietly.

"I'm going to get the contract." He was sure the Cars for K-9s weekend would seal the deal.

She cocked her head, the hair softly framing her cheek. "You're determined to help Security Hounds succeed."

He shrugged. "They're my family and Beth won't get the surgery she needs on her back until we clinch the business."

He'd braced for Emery to be upset at his participation with the Taylors, especially after Hilary's remarks. Instead she leaned her head against the wall, weariness etched in every shadow that played across her face.

"I'm glad you have family around you, Roman." Her voice was soft. "You deserve that."

Deserve? To be loved like he was by people who'd chosen him? He didn't believe that yet, which is why he was working so hard on the K-9 event. He was going to show them he was worthy.

She sighed. "But there's something wrong with the Taylors. I don't exactly know what. For all her faults, Diane wouldn't have gone to the house with murder on her mind and my father wouldn't have taken the blame or shot anyone himself unless he felt there was no other choice."

"I know you want to believe that. I did too."

She blinked. "You stopped believing pretty quick, didn't you? And you walked away."

From Theo…and from her.

The blanket of quiet was smothering.

"I'll get you that crib." He dug his keys from his pocket. As he called to Wally and pushed open the door, he noticed Gino in the bedroom patting Ian's back. He'd obviously been eavesdropping.

Gino darted a look at him just before he closed the door.

If he were still in the Navy, it'd make him take a good long look at Gino and earn the man an up close and personal examination from a nosy dog.

One thing was for certain.

Gino had secrets.

After an hour of the baby's screaming that left her nerves ragged, Ian finally fell asleep in his car seat with Emery curled up next to him on the floor. Eventually, she must have slept as well because her eyes flew open again a few minutes after eight o'clock. Her neck was beyond kinked, body outraged at having been sprawled on the hardwood.

Groggy, she got to her knees. The room was dark save for the small side table lamp and the light coming from underneath the closed door of the second bedroom, which Gino had claimed. She shoved her hair out of her eyes. No need to keep it dyed dark anymore, since her secret was out. Everyone knew she was in town and that made her feel naked, vulnerable. No doubt it was a mistake to stay in her father's cabin, but there seemed no other choice, no one else to tackle the packing. *All on you, Emery.*

Roman hadn't returned with the crib. She probably shouldn't have asked him about it anyway. It rankled her that he was business partners with the Taylors. They might not be criminals, but they surely wanted her father imprisoned for the rest of his life and they had strong opinions about her sister's motives.

So had she. In fact, she'd been convinced Diane's latest appearance in her mommy role was another way to take advantage of her father's good graces, one more mess she expected the family to clean up. Her own guilt left a sour taste in her mouth. Ian twitched in his sleep.

Not a mess. A child. She heaved out a breath and offered a prayer for God to soften her bitter heart.

…honestly she was a good mother, Mason had said.

The sentiment touched her, from a man who had no reason to say one nice word about any Duncan family member. For all her faults, Diane didn't deserve to be comatose with an unwilling sister raising her baby. "Lord, help me do my best."

Ignoring her protesting muscles, she took a knee next to her sleeping nephew. Ian's mouth puckered and she hastily tucked the blanket more snugly around him and rocked the seat until he quieted. As he settled once more, her gaze drifted to the clutter closing in around her, every item in need of packing away and disposing. Books, navy memorabilia, fishing lures, her father's beloved houseplants, now mostly dead after months of not being watered… The magnitude of the job flattened her until she forced a deep breath.

"Not impossible," she told herself with more cheer than she believed. "With Gino's help, I can knock this out in a few days if Ian will cooperate." Then she remembered the basement and the groan made its way past her defenses. How much had her father accumulated since she'd last been down in that dank space?

She shot a look toward the bedroom. Gino had earned a few hours of rest, especially after his marathon bus trip with an infant in tow. She'd allow herself a quick peek while Ian slept.

The front door was secured only by the worn bolt. It was something anyway.

The basement door opened and a rush of cool air bathed her face. She moved Ian away from the draft. "Be right back. I'll be able to hear you if you cry, okay?" Did other parents engage in one-sided conversation with their children?

She flipped the switch at the top of the stairs, which activated a bare bulb, a meager forty watts, but enough for her to use the stairs safely. She knew there were small windows set high in one of the basement walls, which would make the daytime packing easier. Tonight was simply recon, as Roman would say.

Dismissing him firmly from her mind, she decided on her "top three" for the rest of the evening. First, no matter how daunting, she'd scope out the contents of the basement. Second, compile a list of supplies necessary for the three of them to survive the packing phase. That would entail a trip into town, which made her insides quiver. All the haters were stoking their anger, no doubt. Third, call in to her agency and let them know she was unavailable for a few days. *Unavailable and unpaid*, she thought grimly. How long would her money hold out with the majority of it going toward her apartment rent?

One cement wall was floor-to-ceiling with rickety wood shelves holding a hodgepodge of materials. Her father the pack rat…

Against the far wall was a metal desk, tidy, at odds with the rest of the space. On top was an iPad. Odd since her dad was a dinosaur where technology was concerned. Next to it was her father's favorite "Daddy's sweeties" mug, emblazoned with a photo of her and Diane. It was the last school photo before their mother and father divorced.

Marjorie Duncan was now Marjorie Watkin, her second marriage since she'd divorced Theo. She was aware of the situation with her daughter and ex-husband, of course. She'd even visited Diane in the hospital once, but she was the manager of a struggling travel agency. With nothing good to say about Theo Duncan, she'd managed a halfhearted offer.

I could, um, send some money when things pick up again. Or you could move to Virginia and maybe I could help with the baby when I'm not working.

Marjorie Duncan wanted nothing to do with raising a baby or resuming her position with a family she'd left two decades before. Emery appreciated the offer for what it was, polite and insincere. Mom didn't know her daughters anymore, didn't want to revisit any connection with their father and couldn't board the plane back to Virginia fast enough.

Just you, Ree Ree. With tears in her eyes, she moved closer to the desk and attempted to turn on the iPad. Dead. Naturally.

She picked up the mug and caressed it, her fingertip finding the chip. A sound made her clutch it to her chest. The baby? She was three steps toward the stairs when she heard it again. Slowly she swiveled around.

Wrong direction.

The sound was coming from outside. She stared at the small windows. Shifting shadows stretched and undulated outside, wind-driven tree branches caught in the moonlight.

Branches, she decided. *You're in the forest, remember?* Acres of wild Siskiyou County, stretching halfway to Klamath Falls. She was reaching to return the mug to the desk when a shadow took terrifying shape against the moisture-speckled glass. Something white against the pane.

A hand, cupped, pressed to the window, the gleam of two eyes peering in.

With a scream, she dropped the mug and ran up the stairs two at a time, snatching Ian out of the car seat, startling him into a shriek. *Get out or stay in? If someone was out there...*

"Gino," she yelled. She ran to his bedroom. Empty. So was the bathroom. Where had he gone? Panicked, she fled into her bedroom, locked the door and then pulled out her phone, dialing without thinking.

Roman answered on the first ring.

"Roman, there's someone outside."

"Where are you?"

"Locked in the bedroom with Ian."

"I'm five minutes out. Make that three. Stay on the line with me."

She heard the revving engine, imagining she could detect Wally's slobbery panting in the passenger seat. Trying hard to both quiet the baby and her own breathing, she strained to hear any sounds from outside. Were those normal shadows writhing outside the curtains or someone approaching? It was as though she were being tossed in the river all over again, helpless, drowning... Roman's voice on the phone snapped her back to the present.

"Are you hurt? Ian? Where's Gino?"

"We're okay. I don't know where Gino is.

Ian's crying because I woke him up. I was in the basement and..." She froze as a human silhouette glided across the closed bedroom curtains. "Roman," she whispered over her thundering heart. "I think there's someone walking outside."

"I'm almost there. Hold on." In moments she heard his boots pounding over the gravel, a crash as the front door was kicked open, the scrabbling of dog nails on the hardwood.

"Emery," Roman said. "It's me. Stay in there while I check."

With a surge of blissful relief, she tried to calm herself and Ian, patting his bottom. "Shh, baby. Help is here."

Time passed with painful slowness until Roman's tap startled her.

"House is clear. You can unlock the door."

She did, with trembling hands, stepping out and, without any conscious intention, delivering herself into his arms. He embraced her and the baby, wrapping them close while Wally gave them an interested sniff before allowing himself free rein to explore the house.

She pressed her cheek to the rough fabric of Roman's flannel shirt. "I'm sorry for calling you," she whispered.

His embrace tightened. "Nothing to be sorry about. I was on my way here, anyway. Your call just lit a fire."

She realized she was snuggled against him, inhaling the enticing aroma of pine from his shirt. What's more, she was dismayed to find she was savoring the sensations. Quickly she straightened, shuffling the baby on her hip as he started crying again. "Um, my screaming woke him up. He's grumpy, for sure."

Roman cocked a look at her. "Found a trespasser, by the way."

"Who?"

He jerked a thumb behind him. Gino stood with his hands in his pockets. He wore a dark windbreaker and a baseball cap. His cheeks were flushed.

"I thought you were sleeping in the bedroom. Why didn't you come when I screamed?"

"I was outside. I didn't hear you. Is something wrong?"

She gaped. "Why in the world were you out in the cold?"

He shrugged. "I couldn't sleep. When I came out of the bedroom, you were dozing next to Ian so I figured I'd take a quick walk to loosen up. I went out the back door so I wouldn't let in a draft on you and Ian."

Roman was examining Gino's expression with the same intensity she saw in him when he'd been tracking with Wally. "She was almost drowned recently, stalked at the inn, and you left her here alone with a baby? Went for an evening stroll?"

Gino's flush deepened to scarlet. "I was no more than five minutes away tops, on the trail. I could have run back if I'd heard…"

"But you didn't hear," he snapped. "She screamed and you didn't head back until you saw my Bronco roll up."

His brows knitted. "The wind was blowing. I shouldn't have left, but I was desperate for fresh air." He turned to Emery. "I'm sorry. Are you two okay? Why did you scream?"

"I saw… I thought I saw…" She took a breath. "I was in the basement and I thought I saw a face at the window, looking in."

Gino's crimson cheeks paled to white. "Who?"

Emery shook her head and continued to joggle the baby. "I don't know. Roman, was there any sign of someone out there?"

"Not that I could tell. It's heavy grass so no

prints would show, anyway. Wally wanted to drag me into the shrubs, but he was after a racoon or possum, likely."

She took in the two men staring back at her. They didn't believe she'd seen someone. She wasn't sure she believed herself. Had it been a human face at the window or the play of light and branches against the glass?

"I'm sorry. Probably my imagination. I guess I'm jumpy."

"You were almost murdered. Makes sense." Roman's tone was guarded and she couldn't decipher his expression as he strode toward the door. "I'll bring in the crib." He paused and tossed over his shoulder, "And I can stay the night on the sofa, me and Walls."

He didn't wait for her to reply before he headed outside.

Stay the night? She handed the baby to Gino. "Be right back."

She caught up with Roman at the Bronco where he hauled out a neatly folded portable crib. Rain drops spat at her.

"This was up in the attic at the ranch," Roman said. "Chase asked me to store it. He... Well he cared for his girlfriend's baby for a while. A painful breakup. Long story. Anyway, I know he wouldn't mind you using it for Ian."

"Roman, thank you for this and everything, but there's no reason for you and Wally to stay here."

His eyes sought hers. "Yes, there is."

"I was probably mistaken."

Roman stayed silent.

"And Gino's here with me. I know you don't trust him, but I do and I know him better than you." She paused. "My dad did, also."

Roman's frown deepened. "Maybe not a trustworthy character reference."

She bristled. "I'll make my own decisions about whom to trust."

Again, a long silence grew between them along with her kindling ire. She knew her father's heart and Roman had too, but he'd convinced himself he'd been betrayed. Did he see that whatever had happened that terrible night did not erase the goodness in her father's soul?

"Don't stay," she repeated. "We're fine."

"I busted your door lock."

"I'll put a chair under the knob for tonight."

He grimaced and started to reply, then

stopped and sighed. "I'll come tomorrow to fix the lock."

She wasn't going to talk him out of that, she could tell. "All right. I'll pay for the materials. Just let me know how much." She turned to go but he grasped her hand.

"What if Gino is lying?"

She grabbed the crib and backed up a step. "As I said, I know Gino better than you do, like I know my father." What was she doing? Baiting him? Poking him toward a fight because that was easier than acknowledging the strange attraction she'd felt earlier? "I appreciate your help. Thanks for the boxes, and bringing the crib, and…" And holding her while she trembled in fear. She tipped her chin up.

She'd made her decision. She might be attracted to Roman, like she'd always been, but that was surface-level only. He was a bitter person who cast everyone outside the walls he'd built. There was no room for forgiveness or even space to entertain the possibility that her father was acting to protect his children. She didn't want him around to remind her how Theo Duncan had failed. The task in front of her was enough to do that.

"Good night, Roman."

She didn't stay to hear his reply as she carried the crib inside and closed the door behind her.

Chapter Eight

Roman knew he was overstepping, yet he simply couldn't divert his mind from Emery and the baby. Gino wasn't trustworthy. He knew it. He felt it. But it was her choice so he shouldn't interfere. Deep in his soul he was certain the person who'd tried to drown Emery was the same one who'd been lurking at the inn and Theo's cabin.

After a night of wrestling with the covers, he finally landed on something he could do. He'd provide her some independence in the form of a vehicle, a safe way out if things went bad. He'd called her cell at the ungracious hour of 6:00 a.m. She'd answered on the second ring and agreed after some intense convincing on his part. When he pulled up at the cabin at a little after seven o'clock with Wally sprawled in the back seat, she was standing on the porch, dressed in a windbreaker and jeans.

"Not bringing Ian?" He was surprised at his own disappointment. Things would be much less complicated without a baby along, but still...

"Gino's up. With the rain threatening, it's better not to take Ian out since he's had the sniffles." She held up a palm. "Gino loves Ian as much as I do and I trust him implicitly."

No matter what you say, he finished in his head. He shrugged. "Would have been nice, is all."

She shot him a sidelong glance under those impossibly thick lashes. "You're disappointed?"

"Wally is. He wanted to frisk Ian for any loose pacifiers."

Her laugh encouraged his and the tension between them melted. She turned to scrub Wally behind his pendulous ears. "Wally, you are a national treasure. They should put you on a dollar bill."

"He seems to think so."

She straightened and tucked the hair off her face. "I really appreciate the car. I want you to know I'm going to pay you back for all of this, the gas, the crib, everything."

"Nothing to pay back. The crib is a loaner and so is the car. Wait until you see it. It's no great shakes and it smells of dog but Steph hasn't gotten around to selling it. It's just had a rear fender replaced so it's in the shop in town."

"Still, gas and..."

He reached for her hand and squeezed. Her fingers were warm, strong. "No need."

When she answered, her voice was low. "I don't want you to do things because you feel guilt or pity for me."

He twisted toward her, startled. "That's not what I feel."

She cocked a look at him. "Really?"

He didn't know how to reply. His emotions were zinging around like kernels in a popcorn popper, but guilt and pity were definitely not in the bunch.

"We can clear out the elephant in the room, Roman. When you look at me, you see my father's betrayal. It hurts. You don't want anything to do with the Duncans so you must be helping me because you feel sorry for me and Ian."

"It's not like that."

"Yes, it is. Has to be, even though most everyone else won't come near us for any reason." She groaned. "That's the worst thing about it all, really, is the way people have stepped away, like they're afraid of catching something or ruining their reputations by sticking around."

Was she saying he'd done that? He'd stepped away, for sure, but she'd welcomed it. His actions had nothing to do with her anyway. A sizzle of regret lashed him. Whatever the reason, he had indeed sidestepped as far as he could from Theo, and by default, Emery. "I should have explained earlier. I... I mean, my behavior back then had nothing to do with you or worrying about what people might think or anything like that. Your father pretended to be something he wasn't, told me stories about honor and righteousness and self-control when he had none of those things. I don't keep people in my life who betray me."

She shook her head, lips pressed together. "I still believe my dad didn't do what he confessed to, but you know what, Roman?" Her eyes glittered like the crystalline waters of Crater Lake. "This might rock your world but I'd love him every bit as much if he was guilty."

He blinked in disbelief. "You'd love him if he'd planned a murder?"

Her chin went up, the answer short and pained. "Yes."

Attempted murder from a person who'd

spouted on about love and God and the way to be a proper man? Acid and anger churned the coffee in his stomach. How had the conversation taken such a turn in the span of a few minutes? "It's not like we're talking about unpaid parking tickets."

She was silent, staring out the window for several beats before she answered. "Love doesn't turn on and off like that. It doesn't with God and it shouldn't with us. If he's really guilty, would I be crushed? Ruined in my heart? Of course. It would split open my soul." Her voice wobbled. "I'd never get over it but I wouldn't stop loving him." She swiped at a tear in the corner of her eye.

His heart lurched as he tried to take it in. He reached for her hand again, kissed the knuckles, desperate to ease her pain. "I'm sorry to make you cry. You... I mean, it's okay however you feel about it. I guess we're just two really opposite types of people."

She pulled a tissue from her pocket and wiped her face. "Not so different. You still love your uncle Jax."

The words took his breath away. He gripped the wheel. "Yeah, sure, but that's a completely different situation." Uncle Jax hadn't planned to kill anybody.

"So you've forgiven him? You still love him even though you believe he betrayed you?"

Forgiven Uncle Jax? He wasn't sure. Loved him? That was easier. He squirmed. Why did they need to talk about his uncle, anyway? "I've grown up some. I was young and insecure back then. I shouldn't have behaved the way I did."

"That's not an answer to the question."

He didn't like the question, or the whole conversation for that matter. He had to force himself not to exceed the speed limit as they took the winding road into town. This wasn't about him, though she was bent on making it such. He knew most of the fault for the debacle with Uncle Jax was his own stubborn adolescent behavior. He'd let it go, mostly. So why hadn't he ever returned Uncle Jax's calls? Talked to the man in the decade since the day he'd run away? Because Roman had found a new family to love him in the Wolfes? *A new family...* His own angry words rang in his memory as if he'd shouted them only moments before.

You found a shiny new family, Uncle Jax, with kids that are better than me, right? Jax's decision had uprooted Roman's worst fear, deeper than abandonment or pain or failure, the deep down, bone-shivering worry that he was not lovable.

He jumped when he felt her fingertips on his arm. "I'm sorry, Roman. What am I doing? I'm dumping on you. I shouldn't have brought up Uncle Jax."

"No big deal," he said, straightening slightly until she removed her hand.

"Yes, it is." She sighed. "I love my dad and if he did plan to shoot someone, I'll have to come to terms with that. But loving and accepting are two different things. My dad was generous and kind to you. He's still that man somewhere deep inside, no matter what happened. Can you allow for that possibility?"

It was too much. His delay in replying made her twist away from him to look out the window. Her profile was so lovely that he thought the rising sun could not compete. A shiver raced along his nerves. If things had been different, if he hadn't enlisted, gone away…if Theo hadn't done what he did…

No sense contemplating what might have been.

Wally's tail thwacked the rear seat as they arrived. The morning traffic consisted of several trucks cruising the main drag, their drivers in search of coffee or fueling their vehicles at the corner gas station with an attached auto repair place. The mom-and-pop grocery store was opening up for the day. "Got another fifteen before we can pick up the car. Need supplies?"

She huffed out a breath. "As a matter of fact, yes. I made a list."

He laughed. "Ever the organizer."

"That trait has come in handy when I was suddenly in charge of Ian. I went from taking care of myself to raising a helpless miniature human."

"I can't imagine. No other family members to step in and share the load?"

She shrugged. "Not really anyone suitable. My mother made a halfhearted effort but that wouldn't have worked out. He would have gone into foster care."

Like Roman had. The magnitude of her choice to take in Ian swept over him.

"You're doing great with him. He's blessed to have you." Blessed, completely.

She cocked her head in surprise. "Thank you. It's the hardest thing I've ever done."

And would continue to do until Diane recovered, if she ever did. What kind of courage did that take? To leap into another person's life for a season, or maybe forever. Like Uncle Jax had done. Again, his thoughts circled back to the past, his own mistakes.

He drove to the grocery store, jaw set. When he parked, Wally emitted a howl when Roman told him to stay put.

"Last time you knocked over the entire mac and cheese endcap along with the store manager. Your face is on a wanted poster in there."

Wally slammed a front paw into the seat for emphasis.

"You don't get what you want by throwing a fit. Stay."

Roman had a feeling Emery was holding back laughter as they hurried into the store.

She moved quickly, snagging things and tossing them into a handbasket. A stocky man with a barn jacket glanced at her from the bread aisle. Roman recognized him as he turned down their row, gaze still locked on Emery. Before he could say anything, she squared off with him.

"Can I help you with something?" she said to the staring man.

"You just look familiar, like someone who used to live here."

He started to intervene, but Emery spoke up.

"I am someone who used to live here."

The man's eyes narrowed. "I know you. Heard you were back. You're a Duncan."

The Taylors must have been talking. "Yes."

Roman put a hand on her arm. "This is Kevin. He's a mechanic here in town. Works on the Taylors' cars too."

Kevin nodded. "Yeah. And it was a real tragedy what happened to Mason. Guy probably won't ever recover fully." The rest was unsaid. *Because of your father.*

He felt the muscles in her shoulders tense and he eased in front of her. "Kev, Emery has nothing to do with that."

Kevin twirled a bag of bread. "You told everyone it wasn't Daddy's fault. Now where's Daddy? In jail, where he belongs."

"That's enough." Roman moved until he was inches from Kevin's chest, his own fury hot in his veins. "How about you behave like a civilized person? Not the place or time to air your opinions to a lady who's here to get groceries like you are. Is this how we treat people in Whisper Valley? That's the kind of man you are?"

Kevin looked up at Roman, who glowered down at him. The seconds ticked by as Roman considered whether he should escort Kevin out of the store or remove Emery from the situation. Either way, she wasn't going to be insulted anymore.

"Whatever." Kevin yanked himself around and shuffled to the checkout stand.

Emery sniffed and he realized she was fighting to keep from crying. He turned her toward him and embraced her. "Don't let him get to you. He's a hothead."

She leaned in and turned her face to his neck.

"No need to stay," he said, his lips grazing her cheek. "We can get supplies later."

She straightened. "No. No one is going to prevent me from getting Ian what he needs."

His breath caught as she straightened her spine, tipped her chin and blinked back tears. She strode toward the baby aisle and he scurried to catch up. In a few moments she'd grabbed a dozen or so items, including a large package of diapers, formula and some fruits, applesauce and bread. Jars of baby food and a pacifier completed the collection.

He was grabbing for his wallet when she produced hers with a dazzling smile. "Got mine back, remember?"

He knew better than to offer to pay, anyway.

After checking in with the mechanic, Emery

was installed in the loaner Toyota. She was still obviously upset from the grocery store encounter but determined to put it behind her. The rain had begun to fall, swirling the tangle of trees that bordered the garage parking lot. He checked the wiper blades and gave her a thumbs-up as Wally scanned the cracked asphalt. She rolled down the driver's side window. "I promise I'll return it with a full tank of gas."

Desperation tightened his stomach. She was ready to go and he wasn't sure when he'd see her again. He'd told himself he was concerned for her safety, angry townsfolk now added to the list of dangers, but it went deeper. "Cup of coffee before you head on back?" He pointed to the small café across the street.

Her gaze was mournful. "As tempting as that sounds, I'd better scoot. Ian's been fussy lately and it's not fair to Gino to leave him for too long."

The door of the coffee shop opened and Mason Taylor came out, sipping from a cardboard cup, a cane in his free hand. He noticed them and saluted with his drink.

Emery's smile flickered, but she waved back. It had to be weird to see the guy her father had shot. Bad enough when they'd appeared at the cabin. Mason would be heading to the ranch for their morning meeting, which was also probably strange to Emery. The Taylors were prospering in a town where she was greeted with animosity and anger.

Wally's head whipped toward the trees.

Roman tensed. "What's up, boy?"

Wally woofed, a long low sound, a moment before a rock came hurtling through the air.

Emery screamed as something crashed against the glass. Roman and Wally immediately sprinted off toward the trees. She stared around wildly, noting the chip out of the rear window and a rock rolling away until it came to rest a few feet from a sprawl of weeds. A rock... hurled at her car?

In the distance she saw that Mason had dropped his coffee and was sprinting over.

"Emery..." he called out. Before he reached her, he tripped on an uneven spot with his damaged leg and sprawled face-first on the pavement, his cane clattering next to him.

She flung open the door and scrambled over to him. He'd tucked his knees and awkwardly made it to a sitting position before she reached him.

She retrieved his cane.

With her help, he got to his feet and looked ruefully at a smear of mud on his pants. "Great."

The shop owner burst through the door, scanning from Emery to Mason. "Should I call an ambulance?"

Mason waved him off. "Not for me. How about you, Emery? I heard you scream and I came running, or tried to anyway."

"Somebody threw a rock at the car, but I'm completely fine. Are you sure you're okay?"

Mason rubbed his knee. "Just bruised, I think."

Roman returned, breathing hard. Wally's tail wagged as if he'd just had a wonderful exercise, his pink tongue lolling.

"Whoever it was is long gone," Roman said through gritted teeth.

Mason eyed Wally. "He couldn't track him down?"

"Not without a scent to target and I didn't think to take the rock. Wally thought it was a great game of some sort, especially when the squirrel made an appearance." Roman took a photo before he picked up the rock with his fingers covered by his coat and offered it to the dog. Wally took great sniffs of it and sat in a heap, drool ribboning from his mouth.

"Possibly he was wearing gloves, or Wally doesn't feel like tracking anyone since he just had a full-out sprint." Roman was irritated but Emery didn't blame the dog. She'd hardly had time to realize what had happened either.

Roman grabbed a plastic bag from the Bronco and dropped the rock in.

Mason frowned. "Why would someone throw something at Emery's car?"

Emery hugged herself against the chill wind. "Word's gotten out that I'm not Emily Bancroft. My family and I aren't the most popular people in town. A mechanic by the name of Kevin told me as much in the grocery store."

"Our Kevin? Why...?" Mason trailed off. "Oh. I see." He looked away and flexed his knee, wincing. "Look, I liked your sister and I didn't know your dad, but she spoke of him as being her hero. If he came to our house intending to kill my brother, he deserves to be in prison, but I don't hold that against you or Diane."

Emery felt her eyes fill again. Her father was her hero too. Still, in spite of everything. "Your brother and sister-in-law don't share your views."

"They don't share my views on a lot of things.

At least we agree on the business stuff, mostly. I'll talk to Kevin. He's not going to bother you again if he wants to keep his job with us."

"Thank you," Emery said.

Roman nodded his thanks.

Mason tested his leg. "I'm going to pay for my clumsiness, I guess. Not sure I can drive myself to the ranch for our meeting." He rolled his eyes. "Embarrassing."

"I'll drive you." Emery blushed when Roman and Mason stared at her. "I mean, um, unless you'd rather not ride with me. Beth asked me to pick up some baby blankets so I might as well do that now before I go home and I can drop you off for the meeting."

Mason looked startled for a moment. "Okay. Thanks. I'll arrange for someone to pick up my car when it's convenient. Roman, I'll see you at the ranch. I wasn't planning on our meeting starting this way, but as long as it gets done, right?"

Roman still looked uncertain, probably wondering why she'd volunteered. She didn't know why she had either, except she had a burning desire to tell Mason what was in her heart.

"I'll follow as soon as I get the police on the phone," Roman said.

"Should I wait here too, to talk to them?" Emery said.

Roman shook his head. "No. Could take a while for them to arrive and there's not much to see, anyway. You go on to the ranch."

In case there was someone else around with another rock? She suppressed a shiver.

"I'll text the family to let them know you're on your way."

She quickly messaged Gino as well, relieved to hear that Ian was still asleep and Gino was enjoying a bowl of instant oatmeal he'd found in the pantry.

They buckled in. Mason chuckled. "At least I can tell my brother I got a sprint in today. He's always trying to curb my couch potato tendencies."

She laughed. "Lincoln's into fitness, I've noticed."

"Like you wouldn't believe. Me? I'd rather drive than run any day of the week." He surveyed the interior, neat but worn. He was no doubt accustomed to finer vehicles. They drove by his ride, a pristine Ford Fairlane.

He surveyed the interior of the borrowed car. "This color reminds me of the Thunderbird. That was my dad's pride and joy, and he taught me and Lincoln how to drive in it. Not worth much with all the dings and scuffs, but man, I have a soft spot for that old thing." He patted the dash. "This machine's got a great engine. Change the oil every three thousand miles and it will run forever."

His easy manner gave her courage. "Mr. Taylor…"

"Mason."

"Mason, while we have a minute, I want to say I am sincerely sorry for what happened. It seems so inadequate, in light of your injury. But if my father…"

Mason cocked his head. "If…? You think your father is innocent?"

She blushed. "I do. In your statement, you said you didn't actually see him pull the trigger. It was dark. There was a flash and you woke up to find EMS people there."

"That's true, but if your father didn't do it…" He blinked. "Oh. I see. So you believe your sister probably shot me, thinking I was Lincoln, and your father took the blame to protect her. His confession was bogus."

"I don't know. I really don't, but if she did, or if my father took the shot, I am so sorry for your pain and suffering."

"You've suffered too." He jerked a thumb at the chipped glass. "Seems like you still are and you didn't have a thing to do with my injury. Could be we both paid the price for our siblings, right? I'm going to guess you've been cleaning up after Diane's messes for a while, haven't you?"

She blushed. *It's when I stopped helping that things turned catastrophic.* "You could say that."

"And now you've got a baby. Believe it or not, I understand being the person that has to watch from afar while your sibling trashes their life. My brother had a great woman by his side. Hilary would have forgiven his overspending and mismanagement of the car collection, but she couldn't exactly turn a blind eye to his infidelity, now could she? They could have had an amazing life but he threw it away. What a waste."

"I can understand why Hilary is resentful."

"I am too, in some ways. Lincoln inherited the car collection from our father, and instead of growing the business, he sold off cars to pay his debts for school, et cetera. Hilary and I finally convinced him to build a showroom, but by then he was deep in debt and he had to sell more cars and finance the inn so there'd be a place for visitors to stay." He leaned against the headrest. "I love my brother and I'll support him to his grave, but the guy has no mind for business. It's hard not to resent it, right? Having to be your sibling's keeper?"

"Yes, it is." On that subject they could commiserate.

Suddenly he looked pained. "I shouldn't be talking badly about my brother, especially to you. I hope you won't think my whole family is your enemy."

Only if they'd been responsible for driving her off the road and trying to drown her. Maybe Lincoln wasn't what he seemed, an arrogant womanizer. Diane had seen something in him, hadn't she? She remembered the feeling of plunging into the icy water with her wrists and feet bound. Mason was friendly, but blood was thicker than water and there was no reason to trust him completely. His priority was his family. She felt the same. She'd delivered her apology and that was the important thing.

She thanked him and they turned into the drive to the Security Hounds Ranch. This would be a quick drop off, snag the blankets from Beth and get back to her packing.

She parked.

Mason shot her a look, fingers on the door handle. "Hilary says she doesn't think Ian is Lincoln's, but deep down I wonder what she believes. What do you think?"

"I'm not sure. I know he's Diane's, and that's all that's important to me right now."

"Fair enough." Mason pushed the door open. "But if the baby is Lincoln's, he should help."

Emery puzzled as she got out. Did Hilary think Diane was telling the truth about Ian?

She remembered Hilary's forceful demeanor. She must have been humiliated by Lincoln's infidelity. What did she stand to lose if Lincoln really was Ian's father?

Chapter Nine

Roman had left a message with the police. Didn't matter. He'd be able to provide a face-to-face rundown with Hagerty who was also expected to attend the ranch meeting. He wouldn't put it past Kevin to have launched the rock at Emery. Rock throwing, the same kind of juvenile thing he himself might have done as an angry teen, exuding rage from every pore. *Until Theo straightened me out.* Was it progress that he could acknowledge the good Theo had done in his life?

He swallowed and confronted the thought instead of pushing it away.

Theo showed him another way and introduced him to the Wolfes. Emery's words echoed in his mind.

This might rock your world but I'd love him just as much if he was guilty.

And hadn't Roman himself been loved when

he was angry and unlovable? By Theo? And the Wolfes? And his uncle? And God? He rubbed his eyes, gritty from lack of sleep.

And Emery thought he was helping her purely out of pity. Not true. Pity wasn't causing his stomach to knot when she was out of sight, or his blood to warm when she was near. It was something else that he didn't want to mull over at the moment. Why did Emery make him *think* so much?

As he parked next to her loaner car and the Taylors' gleaming Mercedes, his mental gears switched quickly. Lincoln, Mason and Hilary were talking to Officer Hagerty, Stephanie and Garrett. Beth had moved closer to Emery, protectively almost, probably realizing the awkwardness of the situation. Bad start. Somehow he was going to have to make this meeting work. If the Taylors or Hagerty weren't satisfied with the plan he'd laid out, they might drop the whole K-9 component from the car show altogether.

Not gonna let that happen.

Roman rubbed Wally in that special spot under his collar. He'd already slipped on the snazzy Security Hounds harness, which fit the bulky bloodhound perfectly. "Walls, I'm

counting on you, baby. Don't let me down."
He hoped Wally didn't know he was worried.
This was, after all, the breakfast-snatching, pac-
ifier-chewing dog with the brilliant nose and
a dubious work ethic. That's why they'd be
showcasing Chloe, their undisputed champion.

Wally whined, looking as if he wanted to go
exploring. Roman took his collar and urged
him into the fenced area with Chloe. Wally
fired a "you are ruining my life" look at him.

Roman greeted everyone genially. Stephanie
whispered in his ear, "'Bout time you got here.
Mason's been telling us what happened at the
garage. I want more details. And Hagerty has
something for us, he said."

"I'll explain later. Everything set?"

Garrett's quick smile was affirmation.

Time to shine, bloodhounds.

Emery pursed her lips uneasily. "You've all
got a busy morning. How about I snag those
blankets and get out of your hair?"

Hilary seemed as if she thought that was a
grand idea. Lincoln was careful to avoid looking at Emery altogether. His body language
telegraphed his desire to be anywhere but in
her presence.

"Oh, no scooting out now. You'll want to see

this," Beth said brightly. "Won't take long and the dogs have been working like...well, dogs."

Roman heard the velvety steel in his mom's voice. Emery had nothing to be ashamed of, she silently declared, daring with her bold eye contact for anyone to contradict her. No one did.

"Yes," he said, gaze riveted on Emery. She had every right to stay. Her father had helped the ranch stay afloat. Second time today he'd thought of Theo in a more positive way. Odd. "Stay. Please." Before she could reply, he dove into the itinerary.

"For the final event at the showroom on Sunday, we'll have a volunteer hidden in one of your cars," Roman said. "We'll do a quick talk for the guests while the dogs are well away from the showroom, then have them pick in which car she should conceal herself."

"Ah. To make sure there's no trickery," Hagerty said.

"Yes," he confirmed. "We'll give the dogs a scent article and have them track the guest." Two dogs, in case Wally decided he wasn't in the mood.

"All right, that's perfect for the day when the heavy buying will occur." Hilary surveyed the large fenced space where Chloe and Wally were nosing about. The other four were enjoying a nap in their kennels. They needed it, judging from the half dozen freshly dug holes he'd have to fill in after the demonstration. Canine backhoes, the lot of them. He prayed Chloe and Wally would put on a stellar performance for the observers.

"But what about the day before?" Hilary demanded. "That's a nice demo for Sunday, but I'm billing this as a weekend stay for my inn so what's the Saturday entertainment?"

Lincoln finally looked up. "Saturday night we're auctioning off a Rolls so we want all the high rollers there." And Lincoln had pledged a portion of the proceeds to fund the new bloodhound county K-9 team, so Roman had planned an especially dramatic demo. His palms went clammy.

"Glad you asked," Roman said. "Saturday's demo will be something really unusual, including the inn, the estate and the ranch. Lincoln, you said you could show a live feed on the big screen in your showroom?"

He nodded. "Sure. I have top-of-the-line technology."

"Excellent. The Inn at the Pines is two miles from here. Hilary will have already chosen one of her guests to be a volunteer and someone from Security Hounds will accompany that individual to a hiding spot somewhere between our ranch and the inn. We'll put a GoCam on the bloodhound and while the rest of the attendees are enjoying the luncheon buffet you're providing at your estate, they can watch in real time as the dogs track down the guest."

Hagerty raised an eyebrow. "What if the dogs can't do it?"

"Not an issue. They can." Stephanie nodded emphatically.

"No question," Garrett added.

"And we'll have a table on your property so we can be handing out donation info for those who'd like to contribute toward funding our bloodhound team in the county." His mouth went so dry he almost couldn't get it out.

Emery caught his attention. He risked a quick glance at her and she gave him an almost imperceptible nod. Was she proud of him?

"All right," Hagerty said. "So that's two pretty ambitious events. Give us a preview. Let's see your star dogs in action to convince us this is going to work." He gave Roman a close look. "Time's marching on and I need to go take a look at the mechanic's shop, dispatch tells me."

Roman nodded. Later. No need to elaborate with Hilary and Lincoln within earshot. They'd hear it all from Mason, no doubt. "Garrett, can you take the dogs to the run for a minute?"

Garett whistled to the dogs who ambled amiably after him around the corner where they'd installed a covered area to be used during inclement weather. Bored and under-exercised bloodhounds were something to be avoided at all costs.

"He'll give them a treat and some water so they won't hear anything." Roman turned to Hilary. "Would you mind volunteering?"

"Me?"

"Our scents are all over this area so the dogs would have a hard time sorting out which trail to follow. They'll need to smell something you've touched. Your purse or scarf, your cell phone."

She took a silver container from her pocket. "How about this? My business card holder."

"Perfect." Roman pulled a bag from his pocket and asked her to drop it in. "We've got cars parked at the bottom of the road, one by the river on our property and a third beyond the kennels. Which one would you like to hide in?"

She cocked her head. "I've got to interview a new chef today. I don't have time for a long hike."

"The bottom of the road, then. That's a half mile and change, but it's downhill."

"I can do it. That's a short run for me." Lincoln said.

Hilary sniffed. "Oh, please. I'll walk. I don't run the mile in six minutes like you do, Lincoln, but I'm no slouch."

"True," Mason put in. "I've gone running with her and I practically need a taxi to keep up."

She quirked a smile at him. "You do fine as long as I give you a head start."

Mason grinned. "I'll hold down the fort from here. Record it on your cell phone so I can watch later, okay?"

Beth handed Mason and Lincoln binoculars. "These should help."

Stephanie messaged Garrett who returned with Chloe and Wally after Hilary was well away.

Roman clipped them both to long leads and gave them a whiff of Hilary's business card case still in the bag. Stephanie took Chloe's leash.

"Find." Chloe and Wally started in, sniffing in seemingly random circles. Roman let them both satisfy themselves before he gave them another smell. "Find," he repeated. Both dogs snuffled at the scent trail Hilary had left on the road.

Come on, dogs. You can do this. No sweat.

Emery gave him a thumbs-up and Garrett started a stopwatch.

The noisy snuffling, half-frantic parade began. Chloe's pursuit was methodical and straightforward, while Wally got sidetracked by a chittering squirrel and required firm redirecting. Stephanie and Chloe moved ahead.

Sixteen minutes later they arrived at the car, partially concealed by shrubbery. Hilary wasn't visible. Embracing her role, she'd crouched down below the windows. He smiled to himself. You could fool a bloodhound's eyes, but it was nearly impossible to trick their noses. The dogs both jumped up and barked eagerly, until he and Stephanie commanded them to sit. They did so reluctantly, taking the small treats but craving their real reward, the target they'd been tasked to pursue. Wally let loose with a victory howl the moment Hilary emerged from the car, slinging a trail of saliva as he did so.

"All right, I'm convinced," Hilary said.

"You've got two fuzzy Sherlock Holmes detectives there, but they sure do drool a lot. It's gross."

He held back his own yowl of relief and pride and supplied more treats to the dogs before they all walked back to the house.

Beth and Emery clapped at their arrival and Garrett gave each dog a thorough scratch behind the neck.

"Record time," Beth said.

Mason nodded. "Even through the binocs, that was cool."

And Wally had actually completed the mission, squirrel notwithstanding, Roman thought with relief. Extra playtime and maybe some poached salmon was in order.

"Impressive," Lincoln said. "The guests will eat it up with a spoon."

And hopefully donate to the cause. Chloe sprawled happily at Stephanie's feet but Wally avoided Roman's attempts to put him into a sit. Still amped up on the adrenaline possibly? He whined and pulled at the leash.

Hilary collected her business card case. "Let's go, Lincoln. I've got things to do. I'll drop you in town and you can drive Mason back."

Roman moved to let them by and Wally

seized the moment to follow his nose around the parked cars.

"Walls, come on," Roman said, hoping the dog would listen.

He didn't. When Wally was fixed on a scent, Roman could have been hollering into a megaphone and the dog would still ignore him. He'd galumphed right up to the driver's side door of the Mercedes. Wally's wide behind was blocking Lincoln's access.

Lincoln's lip curled. "Can you move your dog, please?"

"Wally," he said sternly, feeling the mortification rising.

The dog glided his nose over the shiny metal.

"He's not going to scratch the paint, is he?" Hilary said.

Not now. Don't show them your disobedient side. There's no way they'll let you in that showroom with all those expensive cars. But Wally would not be dissuaded. His nose left a wet spot on the shiny paint. Roman was about to grab the dog and hoist him aside when Emery stepped close.

"Wally," Emery said. She had her back to the people but Roman saw Wally's attention snap from the Mercedes toward Emery. "Come with me, little man." As if in a trance, he trotted after her and onto the porch.

Roman tried to hide his shock. Wally was taking orders from Emery as if they'd worked together for years. He closed his mouth and waved goodbye to the departing visitors.

Officer Hagerty lingered. "Got something for you."

"Come inside," Beth said. "I'll make coffee."

"I will never say no to a good cup of coffee. Station stuff tastes like we brewed it in a carburetor."

Roman hustled up to Emery where she still crouched next to Wally.

"I have to know. How did you get him to cooperate?"

She opened her hand, revealing a blue plastic pacifier, which Wally immediately began to lick, his tail whipping in happy arcs. "I bought an extra when we stopped at the store. Figured you needed it for Wally more than I needed a spare for Ian."

He laughed. She joined in. For a moment a mountain was removed from his shoulders and he guffawed with everything in him until they both ran out of air. "I owe you, big-time."

"Yep, you still owe me an ice cream and now another favor. Really racking up the debt, Wolfe."

There was nothing more lovely than her pluck, her humor, her light. No rock-thrower, abductor or hateful townsperson had dulled the spark she carried. He held out his hand and she took it. He pulled her to her feet and she delivered the pacifier. They let Wally enjoy it for a few minutes before Roman retrieved it.

"If you're a good boy, maybe Roman will let you have some quality time with your paci later, okay?" Emery crooned.

Seemingly content, Wally let Roman usher him into the gated yard where he joined Garret's dog Pinkerton in excavating a new trench.

"While you're here, see if Hagerty needs any more details about what happened at the garage."

The remark made her go quiet. He felt pinpricks of rage that someone had attempted to injure her again. What if Ian had been in the car? Thinking of harm coming to either one of them was intolerable. His pace quickened as they marched for the house until she put a hand on his arm.

"Slow down," she said. "I'm getting a cramp."

"Sorry." He tucked her arm through his and

it felt like the most natural thing in the world. He decided to enjoy it and let his brain relax for a moment. It might have been his imagination, but he thought she relaxed too, her shoulder pressed to his.

Hagerty was halfway through the coffee Beth had presented him when they entered. Kara was there too, wan and thinner than she seemed only a week before. He noted his mother's worried glance and knew she'd noticed too.

"Hey, K.K.," he said as she curled up cross-legged on the sofa with her laptop over her knees. Barefoot, practically always when inside, even in winter. "How are things going with the case you and Chase are working?"

She accepted his kiss on the cheek. "Chase is wrapping up but I think we have enough to send to the client. His tenant is definitely using the property to move stolen goods."

"Did Tank perform okay?"

"Like a champion, which Chase will tell you all about when he gets back." She looked at Emery. "I'm sorry about what happened in town." She reached out a hand and gripped Emery's. Some understanding seemed to pass between them. Kara knew what it was like to be on the outside looking in.

"Sit here." She patted the sofa next to her and Emery settled in.

"So about the rock-throwing business..." Hagerty said. "We got a confession from Kevin."

Emery sighed. "He was sending me a 'get out of town' message."

Hagerty slugged down some coffee. "Might not be a bad idea. We found a GPS tracker on the rear wheel well of your car. That's how someone knew you were in Whisper Valley."

Her face paled. "Someone's been tracking me?"

Hagerty nodded. "They probably put it on at your apartment would be my guess."

Roman felt a cold chill. Emery had been hunted even before she arrived in town.

Her lip quivered for a moment. "I can't. I have to pack up my father's house. It's being foreclosed. My sister and dad are both in the hospital so there's no one left to do it, otherwise I'd take your advice in a heartbeat, believe me."

Her comment pained Roman. Totally reasonable that she'd want to leave at the first possible opportunity, wasn't it?

Hagerty drank more coffee. "A bad look for Whisper Valley. I'll see what I can find out, but I'm pretty certain it won't be much." He looked at Kara. "Did you get it?"

She nodded and tapped her screen.

Hagerty explained. "Emailed the video of the car that went after us, at least the two seconds my body cam caught before we hit the dirt."

Kara pulled it up on her screen.

"Can you—?" Roman started but she'd already patched it through to the TV. They stood closer to get a better look as Kara froze the frame. He found his shoulder brushing Emery's again and he resisted the urge to loop his arm around her. That didn't stop him from enjoying the light floral scent of her freshly washed hair. He remembered the hot summer between her junior and senior year of high school when she'd let her long waves dry in the sun while she visited the ranch. He'd found it fascinating, the heavy weight of her thick mane and how it would curl as it dried. Same slight curl in it now. Maybe since her cover had been blown, she'd let it return to its natural blond hue. He hoped so. No store-bought color could ever compare.

Would you focus already?

"No license plate or even a partial," Hagerty said. "As you can see, all we got is the front right of a black vehicle, tire impressions indicate it's a quality ride."

"Did your people conclude anything else?" Garrett asked.

"Nope. All over to you hotshot detectives now."

Roman didn't take offense at the tease. Hagerty had made good on his promise to share information with Security Hounds and that was a victory. "The front end plowed through the ground pretty hard. Likely got some scratches or dings."

Hagerty nodded. "Thought of that, but I don't have time to chase it down."

"We do," Beth said.

"For sure." Stephanie turned to her sister. "Kara, if you can get me some names of car detailers or body shops in the area, I'll do the legwork."

Garrett raised his hand. "I'll help."

They settled into a moment of uneasy silence. Roman knew his siblings understood where his mind had drifted.

"Spill it," Hagerty said. "Tell me what you're thinking."

"Wally was real interested in Lincoln's Mercedes."

He looked at Roman over the edge of his mug. "Thought he was just being a pain."

"He was, but he also might be recalling the scent from the car that almost ran us down."

All eyes riveted on Roman.

"You're not saying Lincoln Taylor tried to kill us?" Hagerty said.

"Just noting that Wally's reaction is curious. The car's pristine, like it'd been recently washed and detailed, right down to the tires."

"The Taylors are car people. It's their livelihood. They're not gonna ride around in dirty vehicles. They probably have a detailing facility on the property. And I know for a fact they own several Mercedes."

Roman didn't reply to Hagerty's comment.

Beth said, "Lincoln Taylor, Hilary, Kevin the mechanic, other staff people at the estate, I'm sure they all had access to the car. It could have been cleaned on site or taken elsewhere."

"Uh-huh." Hagerty put down his empty mug. "Not the greatest business move to imply someone connected to the Taylors is a criminal."

Roman hoped his tone was neutral. "Not implying. Sharing Wally's reaction is all."

Hagerty peered out the living room window. Wally was almost up to his tail in the crater he'd dug. He was churning up a blizzard of soil with his sturdy paws. "Trust that hound, do you?"

Stephanie's expression was highly amused as she watched for Roman's response. Did he trust Wally? Hadn't he been trying to offload the stubborn animal before he'd rescued Emery from drowning? He kept his sister confined to his peripheral vision and opened his mouth to answer.

"For what it's worth, I do." Emery's comment startled him. She offered Hagerty a bright smile. "He saved us in the lake, found my car and alerted us in time to keep all three of us from being mowed down. I trust him."

Roman stood a little straighter and fought hard to keep the grin from his face. He tried to put the feelings aside and focus on the case but as he caught sight of his filthy dog sprawled on a patch of sunlit grass, he felt a great surge of affection. Wally might be stubborn and prone to following his own drum, but Roman had the deep-down conviction that the hound had detected something invisible to the rest of them on Lincoln's car.

Was it the same vehicle that had almost run them down? Hopefully Kara's investigations would help discover the truth. In the meantime he intended to keep a very close eye on Emery and Ian.

Hagerty finally nodded. "When you put it that way, I guess I owe him too. I'll keep in mind what you've said and we'll put our info together after you do some of the legwork. I'm sure you'll be discreet, since you're not law enforcement and all…"

A shadow crossed Garrett's face but he beamed a smile anyway. "We are the soul of discretion. Ask anyone. We fly totally under the radar."

"Right. You and your noisy pack of slobbering hounds." Hagerty checked the time on his watch. "I'll talk to you all later."

Beth walked him to the door. "Thank you for coming, Officer. Our coffeepot is at your disposal any time." When he left, she clasped a hand to her lower back. Roman hastened to grab an ice pack from the freezer, knowing she would put it off until they'd left the room.

She shot him a tired half smile. "Thank you, Roman."

She sank onto the sofa and his worries came back in a rush. They had to make the K-9 event work. Had he jeopardized everything with his suspicions before they'd gotten anything resembling proof?

Kara's gaze shifted to Roman and her siblings. "So... I'm looking into this? We're investigating the Taylors?"

Roman blew out a breath. "I don't want to jeopardize our arrangement with them but..."

"I don't want a partnership with anyone who's ready to hurt to get what they want," Beth snapped. "If they're guilty, we need to know." She cocked her chin at Emery. "We'll try to keep you out of this as much as possible, but Security Hounds is diving into this case because we need answers." She was every inch the in-charge flight nurse in that moment before her tone softened. "Do you understand, Emery?"

Emery's shoulders sagged. Was she finally resigned to having Security Hounds officially involved? "I want answers too," she said. "I know you aren't looking specifically for proof that my father isn't guilty, but I can't help feeling this all circles back to that night."

That night...when everything had changed for him, her, Theo, Diane, Ian and Mason.

What really happened in those dangerous moments? With Security Hounds involved, maybe they'd be able to put it all to rest.

"We'll need to go over the details again,"

Garrett said. "Everything you can recall. I'll contact Hagerty for the police reports, Mason's statement, your father's confession, et cetera."

"This is painful," Beth said. "I'm sorry, and honestly I pray that we'll be able to turn up something that might help you and Theo."

Emery's lower lip quivered.

Would they uncover proof of Theo's guilt so even Emery would believe it? Or maybe Diane was the guilty party? Roman's stomach squirmed. Wasn't it possible that things weren't what they seemed where her father was con-cerned?

She'd love him anyway. That thought spun slowly through his mind like a bird floating on the wind. She spoke of an unconditional love, a love closer to the perfect love that God offered. Loving through disappointment.

He thought of Uncle Jax.

"Roman?"

His mother's question zapped him back. He realized everyone's attention had slid to him, waiting to see his reaction. They knew how crushed he'd been at Theo's confession. Did he want to open that poorly healed scab? Confront the feelings he kept buried beneath his reticence?

No, he didn't. He wanted nothing to do with

any of it. There were plenty of problems on today's plate without revisiting agonizing history. But the need to defend his Wolfe family, if necessary, and Emery, was more important than his wish to dodge his own pain.

Emery was the true victim in all this, and the baby she was struggling to care for.

His discomfort was trivial. A predator was stalking her. If he had to, he'd fight through the pain and protect them both, no matter what the cost.

He gave one slow nod.

Security Hounds was 100 percent in…and so was he.

Chapter Ten

At Beth's direction, Kara fetched the blankets. Emery tucked the soft fleece under her arm, thanked them and promised to make herself available as best she could in between packing and baby care. Reality weighed her down. As much as she wanted to assist with anything that might shed light on her father's confession, she had an entire cabin to pack up in a week's time. Beth waved a goodbye from the sofa.

The pain must be intense to keep the strong woman down.

Roman seemed lost in thought as he walked her to the car until she squeezed his arm.

"Sorry, I was thinking." He snagged a look at her. "Why are you smiling?"

"It's an appreciative smile."

"Appreciative of what?"

She shrugged, cheeks warm. "The way you suggested investigating the Taylors' car."

He looked at the sky and then back at her. The light bronzed his neatly cut hair. She'd always thought the ginger color was glorious, though she'd lacked the courage to tell him so. Probably never would.

"Emery, I don't want you to jump to conclusions. The most likely scenario is still…"

She waved away the rest of his comment. "I know…that my dad is guilty of attempted murder and the threats on my life are unrelated, but you were willing to speak up to Hagerty."

He shrugged. "Being thorough is all. Your safety's in question."

"Not just thorough, you're taking a risk since you're business partners with the Taylors at the moment. I know you have a lot riding on the deal."

His mouth tightened and he stroked a hand over his chin. "Mom needs back surgery. As I mentioned, because of the expense and recovery time, she won't agree until the business is more secure. Tough lady."

"That's why she was a good flight nurse."

"Stubborn."

"The perfect pack leader for a bunch of tenacious Wolfes. It's terrible to see her in such pain."

A flicker of worry crossed his face. "I can't

stand it either. She's finally let me take over some of her chores, hauling the food bags and such, but there's no way past the pain unless she has the surgery." He paused. "I more or less put all our eggs into this basket, hoping to get a contract deal with the county for bloodhound services. My sibs don't all agree that it was the right choice. This car show's our best shot, probably our only one."

"And you were willing to jeopardize that? For me?"

"For the truth."

Of course, that was the reason. Why had she even said that?

He straightened to his full six feet and change, shoulders broad and muscled. "Did you think I'd ignore something criminal to protect the interests of the ranch? Is that the kind of man you think I am?"

She went still, stung by his irritation. He was offended that she'd besmirched his honor? "No, but I don't exactly know you well anymore, do I?" The slight reproach in her tone was no doubt clear to him. She could tell in the tightening of his jaw. *Remember who you're dealing with.* Before she'd almost been drowned, she'd seen him only long enough for him to walk away.

Is it true that your father shot a man in cold blood?

Once Roman had been the hero in her heart, the handsome young man who could do everything from building kennels to mountain climbing, and always with a joke or a tease. But now they were grown-ups and she'd taken off her rose-colored glasses. He'd stepped out of her life, along with everyone else, and it hurt. She hadn't realized how deeply until she'd returned to Whisper Valley.

Affection and admiration warred with the bitter echoes of disappointment. He despised her father, maybe just as much as the rock-thrower, the notion of forgiveness as distant and inaccessible as the Cascades. The realization landed on her like a falling tree. Her father's guilt or innocence wasn't the reason for the hurt that spiraled through her. "You know Roman, no matter what you thought about Dad, I could have used your friendship."

He recoiled as if she'd slapped him. "You didn't want me there…" His words died away. His shoulders fell as he heaved out a breath. "I should have stuck around for you, no matter how I felt. I was so wrapped up in my own hurt I didn't consider yours. I'm sorry, Emery."

Her eyes flew wide. He'd apologized? She was

struggling to come up with a reply when they reached the car and he yanked open the driver's door for her. "As far as the Taylors go, if someone in that household had a role in dumping you in the lake, they're going to pay the price."

And that was something else to marvel at. Roman had not only apologized for the past, but he was willing to wade into her situation, no matter how much it upset him. She felt a surge of gratitude poke through the uncertainty. "I hope it doesn't cost you much, helping me."

He looked at her full-on then, reached out and brushed the hair from her cheek. "You've paid a higher price than anyone, Ree."

The nickname, the touch, the look, no anger there, only sorrow and determination. Her heart warmed as she slid behind the wheel of the borrowed car. She felt her phone buzz. Panic nearly overtook her as she recognized the number and answered.

Gino's breathless voice ratcheted her nerves. "Ian's fine, but we have a problem."

Another one? She put it on speaker. "Roman's with me on this call. What's wrong?"

She could hear the drapes rustle as Gino answered.

"There are reporters here. Two of them."

Her stomach knotted up. "Oh, no. This is not what we need right now."

"I didn't speak to them, except to tell them to go away, but they shouted a few questions at me. They're still there, camped next to the driveway."

Emery's spirits dropped with every word. "What did they ask you?"

"Can't you guess? They found out you're in town and smelled a spicy story. They didn't mention your escape from the lake, but they probably caught wind of it. Possibly they're apprised about the foreclosure too. Public record. They asked about the baby."

How was she going to keep Ian out of the limelight now? He'd be a target of hatred too. She leaned her forehead against the steering wheel. "This is all spinning out of control."

Roman took the phone from her hand. "Any way you can get out with Ian and come here?"

"Not without being swarmed," Gino said. "Ian's real fussy at the moment so it's hard for me to think. He won't take his bottle."

Emery sat up. "I'm leaving right now. I'll be there in a half hour."

"But how will you get by—?" Gino asked.

She cut him off, her tone savage. "It's still my

father's house, at least for another week, anyway. I'll call the police if they block my way. Sit tight and try the bouncy seat with Ian, okay? Sometimes that helps."

She disconnected, tried to gather her thoughts. The last thing she wanted was to face down hungry journalists. She'd done enough of that when her father had first been arrested. In her present state of mind, she couldn't predict what would come out of her mouth if she were confronted. Roman stood watching her, thumbs tucked into his belt.

"I'd better go," she said.

He reached through the window and touched her forearm. "Give me one second to grab Wally. I've got a plan."

"What kind of plan?"

He smiled, a boyish grin. "Wally and I are going to be decoys."

Decoys? "How exactly is that going to work?"

"We'll drive right on up to the front, bold as brass. The reporters don't know you're in a borrowed car. You can take the fire trail from the south and park in the woods behind the cabin. I've used that path to train Wally before. The trail leads all the way up to Tule Lake but you can pull off about a quarter mile past the cabin and loop around. It's a short drive to the house. I checked it all out when we first got there."

She gaped at his cunning. "What will you say to the reporters?"

He grinned, a flash of the mischievous teen. "I'll let Wally do the talking."

As much as she wanted to stand up for herself, to send all those reporters packing through her sheer force of will, Roman's offer sent sweet relief coursing through her. She was tired, frightened and feeling more and more desperate to get back to Ian.

"See you in a few. I'll stay for a while and help pack."

"But you've got to—"

He leaned close and kissed her. His lips were soft and warm against hers.

"Help you," he finished. "That's all I'm going to worry about right now. Wait here."

Stunned, she watched him jog away. Her mouth tingled from the kiss.

He was sorry for their past. Willing to put himself out for her safety and Ian's. Perhaps risk the future of the ranch.

What was going on?

And why was her heart skipping as she watched him go?

★ ★ ★

With Emery departing fifteen minutes ahead of them, Roman opened the window halfway so Wally could shove his head out. The wind sent his ears flapping like giant propellers. The dog went so far as to open his jaws and let the breeze inflate his cavernous mouth, gulping in the air as if it were a juicy steak.

"You're turning into a halfway decent dog, Walls. That was some performance, finding Hilary."

The dog turned from his entertainment long enough to twitch a saggy brow at him as if to say, "I know." He considered Wally's reaction to the Taylors' Mercedes. Might be nothing at all. That happened sometimes with blood-hounds. They were attracted to every imaginable scent unless they were encouraged to focus on a particular search. Might be a stray odor from a take-out bag or another dog that had been transported in the car. Then again, what if one of the Taylors had been behind the wheel and tried to plow them down?

But what could possibly be the motive?

Something to do with the shooting six months earlier? It couldn't be, yet his gut would not dismiss the thought. He'd trained plenty of army soldiers and their dogs, and if there was an underlying theme, it had to be *trust your dog and your squad*.

He trusted his Wolfe squad, and he was slowly coming to trust Wally. The Taylors were business partners only.

What about Emery?

He wasn't sure what had prompted him to apologize to her, though it had been exactly right. A God thing, probably. That straightened him up. Interesting, since he hadn't felt very connected to God for a long time. He squeezed and relaxed his fingers on the steering wheel. Maybe Emery's assertion that she'd love her father even if he was guilty had started things percolating inside his own soul. For years he'd thought he'd had a right to his grudge against Uncle Jax, but the adult Roman understood that he'd been the one to walk away from his uncle, not the other way around. And he'd walked away from Emery too.

Man, the growing up thing was torture sometimes. He forced his mind to the details of the Security Hounds demonstration. All the dogs would need baths. That'd be a messy undertaking. The doggy aroma was already thick in the vehicle in spite of the open window.

"If you'd keep away from Mom's chicken coop, you'd smell better, you know."

Wally whacked him with his thick tail as the drive to Theo's cabin came into view. Parked on the rocky shoulder were two vehicles with men in the driver's seats. When they heard Roman's approach, they both got out, phones ready to record. He slowed to give them time to get closer.

Wally eyed them with curiosity.

"You ready for your big moment, boy?" He flicked the radio to the country station. The change in Wally was instantaneous. He yanked his head inside the vehicle and sat in a tidy bundle, nose pointed to the radio. Three, two, one…

As soon as Roman edged up the volume, Wally broke into a plaintive yowl.

The reporters hesitated.

Wally did not. His soulful accompaniment to the music grew so loud Roman's ears pulsed. He rolled down his window as the men drew abreast. "Afternoon."

They introduced themselves, but he only caught a few words. He tapped his ear. "Sorry, can't hear you. Dog's a real performer."

"Can you tell us if Emery Duncan is here?" the taller one shouted. "Does she have her sister's baby with her?"

"What?" Roman said.

Wally started in on the next song with gusto. The howling actually vibrated the glass. Impressive.

The shorter one said something that sounded like a rude suggestion on how to shut Wally up. Roman kept his smile in place. "Hey, fellas. Sorry, but I can't control him when he wants to sing. A regular Pavarotti, you know? I'm just here to do some manual labor so I'd better get on that."

"But..." they both said at once.

Wally let loose with another ripping chorus. Roman pointed to his ear again and shrugged. "Catch you later, huh?"

He was still laughing when Gino let them into the cabin. He immediately shut and bolted the door.

Emery cradled the fussing baby, beaming a smile at him. "It worked, just like you said. They didn't see me come in the back."

He felt a rush of pleasure at her smile. Ian let loose with a scream and launched his pacifier into the air. Roman caught it, just before Wally did.

She laughed. "Thanks. Another excellent save."

Roman chuckled and handed it back to her.

Their fingers brushed, hers warm, delicate. He wanted to clasp her palm in his. His heart thudded hard in his chest. "How about I, uh, pack? Should I start in the basement?"

She nodded.

Relieved to have a quiet place to marshal his unruly feelings, he grabbed some boxes and got to work.

When Emery was almost at her limit, Ian finally dropped into a late afternoon nap in his bouncy seat, which did not bode well for a restful night. Wally snoozed next to him, a comical sight. Emery's nerves were frazzled from comforting her fussy nephew and spending every free moment cramming her father's belongings into the cartons, while Gino did the same in the garage and Roman tackled the basement.

It hurt, boxing her father's possessions, the reels and the piles of books about fly-fishing. Would he survive the heart attack? Spend the rest of his life in jail and never enjoy fishing again? Among a stack of unused envelopes, she found an unframed snapshot of her and Diane, knobby kneed in denim shorts, ankle deep in the mud, her dad photobombing behind them. It was the last family vacation she could remember. Tears fogged her vision as she knelt there. They were so happy in the picture, unaware of the traumas that would follow: divorce, her mother's departure, and now the unfathomable mess with her father, Diane's injury. Her fingers traced their young faces, her father's unruly hair. How had it all unraveled?

"No matter what, I still love you both," she said and though she felt sad, the anger was missing. She'd let go of the resentment against Diane, she realized. Sisters, for better or for worse. She wished she could tell Diane as much.

Warm breath on her neck made her jump. Wally pressed the advantage and licked her chin. She realized Roman was standing in the living room, a mug dangling from his index finger.

"Uh...sorry," he said. "I was craving some coffee, if you have any."

She jumped up. The pendulum clock on the wall read five thirty. "Oh, I'm sorry. I lost track of time. You're probably hungry. I'll fix some dinner."

"No need. I'm okay with coffee."

"You've been packing all day and we might as well eat while Ian's quiet. Trust me, it won't last long."

Roman set the table for three while she scrambled the eggs she'd got at the store and toasted slices of sourdough. Wally opened a baggy eye, nose twitching at the smell of food, but stayed snuggled up next to Ian.

"You didn't let him near Ian's pacifiers, did you? He'll have stolen them all if he got the chance."

She laughed and it felt good to be sharing an easy moment. "Ian prefers his thumb to his pacifier right now, so we're okay for the time being."

The phone rang while she was sliding the food onto plates and handing them to Gino.

"It's Kara." Roman put it on speaker. "You've got me, Emery and Gino. What did you find out?"

Kara's voice was soft so they all leaned forward to hear.

"No surprise that the local auto body shop indicated no repairs to a black Mercedes."

Roman nodded. "Taylors wouldn't risk getting the damage fixed in town."

"Right. There are three other shops within a fifty-mile radius. None was particularly interested in talking to me, but Stephanie took over. Either they didn't do the work, or they're covering up."

"So no progress," Roman sighed.

"There's another avenue," Kara said. "I'll let Stephanie tell you about it."

Stephanie launched in. "I did some digging at the jail."

Emery's eyes flew wide. "The jail?"

Gino repositioned the plates, brows knitted.

"I have a contact there. Unofficial, of course, but I was curious about Theo's activities."

Her father's activities in jail? She'd not anticipated that avenue of inquiry. She wanted to ask more questions, but she forced herself into the chair, mouth closed. She'd agreed to let the Wolfes investigate in whatever direction that took them, so she couldn't exactly complain about their decisions.

Gino voiced her thoughts a moment later. "What does this have to do with the danger to Emery?"

Stephanie seemed unaffected by Gino's clipped tone. "I don't know yet. Maybe nothing, but Theo apparently made calls on a regular basis to someone. My contact didn't know who and couldn't tell us anyway even if they did."

Emery's heart squeezed. Regular calls, yet

her father steadfastly refused to speak to her, his daughter. Roman must have noticed her surge of grief because he sidled around and put a reassuring hand on her back.

"I wish I didn't have to revisit all this right now," she whispered, so low only Roman heard.

He bent and murmured in her ear. "Sorry, Ree. It'll be over soon."

His warmth prickled her skin in goose bumps.

Stephanie continued. "He scribbled lots of notes and my contact found one on the floor after one of his phone calls. Most of it was illegible except for *password*."

"Password?" Emery balled up a napkin. "What could he be thinking?"

"No idea. Prisoners aren't allowed on the internet, so I'm not sure why he'd be focused on that word. I was going to ask if your dad was a big computer guy before…well, before," Stephanie said.

She rolled the napkin between her palms. "He wasn't. The opposite, really. It was always hard to get him to use the computer. But there's one in the basement, an iPad. Do you want me to…?" She caught a strange look from Roman. "What?"

"There isn't an iPad in the basement."

Her mouth fell open. "But...there was when I was down there before. You must have missed it."

Roman shook his head. "Feel free to double check me, but I've packed almost everything down there and there's no iPad."

"Did you borrow it, Gino?"

He shook his head. "Nah."

Emery stood. "I'm going to look again. Can you watch Ian for a second, Gino?"

"Call you back in a minute," Roman told his sister.

Emery flipped on the light and they hurried down the steep staircase.

The air grew cooler with each step.

"It was on the..." She blinked in disbelief. The desk was now cleared off, the drawers partially open and empty. "You didn't see an iPad? Right there?" She traced her fingers over the scarred wood.

He shook his head slowly. "There were no computers down here."

A thought occurred to her and she pulled the desk away from the wall. He hurried to help.

"There," she said in triumph. A charging cord was plugged into the wall.

"Good detective work. So he had a device down here and a way to charge it." His eyes shaded from brown to black in the dim light as they found hers. "Who took it, then?"

"It wasn't Gino, if that's what you're thinking. He wouldn't lie."

Roman hesitated a beat. "Someone else got into the cabin since you arrived here?"

She went cold all over. A stranger might have been poking around. She thought of the shadowy figure she'd seen move past the basement window.

"I'm scared, Roman." The admission came out before she could stop it and she shivered.

He enveloped her in an embrace, tucking her under his chin. "Let me stay the night here with you. Wally and I can sack out on the sofa."

"I can't ask."

"You didn't."

She pulled away to look at him. "And what if I say no?"

He sighed mournfully and pressed a hand to his heart in dramatic fashion. "Then poor Wally and I are in for an uncomfortable night, patrolling in the freezing cold every hour, trying to catch some shut-eye in my cramped Bronco, fending off attacks from packs of coyotes…"

She folded her arms, fighting down a smile. "The coyote thing was a tad over the top."

He raised a brow. "Should have gone with a pride of mountain lions?"

His mischievous look was so reminiscent of her teen heartthrob. On tiptoe she kissed him, a soft quick touch that thrilled through her and awakened a wondering look on his face. Why had she done that? Hastily she turned to the stairs to hide the blush. "Thank you, Roman."

"My pleasure," he said quietly.

Chapter Eleven

Roman felt a ridiculous swell of pride as he handed the baby over to Emery. "Took me sixteen laps but I finally got him to sleep."

Emery flashed him a weary smile. "My deepest gratitude. Let's hope he stays that way." She tiptoed away and laid him down in the porta crib before rejoining Roman and Wally.

"Where's Gino?"

"He's already gone to sleep, I think. Or he's out for a walk now that the reporters have decamped."

Roman refrained from commenting. Gino's behavior was suspect as far as he was concerned. It seemed more likely to Roman that Gino had taken the iPad than it was the work of a stranger. He couldn't fathom a motive.

She yawned, heading for the coffeepot. "I'll refuel and tackle the bookshelves."

"It can wait until morning."

"I wish. I only have a few days left to get this house packed up." He was going to argue but she waggled a finger at him. "And your event kicks off tomorrow so you need some sleep too."

The argument died on his lips. She was right. Tomorrow was a make-or-break day for Security Hounds, the moment when they'd hopefully prove their worth to the community and police department.

"Any way I can convince you to come stay at the ranch while the demonstration is in progress?" For safety reasons, he told himself, but there was some sensation that ballooned in his chest when she was near, a feeling he couldn't put words to, though he was beginning to crave it.

She smoothed her hair and his fingers longed to do the same.

"I have to get things straight here. It's the only thing I can do for Dad."

Her dad, his mentor, the prisoner. In the past the mere thought of Theo would have shot bitter anger through every nerve. Now he felt more subtle sorrow mixed with concern.

"What?" she said softly. "There's a funny look on your face."

"I, uh, was just thinking about your dad." He slouched, then straightened, unsure what to do with his hands. "How you said you'd love him anyway, guilty or innocent."

She nodded.

He lifted a shoulder. "He's blessed, is all, to have that kind of love." The room felt too small, his emotions far too big. "Gonna take Wally out." She didn't reply but he felt her gaze as he left.

Wally hustled outside, eagerly inhaling scents hidden from his handler. He cocked his head, ears trailing, nostrils quivering.

Roman tried to see what Wally was noting.

The quiet rustling of branches drew him. Wally beelined over and Roman caught up and put a hand on his collar. "Wait," he cautioned the dog, but he could feel the stocky body straining against his hold.

He eased forward to the other side of the shrubs but found no one there. Had there been someone a moment before? Or some nocturnal creature who'd made the smart choice to flee from the exuberant bloodhound? Uneasy, he continued to prowl with no further signs that any intruders were in the vicinity.

His phone buzzed and he answered.

"You're up late," he said to Stephanie.

"Can't sleep. I could hear Mom trying to get comfortable in her recliner."

"She needs that surgery."

"Yes, more reason why the event has to be a smash. We've spent enough on it."

He felt the jab and the truth in it. "It'll pay off."

"Sure you'll be here ready to roll tomorrow?"

"Is that a serious question?" Truth be told, he might be awake all night, counting the minutes until morning.

"I've been researching the Taylor family. Patriarch Benjamin Taylor lost his wife to cancer when she was thirty-three. Put his life and blood into the cars he'd collected with the money he inherited from his father. Had a couple of major credit card debts when he died, which his sons had to pay off. Not the best business man is my impression."

"How's the outfit doing now?"

"Hard to say. They've added to their collection steadily, built a premier showroom and all that."

Roman considered. "Expensive."

"Very."

"What are you thinking, Steph?"

"That it'd be pricey to raise a kiddo too."

"Meaning?"

"Meaning that Diane was pressing Lincoln for a paternity test. Hilary had good reason for hating Diane on that count alone. If they wound up marrying, she wouldn't take that well. Mason might have wanted Diane out of the picture too if Lincoln is bleeding money and possibly adding a kid to the list of expenses."

"Yet we've still got Theo Duncan confessing to the crime and all the evidence pointing to him."

"Evidence can be manipulated."

He felt a thrill of hope. "You think Theo isn't guilty?"

"I don't know. That little tickle in the bottom of my stomach is telling me something is not what it appears to be."

"Keep digging."

"I will. See you tomorrow."

As he laid down on the sofa, he tried to stick to the practical, but for the first time since he'd heard of Theo's arrest, he realized how desperately he wanted Stephanie's suggestion to be true. What if all was not what it seemed?

But why would Theo refuse to say what he knew in favor of investigating from prison?

Surely the police were more equipped to handle an investigation than an incarcerated guy. And why had he shut Emery out when she might have helped him? Troubling thoughts. He returned to the cabin.

Emery had fallen asleep in the armchair, the door to her bedroom open in case Ian cried out. Her expression was gentle, the worry lines faded away into peaceful rest. His heart lurched and he took the blanket and covered her.

She needed sleep and he and Wally did too if they were going to perform their best the next day, but it wouldn't hurt to pack up a few more boxes in the basement. If it would help her and Ian, he'd sacrifice. Plus he'd be awake and alert to any danger.

The notion comforted him and he found he was smiling as he headed down the staircase.

Wally's muffled baying startled Emery awake. Wally? What was he upset about? The clock read a few minutes after three in the morning. She didn't remember returning to the bedroom. Fear nibbled at the edges of her consciousness, shrilling an indistinct message until her senses kicked in. The acrid smell... Fire!

She leaped from the bed, landing hard on her

knees before plunging toward the porta crib. Ian was still sleeping. Smoke wafted under the bedroom door.

"Gino, Roman," she screamed as she grabbed the baby.

No answer.

"Roman," she screamed again.

She heard only her own frantic breathing. Covering the baby with a blanket, she put a finger on the doorknob. Cool to the touch, but when she tried to open it, the door wouldn't budge.

Dropping to her knees, she felt a piece of wood wedged in the jamb. She pounded with both fists. "Help."

She forced herself to think. The box cutter she'd been using to dispose of miscellaneous cardboard. It was on the chair. She snatched it up and quickly removed the pins from the door hinges, dropping them both and tugging with all her might on the knob. At first there was no movement, but the disabled hinge finally allowed her to yank the door inward.

The smoke was billowing from the rear of the house in ghostly puffs. Gino's door was open, his room empty. She checked the bathroom and found it empty too. Roman and Wally were not on the sofa. What had happened? Where were they?

Her next scream ratcheted up in volume.

This time there was a thump and a muffled shout before the basement door slammed open with a splintering of wood. Wally and Roman burst through. "Locked in. Wally smelled the smoke before I did. Where's Gino?"

"I don't know. He's not in his room, or the bathroom."

He pulled her to his side and reached for the baby. "Let me take him. Stay low. Crawl to the door." He tucked Ian inside his sweat jacket and zipped it closed.

The smoke made her cough, tears streaming until she couldn't see the way. She heard the kitchen curtains catch with a whoosh as the fire consumed the fabric. The doorframe was next for the gobbling flames. There would be no escape through the kitchen door.

"Hold on." He took her hand and wrapped it around Wally's harness.

"Away," he yelled to the dog.

How would Wally know where to go? But he'd saved her life before and she was determined not to doubt him now.

Wally lunged forward and Emery held on,

trying to follow where he led without weighing him down. The muscular dog guided her around what must be the coffee table, though she could not see it, and past the lumpy sofa.

Wally plowed on, cleaving through the smoke until they reached the front door. She unlocked the bolt and they crawled into the darkness.

The pristine air was delicious, cooling to her overheated face.

Ian, her mind shrilled. She hadn't heard him cry through the whole ordeal. Her stomach clenched into a fist. What if…?

Roman exited right behind her, helped her to her feet and continued urging her forward until they reached his Bronco. Both of them heaved in lungfuls of clean air as he guided her into the passenger seat and handed the baby into her eager arms. She peeled away the blanket, breath held.

Ian blinked at her, his breathing normal and color fine as best she could tell. He whimpered and squirmed and she'd never been so happy to hear him fuss.

"He's okay," she breathed.

Roman's shoulders sagged. "Thank you, God."

She could only nod in silent agreement, cuddling the baby close. She fought tears, pressing kisses to Ian's forehead in spite of his wriggling.

Roman touched her. "And you are too, Ree?"

The press of his fingers made more tears crowd her eyes. She nodded and forced out a breath. "A-okay."

He bent and kissed her forehead, trailing a finger over her tearstained cheek. If he hadn't been there... But it was more than gratitude and relief. For one frightening moment she felt such a flood of affection for him, it was as though her anger and disappointment with him had all but disappeared.

Confused, she could only huddle there, against his chest, and wonder until he pulled away.

He locked her door and closed it. Going around to the driver's side, he started the engine, flipping on the heater. "Do you have a phone with you?"

She shook her head. "It's on the bedside table."

"Take mine. Call emergency and then the ranch. It's programmed in. My sister or Mom will answer. Tell them what happened and if I'm not back in ten minutes, they need to send backup."

"Where are you going?"

He trotted to the porch and grabbed the jacket Gino had left there. "To look for Gino. He might be on the grounds, out for a walk, or in the garage. If there's trouble, if anyone approaches, drive away from here."

Trouble? More trouble than her father's cabin burning down? The grim reality spread through her consciousness. Someone had locked Roman in the basement, her in the bedroom and set the place aflame while she was sleeping, hoping she would die. The baby too?

Before she could ask anything else, Roman closed the door. Through wisps of smoke, she saw him bend down and offer the jacket to Wally for a sniff.

"Find," he said.

Without hesitation, Wally beelined, not for the house but into the night.

Emery's whole body went cold as she soothed the baby.

If Wally hadn't alerted, they all might have died in the fire.

Out in the darkness, would Roman and Wally encounter the person who'd set it?

Clutching the baby, eyes trained into the night, she prayed.

★ ★ ★

Officer Hagerty arrived on scene and took a report. It became clear that the culprit had entered through the rear of the house after breaking the side window. Roman talked to Hagerty a few feet from the Bronco where Emery sat with the baby. His expression was grim. "Seems someone really wants her dead," he said.

"Someone who knew where to find her, how to get in. Waited until I was in the basement, maybe."

Hagerty was quiet. "Gino?"

"I don't know for sure, but it's odd that we can't find him at the moment. And there's the missing iPad, which he had easy access to."

"Yes," Roman said.

"If this involves the Taylor family…" Hagerty held up a rough palm, "And I'm only saying if… We should look at it through the three big motives…money, power, love."

Roman thought aloud. "Taylors might have money problems—certainly Lincoln created a mess when he betrayed his wife with Diane. Emery said Mason told her Lincoln is a poor businessman."

"And maybe the brothers are in a power

squabble over the car collection, but none of those motives indicate why Emery Duncan would be in the crosshairs."

"That's the problem I keep running into also."

Hagerty stuck his pen in his breast pocket. "Enough for now. I gotta talk to the fire chief."

Roman hustled back to the Bronco with Wally. Emery did not argue this time when he drove them back to the ranch. How could she? The fire department had contained the fire but the house was a sooty mess. They would be able to salvage some things, probably, but certainly not until the building was cleared and the smoke had dissipated.

One firefighter had graciously located the bottles of formula in the fridge and delivered those to Emery along with a package of diapers and a handful of tiny clothes he'd been able to save. In her gratitude, she'd almost cried.

"We'll get whatever you need," Roman said as they drove to the ranch.

She turned a stricken face in his direction. "What about Gino? Where could he be? He hasn't answered my phone calls or texts. I'm really worried."

"We'll find him." Roman hoped his words conveyed more optimism than he felt. Gino could not be unaware of what had happened. If he'd been in the vicinity, he'd have heard the cacophony of sirens and responded. Unless he couldn't...or didn't want to.

He set that thought aside and ushered Emery and Ian into the house where Beth waited. "I borrowed a porta crib from the neighbors and Kara helped me set it up."

Kara nodded shyly. "We zipped out to the store and bought more formula and bottles too. Roman told us what kind."

Emery looked on the verge of tears again. Reluctantly he watched her disappear into the bedroom.

Garrett clapped him on the shoulder. "Done all you can for one night. Party starts early tomorrow. Better get some shut-eye."

"I'll sleep on the couch in here, instead of my trailer," he announced.

His brother arched a brow but didn't comment.

Wally slunk to the fireplace and made himself comfortable on the carpet. Not like he would be upset about staying inside instead of in his kennel, and Roman had the overwhelming need for them both to be close to Emery and Ian.

He was glad his brother hadn't asked why. Because he couldn't have explained it, anyway.

Chapter Twelve

The morning came all too quickly. Roman gathered his family before Emery emerged from the bedroom. "I know it's a lot to ask, but I don't want Emery alone, even for a moment."

"You worried Gino's behind this?" Stephanie said.

He scowled. "I don't know but someone wants her dead and I don't trust the guy."

"Why would Gino want to get rid of Emery when he's been helping her care for the baby all this time?" Kara distributed mugs of coffee.

Garrett, always affectionate, squeezed Kara's arm in gratitude. "He might have motives we know nothing about. Can you look him up, sis? See if anything jumps out at you?"

"Sure." Kara's fingers were already tapping away.

Ian's crying filtered through the door and Garrett lowered his voice. "In the meantime, there are enough of us around. One of us will have eyes on her and the baby."

Reassured, Roman and Stephanie let their dogs out for exploration time in the yard. Garrett helped Kara and his mom set a table outside with the agreed upon coffee, lemonade and cookies for whoever arrived for a tour of the ranch before the main event.

Maybe no one would come, he thought in a panic as the time ticked by. He'd overestimated the appeal of a combined dog and car program. It would be a flop. What had he been thinking? Taking such a risk with their minimal funds? The midmorning sunlight did not warm away the ice in his gut. At the sound of approaching vehicles, Wally glanced up from the hole he was excavating.

Roman plastered on a pleasant smile and let himself out of the gated yard. He watched the first car roll up, the black Mercedes with Mason and Lincoln.

"We ready?" was all Lincoln said.

"Absolutely." *Please, let us be ready.*

Mason snatched two cookies, waving away his brother's objection. "I know, I know. I shouldn't be eating cookies since I'm unable to exercise at the moment, but we can't all be fitness machines and you rushed me out the door." He took a bite and jutted his chin at Roman. "Rumor has it Theo Duncan's place burned last night."

Roman watched the two brothers for any sign that they had inside information but Mason was his usual friendly self and Lincoln was unreadable. "Rumors spread fast."

"Faster than a six-minute mile," Mason agreed. "What's going on? The fire, someone throwing rocks?"

"I don't know."

Lincoln scowled. "You don't know, or you won't say?"

I wouldn't tell you either way. He wasn't sure exactly where his dislike of the Taylors sprang from. Until recently he'd looked at them strictly as business partners. But what if one of them was involved in threatening Emery?

Roman was saved from breaking the awkward silence when Hilary showed up in a large van along with a dozen guests from the inn. Four of the arrivals were women, jauntily outfitted. They chattered cheerfully. The men headed straight for the coffee. Lincoln strolled toward the women.

"There goes Romeo. Doesn't take him long,

does it?" Mason sighed and wiped his hands. "I'd better do my part to grease the skids with the men. Happy visitors are more likely to open up their wallets and purchase classic cars aren't they?"

"How many are you looking to sell?"

"Five would break even for what Lincoln spent on the showroom, but that'd be a stretch."

"Overextended?" Why had he said that? Absolutely inappropriate.

Mason stiffened. "Who isn't?" His penetrating look seemed to laser right through Roman. Truth. He'd overextended Security Hounds too, hadn't he?

Mason shrugged and relaxed. "Cars are expensive investments. Even rich people are content with window-shopping, it seems." He beamed at a bewildered-looking man with a leather jacket and boots. "Duty calls."

Officer Hagerty arrived and chatted with Lincoln and Mason before he sought out Roman. "Accelerant, fire department confirms. They're still sifting through the debris." He nodded to Emery who'd come out on the porch, holding Ian.

"This might not be much encouragement,

but the department is ready to release your vehicle, Miss Duncan."

Emery's hair was glossy in the sunshine. Her smile was tired, but bright nonetheless. "That's something, anyway. Thank you."

"Got a few folks from the police board and county officials here amongst the visitors," Hagerty said. "You and the dogs gotta shine, Wolfe."

He tried to keep the tension from his voice. "We're ready."

Hagerty gave a mock salute and wandered into the crowd.

"You're going to be great," Emery said. "I promised Wally a pacifier if he tried super hard."

He laughed, ridiculously pleased at her optimistic tease. "That should do it." He bent to tickle Ian's cheek, gratified as the baby gave him a gummy grin. "And you'll be pulling for us, won't you, baby boy?"

"We both are," Emery said quietly.

He embraced her, both of them, heedless of the gathering group. It felt so right. The urge to kiss her rolled over him, but Stephanie had climbed up on the porch and commanded attention. She introduced Chloe and Wally and taught a mini lesson on the attributes of the bloodhound. The guests appeared to be interested, he was thrilled to note, and peppered them with questions.

"And you'll see the dogs in action from the big-screen live feed at the showroom," she said. "Lincoln's enlisted the help of…?" She looked at the crowd.

"Me, Vivian," an attractive blonde said, shooting up her hand. "All for a good cause, right?"

Lincoln grinned at her. Roman noted Hilary's glower. He could see that Emery had noticed too. Romeo, indeed.

"Yes," Mason piped up. "It's for a great cause. Taylor Autos is donating ten percent of all our proceeds this weekend toward funding a local search and rescue team. We appreciate your participation, Vivian."

"Happy to help," the woman said, but her gaze was still on Lincoln.

Stephanie nodded. "Lincoln and Vivian will make their way to the car…"

"The beautiful Bel Air our employee has brought over and hidden, disclosing the location only to me," Mason added in dramatic fashion.

Stephanie smiled. "They'll hike over to

the car and hide inside. Our hounds, Chloe and Wally, will track Vivian's scent, using her glove."

Vivian held it aloft for all to see.

"But before that, we'll whisk the rest of you right off to the showroom and you can follow the dog's progress via Chloe's Go Cam," Hilary said. Her tone was cheerful but she stared daggers at Lincoln. "Has everyone finished with their snacks and gotten to meet the dogs?"

Mason provided the location to Lincoln and Vivian who set off immediately.

After a half hour, the visitors loaded up and drove off for the showroom. Roman returned to his dog and massaged Wally's ears. "Ready to rumble, Walls?"

Beth and Officer Hagerty climbed into the ATV.

"Mom..." Roman started.

She held up a "don't even try it" finger. "We're not going to miss this." He was surprised when Emery settled in the tiny rear seat after Kara took Ian from her.

His uber shy sister joggled the baby and began to coo at him. They'd be secure on the property with Garrett who was staying behind in case anything went wrong or they needed another dog. And as far as Emery's safety went, with Hagerty accompanying them, he didn't see how the situation could be much improved. He and Stephanie donned their Security Hounds vests and checked their gear. They gave the dogs a good hydrating drink and a few jerky treats they used only during missions.

A half hour later, Hilary texted that the guests were assembled in the showroom for the live feed. Steph activated Chloe's Go Cam and they attached the long leads to the harnesses.

"Ready or not, here we come," Stephanie said.

The dogs were enthusiastic as Stephanie offered them both a deep whiff of Vivian's glove nestled in a plastic bag. A few moments to soak in the scent, and a loud command to "find" and the dogs were eager to go.

They hustled off, not stopping to reconsider the smells as they did when they were uncertain. Roman's heart raced. Maybe, just maybe, this plan would work. Since he was sprinting to keep up with Wally, he was soon hot and sweating, struggling to keep from tripping on the rocky ground. Trees and thick foliage were not a problem for the bloodhound bulldozers, but Roman was glad he'd worn his heavy-duty pants and boots. Even so, he took a branch to the face that made his eyes water.

The ATV was out of view since it had to keep to the more level trail. Five minutes stretched to ten, then twenty. Excellent. It needed to be a long enough mission to keep the remote viewers interested.

Down a brushy gully they went. They stopped the dogs for a rest period, watered and gave them a treat and reassured them of the scent. Chloe leaped up at the end of the break, but Wally trailed off toward the far end of the gully, which was almost completely swamped in shrubbery, way too small a space to hide a vehicle.

"Wally," he said sternly. "Find."

Wally continued to strain away from the departing Chloe and Steph.

Stephanie turned and tossed him the scent bag. "Try to redirect. I'll keep going."

He nodded, remembering ruefully that all the guests would now have seen footage of his dog going on a walkabout. On the trail above him, he saw the ATV, the glint of binoculars. Three more sets of eyes trained on his location. He wished they would keep going, follow Chloe, not his wandering hound.

It took all his strength to pull the dog to a

stop and put him into a sit. When he opened the scent bag to refocus him, Wally used the opportunity to take off in an all-out sprint for the shrubs. Roman barely caught the end of the lead. Thankfully that hadn't been caught on the Go Cam.

"Wally," Roman shouted. Of all the times for the dog to go after a squirrel or rat, this had to be the worst. Why had he thought Wally was ready for a public mission?

He ran in pursuit.

In the far distance he heard Chloe's joyous baying, loud as a trumpet blast as she neared her target. He hauled on the leash, but trying to pull Wally to a stop was like trying to harness a freight train. There was no help for it but to let the dog follow his trail until he got it out of his system. At least Chloe had saved their skins.

The dog stopped abruptly. Roman was able to catch up.

He had just started in on his tongue lashing when he saw what his dog had been after.

The toe of a boot pointed up at the sky.

Heart sinking, he grabbed his phone.

Emery stared through the binoculars as Hagerty dropped his, leaped from the ATV and disappeared over the rim of the gully.

What had he seen? What had Roman found?

When she got the lenses into focus, her heart stopped.

She didn't hear what Beth shouted, nor thought out a plan. She simply tumbled from the ATV and prayed that she'd been mistaken. Pulse slamming, breath heaving, she scrambled down the slope, heedless of the dirt infiltrating her shoes and socks.

Roman held up a palm as she approached as if to stop her. Despite him, she collapsed to her knees next to Gino's crumpled form. Blood smeared his forehead and his leg was twisted at an odd angle.

"He's alive." Roman's words finally penetrated.

She took Gino's fingers in hers. Cold, so cold. "Oh, Gino," she whispered. "It's Emery. Can you hear me?"

Hagerty talked quietly on his radio. Roman took a knee next to her, touching Gino's wrist.

Gino's eye cracked open. "You shouldn't be here."

Emery leaned close. "It's all right. You're going to be okay."

He stirred, winced.

"Stay still." She blinked back tears. "Help is coming."

"How'd you'd get here, Mr. Kavanaugh?" Hagerty said.

"Dunno," Gino rasped. "I was at Theo's. Heard a noise and went outside to check. Someone hit me over the head, went through my pockets, my phone. I think they thought I was dead when they dumped me."

Emery stroked his arm. "Don't try to talk. It's okay."

He shook his head, sending the leaves in his hair scattering. "Need to tell you. Should have before."

She was going to stop him again, but Roman caught her eye and she pressed her lips together.

"I've been keeping something from you," Gino said. "Something big." He was talking so low they both knelt to hear. Hagerty edged closer.

"We're listening," Roman said.

He breathed in and out, shallow and pained. "I love Diane…have since the eighth grade. When she blew back into town with a baby… I was stunned. I dove right back into the best friend role. Figured I still had a shot, if things didn't work out with Ian's father." He groaned.

"Never should have let her go to the Taylors alone. I thought Lincoln would boot her right out but he let her stay there. I kept telling her something wasn't right. He didn't want the baby, or her, wouldn't even take a paternity test."

And certainly his ex-wife didn't want Diane and Ian around, Emery thought. But what had Gino been keeping from her? And why? And who could have left him for dead?

Roman frowned. "You've been lying to Emery? About what?"

He blinked, wriggled, eyes on Emery. "Your dad asked me to keep you out of it. I promised I would."

"My dad?" Nerves flared up and down her spine. Her father had been keeping secrets with Gino?

Gino blew out a deep breath. "Theo didn't shoot Mason," he croaked. "Diane did, but your father believes it was self-defense. That Lincoln arranged to meet her and murder her by shoving her over the balcony rather than marry her. Her text convinced Theo she'd been threatened somehow. That night... Theo thinks Diane was lured to the house where Lincoln was waiting and she shot the gun to protect herself but got Mason instead before she fell."

She gaped. "Lincoln wasn't even on the property that night according to the police report."

"Your dad sensed there was someone else there in the upstairs hallway. He thinks it was Lincoln but he knew no one would believe it." Gino gulped. "That was Theo's mission. Take the fall for Diane and use his time in prison to prove Lincoln set Diane up to kill her. He couldn't afford a private eye so I was helping."

Hagerty was hanging on every word. Emery hadn't realized Beth had joined them until she squeezed Emery's shoulder. "Ambulance will be here in a few minutes."

Emery's mind was reeling. Her father hadn't shot Mason. Diane had, but it was self-defense? And he was working to prove Lincoln intended to murder Diane?

Roman looked incredulous. "But Theo's fingerprints were on that gun."

Gino took a shuddery breath. "Theo told me he arrived on the property to find the front door open and Diane lying on the bottom floor with the gun still in her hand. He checked her, heard a groan from upstairs, ran to find Mason shot. He realized Diane would be sent to jail so he wiped the gun and left his own prints, fired once more into the floor to be sure he'd test positive for GSR. He had to hurry back to Diane so he couldn't take time to search the property, but he was certain there was someone there. Figured it was Lincoln since Diane said in her text she was all wrong and scared."

Emery realized she was squeezing his wrist so she relaxed her grip.

Hagerty asked permission to record with his cell phone. "So what proof has Theo been pursuing to incriminate Lincoln?"

Gino closed his eyes, breathing hard. "His location that night. If he could catch Lincoln lying about his whereabouts, the police might investigate further."

Emery couldn't follow. "How?"

"The fitness tracker. Lincoln wears one all the time. He's a fanatic, Diane told Theo when she called him the day before the shooting. Always wanted the newest and best model. Even wore it when he was asleep. Your dad asked me to see if I could hack into Lincoln's fitness tracker account."

Emery could only gape in surprise. "A fitness tracker?"

Beth nodded. "I get it. I have one also. It not

only monitors your steps but your location too. It's got a GPS in it."

"Which would prove Lincoln was at home when his brother was shot," Emery finished. "That he'd been lying."

Gino shivered and Emery chafed his arm.

"The info only stays for thirty days on the device, but it's stored on the website until it's erased," he said faintly. "Theo figured if I could hack into the account, he'd have enough to at least convince the cops to open an investigation. Maybe serve a warrant and discover threatening messages from Lincoln to Diane."

"Info acquired by hacking isn't going to put Lincoln away," Hagerty said. "And we're not going to get a warrant with hacked information either."

Roman frowned. "Maybe Theo was hoping to put pressure on Lincoln and force him to confess to threatening Diane."

Emery sank back. "All this time, you've been working with my dad while he's been in jail and neither of you ever said a word."

"Yeah." His smile was faint. "Trying to be some kind of Dick Tracy hacker. Lincoln's sign-in was easy but I've not been able to figure out the passcode."

"And to repeat, that's illegal," Hagerty said.

"I know. Emery, I think there's someone in the jail feeding Lincoln info about your dad's calls and visitors. All the danger lately... Lincoln must suspect your dad is onto him, and that he might have shared some of his suspicions with you. He could have been the one spying on us, burgling the mail at your apartment. I think he set the fire too...did this to me to try to get me out of the way. Could be when he knew you were coming to town, he panicked, tried to drown you to prevent you from returning and stirring it all up again. Or to suppress any proof Theo might have passed on to you."

"The iPad?" Roman said.

Gino sighed. "Mine. Snuck into the basement to do some research and accidently left it there when Emery saw it. I was looking at it when I was attacked and now it's gone."

Emery bit back a groan. "There is no proof in the cabin or anywhere. Only speculation. All this is for nothing. Why did Dad tell me to go home, anyway?"

"I wondered that too. I'd told him I thought I was being followed and the mail had been gone through. He must have gotten scared. He'd heard about Security Hounds. Maybe he wanted you to get help from the Wolfes since I couldn't crack the case."

Roman's eyes went wide.

Gino squeezed her hand. "I'm sorry I lied to you. I never should have agreed. Should have stopped you from returning in the first place but I didn't know how without spilling everything."

It made sense now, how he'd tried to talk her out of going, offering to come with her to Whisper Valley. "It's okay," she forced herself to say. "You were trying to help my family. Right now, all that matters is getting you to a hospital."

The rescue crew arrived and Roman assisted them in strapping Gino to a stretcher.

Before he was moved, Hagerty leaned in. "Not approving what you did, Mr. Kavanaugh, but for the sake of Emery and Ian's safety, don't talk to anyone. I'll see what we can do to keep this between us until I've got some evidence to move on. Got me?"

Gino nodded.

Emery could only give him one more squeeze before he was hauled up and out and driven away.

She stood on shaky legs, trying to process.

Should she feel hopeful? Angry? Worried? All of the above? If Lincoln was the one who had threatened Diane and left Gino for dead, what would happen once he figured out Gino was alive?

"Will he be safe?" she said to Hagerty.

"I'll see to it. I'll roll with the ambulance to the hospital and make sure."

He climbed out of the ravine.

Wally poked her thigh. She cradled his squishy head. "Wally, you found him." She looked at Roman and Beth. "I know it wasn't what you'd hoped, but Gino might have died without Wally."

Roman's smile was half pleasure, half chagrin. "Typical Wally. He chooses his own mission."

But she knew the dog's deviation might reflect badly on Security Hounds. Everyone was paying the price for what had happened at the Taylor estate on that terrible night.

Roman consulted his phone. "Chloe finished. The guests were impressed."

Beth bent with a twinge of discomfort and patted the dog. "See? All is well. Nothing to worry about."

Her stomach knotted. Nothing to worry

about…unless Lincoln had really threatened Diane and escaped looking completely blameless. Was he trying to kill Emery now too because of her father's prying?

Was he the reason her sister was in a coma and her father in jail?

From Roman's distracted demeanor as he collected Wally's leash, she knew he was wondering the same thing.

He took her hand and she clutched his warm fingers.

"You were right about your dad," he said.

"He was right about you too," she said, throat thick.

Tears blurred her vision. She should have been filled with relief.

Instead all she felt was fear.

Chapter Thirteen

Stephanie and Chloe returned late afternoon, aglow. Roman felt a thrill that part one of their business plan had gone brilliantly, in spite of Wally's detour rescue. Roman eyed his family seated around them. His mom, Kara sitting cross-legged with her iPad in her lap, the twins Stephanie and Garrett. Emery stood by the sliding door, hugging herself. It should have been a celebratory moment. Instead his body hummed with the aftermath of Gino's rescue.

Gino's confession was so farfetched, wildly improbable. Lincoln had been trying to lure Diane to her death? Simply proving Lincoln was on the property that night wouldn't necessarily convince the police to investigate. But what if? What if they were actually partnering with a man who'd planned to murder Diane? Gino? Emery?

He snagged a look at Emery, quiet, troubled.

Theo wasn't what Roman and everyone else thought him to be. Guilt chewed at Roman. What if all this time his mentor had been sacrificing himself for his daughter? That was consistent with the man Roman knew or thought he did. He'd believed Theo to be a man of service, compassion, courage.

And maybe that's exactly what he was. A thought stabbed at him. If Roman had gone to see Theo in jail, showed the slightest sign of support, maybe Theo would have broken his silence and come to Security Hounds for help.

Water under the bridge. Right now, Theo could be depending on them to save his daughter.

He caught Emery's gaze and smiled.

She offered one in return.

Hagerty's arrival interrupted.

"How's Gino?" Emery asked.

Hagerty accepted coffee from Beth. "He's stable, with a broken leg and a concussion. I've asked the hospital to state only that he's under sedation, not to divulge the severity of his injuries. He's got an officer posted at the hospital door."

Stephanie frowned. "Gino's story is so convoluted. If Lincoln is guilty, why would he risk everything to kill Diane just to avoid a paternity test? He doesn't have to marry her, only meet his responsibility to support their child if Ian is his. Murder seems extreme."

"Murder is extreme," Kara said, without looking up from her computer.

Roman resisted the urge to pace. "Okay, let's say hypothetically Lincoln did do it for that reason. And he's lying about being off the property altogether. Did he have help or is he acting alone?"

"Hilary? Mason?" Garrett tapped a pencil on the coffee table. "Those are the two likeliest coconspirators. His ex-wife doesn't have much good to say about Lincoln, so would she aid and abet?"

Stephanie frowned. "She might if Diane planned to force a court paternity test. Revenge might be enough motivation for her to want Diane dead."

Garrett nodded. "Okay. What about Mason?"

"Maybe he's got a motive too," Stephanie said. "Diane shows up and Lincoln's forced to pay child support. Lincoln's already imperiled the car business with his spending. Maybe Mason sees a way to stop him? Or maybe if

Diane marries Lincoln, it affects a will or something and Mason loses out."

Officer Hagerty settled onto the love seat with Wally crammed as close to his side as the dog could manage. The object of Wally's interest was Hagerty's leather belt. Leather was one of Wally's two favorite items. Good thing he didn't carry pacifiers around or Wally would have never let him get up off the furniture.

Hagerty stroked the dog's ear. "You all see how this looks though, right? A man jailed for attempted murder is eager to pin the blame on someone else. An upstanding citizen, I might add, who's bringing business and tourists to the area." He narrowed his eyes at Roman. "As the voice of the law here, I need to remind you all that Theo confessed to shooting Mason Taylor and he hasn't offered one word to the contrary except what we've heard from Gino. Not generally how an innocent man would behave, is it?"

The room fell into an uneasy silence.

Unable to stand still a moment longer, Roman got up and rolled his shoulders. "I agree it's wild that Theo thought he could prove Lincoln's guilt from jail. That he'd allow himself to be arrested rather than reveal his suspicions to the cops."

"It's not." Emery's statement blasted through his thoughts.

He blinked. "But having Gino try to hack into the fitness app? It's ridiculous to think that would work."

"He would do it to protect me and Diane."

He saw the beginning of her tears and realized he'd wounded her. "I didn't mean…"

"It's not ridiculous or farfetched. Don't talk about him like that. Now that I know how he's been trying to find evidence…" Her lips trembled. "He sacrificed for us, gave up everything." One tear slid down her cheek, and before he could say another word, she got up and banged through the porch door.

He looked at his family. "Was what I said that bad?"

Garrett shrugged. "Doesn't matter what you said. Matters how she feels about it."

He closed his mouth and walked outside. She stood near the fence, watching the dogs, arms folded around herself like a bulletproof vest.

"I'm sorry, Ree."

She didn't answer, didn't look at him. "Deep down you don't really believe he's innocent."

"It's not that…"

She turned on him. "Because you don't want to believe it, do you? You still want him to be punished because he disappointed you."

"No."

"Yes." Her eyes flashed. "You want punishment because you want him to hurt like you were hurt."

He had no idea how to reply. "Emery, I loved your dad, but…"

"Loved? Past tense?" Her eyes glittered. "That's at the bottom of it, isn't it? You were hurt, by your birth mom, by what happened with Jax and now my father. You won't forgive them. Maybe deep down you think if you let go of that anger, you'll discover you aren't worth loving? Punishment is better than vulnerability, right?"

Anger stirred in his belly. What did she know about what he'd experienced? The scars it left behind? "Maybe this isn't about me. Maybe it's you that's angry for what your family set in motion. You had to take in your sister's baby after she train-wrecked herself. You said she made messes her whole life that you had to clean up and here you are doing it again. Now you're going to forget all that?"

She smacked the fence post. "I haven't forgotten it. I live with the unfairness of that every single sleepless night, each exhausting day and every moment in between."

"How?" And in that moment it seemed as if he'd never wanted to know an answer so badly in his entire life. How did she live with the circumstances thrust upon her?

She dashed at the tears with her sleeve and let out a breath that sagged her shoulders and seemed to drain away her anger. "God set me on the diving board and said, all right, Ree. I've loved and forgiven you all your life. Now I'm asking if you can do the same by forgiving your sister and loving Ian."

"And you answered yes."

"I'm trying to. Every day." Her words were high and choked. "I wasn't there for my sister because I was angry at her and happy to dump it all on my dad. That's the truth, I'm embarrassed to say. Now I'm trying to show up like I should have done then."

The catch in her voice cut at him and he longed to take her in his arms but he wasn't sure where he stood, where they stood. Instead he simply stared at her, willing his mouth to fashion words around his feelings. Nothing came.

Emery exhaled, her shoulders slumping. Slowly her chin came up. "Roman, I don't know how everything has gotten to this point, but one thing I'm sure of. You have to look in the mirror and decide you're worth loving because God said so and He's the only one that's going to do it perfectly. No man, or woman, can deliver." She turned that blue-green gaze on him and it took his breath away. "I think you're worth loving and so did my father. I'm sure he still does."

She walked slowly away, into the house, leaving him open-mouthed.

He sought the solace of his trailer. Flopping down in the chair, his mind buzzed with uncertainty. Theo, Emery, Eli. Pain from his past rushed through him in an angry tumult. The photos in his bedside drawer called to him and he pulled them out, two of very few photos he possessed.

His sister Stephanie's nickname for him was the Photo Fugitive. True, he had a visceral reaction to having his picture taken, a fact that the women he'd dated in and out of the service had found off-putting.

No fun.

Party pooper.

Wet blanket.

He'd heard all their remarks.

Roman fingered the photos.

Gonna hurt. Why look?

But he did, anyway. In the first he was a gangly teen with spotty skin, grossly overdue for a visit to the barbershop, grinning up at Uncle Jax, similarly unkempt, muscular from his days working on various rigs and pipelines. It was his own expression that got him, the love in it, the trust he'd given so willingly.

It had hurt so profoundly, like a bullet punching through his rib cage, when Uncle Jax introduced him to Melissa and her three kids. One older than him, two younger, a whirlwind of soccer trophies, straight-A report cards, a pending college scholarship. Roman had handled it terribly. Jealous, reactionary, finding fault with the woman who tried to discipline him until Uncle Jax tearfully told him to straighten up or get out.

He'd left.

Over the years Jax had called and he'd ignored the messages, at first out of hurt that Jax had brought in a whole new family, but then out of shame at his own behavior.

He drew the one from underneath.

An older Roman, starting to fill out with muscles, his hair cut military short, though it would be another year before he enlisted. This time he was standing beside Theo Duncan, the man who'd helped him sort out his own anger into manageable portions, set him on the road to honorable military service, screwed his head on straight enough that he could accept love from him and the Wolfes.

Try as he might, he could not see anything but gentleness in Theo's face.

I would still love my father even if he was guilty.

Emery's pronouncement had stunned him.

Love doesn't turn on and off like that. It doesn't with God and it shouldn't with us.

Yet Roman had turned his off tightly, sealing it closed. The images of Jax and Theo showed him flawed men, with a mixture of strengths and weaknesses instead of the caricatures he'd reduced them to.

Uncle Jax the Betrayer.

Theo Duncan the Murderous Hypocrite.

The photos came into clearer focus, two men who had offered love and acceptance to a lonely youngster. Jax and Theo had both loved him generously, offered what they could.

You have to look in the mirror and decide you're

*worth loving because God said so and He's the only
one that's going to do it perfectly. No man, or woman,
can deliver, Roman. Only God.*

He closed his eyes, sank to the floor, back
pressed to the mattress, praying as the tears
began to fall.

At sunrise, Emery tapped on Roman's trailer
door. Wally stood at her shin, tail swinging,
paws muddy.

Roman looked from her to his dog. "Did you
dig your way out of the kennel again?"

Wally didn't wait for an answer but pushed
in and snuffled around the kitchen in search of
crumbs.

She'd had a whole speech planned out, calm
and controlled. Instead everything evaporated
the moment Roman opened the door. "I'm so
sorry. I was horrible to say those things to you."
And then the tears started in again, fountain-
ing out of control.

He didn't reply, simply reached out and
guided her inside before wrapping her in an
embrace. "No apologies," he said over her sniffles. "You were right. I needed to hear it. Probably I've needed to for a long time."

She clung to him, feeling the beat of his

heart against her cheek. When she raised her tear-stained face to his, he closed the distance and kissed her. There was a river of sweetness in that kiss that warmed and soothed her, circled around the aching places in her soul like a healing balm. They'd both sustained so many wounds, upheavals, violent u turns, but here they were together and she wondered for a moment if that's what God had intended all along.

But he eased her away and into a chair and her daydream floated away. Friendly understanding, nothing more. She attempted a calm smile, wiping her tears with the tissue he offered. She saw the photos taped to the refrigerator, Roman and a man who had to be his uncle, Roman and her father. He caught her look.

"They're two important men in my life," he said. "No matter how things turned out."

The sun crept through the tiny kitchen window and straight into her heart.

He cleared his throat and shuffled to the kitchen, poured a bowl of water for Wally. "Thought I'd maybe call Uncle Jax later after the event is over." He didn't look directly at her when he said it but she caught the shine in his eyes, anyway.

"I think that's fantastic."

Several silent moments ticked away between them. Roman fiddled with the blinds. "How is Gino?"

Emery wiped her eyes. "He's holding his own. He has to be very still and quiet to give his brain a chance to recover from the concussion. His leg will heal fine, the doctor said."

Wally slurped water, sending it sloshing over the floor, which made her laugh. "Is he going to have a role today?"

"Considering he went rogue yesterday? We'll let Chloe take the lead again, but Wally will be on the premises to answer questions and meet and greet."

She steeled her spine. The moment had arrived. "Roman, I want to come with you today."

He jerked. "Uh, no. I don't think so."

"I have to see it, the place where it all happened. To try to make sense of it in my mind. This is my only opportunity."

"Emery..."

"I'm not being irresponsible. I know someone is determined to kill me and if Dad is right about Lincoln, I'll be walking right into his home, but Hagerty will be there and you and Stephanie and Garrett and all the guests. Very public. Very safe. Kara will stay with Ian again and there will a police officer checking periodically."

Roman heaved out a breath and rested his hands on his hips. "You've thought this all out. I get the sense whatever I say is going to be a waste of breath."

"That's about the size of it."

He shook his head. "You're as stubborn as Wally."

She laughed and headed for the door, but part of her spirit lagged.

His kiss had made her feel loved, she realized, in a way she'd never experienced before.

But it hadn't meant the same to him, clearly.

"Something else?" he asked.

No, nothing else. "Um, no. I'll see you later."

She kept her smile bright anyway, the rising sun chasing the shadows away as she returned to the ranch house.

Chapter Fourteen

Emery. Roman simply could not get her out of his mind. The kiss, her tears of remorse, the peace she'd prompted him to accept that felt like putting down an anvil he'd been straining to hold for more than a decade. It left him off balance, confused.

"You're adding to the chaos."

Garrett's voice snapped him out of his reverie, along with the rivulets of water Wally was shaking off from the bath he'd just received. Wally trundled a safe distance away from the hose and shook violently again.

Roman laughed at the dripping dog. "You aren't the best at obedience, but at least you're clean." The dog sent Roman a look of pique.

Chloe received similar treatments before they were loaded up into the special trailer Roman had painstakingly converted for their use with comfortable stalls that opened onto ramps from the outside for ease of loading and unloading. He climbed aboard and followed Stephanie and Emery in one vehicle and Garrett and Beth in the other.

On the porch Kara joggled Ian and waved the tiny baby's hand at them as if he were sending them off. They wouldn't be alone. Hagerty had, indeed, posted a cop at the end of the drive and Roman appreciated the precaution. It didn't quite ease all the tension away. Emery's safety, the event's success, Beth's pain, all weighed heavily as they made the journey to the Taylor estate.

Several pristine classic cars were visible, parked on the grounds to the side of the main house and guests were strolling around them, sipping and snacking. The showroom itself was set back from the fence line, all glass and sleek angles, the doors propped open to encourage visitors inside. They'd agreed on a staging area for the dogs under a cluster of towering pines. Garrett set up an information table with Security Hounds flyers and business cards. It didn't take long for the dogs to attract some people. Chloe basked in the attention. Wally surprised him by hanging back, close to Emery. Roman had made sure she was securely situated near his elbow as he fielded questions and kept an eye on the proceedings. Apparently, Wally had decided she needed canine protection. At least on that priority they agreed.

Good dog, Walls.

Lincoln gathered his flock of visitors with a hearty, "Are we living the life, or what?" There was general laughter and a chorus of approval from the crowd. Vivian, the blonde who had hidden in the car, let loose with an enthusiastic "woo-hoo" that got her a thumbs-up from Lincoln.

Hilary wandered toward them. "We'll get the demo started after Lincoln's done being the rock star."

"Seems like a natural born salesman to me," Garrett said amiably. Roman recognized his brother's technique. People would tell Garrett anything because he was the textbook example of approachability.

"A natural born salesman but not a businessman, or a faithful husband, of course." Hilary's words dripped with bitterness and she cast a hostile glance at Emery.

Emery lifted her chin. "I'm sorry for what my sister and Lincoln did and how it affected your marriage."

"Not affected, ruined."

Emery's face reddened, but she didn't reply.

Hilary's gaze narrowed as she looked away. "Mason is more of a man than Lincoln. The car collection would have been in much better hands with him but their daddy never bothered to update his will after Mason was born. A charming procrastinator, and he passed all those genes down to Lincoln." She shook her head. "Anyway, don't know why I'm dumping all this on you. Let me see if I can rein in Mr. Charming and we'll select another volunteer to hide in one of the cars. Dogs ready?"

"Yes," Stephanie said. "This will be a piece of cake for Chloe."

Hilary left without another word.

They all exchanged looks. So Lincoln had inherited and never arranged to legally share the wealth with Mason? He wondered what Lincoln's financial arrangement with Hilary had been upon their divorce.

Stephanie harnessed Chloe and waited for the scent article.

"So we've got Lothario Lincoln holding the purse strings," Garrett said. "That's interesting."

"And don't forget the scorned wife, and perhaps a resentful younger brother," Beth added.

"An unhappy family for sure." Roman was grateful once more that God had given him a second chance and he intended to do the best he could for his family, and to try to repair what he'd damaged with Uncle Jax. He'd wasted too much time already. He unfolded a card chair. "Sit down, Mom. Please."

She obeyed with a pat to his hand. "All right. I'll hold down the fort."

He looked over at Emery. "I know you want to see inside the main house."

She flushed. "I was thinking it's a good time for me to visit the powder room."

"Wally and I will walk you over."

"I was hoping you'd say that." She smiled, which added that little dimple to one side of her mouth. He remembered the kiss in his trailer, soft and tender. A fond gesture only, wasn't it? Purely his instinct to comfort? He was still mulling it over, inert with the confusion of it when she squared her shoulders and headed toward the main house. He decided to let his instincts take over for a while and managed to snag her hand, holding Wally's leash in the other.

"I can imagine this is going to be difficult for you, seeing the place where it all happened."

Her mouth was tight as she nodded. "I need to do it for both of them."

He squeezed her fingers, awed at her courage. He'd dismissed his uncle and all the past mess because it hurt too much to face, and here she was, walking right to the place where her family had been demolished. Amazing, that's what she was.

They entered the foyer, which featured a massive spiral staircase in black-and-white marble leading to the upper floor. The lower-level featured a round table housing a flower arrangement and in the corner a bay window flanked by a massive potted tree. Paned windows flooded the room with light.

"Best behavior, Walls," he whispered. The last thing he needed was Wally running rampant. Emery still held his hand, but her skin had grown cold.

"Living the life for sure, aren't they?" His half-hearted attempt to lighten the mood.

She didn't appear to hear, her gaze riveted on the upper-story railing. "They must have replaced it after she…"

After Diane fell.

When he heard her breath catch, he moved to her side, letting the leash out so Wally could explore within limits. He beelined to the indoor tree. "No peeing," he cautioned.

Emery was still staring. Her words came out singsong, as if she were telling herself a story. "Diane was scared of someone so she took her gun to the Taylors' house. She encountered Mason upstairs. It was dark. She fired. Mason was struck and she fell. My dad arrived and found Diane downstairs. He ran to the top floor and discovered Mason bleeding, heard someone else on the premises. He returned to Diane, wiped her prints off the gun and added his own."

"And then he confessed." Roman rewound the tape in his mind. "But your father's theory that Lincoln scared Diane, lured her over there somehow, it's all just conjecture."

Emery sighed. "Lincoln probably discarded the tracker already and deleted the account."

"Possible."

"Then we have nothing." She sagged. "My dad might not survive, nor my sister. Even if I did figure out the website password and the account is still active, the evidence wouldn't be admissible. I don't know why I thought coming here would make any difference."

Her defeat felt like a physical blow. Security Hounds hadn't been able to help, nor had he. Wally pawed at the heavy terra-cotta pot. Through an interior doorway, a woman entered in a housekeeping uniform. She headed straight for them.

"I'm sorry, sir. You can't have a dog in here."

"He's a working dog. We're here for the demo." Wally didn't help Roman's case by trailing a ribbon of saliva down the side of the pot and whining.

"I'm sorry, sir," she said firmly. "No dogs."

"It's okay," Emery said. "I'll visit the powder room and come right out."

"We'll wait for you on the porch," Roman said. "Use the front door only, right?"

She nodded. "No wandering, no exiting through a rear door. I know."

He lugged Wally to the shaded front steps. In the distance he could hear a sudden ripple of excitement from the showroom. Chloe must be doing her thing. The murmur rose to a cheer and he silently added his own. "You'll get there someday too, Walls." The dog was far too annoyed at being pulled from his potted plant to listen.

His phone buzzed, a group text to all of them from Garrett.

Guess what? With the police department's blessing, a county administrator has officially offered Security Hounds a trial search and rescue contract.

Roman pumped a fist in the air. He realized the only person he was burning to tell was Emery.

Emery emerged from the restroom to find the housekeeper gone. She gazed around the pristine flower-scented space. Living the life. Would her family ever be able to do that? Whatever secrets this room contained, they would remain there forever. She started for the front door, distracted by the dark patch of Wally's drool on the terra-cotta pot. Why had the dog been so interested?

She gazed up at the balcony one more time, imagining it giving way, the failure sending debris raining down from the upper floor. A strange thought occurred to her. What if…?

She hurried to the plant and looked all around its mossy base. Nothing there. Of course not. What had she expected? Still, the urge for further examination needled her. After making sure the housekeeper hadn't returned, she knelt next to the pot and shoved her arm into the dark space. Her fingertips met only slick tile. Hunkered down, she stretched a few inches farther and touched a pliable rubber object. Quickly she snatched it out of its cubbyhole.

Unable to believe it, she stared down at the exercise tracker with the half-detached wristband. It had to be Lincoln's. Nerves zinging, she quickly wrapped it in a clean tissue from her pocket, praying she hadn't ruined any evidence. "Roman," she called as she got to her feet.

A hand clamped over her nose and mouth, an arm cinching around her neck. She tried to struggle, scream but the grip was fierce. Sparks danced before her eyes.

Roman…

Her shoes skidded uselessly on the slippery tile.

The pressure on her windpipe increased.

She couldn't make a sound as she was dragged away.

Too long. Now that the euphoria of Garrett's text was fading, Roman became more aware of the time.

The visitors were spilling out of the showroom and Emery still hadn't exited the house.

He shoved open the door. There was no one in the foyer. Heedless of annoying the house-keeper, he and Wally burst inside and raced down the hallway that led to the powder room. No sign of Emery.

He was about to shout for her when Wally nosed hard at something and barked. It was one of their flyers, crumpled. Emery had dropped it. He knew it in his bones. He knelt next to the dog and offered him a proper sniff.

"Find," he said. *Please, Wally.*

The dog launched down the hallway. They raced past rooms, which Wally ignored com-pletely, until they burst into an enormous kitchen. A caterer arrived one moment after them, holding an empty tray, startled. "Can I help you?"

"Did you see someone come through here? A dark-haired woman?"

"No, I was out with the guests."

Roman plowed through the exit door, which funneled him into a well-tended backyard. He clutched his phone as Wally dragged him across the grass toward a cement sidewalk.

"Garrett, Emery's gone. Lincoln must have snatched her from the main house."

"Not Lincoln," Garrett snapped.

"What?"

"I'm looking right at Lincoln and Hilary. Not them."

He gaped. "Can you see Mason?"

"Negative."

His blood ran cold. "He's our guy. I'm heading west with Wally tracking. Get Hagerty."

"Copy that."

Garrett would locate the cop, but by the time he caught up, it would be too late for Emery. He didn't know why Mason would have snatched her. Something to do with his inheritance or protecting his brother? Either way, if he was desperate enough to try an abduction in a public place, he wouldn't let her live. Wally galloped along the cement sidewalk. Roman rushed as fast as he could to keep up.

Unless he overtook Mason, there would be no last-minute rescues this time.

Emery swam to consciousness, her thoughts jumbled, her throat raw where he'd choked her. Her senses cleared and she realized she was in the rear of a car; she'd been dumped into the back seat. Her ankles were bound with duct tape. Not again. She managed to wriggle to a half-sitting position but her hands had been

taped with messy loops to the passenger headrest and tugging only compacted the strips into
wiry ropes that cut into her skin. How much
time had passed? Would Roman have noticed?

"Lincoln, please," she called into the front
seat. "I won't tell if you let me go."

"About the exercise tracker you found behind the plant?"

Wrong voice. It hit her like a brick. It wasn't
Lincoln who'd abducted her.

"I simply could not figure out where it had
gotten to," Mason said. "Even without it, your
dad was getting close. I have a friend who
works in the jail who told me Theo was poking around, asking someone he called to contact
companies that sell fitness trackers. I figured
he was talking to you." His tone was chatty,
friendly. "When he had the heart attack, he
mumbled something about proof. I assumed it
was something he'd mailed you or spoken to
you about. I would have liked to kill him then
but it's hard to get to someone in a prison hospital, so I decided to get rid of you and the potential proof. I stole your mail once but whatever
he sent is bound to arrive sometime and I can't
stake out your mailbox forever."

Her father was truly innocent. All this time

she'd known it and now it was confirmed. "He didn't tell me or send me anything."

Mason shrugged. "Too late now, isn't it? No one would believe him if he does happen to recover, but they might believe you. So…" He grinned at her in the rearview mirror. "When the drowning failed, I decided I could get you at the inn. That was a bust."

"So you tried to burn down my dad's cabin? Attacked Gino?"

He shook his head. "I didn't know that Gino clod was working with your dad until I heard him on the phone outside your cabin. He was chatting with a fitness-tracker company, trying to convince them he needed to recover a lost password, so I took action. He was supposed to die in that ravine. I never planned on any of this. It snowballed. I had to act before it was all gone."

"What?"

He lifted a shoulder. "Everything. The cars, house, showroom. Dad left all the assets in Lincoln's name and never revised his will when I was born. Oh, sure, my brother was going to get around to making things equitable like Dad intended. Every year he'd mention it, and did he ever follow through? Of course not. There are too many slackers in this world."

She slowly put the pieces together. "Lincoln cut you out of the assets."

"Not purposefully. He's a procrastinator like my dad but he also doesn't know how to run a business, or a marriage for that matter. Between alimony and dithering around with the cars, I'll be fortunate to have anything left when he does sign half over to me, which he's been promising to do for the last thirty years."

She could hardly make herself believe it. Mason was the exact opposite of the friendly community-minded local he'd pretended to be. "I won't tell anyone anything. I'll leave with Ian. I promise." She hoped her voice didn't quiver.

Mason didn't appear to hear. "Theo's false confession was too easy. I knew he had something planned, that weasel."

The right crime, the wrong man. Mason, not Lincoln, all this time. "You're wrong, Mason. My dad thought Lincoln lured Diane to the house to kill her."

He didn't answer for a moment. "If only I'd known that. I was the one who got her to come that night."

"Why?"

"To kill her, of course."

Emery shivered. "I don't understand why you'd risk committing murder."

"Lincoln decided to take that paternity test. He was going to find out Ian was his and marry Diane. He always felt bad that his infidelity ended things with Hilary. That's why he paid for her inn to be remodeled. He said he was going to get it right the next time he married, be the better man. What do you think would have happened to the remainder of the collection if he married a second time? You think I'd ever get my share? Not until after he sold it all off to pay for a wife and kid."

"You figured you'd kill Diane, make it look like a fall?" She continued to flex her hands, stretching the tape a little more. A hot trail of blood oozed down her arms.

"The afternoon it all went down, I followed Diane to her favorite coffee shop. She called your dad, I heard her blabbering about her plans to get together with Lincoln, that he was coming to love Ian, et cetera, et cetera. He was softening on the paternity test idea."

She caught a glimpse of his sly smile in the rearview mirror. "So what exactly did you do, Mason?"

"What I had to."

And now he thought he had to kill her.

Each minute brought them farther out of town, deeper into the wilderness that had almost been her grave before.

Desperately she yanked on the tape.

He wasn't going to get another chance.

She had to find a way to save herself or her father's sacrifice would have been for nothing.

Chapter Fifteen

Roman was covered in sweat when they emerged at the outbuilding at the end of the walkway.

Wally pawed at the door of the neatly tended garage. It was placed well away from the house, probably designated for employee cars and utility vehicles.

His phone rang.

"Wait until I get there," Hagerty puffed. "Got units responding."

Not waiting. He pocketed the phone. The panel on the roll-up door was a numbered keypad. Kara could undoubtedly crack the code since she loved number puzzles more than breathing but there wasn't time for that either.

Instead, he hustled to the side window, concealed by a curtain. Finding it locked, he put Wally into a sit, picked up a rock from the ground and bashed it through the glass. The hole enabled him to reach in and force the window and drop down inside. He saw immediately where the car had been parked. Slamming the garage opener from the inside, he raced out and texted the group.

He's got her in a vehicle.

Steph's reply popped up immediately. Direction?

"Wait one second." He dropped next to Wally and reminded him of the scent. "This is it, boy. No squirrel chasing or stubbornness. I need you to help us find her. I'm counting on you." Wally's nostrils quivered as he smelled the crumpled flier again. "Find," Roman said.

If they failed…

He shook the thought away. After what seemed like an eternity, Wally decided on a direction, nose glued to the ground. He circled, looped twice and stopped after only a couple of yards. Logical. He'd lost the scent at that point. Even bloodhounds could not track subjects in speeding cars. But it was enough. Had to be.

Northbound, along the frontage road, he texted.

No response dots immediately popped up, and he knew what they were thinking. Was

Wally accurate? Should they bank all their resources on it?

He tried to clear his mind. Garrett, head
south, in case we're wrong.

Got a unit at the junction, Hagerty texted.
He won't get to the freeway.

What was between here and the junction?
His heart fell.

The lake. Would he take her there again?
Finish what he'd attempted?

His legs felt like rubber. Borrowing a vehicle.
Heading north toward the lake with Wally, he
messaged.

He felt the thrill of fear in his mother's reply.

Stay safe. He's desperate.

Desperate. Well, so was Roman.

Desperate to capture Mason, make him pay
for what he'd done.

Desperate to capture the most radiant light
in his world.

Desperate to save her.

He grabbed a nearby motorcycle by the han-
dles and rolled it out of the garage. The keys
were in the ignition.

Wally barked and jumped. Roman grabbed a
rope and climbed on the seat. The dog's wrin-

kled face broadcast his fear that he would be left behind.

Not leaving you, Walls. Roman scooted back and patted the space in front of him.

Wally sailed into the spot and Roman awkwardly tethered his companion to him, like a mother carrying her baby. It was ungainly, but it would provide enough protection that Wally wouldn't fall. "I got you, Wally."

He gunned the engine. The dog howled. In a frenzy of noise, they jetted away.

Emery's arms ached from tugging at the tape. She'd almost succeeded in freeing one of her wrists but the car was now bumping and jostling, indicating Mason had driven off the main road. She needed to cover the sound of her yanking.

"Why were you wearing Lincoln's exercise band that night?"

"I took it when he was in the shower before he went out. I used it to send Diane a text, pretending to be Lincoln. Did you know you could message with those things? It said he'd decided to take the paternity test and sue for full custody and he'd win because of her seedy past, that he'd pay people off if necessary to prove she was an unfit mom."

Full custody? How that must have terrified Diane. Ian was the best thing in her life. "My sister thought Lincoln was out to get her but it was you all the time. And everyone thinks you're such a nice guy."

He sighed. "Good plan though. That part worked, she came charging up the stairs. I was going to give her a shove and be done with it. That old railing was weak. No one would know it wasn't an accident. If she didn't die, I could help her along before calling the cops. Never would have guessed that she carried a gun. I took a step toward her and she shot me as I shoved her over. I bled like crazy, but I saw her phone near me. I deleted my text from both the fitness tracker and her cell. No trail back to me. I was in the process of wiping my prints off the exercise band when I got lightheaded and collapsed. Dropped the silly thing."

Emery felt like screaming. It had been Mason all along.

"Your father barreled in but I pretended to be unconscious. His confession to protect Diane worked in my favor. Cops didn't delve too deeply into the details."

They wouldn't. Mason appeared to be the victim and they had a confession.

Her thoughts spun faster and faster. The app could put a person at the scene of the shooting, but it couldn't identify who was actually wearing the exercise band, not without fingerprints. The wristlet she'd found was the smoking gun. It was gone from her pocket, of course. He'd taken it when he'd choked her at the mansion. She held back a groan.

Mason seemed to read her mind. "I didn't think there was any way I could be implicated. That's when it dawned on me that the lost exercise band would have my prints. I couldn't delete the app either because it's in my brother's name and I don't know the password. The only loose end."

His tone was hard; she could barely believe it was the Mason she'd known. A terrible thought dawned in her mind. "Wait a minute. That's your plan B, isn't it? If Dad's sleuthing made the cops reopen the case, or you couldn't get rid of me and whatever proof you thought I might have, you were going to let Lincoln take the fall."

"My first choice was to keep us both out of jail, but…" He shrugged. "The app was in his name, like I said. It was on the property the night of the shooting. He had a strong motive to want her gone. If he continued to refuse me my fair share of the inheritance, that little tracker would be my insurance policy, providing I could find it. If I did, I'd wipe my prints to clear myself and if necessary, arrange for it to be found by someone else. I'd suddenly remember seeing my brother threatening Diane. The cops would get a warrant and retrieve that deleted text that looked like it came from him. I've been waiting on Lincoln to take care of me for decades and he's ready to jump in with both feet for a woman who isn't even his blood? How much can a man take?"

"You'd sell out your own brother."

"He sold me out first." The car jerked to a stop. Frantically she hauled on the duct tape but she was out of time. He yanked open the door, cut the loops around her wrists and dragged her out by her taped feet. She fell onto the muddy ground, terror ribboning through her.

The lake.

He'd brought her back to drown her.

And this time he wouldn't botch the job.

"They'll know it was you," she panted, getting to her feet.

"I don't think so. I'll cut off the tape after you're dead so it looks like you jumped in yourself, return the car, change clothes and sneak back to the showroom before anyone's the wiser. I'll be just as shocked as everyone else when your body is found. They won't pin it on me."

He held up the wristlet. "But thanks for finding this. Never would have thought it could have landed behind that potted tree." Before his smile had time to dim, she shoved him as hard as she could. He cried out, doubling over, the wristlet flying from his fingers. She grabbed it and hopped frantically away. Hide. She had to hide or maybe outpace him if she could.

"Stop," he shouted.

She was at the edge of the trees, hopping, leaping, throwing herself into the covering foliage. Slithering as deep as she could into the branches, she searched for a sharp rock. Thorns and branches tore at her, but she located a stone with a jagged edge. Immediately she sawed it against the ankle tape. It began to give way, but Mason was staggering toward the bushes now, muttering. She saw glimpses of his genteel face, twisted in hatred, his neatly cut hair mussed along with his clothes.

Hurry.

One more inch of tape to go. She sawed for all she was worth until it came loose. Then she was up and running, slapping at the branches that barred her way. If it meant surviving, she could run like this forever and Mason was recovering from a gunshot wound. She'd make it. She'd...

And then a shot whistled by her cheek. She turned, stopped dead at the sight of the gun in his hand.

He smiled. "Diane was smart to carry a weapon. Took a page from her book, so to speak."

A sob escaped her and Mason offered a sad smile.

"I'm sorry it had to work out this way."

She pressed her lips together. She wasn't going to beg. Ever.

As she closed her eyes, the roar of an engine swept over her. Roman appeared on a motorcycle with Wally tucked against his stomach, heading straight for Mason.

Mason held up the gun to fire. Emery hurled the rock she still clutched. It deflected off Mason's temple and he fell.

When he rolled over to get the gun, Roman slid the bike to a stop, freed Wally and leaped off, diving onto Mason. It was a short battle, punctuated by Wally's ear-splitting bays and howls as he darted around the men.

Finally Roman turned Mason over onto his stomach and knelt on his lower back.

Wally trotted over to Emery and slobbered all over her with his massive tongue.

Roman's frantic gaze found her, sirens wailing in the distance. "Emery..."

She struggled to breathe. "I'm okay. You did it. You two tracked me."

He smiled and nodded. "Piece of cake," he panted.

Wally howled.

She felt like sobbing, but instead she laughed.

Roman sat in the waiting area of the county hospital while Emery visited her father. Theo's prognosis was guarded but improving. There were subtle indications her sister might be showing signs of recovery as well. Lots of prayer and a long road ahead for both of them, he thought.

His fingers still tingled from the last text he'd sent.

Uncle Jax, been doing a lot of thinking. Can I talk to you sometime?

The reply popped up within sixty seconds.

Absolutely. So glad to hear from you, Baby Boy. You name the place and time.

He smiled at the tiny screen.

Gino had insisted on watching the baby while they visited the hospital, hobbling around with Kara's help, his foot encased in a cast.

Emery came out and he held her, let her wipe her eyes before he guided her into the Bronco. They drove to a peaceful spot, a grassy meadow fringed by trees, far away from the lake. He'd brought a picnic for them, a bowl of treats for Wally.

They sat on the blanket and chatted, eating their sandwiches while Wally meandered around, reveling in the scents.

"This is the perfect way to spend an afternoon," she said. "After everything that's happened."

"I still can't believe Mason was behind it all."

She shivered and he snuggled her closer. "And the horrible thing is, my father didn't have any proof and hadn't sent me anything or even told me his suspicions. Gino couldn't hack into Lincoln's account. Mason might have gotten away with everything if he hadn't decided to go after me."

Roman exhaled. "I don't want to think about Mason right now."

"Me neither."

But he knew it would take a long time to get past what had happened, for him, but mostly for her. They focused on the picnic, enjoying the breeze that whispered across the grass. She enjoyed his offering, humble peanut butter and jelly though it was. When they were done, he ceremoniously presented her with an empty ice-cream cone and pulled a scooper from his jacket pocket. "I am finally keeping my promise."

She chuckled, the light in her face igniting joy in his heart.

"Ice cream?" she said. "I knew you were good for it."

He opened the cooler with a flourish. In shock, he did a double take. "Wait. What?" He spun around. Across the meadow, Wally sat with his purloined strawberry ice cream, slurping from the container he'd torn in half for better access.

"Wally," he shouted. "This is abominable. You are grounded for the next year of your life. Do you hear me, dog?"

He turned back to find Emery laughing so hard she was unable to speak. In a matter of moments he was breathless with laughter too. They guffawed until the tears ran free and they were both out of breath. "Aww man. I'm real sorry about the ice cream."

Her cheeks were rosy. "Honestly, I think there is nothing better in this world than a bloodhound."

"Almost nothing."

She looked a question at him.

"I mean this." He gestured to the landscape. Words bubbled out, in fits and spurts. "All this beauty, being able to live here, with a family." He tried to calm himself. "And having you in my life again, and the things you've taught me."

She quirked a brow. "Me?"

His stomach tightened. "Uh-huh."

"But I haven't taught you anything."

"Yes, you have." He took her hand. "How to hold a baby, the power of a pacifier…"

She giggled. "That's nothing."

He swallowed a lump in his throat. "You taught me that God loves me no matter how I blunder, just like you love your father."

Her eyes went wide.

He pressed on. "You said you'd love him

guilty or not. Reminded me that's the way love is supposed to be, not conditional, not something that ends when someone disappoints you." His throat felt tight again. "I texted Uncle Jax. I'm sure he'll let me know it's taken me a dog's age to realize what I should have known all along."

She grinned, a brilliant smile, and reached to put her palms on his cheeks. "I'm absolutely thrilled that you're talking to Jax."

He pressed her hands in his and drew them to his lips for a kiss. "Me too. We're going to meet soon."

"That's fantastic, Roman. Really wonderful."

He paused, touching his cheek to her fingers, not daring to look her in the eye. "Want to come?"

She hesitated, confused. "Of course, if you want me to, but isn't that a family moment?"

"Yes, it is." He looked at her and inhaled until his ribs creaked. "And I want you to be my family."

Her mouth opened. "Your…family?"

"Yes, ma'am. I love you." He gripped her hand. "I love you, Emery. I don't ever want to lose you again."

Tears glistened under her lashes and she stared

at their joined fingers. And then he heard it, the smallest of whispers that shouted louder than a blast of thunder. "I love you too, Roman."

For a moment he couldn't move at the sheer joy that was so overwhelming it bordered on pain. "I'm sorry I wasn't there for you earlier. When I think of how..."

She squeezed until he stopped talking. "Let's go forward, not backward. We've learned and moved and grown. Tomorrow's more important than yesterday, right?"

"Right."

"Forward," he said. "As long as I get to spend my tomorrows with you."

She bit her lip and eased from his grip. "But it's not the right time."

His spirit plummeted. "What do you mean?"

She hung her head and her voice dropped to a whisper. "My life is a mess. The police will have to unravel all the threats before Dad is exonerated. His cabin needs to be dealt with, and my sister's care is ongoing. And Ian... He needs so much. It wasn't what I chose, but he has to be my first priority now."

His spirit filled with pride at her commitment, her love for others.

"I'm in."

"You're in? For all that? The mess and the baby and—"

He kissed her until she stopped talking. "I'll try to be the best uncle I can to Ian, like Uncle Jax tried with me."

Her expression was still somber, but wondrous too. "I know you will, but…"

"And when your sister is better…"

"That's just it. She might never be," Emery said in a strangled voice. "If she can't take care of Ian, then I will be his mom and whoever marries me…"

"Will be a stepdad."

"Yes." She looked at him half-fearfully.

Last he'd heard, the distraught Lincoln had professed some sort of interest in staying connected with his son. That wasn't enough, not nearly. The boy didn't need a connection; he needed a "boots on the ground" dad. "Like I said, I'm in."

Now the corner of her mouth lifted a tiny bit. "Are you sure?"

He stroked her cheek with a finger. "If that's how it works out, I'll be the best father I can be to him. I don't know a ton about parenting, but Uncle Jax can advise and Beth is the epitome of an amazing parent. They'll help me learn and so will you. Whatever it takes. I don't know how, exactly, but I'll make sure Ian always knows he's loved by me, and by God." He swallowed a swell of emotion. "Period."

He leaned in and kissed her and the sensation of unbridled joy consumed him again. Her response told him she believed him. She would belong to him and he to her and through their mistakes, blunders, missteps, they'd hold on to that bond that God had given them and try to instill it in Ian.

Tears splashed down her cheeks and she flung her arms around his neck and kissed him. "Roman, I can't imagine my life without you."

"Me neither," he said with a cocky smile. "In every photo I'm gonna be right there with you and Ian too." He kissed her again.

Wally finished licking the ice-cream container and yowled.

Emery produced something from her pocket, which set Wally's tail wagging.

"May I?" she said to Roman.

Roman laughed. "He doesn't deserve it. He's just consumed an entire pint of stolen ice cream."

"A treat, for all he's done for me."

"Wally come over here, you disobedient

bloodhound," Roman said. The dog cast aside the empty container and sauntered over without a trace of guilt.

"Sit," Emery told him.

He did.

She held out the shiny red pacifier.

Wally almost knocked himself over in his eagerness to accept it. He licked and sniffed and snuggled it between his two massive front paws until they were both breathless from laughing.

Emery took a selfie of the three of them together. He found he didn't mind at all having his picture taken this time. He pressed her cheek with a kiss in the next one.

Wally whined in happiness.

"It wouldn't be a family picture without Wally," she said.

Roman chuckled. "I suppose he'll worm his way into every photo now."

As if he realized he was being talked about, Wally woofed.

"But no more pacifiers, Walls," he said sternly.

"At least not when anyone's looking." Emery smiled slyly as she slid another one from her pocket. Wally perked up as if he'd heard the dinner bell ringing. "This one's blue. Totally different flavor. No harm in a little spoiling is there, Mr. Wolfe?"

He laughed loud and long before he swept her into another embrace.

"No harm at all."

★ ★ ★ ★ ★

Rocky Mountain Survival

Jane M. Choate

MILLS & BOON

Jane M. Choate dreamed of writing from the time she was a small child when she entertained friends with outlandish stories complete with happily-ever-after endings. Writing for Love Inspired Suspense is a dream come true. Jane is the proud mother of five children, grandmother to ten grandchildren and staff to one cat who believes she is of royal descent.

Visit the Author Profile page
at millsandboon.com.au.

And this is the confidence that we have in him, that, if we ask any thing according to his will, he heareth us.
—*1 John* 5:14

DEDICATION

Those who have read my other books know how I deeply admire the men and women of the United States Special Forces. They make it possible for us to sleep safely in our beds at night while they fight America's enemies. SEALs, Delta, Rangers, Marine Force Recon and others, this book is for you.

Chapter One

Cold.

Kylie Robertson had never minded the cold. Had, in fact, always enjoyed the bite of a Colorado winter. Until a year ago. Until...

Her hands ached. The cold aggravated the pain. That was to be expected. She didn't need to remove her gloves to see the scars that crisscrossed her palms like twisted barbed wire.

With one more violent shiver, more from the memory of how she'd gotten those scars than from the cold itself, Kylie let herself inside her condo.

She'd returned from the event early, realizing she'd forgotten to bring a different camera lens for the photos she wanted to take for her next story, those of a children's chorus singing at the birthday party of a 101-year-old veteran.

She turned the heat up and waited for warmth to fill the small space. The doll-sized condo had been all she could afford, but that would change—she hoped—when she sold her next series of photographs, especially those she'd taken today. She had high expectations for them, capturing expressions of those attending a speech concerning shootings in shopping malls and grocery stores, schools and churches.

Violence in the nation had grown to alarming proportions. By showing the pain and the grief, the bewilderment and the anger on the faces of the hundreds of individuals who had attended, she hoped to raise both awareness and outrage of what was happening.

She moved through her condo. Even the heavy coat she wore didn't completely ward off the cold. She'd turned down the heat before she left, trying to save on the gas bill that seemed to go up exponentially every month.

A highly charged mix of cheap aftershave and adrenaline-infused sweat alerted her that someone was in the condo with her. In the next instant, a thick arm clamped around her neck, threatening to cut off her air supply.

Panting, she fought against the attacker. She thrust her elbows up and back. He grunted as she connected with the soft tissue of his throat, but it wasn't enough to make him release her.

Her brain struggled to take in information and process it as her air supply diminished with every passing second. A few more seconds and she would pass out. Another couple of minutes would equal death.

She had survived six months in a prison camp run by a commandant so inhumane that even the guards flinched at what they were ordered to do. No way was she going to let some local goon snuff out her life now.

She needed to stay alive. She jabbed back at him again.

"Where is it?"

"Where's what?" she asked in a hoarse voice.

Her attacker loosened his hold on her enough that she could breathe. She let the oh-so-sweet air in and found she could think again.

She'd bide her time and strike when he least expected.

"The SD card."

Her SD card. It contained only the pictures she'd taken today of the crowd gathered to hear the governor's speech, and though she felt she'd captured some good images, there was nothing that warranted a threat to her life. "Why?"

"That don't concern you. Just give me the card, and you get to live."

"Big of you," she muttered.

In retaliation, he tightened the arm around her neck once more. "Do you want to play rough? 'Cause I'm good at that. I'm *really* good at it."

"No." She gasped out the single syllable in a desperate bid to suck in air.

"Okay." He eased the pressure on her windpipe. "Hand over the card and forget you ever took those pictures."

What made those pictures so important? "I think there's been some kind of mistake."

"Yeah. And the mistake is yours."

He didn't sound like the kind of man she could reason with, but it wouldn't hurt to try.

"I don't know—"

His grip on her tightened. "Hand it over."

"I'm trying to tell you that I don't know what you're talking about." The words came out in a rush. She strangled out a gasp that nearly caused her to choke.

"The SD card with the pictures you took today. I want it." Her attacker's voice thrummed with menace, and she shivered. It wasn't just fright; it was losing control. She had no idea what she was mixed up in and didn't like being in the dark. If he was going to kill her, she at least wanted to know *why*.

When she got her voice back, she asked, "What do you want with it?"

"My orders are to get that card. If you want to live long enough to take your next breath, you'll hand it over."

She believed him. She'd encountered bullies in school, in the workplace and then again in the hot spots of the world where despots and tyrants exerted their will on helpless people— and recognized the same swagger and meanness in her attacker. She wouldn't allow this one, with his bad breath and bossy attitude, to intimidate her.

She inhaled sharply. Not so much because she needed air, but because she was stalling for time. Time to decide what to do.

Despite that resolve, tremors invaded her body, making her all too aware of the weakness that had been her constant companion since she'd returned to the States.

She tried for meek to disguise her growing fury. "Please. You're scaring me." She didn't have to fake sincerity as that was the truth.

He leaned closer. "I'll do a lot more than that."

"They're just pictures of the crowd waiting to

hear the governor speak." Though she doubted she'd convinced him, that was the truth. She had wanted the honest reactions of people who had gathered to hear the governor talk about shootings in the community.

"Quit lying."

"I'm not—" She wasn't given the opportunity to complete the sentence.

Her vision grayed; her skin grew clammy. Worse, her brain grew fuzzy. She was once more on the verge of passing out when he let up. Greedily, she sucked in what air she could.

"Like that?" he asked. "There's more where that came from. In fact, I can keep it up all day."

"Why?" She barely croaked out the word in a voice that sounded as raw as her throat felt. She should just hand over the card and hope he let her live, but something in her refused to obey the sensible advice. Could she be making someone captured in the pictures a target if she gave in to the man's demands?

"You don't need to know why. You just need to do it."

He tightened his hold again. Lack of oxygen shut down brain function. She felt it happening and was powerless to stop it. With the last remnants of her energy, she flailed her arms, but it did no good. Where were her carefully earned self-defense skills when she needed them?

"You act like you have a choice about this," the man taunted. "You don't. If you want to keep on breathing for another minute, you'll do as I say."

"You'll kill me anyway," she managed to get out.

"But there's dying, and then there's dying. Your choice."

The total lack of emotion in his voice frightened her far more than if he'd screamed at her.

"Okay. It's in my purse. Let me catch my breath, and I'll get it for you."

In truth, the card was in her pocket, but she wasn't about to tell him that. She'd put it there when her hands had been full as she'd switched out one camera for the other.

"No tricks," he warned.

"No tricks."

While she was talking, Kylie edged her right foot backward. She needed leverage if she was to make her move, one she'd learned in her Krav Maga classes. The instructor had drilled into her students to use whatever means they could to protect themselves. She'd have one opportunity to save herself and only one. She had to make it count.

When she still had made no attempt to retrieve the card, he snapped, "I'll get it myself."

She pointed to the kitchen table where her purse sat.

When he turned his back, she shifted her weight to her left leg and got ready.

He grabbed the purse, dumped the contents on the table. "There's no card here."

"I'm sure I put it in there." She worked to make herself sound confused, as though the situation had traumatized her.

If he only knew the truth, that she had already been broken both physically and emotionally, he might have pushed her harder. As it was, she was doing her best to hold it together and come up with a plan to come out of this alive.

He'd kill her once he had what he wanted. She saw it in the cold intent in his eyes, heard it in the dispassionate tone of his voice.

This was a job for him. No, *she* was a job for him. No more. No less.

He turned back to her. "You're asking for it, lady. Give me the card, and we'll end this."

"You'll let me go?" she asked with what she hoped was a convincing whimper.

"Yeah. I'll let you go. Why not?" The words were said on a sneer that made no attempt to be anything than what it was.

"You're not lying, are you?" She was stalling for time, going through the sequence of moves she needed to make.

"Lady, just shut up and give me what I came for."

"Here it is." She pivoted on her foot, then raised her knee and hit him squarely between his legs. The resounding thump felt good.

He shrieked like a wild animal that had gotten his leg caught in a trap. He dropped to the floor, screaming at her. The look in his eyes was one of pure agony. Beneath that, though, was the promise of retribution.

But she didn't waste time gloating. Instead, she grabbed her laptop.

He seized hold of her coat as she passed, but she didn't let that stop her and yanked herself free.

"You'll pay," he croaked out, still clearly unable to get up. "You'll pay for this."

The frigid morning air bit into her, all teeth and claws. Fortunately, she hadn't removed her coat as she had just walked in the door when her attacker grabbed her. Still, the cold was enough to cause her to gasp.

The fight-or-flight instinct kicked in. She had already fought. Now it was time for flight. She had one choice.

Run.

Even with her training, she knew she was no match for the man who had broken into her home. She'd gotten the better of him earlier because she'd taken him by surprise. He wouldn't be fooled again. Pain and probably a good dose of humiliation would make him want payback.

Her car was in the garage, which meant she'd have to go through the condo again to get to it, so that was a no-go. He'd be anticipating that.

Think.

Her cell was in her pocket. She pulled it out and punched in 911 and spat out the information.

"Can you get somewhere safe?" the operator asked. "I'll dispatch a unit to you, but it will take them five minutes to reach you. The storm has us spread pretty thin."

A block away was a local grocery store. If she could reach that, she could wait for the police to arrive. She gave the location of the supermarket.

And ran.

Snow-packed sidewalks from an unseasonal early storm made the going treacherous, but she couldn't slow down. A cold blast of wind whipped her exposed face. She heard the pounding of footsteps behind her but couldn't afford the seconds it would take to look back. Instead, she gave an extra burst of energy, increasing the distance between her and her pursuer. He wasn't as fast as she might have suspected; no doubt his injury had slowed him down.

She hadn't stopped him, no, but she'd given him something to think about.

Only a few yards more.

When she reached the store, she pushed open the door. The people there gave her odd looks with her wild eyes and windblown hair, but she didn't care and ducked behind a counter. The clerk must have sensed her desperation because he didn't say anything.

She decided her hiding place was too obvious and hid behind a large cart filled with items to be stocked. Her heart was beating so rapidly she feared she was having a cardiac arrest as she wondered whether the cops would show up before her attacker. Had he followed her into the store or had she lost him?

A couple minutes later, the police arrived, and she took her first easy breath since she'd felt her attacker's arm at her throat.

Two officers questioned her at length.

"You say you don't know why he wanted your card?" the patrolman asked for what seemed the fiftieth time.

"No." Her throat hurt, and she could barely get out the word.

"Do you have anywhere you can stay until we find out what's going on?" he asked.

"I don't know." That was the truth. Upon her return to the States six months ago, she'd rebuffed attempts from friends to connect with her. Eventually, they'd given up calling or dropping in on her. As one friend had put it, "If you don't want company, I won't bother you anymore."

She couldn't stay here. What's more, she needed transportation. Dare she return to her condo to retrieve her car? She walked back home, all the while checking over her shoulder. After circling the condo several times, she used the code to her garage and got her car.

She needed help…and the one man who could help her was the same one she'd never thought to see again.

* * *

Josh Harvath finished packing his duffel bag. He was taking a much-needed vacation, heading to the warmer temperatures of Arizona. Away from the brutal cold of a Colorado winter. Away from the demands of working for S&J Security/Protection, where he could serve as a bodyguard one day and a computer hacker the next. Away from his mother's meddling in his social life. Away from the pressures of always being on call, whether at work or as an eligible single man whom every aunt, friend and female coworker had on speed dial.

And though he liked his job and loved his mother and didn't mind serving as the occasional plus-one, he needed to get away. The last year had been a hard one. He'd been wounded while serving as a bodyguard for a visiting member of European royalty and had spent six weeks in rehab. That, plus going undercover as a computer whiz at a high-tech company to ferret out who was selling secrets—and getting his butt whipped along with three broken ribs by the two men intent on not going to prison— had taken its toll. He was back to full strength, but it had been a grueling process.

So when someone pounded on his door with

annoying persistence, he was tempted to ignore it. His training and, yes, a dose of curiosity finally kicked in. Who would be knocking on his door today when he'd told everyone he knew that he'd be out of town for a week? If his employers at S&J Security/Protection wanted to contact him, they'd have called his cell. The same for his mother. Was it sad that they were the only people he could think of who might want to get ahold of him?

Though he didn't expect trouble, he kept his Glock at his side. No sense in playing the fool, not when burglaries and muggings had increased substantially in Denver, even in the daytime.

Outside the door stood a woman he'd never expected to see again. The woman he'd walked away from eleven years ago. His body tensed, his heart picking up its beat and stomach clenching. How many times had he told himself to forget her, that it was best they'd gone their separate ways? Not a day went by that something didn't trigger a memory of her, even for a moment. A song. A passage from a book. It didn't matter what.

"Are you going to invite me in?" she asked when he made no move to do so.

He opened the door wider, allowed her to slip past him. "Kylie. What are you doing here?"

"Gracious as ever."

And she was as beautiful as he recalled. Maybe even more so.

There were differences between then and now, slight, but he could see them. Her cheekbones were more pronounced, her once long hair was cut in what he supposed was called a pixie, and her waist, always slender, was now so narrow that he could probably span it with his hands.

But her eyes hadn't changed, dark eyes that seemed to see straight through him. Eyes that had once held tenderness and were now filled with confusion.

He gestured to the sofa and took a chair across from it. "Are you going to tell me what you're doing here?"

She bit down on her lip. He recalled her making the gesture when they were kids, whenever she was about to cry but didn't want to give way to tears.

"Kylie. Tell me what happened."

She shuddered before abruptly standing up as though she'd been scalded. "I'm sorry. I shouldn't have come here, but I didn't know where else to go."

Now he was concerned. Why had she come? "Tell me."

"Someone attacked me in my condo this morning."

"Are you all right?" He pushed the past back where it belonged and barked out the question, the only thing that mattered now.

"I'm fine." But her voice didn't sound fine. It quivered in a very un-Kylie manner.

"Do you know what he wanted?"

"An SD card. He wanted the pictures I took at the governor's speech today."

He nodded, a silent invite to continue.

"I don't know why he wanted it. It's just pictures of the crowd and their reactions."

He'd kept up with Kylie and knew she was an award-winning photojournalist. She'd visited hot spots all over the world. Her photographs caught both the horror and the occasional glimpse of compassion in such places as Ukraine, the Congo and other countries under siege.

Though he'd never admit it to her, he had two of her photos, which he'd scraped up the money to purchase and had hung in his bedroom. Lately, she'd been focusing her attention on the angst in America, on everything from racial strife to public shootings.

"Start at the beginning."

She took him through it step-by-step, including her trip back to her condo to retrieve her car.

"You took a risk going back to your place," he said.

"I was careful, made sure that the creep was gone."

By the time she'd finished, he was more than worried. For someone to break into her condo and threaten her, then demand an SD card, meant that something more serious than merely wanting pictures of a crowd at the governor's speech was going on.

She must have caught something else in her lens, something that was worth killing for.

"Think. Did you see anything, anything at all, that gave you pause when you were taking pictures?"

"Don't you think I haven't asked myself that question?"

That was the Kylie he remembered. Giving as good as she got with a healthy dose of tart thrown in for good measure.

"I don't know," he said calmly. "That's why I'm asking."

"I'm sorry. The whole thing has me rattled."

Another un–Kylie thing. The Kylie he remembered would have never admitted to any weakness. She went from fragile to sharp to fragile all within a breath.

His gaze softened. "You have a right to be rattled."

"I didn't know where else to go."

An awkward beat of silence bounced between them.

For her to come to him told him just how frightened she was. When they'd parted so many years ago, he'd never thought to see her again. Angry words and hurt feelings had torn their relationship apart.

"You did right in coming here. How did you know I still lived here?" He'd bought the place from his mother when his dad passed away a few years ago.

"I'd hoped your parents might still be here and could tell me where you were." She gazed at the suitcase. "Were you going somewhere?"

"Not anymore."

"I heard you were working for a protection agency. Thought maybe you could help me find someone to protect me…until I get this sorted out."

"No."

"No?"

"That's right. No. I'll be taking care of you. That's why you came here, isn't it?"

"But we…" She didn't finish.

"Yeah. We didn't part under the best of circumstances." You could say that again. The last time they'd seen each other, he'd ended up walking away. He'd wanted Kylie to come with him to California, where he'd be undergoing SEAL training. His dream for them to marry and have a family remained just that: a dream.

He knew the statistics regarding navy SEALs and marriage, but he was convinced that it would be different for him and Kylie. They were so much in love. How could it not work?

Kylie had had her own dreams, though, and following him to California didn't fit with them. Looking back, he could only shake his head at his selfishness. He'd expected her to drop her dreams so that he might follow his.

They'd gone their own ways. Following a seven-year stint in the SEALs, he'd worked as a US marshal on the East Coast, and had only returned to his home state when he'd received the offer to work at S&J's Denver office.

He'd changed from the self-centered man

he'd been back then. But he wasn't going to get into that with Kylie. Not now.

"I don't know what to do." The words were said so softly that he almost didn't catch them.

This wasn't like the Kylie he remembered. She'd always been so sure of herself, of what she wanted, of how she planned to go about getting it. The frightened woman standing before him was vulnerable in a way the Kylie of eleven years ago had never been.

"We'll work it out."

"Will we?"

He was about to reassure her, but the window shattered and the room filled with smoke. A flash-bang.

He grabbed her hand and pulled her into the kitchen. "Stay down." He drew his weapon. And waited.

Kylie didn't like the role of damsel in distress. She didn't like it at all. Like it or not, though, it had been her default role ever since she'd been freed from the prison camp.

So when Josh told her to stay down, she did. And hated herself for it. She then gathered up the tatters of her courage and looked for a way she could help. She knew how to use a gun; in fact, she was more than proficient at it. She'd made a point of learning how to use various weapons after her first assignment overseas. Witnessing warlords attack villagers in the Congo and other war-torn countries had convinced her that she needed to be prepared to take care of herself.

"Do you have another weapon?"

He handed her the Glock he held and grabbed the Sig Sauer he kept strapped at his ankle.

She was familiar with both but preferred the Sig. "Let me have the Sig."

What she didn't tell him was that she hadn't handled a gun since her time as a prisoner.

"Don't fire unless you have to," he said and handed her the weapon.

"Don't worry." She didn't relish the idea of shooting anyone, but she would if it came down to protecting herself and Josh. She'd brought this trouble to his house. How had her intruder found her here?

There'd be enough time to worry over that later. For now, she just wanted to stay alive.

The crack of wood alerted them that the front door had been breached.

Josh put a finger to his lips, then motioned her to head to the pantry. There, he pulled out a bag of sugar and two matches. She got it. Sugar, with its chemical formula, and matches produced a combustible reaction.

"When I give the mark, throw the bag," he said.

He gave the signal at the same moment the bad guys burst into the kitchen. The blinding light and flames shocked the men. In their confusion, Josh managed to disarm them. He handed their weapons to Kylie.

"If either one moves, shoot 'em."

"Gladly."

She kept the gun trained on the two intruders, neither of whom she recognized as her attacker. So there were at least three men involved.

One man, the bigger of the two, got to his knees and glared at Josh. "Quit pointing that gun at me, or I'll show you how smart I am."

Josh knocked him back down. "Stay down if you know what's good for you."

After grabbing a couple of flex-cuffs, he bound their hands. He then undid the men's belts and used them to bind their feet. He clearly wasn't taking any risks they might escape.

She admired his efficiency and, wanting to help, found two dishrags and stuffed them in the men's mouths. One aimed a hate-filled glare at her. She gave as good as she got and glared back at him, having the satisfaction of seeing him lower his gaze.

Josh gave her a short nod after glancing at the rags. "Good thinking. We don't want them yelling for help and attracting the neighbors before the police get here. The longer they stay out of circulation, the better."

He searched the men and came away with a set of earbuds, which he handed to her.

The earbuds seemed to be connected to a cell phone. She listened. "Mackleroy, did you get the card?" The voice thrummed with impatience. "Mackleroy, Washington, talk to me. Tell me you got it."

When no answer came, the speaker abruptly hung up.

"That's the man who attacked me," she told Josh.

"You're sure?"

"I'm sure." She shuddered. "I'd recognize that voice anywhere."

"These two aren't carrying any identification, not that I expected it. But there's another way to identify them."

Initially the two men had fought against the

restraints, but they had given up and sat there, resentment oozing from them.

Josh pulled a device from a drawer, what looked like a digital scanner. With the dishrags stuck in their mouths, the men couldn't even protest when he took their fingerprints and sent off the images.

"Where are you sending them?" she asked.

"S&J. They have the equipment to identify these yahoos if they're in the system. I'll be surprised if they aren't.

"My guess is that they're just hired help." Josh sent a disgusted look their way. "They don't look smart enough to do anything but take orders. And they're probably not very good at that."

When Josh's phone rang, he listened. "Fingerprint report," he told her after hanging up.

It surprised her how quickly the results had come in.

"S&J has access to police databases," he said in answer to her unasked question. "Our boys..." he gestured to the two trussed-up men "...are low-level hoods. Both have served time, but there's no record of who they've worked for in the past. My guess is that they were hired re-

motely for the job and don't know who's foot-
ing the bill."

"What now?"

"We put a whole lot of gone between us and
whoever is after you."

Chapter Two

Josh gathered up supplies from the kitchen, focusing on high-energy foods that required little or no preparation.

"There are two sleeping bags in the front closet," he said. "Grab them and any blankets you can find. There's a tarp along with the sleeping bags. Better get that, too." They were going to need them.

"Where are we going?" Kylie asked.

"Away from here."

He threw some winter clothing into his duffel bag. They'd need changes of clothes, and though his would swallow Kylie, they didn't dare go back to her place to get some of her own. She'd have to make do with his. The last thing he grabbed was several lengths of rope.

He looked about and wondered what he had forgotten. Preparation for a trip to the mountains was everything. It could mean having enough to eat or going hungry. More, it could spell the difference between surviving and not surviving.

The warmer temps of Arizona would have to wait.

He wondered what the police would make of the scene. He called S&J and asked that an operative be sent to his house and then contact the police to have the men picked up. It wasn't that he didn't trust the police, but he didn't want to spend the time it would take explaining the situation.

He wanted to get Kylie out of there as quickly as possible. Just as important, he needed to find out how the men had found her.

It could be as simple as they had picked up her tail and followed her, but Kylie had always been street-smart. She would have noticed a tail first thing.

"Let's go," he said and hustled her out of the kitchen door leading to the garage. His big Expedition could handle most terrain. They'd need it where they were going.

"Make yourself comfortable," he said once she was strapped into the vehicle. "It's a couple hours' trip."

"Where're we heading?"

"The mountains. My uncle's got an off-the-grid cabin in Rocky Mountain National Park."

It was her life on the line, and she followed without further questions. Twenty minutes later, they'd left the city behind. The relief of leaving city driving and being on the open road eased the tension in his shoulders, and he was at last able to focus on Kylie.

"You holding up all right?" he asked.

She nodded. "Considering I've had a man threaten my life, two others show up at your place and I'm heading to I-don't-know-where, I'm doing fine." She flushed at the bite in her voice.

"Give the smart mouth a rest, why don't you?" he suggested gently. "We're going to be together for a while."

"Sorry." She ducked her head. "I didn't mean to snipe at you. I guess I'm more rattled than I thought."

"You have a right." He understood Kylie well enough to know that she abhorred being dependent upon someone else. It wasn't in her nature to hand over control. To him. To anyone.

She sighed. "I brought trouble to your door, and now you're paying the price. I should be thanking you rather than picking at you."

"No need for thanks."

"I'm sorry about falling apart on you," she said in a stilted voice. "That's not me. At least, not usually."

"Hey, it's okay. And you didn't fall apart. I'd say you handled things really well, considering."

"Thanks."

She loosened her jacket, revealing bruising around her neck. His mouth tightened, but the marks weren't what he focused on. No, it was the thin gold chain he'd given her eleven years ago. He didn't know she still had it, much less that she continued to wear it.

Not the point, he reminded himself and focused his attention on the bruises. From the look of it, her assailant had had large hands. The man who had put his hands on her would pay.

"Put your head back and try to get some rest," he said.

She sent him an incredulous look, clearly asking how she was supposed to rest when her world had been turned upside down, but she did as he said. Soon, he heard soft, even breathing that told him she had slipped into sleep.

Good.

He had some thinking to do, and he didn't want her peppering him with questions. Kylie had always been curious, wanting to know everything immediately.

It was a good quality for a journalist, and he even admired her for it, but now wasn't the time.

Right now, he had his own curiosity to satisfy and he lined up the questions as best he could.

What had Kylie caught on her camera?

Who wanted the photos?

Why?

And, most important of all, how far were they willing to go to get it?

Kylie woke, startled to find herself in a truck with Josh Harvath. *What's going on?* When the memory of a man trying to strangle her returned, her breath hitched in her throat.

"You okay?" Josh asked.

"Y...yes." She didn't sound okay and tried again. "Fine."

The doubtful look he sent her way told her that she'd been less than convincing.

She couldn't shake the memory of her attacker's hands around her throat. She'd run from him. The last thing Kylie wanted was to run, but it looked like that was exactly what she was doing. Running.

Worse, she'd run toward Josh—the man she'd left years ago. She glanced at his profile from the passenger seat. She couldn't believe she'd managed to get a few moments' rest on the drive. She felt safe with him.

She'd always felt safe with Josh. Though he'd been scarcely more than a boy when they'd parted, he'd had the same steady air about him, saying that you could count on him.

Admit it, girl. You're scared. She'd faced warring tribes in Africa. Stared down gangbangers in cities all over the world. Even run with the bulls in Pamplona. But knowing that strangers wanted something from her enough to kill her for it took fear to a whole new level.

For seven years, she'd traveled the globe, capturing the world's people on her camera and sometimes her phone. She'd encountered the best in people…and the worst. She thought she'd seen everything.

So much for the intrepid journalist she'd worked so hard to become. Face it. That woman had died in a prison camp halfway around the world. She'd lost the essence of herself and a man she'd grown to care deeply for.

She didn't allow herself to think about Ryan very often. They'd met during a trip to

Ukraine. He'd been a war correspondent. Their careers had complemented each other, and they had found they shared much in common on a personal level, as well. After that first meeting, they'd worked together on numerous occasions. With his connections, he was able to pick and choose his own assignments.

When she'd received permission to accompany an NGO to a war-ravaged village in Afghanistan, Ryan had done the same. Terrorists had invaded the village, killing the boys and men and rounding up the young girls. Ryan hadn't been able to stand by while innocent people were murdered, and had fought back. He'd been shot for his trouble and had bled out in front of her.

Scant minutes later, she had been captured along with the villagers and taken to a prisoner camp.

Images of prisoners being abused had imprinted themselves on her mind, refusing to let go, while smells, ripe with raw sewage and molding food and blood, always blood, wound their way through her thoughts.

Horrific memories crossed her mind.

The constant sting of sweat on the wounds that covered most of her body. The cries from other captives. And then the unthinkable had happened. She became so accustomed to them that they no longer bothered her, and that frightened her almost more than anything.

"Kylie?" The sound of her name brought her back to awareness. "Hey, where'd you go?" Josh asked.

"Nowhere."

For a moment, she lost track of where she was.

The look he sent her told her that he recognized she'd sidestepped the truth, but that he wouldn't call her on it. For that, she was grateful.

"Sorry. I must have zoned out for a minute."

"No problem. It happens."

It had been happening ever since she returned from the Middle East. Her therapist said it was the result of trauma, but she'd been back in the States for almost six months. Shouldn't she be over it by now?

The question had taunted her relentlessly, causing her to doubt herself. The hard-earned self-confidence that had seen her through plenty of tough situations had disappeared, leaving a shell of the woman she'd been.

"Hey, it's going to be all right. I'm not letting anything happen to you. That's a promise."

The quiet resolve in his voice settled her nerves. Josh was a man of his word. When he gave a promise, you could count on him to keep it.

He'd been the same when they'd been youngsters together. That was why she'd turned to him even after all the years they'd spent apart. Going to him hadn't been wise. She couldn't afford to fall for him again. Especially not when her sense of self was now so damaged. She was too vulnerable to let him back into her life in any but the most practical sense.

"Thanks." She flushed at her grudging tone. He had gone out of his way to help her, and she couldn't even be gracious. She chalked it up to being terrified. "Seriously. Thank you."

She thought about what had prompted her to go to Josh in the first place. It had been over a decade since they'd parted, but she'd never forgotten him. He had been her first love, but that was over. She could have turned to a friend, but it was Josh's name that appeared in her mind when she'd been threatened.

Needing to change the subject, she asked, "Where are we going? I know you said the mountains, but just *where* in the mountains?"

"A cabin just west of Rocky Mountain National Park. My uncle owns it. Nobody will know we're there. It'll give us time to figure out who's after you and what they think you have on your SD card."

"I keep telling you that I don't have anything but pictures of anonymous faces."

"Maybe you caught some faces that shouldn't be seen…or shouldn't be seen together."

She'd thought of that but hadn't come up with any ideas of who it could be.

"Like who?"

"That's what we have to find out."

Could he be right? She hadn't noticed anything out of the ordinary in the sea of faces she'd captured. The pictures were of people expressing their shock and anger over the latest school shooting and what the governor was going to do about it.

She hadn't had time to go through the photos, especially not with an eye to who might not want his or her picture taken. If someone didn't want to be seen, why attend such an event? To meet somebody? But then why not meet privately? Certainly, that made more sense.

Didn't it?

Maybe that was exactly why individuals who didn't want to be seen together would arrange to meet in a crowd. They would be but two more faces in a mass of faces.

No one would attach any significance to them.

"You could be right," she said slowly, thinking it through.

Josh opened his mouth, but his response was drowned out by a jolt from behind. She turned her head to see a semitrailer barreling straight at them.

There was no question as to who would win in the dogfight that was certain to come. She inhaled sharply, held her breath, and wished she and God were still on speaking terms.

Josh fought to hold the Expedition steady. It was a good-sized vehicle, but the semi that was riding his tail was huge. There was no way he could hold out against it. What's more, the tractor-trailer appeared to have a beefed-up engine that handled the speed they were going with ease.

He had been in high-speed chases before, as a SEAL, then with the Marshals Service and now S&J, and knew what to do. He didn't fight the wheel as his SUV spun but rather steered it in the direction of the spin.

Minutes stretched into what felt like hours before he gained control and gestured for Kylie to take the steering wheel. "Hold it steady while I get a shot off."

"How're you going to do that?"

"Like this."

He pushed the button to roll down the window, pulled himself half out of it and took aim. Maintaining his position and sighting his weapon was a balancing act on its own as the wind tore at him, nearly yanking him out of the window and throwing him to the ground.

Two shots to the engine should do the trick.

Shooting out tires as was shown on every TV cop show ever made wasn't an option. Trajectory and motion were against the shooter every time, but hitting an engine block was doable.

He couldn't hear the ping of the bullet against metal, but the smoke streaming from the semi's engine in angry black billows told its own story. Back at the wheel once more, he could see the truck grinding to a stop.

"Showing off, Harvath?" Kylie asked.

"Doing what was needed."

"You always were a good shot. Even when we were kids you could hit whatever you aimed at."

He and Kylie had whiled away many a summer afternoon honing their shooting skills. There wasn't money to go to a shooting range, and neither could stomach the idea of shooting at wildlife, so cans and bottles it was. He'd become proficient at shooting with either hand. That particular ability had stood him in good stead when he'd made the Teams.

"They won't be going anywhere anytime soon," he said, "but I'm guessing they're on the phone right along now to call in reinforcements."

"How did they know where we were?"

That was a good question.

He'd made sure they weren't being followed, employing surveillance detection routes. The SDRs weren't foolproof, but they normally defeated any but the most experienced of tails. Had he missed something?

No one was infallible.

"Did you stop anywhere on your way to my place?"

"No. I was running for my life." Her wry tone didn't mask the worry in her voice that the bad guys were somehow tailing them.

Was it possible the man who'd tried to choke her had put a bug on her? But that didn't make sense. From what she'd said, the assailant planned to kill her after taking what he wanted from her. Why would he put a tracking beacon on her?

Had he only wanted her to believe that he planned on killing her? But to what purpose?

While he focused on navigating the winter roads, she spent a few minutes checking her clothing but didn't find anything. Nothing about this made sense.

They didn't have time to worry over it; they had to get out of there. Now.

Kylie knew they weren't out of danger. The hard set of Josh's jaw told her more than could any words that he was preparing for the next attack. Even though she was a strong, independent woman who had been taking care of herself since she was eighteen, she was grateful to have him on her side.

She asked what they were both thinking. "How did those men track me?"

Josh's mouth was a tight line of consternation, and she knew he was bothered by the same thing. He avoided the question and said, "We have to keep moving."

"Even if someone is following?"

"Even if."

The question of how the men had found her continued to tumble through her mind, but she had no answer. Why was it so important to someone to get those photographs?

"I smell a story," she said, "though I can't think what it would be. All I did was capture expressions of the people in the crowd. Some were troubled. Many were so full of grief that I could barely bring myself to invade their privacy. I probably won't end up using a lot of the pictures for that reason." That had always been a problem in her work, her unwillingness to use pictures that had captured too much.

"Is there someplace with a restroom near here?" she said a minute later. She needed one. Now. And it wouldn't hurt to check again for a tracking device.

"What's the matter? Can't you use a bush?" The glimmer in his eyes was rich with amusement.

She glared at him. She'd used plenty of bushes in her travels and had gotten bitten, pricked and stung for her efforts. "I can, and I have. I've also used a bucket for a shower and a hole in the ground for a toilet. But I prefer a real bathroom with a real toilet and a real sink if possible."

"Gotcha covered," he said and within ten

minutes turned into a rest area complete with restrooms, a convenience store and a fast-food place. "I wouldn't mind using a real restroom myself."

After taking care of business, Kylie patted down her clothing once more. Nothing. She checked her phone for an app that could be tracking her or sending out a signal of her location but again found nothing. She wandered into the small store and purchased snacks for the rest of the trip. Chips, cookies, soft drinks. High energy foods, though they lacked any real nutrition.

Josh emerged from the men's room. "I see you picked up the necessities," he said after peeking into her bag.

"Nothing but the best." She smiled. "Did you want something special?"

"No. Although I did develop a taste for grubs when I was stationed in the Pacific for eight months. They've got a nice crunch to them and are high protein along with it." The crinkle at the corner of his eyes told her he was teasing.

She made a face. "No grubs. But I got chips, and they're crunchy."

The banter felt good after the last tense hours.

Josh looked at the sky and frowned. "There's a storm moving in. We need to get on our way."

While they munched on the snacks, she snuck the occasional glance at him. He was still the same straight arrow she remembered. Over the last eleven years, he'd grown even more appealing, with craggy lines around his eyes and mouth, adding character to his face, and a muscular frame that would make Hollywood hunks envious.

The boy she remembered had been cute. The man was rugged-looking, with leathery skin, no doubt due to long days in the heat and cold of wherever he'd been deployed.

But it was his steady gaze that told her and anyone else bothering to look that he was a man you could count on when trouble came knocking.

"We've got another two hours," he said once they were back in the Expedition and he had checked for bugs. "Talk to me and keep me from going to sleep."

She snorted at that. Josh wasn't one to fall asleep on the job.

"Is there anyone special in your life?" she asked.

"No."

The answer was clipped, bordering on rude.

"Sorry. I didn't mean it to come out that way. But, no, there's no one special. There hasn't been in a long time."

What did he mean by that?

A man like Josh would have dated, could well have married in the years since she'd seen him.

"What about you?" he asked.

"There was someone."

"What happened?"

"He was killed."

The bald words shocked her. She hadn't meant to be so blunt, but the words had come out before she'd thought better of them. She never talked about Ryan's death. The circumstances had been so horrific that she feared she wouldn't be able to get the words out without breaking down in tears.

She didn't say that Ryan had died in her arms while protecting villagers from the terrorists. Or that he had asked her to marry him several times over a two-year span and that she'd never given him an answer. Most especially, she didn't tell Josh why she hadn't accepted Ryan's proposal immediately. And she certainly couldn't tell him that he was the reason.

So she left it at that and hoped he wouldn't pry.

"I'm sorry," he said softly.

"So am I." She might not have loved Ryan as she'd once loved Josh, but she'd cared for him a great deal and had grieved his death. He'd deserved better than to die by the hand of a terrorist who was only a coward at heart and had not an ounce of Ryan's courage and compassion.

Josh was close enough that she could see the gold flecks in his dark eyes. She'd always loved his eyes, so deeply brown that they appeared almost black.

Did he remember how she used to look up to him? He had been a hero in every sense of the word. For that matter, he still was.

He cut short her musings. "You know that the people who want that SD card aren't going to give up, don't you?"

"I know."

"The question is how far do you want to take it?"

"As far as I need to." Her words were put to the test when the Expedition picked up speed and careened wildly down the mountain road.

Chapter Three

Josh tapped the brakes. Mountain driving wasn't a spectator sport. When the road curved sharply, he tapped the breaks and realized he couldn't control the vehicle. As it veered toward a drop-off that descended into a canyon, he pulled the steering wheel in the other direction and stepped on the brakes with everything he had.

He managed to correct the vehicle's direction, but the road's sharp descent caused it to pick up even more speed. With little hope, he tried the brakes again.

"Josh?" Kylie's voice held a question.

"Hold on."

The narrow road was flanked by a sheer cliff on one side and the canyon on the other. Neither looked promising.

He pulled the emergency brake, but it barely put a beat in the Expedition's momentum. He jerked on the wheel as his vehicle veered to the edge of the road again and did his best to muscle it away from the steep cliff.

They were going over. The words of a childhood prayer found their way into his mind as the SUV toppled into the steep canyon. The Expedition tumbled over on itself. The sensation caused waves of dizziness to dance through his head, but he didn't panic. Experience in similar situations had taught him that the dizziness would pass, but as he and Kylie were jerked around, he knew that they were going to be roughed up by the time the vehicle came to rest.

No, it wasn't the light-headedness he feared, but there was a real possibility of injury, and though the Expedition was made for heavy-duty wear and tear, even it might not protect them from broken bones or a concussion. He didn't worry so much about himself as he did for Kylie.

Always Kylie.

He'd promised to take care of her. The idea of her being hurt on his watch was anathema to him.

A hard impact jarred him when the vehicle stopped its wild descent and the airbags deployed. He tasted blood as his teeth bit down on his tongue. Neither he nor Kylie moved for long seconds. They were hanging upside down, only their seat belts holding them in place.

"Kylie? You all right?"

"I think so."

He gave a silent prayer of relief that she hadn't been hurt. "Give me a minute, and I'll get us out of here."

He yanked on the door handle, but the door was jammed shut. He reached for his weapon and, using the Glock's butt, broke the window. A yank on his seat belt confirmed his suspicion that it was also jammed, and he reached for the knife he kept tucked in his boot. After cutting himself loose, he climbed out, careful of the jagged edges of glass. Testing his arms and legs, he found them working and then rounded the vehicle's front end to free Kylie.

Despite her assurance that she was all right, she was pale. Fortunately, the passenger side door worked, and after opening it, he cut away the seat belt and carried her away from the SUV. He didn't expect it to explode—once again that was the stuff of TV shows—but he preferred erring on the side of caution.

He then went back and gathered up their supplies. They'd need the food and other goods they'd brought along. The Expedition was totaled, and he gave a small sigh over the two years he'd saved to buy it, but it wasn't important. Not in the grand scheme of things. What mattered was that he and Kylie were unharmed.

He wanted to lift the hood and check the brake line, but with the vehicle coming to rest on its roof, he couldn't get to it. If he had to guess, he'd say the brake line had been cut.

Someone had deliberately tried to kill them.

Arms full, he went back to where Kylie waited for him. "We've got to get out of here. Whoever did this is going to come looking to see if we survived. If they find we have, they'll want to pick us off. We're sitting ducks where we are." One of the key rules in the SEALs was not to make yourself a target.

They divided the supplies into their bags. If he'd known they'd have to scramble up a cliff, he'd have brought backpacks.

He scanned the cliff they'd have to scale. There was no way they could climb it straight up. They would need to make the climb diagonally. That would take longer, but it would be far safer. As though to punctuate his gut feeling that the men who sabotaged the brakes were coming after them, shots fired in their direction.

He pushed Kylie behind a copse of scrub trees and, after returning fire, followed her. Noises from above alerted him that someone was scrambling down the cliff after them.

"Let's get out of here," he said.

He plotted their course in his mind. If they kept to the far side, they could take shelter from shots in the scrub oak and bushes that dotted the rough terrain.

The first leg of the trip went smoothly enough, and they reached a narrow ledge where they rested for a few minutes. The second leg proved more difficult as the climb grew steadily steeper.

Looking for a handhold, Josh grabbed onto a sturdy-looking shrub. As he tried to haul himself up by it, it proved itself anything but and pulled away from the dirt. He toppled backward and would have fallen, but Kylie grabbed his wrist and stopped his descent.

Lines of strain etched themselves into her face as she fought to keep him from tumbling down the cliff.

He knew she couldn't hold him for much longer. When her hand slipped, he yelled, "Let go." There was no sense in both of them falling. He might survive a tumble down the cliff.

He might not. But he wasn't taking Kylie with him. SEALs put their teammates first. Always.

"No." The single word held enough resolve to convince him to not bother arguing with her.

It would take time he didn't have. His free arm flailed wildly until he finally grabbed hold of the edge of a large rock. Once he got a grip on it, she released his other arm, and he pulled himself onto it. He lay there and panted.

That had been close. Too close.

"Thanks," he said once he got his breath back.

"No problem," she answered with a calm that belied the fact that she'd probably saved his life. Another minute passed before he registered the series of shaky breaths she took.

So she wasn't as casual about the incident as she pretended to be.

They continued the climb and within twenty more minutes of reaching the road, they encountered men scrambling up the cliff. When shots were fired at them, he pushed Kylie behind a thicket of brush and, after returning fire, followed her. After several minutes, he wondered if they'd lost the gunman tracking them or if he'd given up only to try again at a later time.

Josh had no doubt that there would be another time. He tried his cell and discovered he didn't have coverage. No surprise there. He needed to get to a phone and call for help. The gas station/convenience store where they'd stopped had a phone booth, a rarity in today's world.

They kept to the road's bank in case their pursuers came looking for them. When a truck's engine sounded, they took to the trees in a ditch. It was a little-used stretch of road. What was the likelihood that the truck's driver was just someone who happened to be using the road at that exact time?

Not good.

"The brake line was cut, wasn't it?" she asked as they hunkered down in some scrub oak and brush.

"I can't say for sure, but, yeah, that'd be my guess. Probably when we were in the store."

Cutting a brake line wasn't difficult. All it took was a sharp tool and a little time. The men after them had probably cut the line partway through, making it appear that everything was all right until the fluid ran out. By then, the damage was done and the vehicle left without any braking power at all.

He checked the sky. It had darkened while they'd climbed to the road. They'd be fortunate to hoof it back to the store before it was pitch-dark.

Their gear wasn't made for hiking, but it couldn't be helped. When Kylie lagged behind, he called over his shoulder, "You doing all right?"

"Fine." She jogged a few steps to catch up with him. "You really know how to show a girl a good time."

His lips quirked. "Yeah, I'm known for that."

"I remember."

The two words pulled him back in time to when the two of them had been dating. They'd been so wrapped up in each other that they barely noticed anyone or anything else. That last summer had been filled with such sweet memories that he'd wanted to store them away. Lazy days spent by a lake had invited the kind of sharing between young people filled with dreams and hopes of what they yearned to be.

The quiet hours had been interspersed with waterskiing on the lake and hiking in the mountains. Kylie was a born athlete and always up for a challenge, including climbing some of Colorado's famed mountains.

The days had been touched by a charmed delight that promised a future of happiness and togetherness.

A half smile nudged his lips upward as he thought of how his SEAL teammates and fellow operatives at the Marshals and S&J would razz him if he had ever shared that with them.

The simple joy of that time had come to an abrupt end when he'd asked her to go with him to Coronado to pursue his dream of becoming a SEAL. They had separated, going their own ways, and he hadn't been able to help wondering what would have happened if she'd accepted his invitation.

He pushed the thoughts from his mind and focused on the here and now.

When they felt the first flakes of snow, he prayed it wouldn't turn into more. They'd done all right so far, but getting wet spelled trouble, especially in the mountains.

"Another mile and we'll be there," he said.

He didn't say what they were both thinking: another mile of hiking in the freezing temperatures plus snow would put them in a bad way.

Twenty-five minutes later, they reached the store. Josh found an old-fashioned phone booth tucked near the restrooms and made a call to

S&J and asked for a vehicle to be delivered. S&J didn't stint on their employees and helped out whenever they could on personal matters. He watched Kylie as she picked up more snacks and then saw her come to a hard stop.

The look on her face told him something was wrong.

Something was very wrong.

Kylie ducked behind a display of wildlife pamphlets. The man who'd attacked her in her condo stood only six feet away. She'd recognized his smell before she'd seen him.

Her attacker hadn't spotted her. She was certain of that, but if he moved a couple of steps to the right, he couldn't help but notice her.

She sent Josh an urgent look, pointed to the man, then held a hand to her throat. He got the message and motioned her to walk his way. Cautiously, she moved out of the man's line of sight and joined Josh.

He wrapped an arm around her shoulder, and she felt much of the fear-induced adrenaline dissipate.

They exited through the back door. The whoosh of cold air came as a relief to the anxious tension that had gripped her from the moment she'd seen the man.

"Did you see anyone with him?" he asked once she'd assured him that, yes, that was the intruder who had tried to choke her.

She shook her head. "There was a man standing close by who might have been a partner, but I can't say I really saw anyone with him."

"I'd say we found at least one of the men responsible for cutting our brake line."

Cold settled in her gut at his words. Having the SUV tampered with was the fourth time in only a day that someone had tried to kill her. Not for the first time, questions of why they wanted that SD card so much tumbled through her mind.

"What now?"

"We turn the tables on them." The glint in his eyes told her he had something in mind.

"What is it?" She was dirty, tired and more than a little discouraged, but she could feel her fight coming back. She relished it. It was time she took action instead of just reacting to what whoever wanted her dead did.

"When he comes out, we take him. Then we ask questions until he coughs up some answers."

"That's your plan? What if he has a partner?"

"We take him, too."

"After we take them—" and she was feeling pretty iffy about that "—what do we do with them?"

"S&J operatives will be here in an hour with a new vehicle for us. They'll take him—or them if there're two of them—back to Denver and drop him off at a police station."

"And all we have to do is capture them and tie them up in a bow." She didn't try to hide her skepticism.

Josh sent her a quick grin. "That's it. Hey," he said, apparently picking up on her sarcasm, "we can do this. We survived a semitruck trying to run us off the road and then having our ride go head-over-tail down a canyon. What's taking out a cheap punk or two?"

"You're right." Embarrassed by her doubts, she grinned in return. "We're two tough dudes."

"Tough dudes, huh?" He looked her over. "Never thought of you as a dude. Tough or not."

"Too bad. Right now, that's us." She leaned in. "Tell me the plan."

"Well, it's like this." And Josh proceeded to fill her in.

Ten minutes later, their quarry walked out of the store, alone.

Josh intercepted him with Kylie coming up from behind. She held the gun at the man's back.

"Don't move." Her voice had a decided quaver to it, and she hardened it. "Don't move."

Despite her bragging, the gun felt unfamiliar in her hands. It had been a long time since she'd held one, much less used one. She wondered if she could fire it if she needed to.

The knowledge sat uneasily on her shoulders as her thoughts drifted to the past and she was once more a prisoner. A guard had held a gun to her back as she was doing now. She'd done her best to swallow back her fear, but she'd lost control and had vomited up everything in her stomach. The guard had cuffed her at the side of the head, and she'd been sick again.

Feeling that helpless, that filled with fear, had shaken her belief in herself. And though she'd told Josh that she was confident with a gun, pointing it at someone shook that conviction.

Just hours ago, she'd held a weapon on the two men who had broken into Josh's home and hadn't flinched. That was the thing with PTSD. She never knew when or how hard it would strike. She bit down on her lip, hoping the pain would snap her back to reality.

"Kylie? Kylie? You with me?" The sharp note in Josh's voice yanked her back to the present.

Startled, she looked up. How long had he been calling her name? She stared at the weapon in her hands, a weapon still pressed against her intruder's back. Had she been holding it the entire time? She might have killed the man if she'd been careless, gotten startled, and it had gone off accidentally.

"Kylie. You all right?" Josh asked.

She cleared her throat to buy a moment's time, but the question in his eyes had her squaring her shoulders. "Fine."

"Great." But the worry in his voice gave doubt to the single word. He had his own weapon trained on the man now, so she knew it wasn't concern over him. It was worry for her.

"Walk to me." When she did, he said, "That's right. Give me the gun." Concern was plain in his eyes. "You're sure you're all right?"

She wanted to meet his gaze straight on but

couldn't manage it. Instead, she put an extra snap in her voice. "Of course I'm sure."

She had never been less sure of anything in her life.

Chapter Four

"Keep walking," Josh ordered and directed the man to the far side of the gas pumps. "We have some talking to do." He pulled a pair of flex-cuffs from his pocket, yanked the man's wrists behind him and slipped them on him none too gently.

"You've got no right." Outrage rimmed the man's voice.

"No? Try me. You tried to kill the lady and me." Josh motioned Kylie to stand by his side. "I think that gives us the right."

"I'm sure you remember me," she said. The fiery look in her eyes assured Josh that whatever had happened to her a few minutes ago was now gone and she was back to herself.

Still, he was intensely aware of every move he made, every breath he took. He recognized the signs of PTSD and knew that an abrupt move, an ill-spoken word, could trigger an attack.

He returned his attention to the man, who sent Kylie a grudging glare. "I don't know what you're talking about," the bully said. "And you ain't got nothing to prove otherwise."

She pulled down the collar of her shirt and pointed to her neck. "Does this jog your memory?"

He shrugged.

"How do you feel about picking on somebody your own size?" Josh asked.

"Why don't you mind your business?"

"The lady *is* my business."

"I'm just a hired gun," the thug said with surprising frankness.

"Where's your partner?" Kylie asked.

"He—" Too late, the man stopped. "I don't have a partner."

Josh searched him and found a set of keys. He pushed a button on the fob and was rewarded when a mud-splattered SUV chirped. "We'll wait for a while."

With the temperature steadily dropping, the three of them climbed into the SUV, Josh and the prisoner in the front and Kylie in the back.

Almost an hour had passed with no sign of the partner. Any attempt to extract more information from the man was met with failure, and Josh and Kylie gave up.

When two shiny pickups showed up in the parking lot, he signaled to them. Two men stepped out.

With their prisoner in tow, Josh and Kylie went to meet them.

"About time," Josh said.

"Hey, we got here as soon as we could," Luca Brady, his colleague at S&J, said. "We didn't know you were up in the mountains playing Grizzly Adams."

Josh turned to Kylie. "Boys, this is Kylie Robertson. Kylie, meet Luca Brady and Matt Henley. Two of S&J's finest. Kylie ran into some trouble, and I'm helping her out for a few days."

Kylie stuck out her hand.

Josh tried not to smile when both men shook it with careful restraint, obviously trying not to crush her smaller hand with their much larger ones. They were tough men who used their strength to help others, not to hurt. Their squared-away hair and ramrod straight posture hinted at their military background.

"Thank you both," Kylie said.

"It was our pleasure," Matt replied. "Josh

would have done the same if the roles had been reversed."

"I know." She nodded. "Still, thanks."

"This the same trouble you had earlier?" Luca asked Josh.

Josh gave a short nod. "Same kind. This guy—" he pointed to the man in the flex-cuffs "—did his best to choke Kylie to death."

She tugged down the collar of her shirt to show the marks made by bruising hands.

Both operatives sent her attacker dark looks. "We'll take care of this yahoo for you," Luca promised. The tone of his voice said that the yahoo in question probably wasn't going to like their methods.

Josh clapped both men on the backs. "You came through, like always."

"Glad we could help," Luca said.

"Just sorry we didn't get to mix it up more with your playmate," Matt added.

"You get those lowlifes at my place delivered to the police all right?" Josh asked.

Luca slanted him a look. "What do you think?"

Josh grinned. "Thanks. Got another favor to ask. Can you get this goon to the police? I don't want my name out there any more than I can help. Tell them that he's the one who attacked Ms. Robertson."

Luca glanced at Matt. "They're gonna want a statement from her. What do we tell them?"

Josh shrugged. "Anything you want. The important thing is that I get her somewhere safe. I have a feeling this won't be the only man who's looking for her." Kylie needed time to catch her breath and to go through the pictures. She couldn't do either if she was subjected to lengthy questioning by the police. He knew how they worked. They'd want a statement, which they would then pick apart. Though he recognized the tactic as a way to get at the truth, he didn't want to see Kylie put through it. Especially not now after she had just suffered a PTSD episode.

Matt nodded. "Can do, though it's going to take some explaining when we turn in another guy."

Josh grinned. He knew Luca and Matt would come through. "See what you can get out of him before you turn him over to the authorities."

"Not a problem," Matt said, gaze hard as he looked at her attacker. "Men who beat up women deserve what they get."

Josh had no doubt that they would get what information they could from the man.

After handing over the keys to one of the trucks to Josh and each grabbing an arm of their prisoner, Matt and Luca took off.

"I like your friends," Kylie said, watching them go. Their new ride was a beefed-up Ford, not much to look at but plenty of power.

"They're good to have around." Once they were in the truck, he said, "Want to tell me what happened back there?"

She stared ahead, not sure what response to give. She tried for nonchalance. "I pointed a gun at a man's back. No big deal." She could scarcely wrap her mind around the events of the day, much less the last few hours.

His silence told her that he wasn't buying it.

"Nothing happened—" She stopped, admitting to herself that she hadn't fooled him. Not for a minute. She pushed the words out in a rush before she lost her courage. "I couldn't breathe. My vision went blurry. For a minute, I forgot where I was, and then I realized I was having flashbacks to being in the prison camp."

"PTSD." At her nod, he said, "It's nothing to be ashamed of."

"Who said I was ashamed?" She felt heat rushing to her face at the snap in her voice. "Sorry. It won't happen again." She realized there was no way she could promise that and flushed once more.

His gaze found hers. It wasn't probing this time but was filled with compassion. "Don't apologize to me. I've had my share of moments where I didn't know where I was. It takes time."

"You've had PTSD?" She found it hard to believe that a strong man like Josh had ever suffered from it. Since her return to the States, she'd blamed herself for what she saw as a weakness. Could she have been wrong?

"A lot of operators have. We've been trained for being taken captive, surviving torture. You didn't have any training. It's no wonder you're having flashbacks."

"I thought I was over them, but this one came roaring back like it all happened yesterday. I wasn't always so fragile. Now it seems I jump at my own shadow."

"Don't sell yourself short. You endured more than most people could ever imagine. Being held prisoner for six months is nothing to be taken lightly. Some people never come back from that. Physically or mentally. But you did."

Josh gazed at her with such empathy that she nearly cried. Every cell in her body wanted to hum at the genuine caring she read in his gaze. Crying wasn't going to help her and would probably only embarrass him. When he reached over and squeezed her arm, her first impulse was to pull away.

But she didn't.

She let his hand remain there for long seconds, absorbing the comfort she hadn't known she needed. When she did pull back, it wasn't out of fear, but because she was dangerously close to leaning on him.

While the earlier anxiety and fear had subsided, Kylie still felt the residual effects of the flashback. Her therapist had told her to expect them off and on while she was in the recovery process.

The problem was, she couldn't predict when a flashback would happen. It could come when she was tucked away in her condo and could deal with it in private, in quiet. Or it could come as it had today, when she was in a crisis situation and needed her wits about her.

Post-traumatic stress had already stolen so much from her. Once, a particularly severe episode had left her unable to write and she'd missed a deadline, something she'd never done before. More troubling, though, she was no longer taking pictures in war-torn countries, preferring to stick close to home. To safety. Or so she'd thought.

Her work today consisted mainly of free-lancing, selling to various news outlets. Her previous work—taking photos for a paper and working closely with her editor, Bernice Kyllensgaard—had earned her a well-deserved reputation, seeing to it that she had no trouble in earning a living by going out on her own. Bernice had been supportive when she'd decided to go freelance.

She had handled the flashback, perhaps not well, but she'd handled it all the same. She called that progress. So what if she'd been holding a gun at the time. Okay, that wasn't good, but how many times was she going to be holding a gun, anyway?

A flash of macabre humor took her by surprise. If things kept going as they were, maybe more than she thought.

"Must have been some mighty deep thoughts," Josh said.

"What makes you say that?"

"I told you. Your eyes give you away every time." He quirked a brow. "Care to share?"

"Not now." Maybe not ever. "Don't worry. I'm okay."

He didn't call her on the lie.

Josh watched the play of emotions as they chased across Kylie's face. Her features had always been expressive, revealing her every feeling. At that moment, he read fear and a fierce determination not to give in to it.

What had happened to her in that camp? He'd been on several missions with his team to rescue hostages from such camps. After one successful rescue, he was feeling good about a job well done.

Until he interviewed the prisoners.

The hostages, who were missionaries, had come away so physically and emotionally damaged that they hadn't been able to answer any but the most rudimentary of questions. When they had been able to talk, their stories of abuse were heart-wrenching. Though he'd thought himself hardened to even the most horrific of accounts from prisoners, he had been hard-pressed not to bawl like a baby.

What had happened with Kylie? He'd noticed

the scars on her hands, which she was even now rubbing, probably unconsciously. Were they a reminder of her time there?

What had made her doubt herself? That wasn't the Kylie he remembered. That Kylie had been ready to take on all comers, to fight to the last breath. This Kylie was unbearably fragile, looking as though she might break at the least provocation.

He wanted to see the feisty glint in her eyes, the one that told him and everyone else that no one was going to get the better of her. That Kylie had believed herself to be invincible. He'd seen flashes of the old Kylie, but the PTSD had stripped her of much of her self-confidence.

It shredded his heart to see her so brittle. She didn't look just rattled. She looked shell-shocked. The adrenaline of the last few minutes had worn off, and now she was crashing. Hard.

He couldn't help darting concerned glances her way, needing to reassure himself that she was all right. For a moment, she'd looked so vulnerable that he longed to wrap her in cotton wool and carry her away from the danger chasing her.

Minutes later, she closed her eyes. Her breathing leveled out. Her lashes swept over her cheeks; her mouth was slightly open, and her hair was tousled.

She was everything he remembered. At the same time, she was more, and despite the attempts on their lives, he smiled briefly, grateful that she was back in his life, if only temporarily.

His smile faded as he acknowledged that they were in trouble. He'd done his best to downplay how worried he was about what she'd gotten herself into. She was now a target.

Having served in the SEALs, where being a target was an everyday occurrence, he understood what it meant. An Afghan warlord had put a bounty on him and two of his teammates when they had taken out a key weapons stronghold. Then there were the terrorists who had vowed revenge upon Josh and his team when they had captured thirteen leaders. Being a target wasn't out of his wheelhouse, but Kylie had no such experience that he knew of.

The men after her were clearly professionals. What's more, they had backup teams to call on. They'd missed, but they would return. He had no doubt of that. His job was to protect her while at the same time figuring out why they wanted her SD card.

Kylie was as sharp as they came, so if she said

she didn't know what was on the card, he believed her, but there had to be something there, something worth killing over.

When they found out what that was, it would go a long way to keeping her safe. The temptation to push harder to reach the cabin was great, but he rejected it. An early storm had slicked the roads with a thin sheet of ice, which was nearly as deadly as bullets. He was a pro at winter driving, but he hadn't expected to need those skills in early November.

Playing it safe wasn't normally a SEAL move, but he had precious cargo aboard, and once more he looked over at Kylie.

I'll take care of you, he promised silently. Abruptly aware that he was in danger of losing his heart again, he made another promise, this one to himself. He wouldn't fall for her again.

He couldn't.

When Kylie woke, it took a few moments before she realized where she was. And why. The man in her condo. Men breaking into Josh's home, trying to run them off the road and cutting the brake line. All because of an SD card. An SD card that was important for reasons she didn't understand.

From the moment the intruder in her condo had wrapped his arm around her neck, events had moved at warp speed.

"You snore," Josh said.

Denial was swift. "Do not."

"Don't worry. It was cute, just a puff of air with a little gurgle at the end."

"Why didn't you wake me?"

"Why? It made me smile."

"How far away are we from your uncle's cabin?"

"Not far now."

She stretched, then wet her lips. Her mouth was dry. "Are you sure this is a good idea?" she asked. "I mean running away instead of investigating what's going on."

"We need a place to regroup, a place where you can look at the pictures you took. Once we learn what they show, we can start making plans."

"What if we don't discover what it is they're after? I took hundreds of pictures today. None of them stood out."

"Then it's a good thing that you have a second pair of eyes."

Josh had always been practical. She was counting on that now. "Okay. After we find out what those men are after, what then?"

"Then we investigate."

"Call in the police?"

"We can," he said, but he sounded doubtful. "Or we can investigate on our own. You're a journalist. I work for a security firm. Between the two of us, we should be able to dig up what we need."

"Is there some reason you don't want to call in the cops?"

He hesitated, then said, "One of my buddies ran into a case a while back where the cops were as dirty as the bad guys." His eyes darkened.

"What happened?"

"He died because he trusted the wrong person. Turned out to be his police contact."

"I'm sorry," she said quietly.

"Then there was the Lawson case," Josh said, naming one of the biggest cases ever tried in Colorado. "He had more cops on the payroll than a precinct station."

She recalled the notorious case where Douglas Lawson had been found guilty on multiple counts of murder, attempted murder, money laundering, human trafficking and a host of other crimes and was now serving several consecutive life terms in a federal prison.

"I thought Lawson and his people, including a bunch of dirty cops, were all brought in."

"They were. But who's to say there aren't more out there?"

"Okay. I trust you." She flushed at that and averted her gaze. Eleven years ago, they had broken up because she hadn't trusted that they could have a life together.

"Thanks." His smile was wry, as though he knew what she was thinking and was amused by it.

"I don't know if I've really thanked you for dropping everything to help me." It was a struggle to get the words out, but she had to say them. It was bad enough owing him, but it would be far worse if she was ungrateful, as well.

Josh had always been a stand-up guy who was ready to lay it on the line to help a friend. She could hardly be termed a friend anymore, but he hadn't hesitated. Why hadn't she appreciated that about him years ago?

The answer was simple enough. She'd been young and eager to start her own career. At the time, her path had seemed so separate from his...but maybe she could have pursued her dream of being a photojournalist anywhere.

Including Coronado, California, where SEAL training took place. There was no point thinking on that now.

"What did you think I'd do?" he asked.

"The same thing you're doing. I guess that's why I came to you in the first place. You were the one person I knew I could count on."

He studied her for a moment. "Hey, it's okay. You're not alone."

"Thank you." That was the only thing she could think of to say.

She felt as awkward as a middle school girl talking with a boy she liked but didn't want him to know it. *Grow up, girl. You're almost thirty years old.* Men didn't intimidate her. Even a man as good-looking and self-assured as the man she'd given her heart to so many years ago.

At that time, he had been everything to her. With her home life a shambles, she had relied on Josh in countless ways. He was strong, confident and so certain of his path in life, while she floundered in making the slightest decision. She'd turned to him repeatedly, until she feared she was losing herself. It had been then that she'd made the decision to pursue her own path. A journalism teacher in her senior year of high school had sparked her interest in photojournalism.

Now she was running back to him, wanting him to solve her problem, and felt that she hadn't made any progress at all. Disgust with herself had her throat closing up.

She'd grown since then. Grown in knowing who she was and what she wanted. She no longer needed someone to lean on as she'd once leaned on Josh, but there was more. The risk to her heart if she let him into it again was too high. Far too high.

Yet the butterflies in her stomach, the hands that clenched and unclenched, were mute evidence that she wanted to lean *against* him. To feel his arms around her.

It was nonsense, of course. The events of the last twelve hours had scrambled her thinking until she wasn't sure of anything.

She needed to remember who she was—Kylie Robertson, award-winning photojournalist. She had survived a deadly fever in the Congo, tribal wars in Afghanistan and six months in a prison camp. If that hadn't broken her, nothing would.

She closed her eyes to regroup her rambling thoughts. She needed to keep her mind on the present.

They took turns driving. Josh took the last leg of the trip and shortly before midnight pulled into a narrow road that led to a rough driveway. At the end sat a ramshackle cabin that looked like it had seen better days, but it appeared sturdy enough and would provide a place for them to rest.

Josh pulled his truck to the back of the cabin out of sight.

The cabin was a simple structure with four rooms, the only heat coming from the wood-stove. Amenities included a tiny bathroom and kitchen.

After cleaning up in the bathroom's minuscule sink and, pleasure of pleasures, brushing her teeth with the extra toiletries Josh had packed, she felt ready to face what came next.

She'd made do with a lot less. What mattered was that she felt safe. That had more to do with Josh's presence than the cabin itself.

"It's not much," Josh said.

"It's fine." Life was too fragile to complain about small inconveniences. And if she had to make do with sleeping in a cabin that was heated only by a wood-burning stove, she'd do so. "Compared to some of the places I've stayed, this is a palace."

"Same here." He grinned. "SEALs can't afford to be picky about their accommodations. I spent more than one night curled up in the branches of a tree, trying to stay out of sight of the guerillas looking for us. When I woke up one morning, I found a snake staring at me."

"What did you do?"

"Stared right back at him."

"You're making that up," she accused.

"Maybe a little."

Appreciating the story and him, she laughed, knowing he'd told her this to lighten the mood.

Josh rejected her idea that they look at the pictures first in favor of eating. With her stomach making impatient noises, she agreed.

From his duffel bag, he pulled out an assortment of canned goods. "What about beef stew?"

As though in answer, her stomach rumbled again. The rumble turned to a growl. Embarrassed, she placed her hand on it.

"When was the last time you ate?"

She had to think about it. "You mean besides the snacks?" At his nod, she said, "Before going to hear the governor."

"No wonder you're hungry. Let me heat this up."

* * *

Fifteen minutes later, he was ladling stew into chipped bowls.

When she took her first bite, she nearly sighed her pleasure. "It's the best stew I've ever tasted."

"It comes from a can," he reminded her.

"Doesn't matter," she said between bites.

When they'd finished and cleaned up, he said, "Now we look at those pictures."

She brought them up on her laptop.

Nothing stood out or appeared unusual. Just a sea of faces. She'd gotten a few close-ups, capturing the angst on one, anger on another. That was to be expected. The governor had spoken on an emotionally loaded topic.

Josh had been deployed in Afghanistan, Croatia and Ukraine along with a number of other hot spots and had seen the worst the world had to offer, but the shootings in his own country had shaken him in ways he'd never imagined.

Flanking the governor were huge screens depicting pictures of victims of violence. When a child's face was shown, Josh heard Kylie's mew of pain. He studied her while she gazed at the picture, saw the taut lines bracketing her mouth. Her eyes were dry, but he knew tears were close. From the tight grip in which she held her hands, he knew she was doing her best to keep her emotions in check.

She shouldn't have been embarrassed at her reaction. He'd seen similar pictures, had even witnessed the actual shooting of children, as had she, he knew, but it never got easier. If anything, it only got harder. You thought you got inured to it, but that was a lie. And he realized he didn't want to become desensitized to such images. To do so would mean he'd lost the ability to feel.

He turned his attention back to Kylie when she said, "Weapons are available to anyone who decides they want to shoot up a grocery store, a mall, even a church. In the governor's speech, he talked about how kids think they're invincible. Their brains aren't yet fully formed, yet they're able to get their hands on these weapons and destroy the lives of others as well as their own." Kylie shook her head. "He gave a description of the problem, but nowhere in his speech did I hear a solution."

She blinked several times, an attempt to hold back the tears he knew were threatening.

He pretended not to notice and waited until she was able to speak.

"Don't worry about me. I've seen pictures of children killed by violence and the anguished faces of parents before." Her voice was steady. Somehow he'd have preferred it if she'd given way to her feelings. He didn't want her to have to exercise such tight control over herself. Not with him.

They turned their attention back to the screen, where pictures of children and parents and grandparents predominated. Some carried signs saying "Protect our children." Faces filled with anger were interspersed with expressions of unimaginable grief.

A child's face filled the screen. He couldn't have been more than three or four years old. The bewilderment in his eyes was as heartbreaking as the grief on his mother's face when the shot switched to her. She held a sign showing a picture of an older boy with the caption "He was only seven." It didn't take much guessing to know that the boy would never make it to eight.

A heavy presence of police reinforced the grim subject of the conference.

Josh sat up straighter as another image appeared on the screen. "Go back," he said as she scrolled through the pictures. "There. Look."

She focused in to better see the persons involved. There, in the corner of one of her photos... Colorado's lieutenant governor was in close conversation with the biggest mob boss in the state.

Chapter Five

That couldn't be right. Granville Winslaw, the second-highest official in the state government, couldn't have business with George McCrane, the boss of Colorado's biggest organized crime organization, but there they were. Heads together, bodies leaning into each other. The picture hinted of a confidential meeting.

This was no accidental encounter.

She and Josh stared at two people who shouldn't have been together. The two men stood in the shadow of a doorway, partially out of sight, but they were plain enough for her to see. Was it only by coincidence that her shot caught them standing side by side? No, they were obviously talking, and, from the expressions on their faces, not very amicably.

She looked more closely, saw an envelope being passed from McCrane to Winslaw. No, this was not an unintended happenstance.

"What are the lieutenant governor and a mob boss doing together?" she asked. "And why didn't I see it earlier?"

"You were taking pictures of the crowd, right?" At her nod, he continued, "You weren't zeroing in on any one person."

"I was trying to capture emotion. To understand the story of real people with real grief. So, yes, I was looking at the people, but only to identify expressions."

"They wouldn't have stood out to you then. They were just two men talking."

"Are you patronizing me?"

"No. I'm trying to get you to give yourself a break. It's no wonder these men want the SD card. They'd want anything that puts them together."

Of course the lieutenant governor couldn't afford to be seen with a well-known mobster, especially since she'd heard that he was considering running for governor next term. Why were they meeting here? Hers wasn't the only camera at the event.

"McCrane has his hand in every corrupt enterprise in the state," Josh observed. "Probably the whole Southwest."

She nodded, thinking of how far the man's

interests extended, including embezzlement, drugs, money laundering, fraud, gaming, human trafficking, prostitution and more. Though charges had been brought against him numerous times, none had ever been made to stick.

Slick lawyers and a seemingly unlimited supply of money saw to it that he had never seen the inside of a prison cell. Witnesses, those who hadn't been killed or disappeared, had changed their testimonies or refused to testify altogether. And who could blame them? There had been talk of cops and even district attorneys being complicit with McCrane's organization, looking the other way when his name was linked to a crime.

"Why meet in such a public setting?" she said aloud this time, more to herself than to him. "It's like they're asking to be spotted."

"A public setting is exactly the kind of place that two people wanting to keep their meeting a secret might choose."

She tried to make sense of that. "How so?"

"Because most people won't ordinarily notice two people together in a crowd, but put them alone in an out-of-the-way spot, it's like hanging a big neon sign around their necks and announcing that they have a secret."

"Okay. I get that. It still doesn't answer the question of why those two men would be together in the first place." The idea of Winslaw and McCrane working together was beyond terrifying.

Josh smiled grimly. "I'm guessing it's not to plan the next church bake sale."

She almost laughed at the idea of the LG and the state's biggest crime boss planning a church bake sale.

What did Winslaw have to offer? He was a relative unknown in the political field, sent on ribbon-cutting ceremonies and other negligible assignments by the governor. He had a reputation of putting his foot in his mouth and then leaving it there. Because of that and his lackluster appearance, he was frequently the butt of jokes.

She went back to her original question: Why should McCrane want to meet with Winslaw? The LG didn't have the juice to do much, so it wasn't like he could help the mobster out of a jam. And why should Winslaw agree to meet with McCrane in the first place?

Did McCrane have something on him, something to use as blackmail? And if so, what was it, and more importantly, what was he forcing the lieutenant governor to do?

Another thought occurred to her. Maybe McCrane didn't have to force Winslaw to do anything. Maybe Winslaw was in it for the oldest reason in the world: money.

Some said the governor had made a mistake in making Winslaw his running mate. Others said that the state's top official had known exactly what he was doing, that Winslaw made him look good by comparison. Whatever the reason, he held the second-highest position in the state. Despite his ineffectual manner, his presence carried some weight.

"I need to take this to the authorities," she said. But how was she to get it to the right authorities? How far did the corruption go? Police, judges, state attorneys?

She voiced the question aloud. "How do I know who I can trust?" If the lieutenant governor was chummy with a crime lord, it stood to reason that there could be others down the line in state government who were on the take, as well.

Another thought occurred to her. "Do you think the governor's involved, too?"

"I don't know."

The frustration in Josh's voice mirrored her own. They had too many questions and no answers to go with them.

"What would the lieutenant governor want with the biggest crime boss in Colorado?"

"It's more like what would the biggest crime boss in the state want with the lieutenant governor," Josh said.

The journalist in her itched to write the story, but there wasn't a story. Not yet. All they had was a picture of Winslaw and McCrane with their heads bent together.

"We need more," she said, her investigative instincts taking over, "before we take this to anyone. We'd be laughed at out loud if we went to the authorities with what we have now." She knew that, given time, she could dig up the story. If she could take hard evidence to the police, there was a chance this might not get swept under the rug like other crimes surrounding McCrane had.

"You're right. That's why we're going to find out everything we can about Winslaw."

"What about McCrane?" she asked.

"Him, too. But the key here is Winslaw. Maybe he was being blackmailed by McCrane, and when they got to talking, the two of them decided they could do better as partners than enemies."

She considered that theory. "If Winslaw's elected, McCrane has the fast track to get legislation passed that would benefit him... You don't seem very surprised."

"It had to be something like this," Josh said. "I just didn't know the players."

"You must've seen a lot in your line of work."

"More than I wanted to." His tone told her that he'd rather forget much of what he'd witnessed over the years. She felt the same. While she'd observed many acts of true Christian service in her travels, she'd also witnessed scenes of such pain and despair that she'd wanted to wash her eyes out with sand, hoping the grit would remove the images.

Mothers and children, even infants, sent to refugee camps that had no running water, little food and no electricity. That was, if they were fortunate. Too many were slaughtered in the name of revolution, which was really just another term for war.

Her camera had captured too much misery, too much anguish. When she'd returned to the States after her time in the Afghan prison camp, she'd found yet more killing and senseless violence in her own country. When did it end?

Or did it?

She'd been disheartened by today's speech, to see that nothing had changed to end the violence in the nation. Politicians gave glorified speeches while children died and parents wept.

Normally a subject like this would motivate her to create change, but instead, she felt tired and scared. Part of her wanted to retreat from the story. That wasn't like her. It wasn't like her at all.

She turned to Josh, wanting to explain, to apologize. Could she tell him of the horror of being in a prison camp for six months, of witnessing acts of such cruelty that she'd been brought to her knees?

But the words didn't come. Instead, she felt a tear, then another, trickle down her cheek.

"Hey, it's gonna be all right," he said.

"This isn't who I am." It was important he knew that, more important that she said it. The tears came harder, faster. She gave a furious swipe at her eyes. "I hate crying. I ugly cry."

"I don't see anything ugly," he said softly. "I see a woman who's been through a lot of bad stuff and is still going through it.

"You're strong and smart, but even the strongest and the smartest of us can have a breaking point. I'm thinking that after you were rescued from the prison camp, you came home and scarcely gave yourself time to recover. Then you jump right into the whole violence thing that's taking place all over the country. You didn't give yourself time to decompress. You were hurting. Physically and emotionally."

He was right.

She'd seen a therapist but had still waded right into the next assignment without taking the time to process what she'd endured overseas. Right now, she could feel the return of the horror of what she'd witnessed and undergone.

She'd seen far too much of it to be surprised; yet, the calculated cruelty she'd witnessed in the camp had shaken her to her core. Then there were the injuries to her hands. The doctors had warned her that she might never regain total movement. Physical therapy had helped, but the tendons had been damaged to the point that her fingers were still constricted and ached after prolonged periods of use.

And covering stories about the suffering throughout America only affirmed what humanity was capable of.

Josh gave her a one-armed hug, which should have been a perfect blend of comfort and support, but she jerked away. She didn't want to lean on him. Not now. She was only beginning to reclaim the woman she'd been before her capture. She couldn't jeopardize that.

Embarrassed at her response, she made a show of pulling her coat more tightly around her. In wrapping herself in the coat, she noted a smudge at the side. She rubbed at it, frowning when she discovered it was sticky to the touch.

She could have picked it up at any number of places since this morning—had it only been this morning?—when she'd run from her condo. Still, she couldn't place what the smudge was and where she'd gotten it.

The down coat was a new one, a splurge for herself after selling a series of photos to *National Geographic.*

"Wait," Josh said. "Don't rub it." Gingerly, he touched the spot. "I think we figured out how the bad guys have been tracking us."

She looked at the smudge. Was Josh saying what she thought he was? "What is it?"

He frowned. "It's a very high-tech tracking device. All someone has to do is rub a bit on their fingers and then touch something the person they want to track is wearing. The nylon shell of your coat is perfect."

"You're kidding, right?"

"Afraid not. This is the cutting edge in tracking. I think your attacker knew the stakes of getting you and that card. This was his backup plan if he failed." The expression in Josh's eyes turned grim. "Whoever put this in action had access to the latest in military technology, plus a whole lot of money."

"How much money are we talking about?" Her chest tightened and her throat closed; along with it, a sinking feeling settled in her stomach.

"More than you or I make in a lifetime."

Josh took his knife from its sheath and cut away the piece of fabric containing the device and then tossed it in the stove.

"We've got to get out of here," he said. "We can't afford to wait until they track us down again."

The rumble of an engine caused her to go on alert.

Josh did the same, turning toward the window. "Too late. Get on the floor." He pulled aside a curtain and peered outside. "An SUV is blocking the driveway."

"At least we know how they found us." But that was scant consolation in the circumstances.

"We have to move and move now if we're going to get out of here with our skins intact."

She knew there wasn't a back door. She could climb out the bedroom window, but Josh was too big to fit. "What do we do?"

Two shots took out the front windows, followed by two Molotov cocktails being thrown inside. The cabin's all-wood interior swiftly ignited. Smoke and flames filled the cabin. As the smoke thickened, she struggled to breathe.

"Grab your bag," he said. "Don't forget the SD card."

She groped her way to where she'd left her bag and stuffed all that she could inside.

Josh began running his hands over the rough pine flooring and she wondered what he was doing. Now wasn't the time to go looking for dust bunnies. Seconds later, he stopped and pressed his fingers against the floor. A large square of wood came up.

A trap door.

She didn't need Josh to tell her what to do next. She tossed her bag into the darkness. With more speed than grace, she scrambled down two steps carved into the ground. There wasn't room to stand upright, so she sat back on her haunches as she waited for Josh. The air was colder here, and she shivered violently.

He threw his duffel bag down and jumped to the floor, grunting as he did. A sharp gasp of pain alerted her that he'd hurt himself.

"Are you all right?" she asked.

"Fine." But he didn't sound fine. He didn't sound fine at all.

She started to ask him what had happened when he pulled a rope attached to the door, closing it. The blackness was complete, and she had no idea which way to go.

"This way," he said.

After she slung her bag over her shoulders, she did her version of a military duckwalk as she navigated her way through the narrow tunnel. Her thighs burned with the effort, but it was better than crawling over the cold ground that would seep through her clothes and leave her colder than ever.

Josh followed.

The air grew cooler, and she knew they were no longer under the cabin. "Where are we?" she whispered.

"West of the cabin. Uncle Hal was a conspiracy theorist. He built the tunnel in case enemy forces came after him. The family used to tease him about his 'forces.' Turns out he was pretty smart after all."

Each of Josh's words seemed to come with an effort. "You're sure you're all right?"

"I told you, I'm fine. So leave it." The sharpness of the order convinced her that something was definitely wrong, but she didn't press it. Not now when they were making their escape.

When the roof of the tunnel abruptly lowered, she got to her hands and knees, her progress hampered by dragging her bag behind her. With no light, she was dependent upon touch. The walls felt like they were closing in on her, causing her to stop.

From the time she'd been a small child and had fallen into a toy box and couldn't get out, she'd suffered from claustrophobia and now shivered as much from fear as from the cold. She tried to swallow the lump that was stuck in her throat, but it refused to go down. How did she tell Josh, a man who had never been afraid of anything, that she couldn't move and that she was afraid that the PTSD would kick in at any moment? If that happened, she'd be totally useless.

"Breathe slowly," Josh said. "You're okay. I'm

right behind you. If you need to stop again, we'll do it."

His voice steadied her, and she dragged in breaths of stale air. She knew they couldn't afford to stop repeatedly while she dealt with her fears. They needed to get out of there before the men discovered she and Josh hadn't died in the fire.

They kept at it until the tunnel sloped upward. Digging her fingers in the dirt, she pulled herself out. Fresh air filled her lungs, and she breathed deeply, not caring that the air was so cold it felt like shards of glass were filling her lungs.

While they had been clawing their way out of the tunnel, the storm had worsened. Moonlight shimmered over mysterious snow-covered shapes. The eerie effect unnerved her until she realized the shapes were only dead trees, fallen branches, boulders. Every step had to be painstakingly maneuvered over and around the lumps.

She fell twice, tripped by branches hidden in their cloaks of snow.

"Careful," Josh said as he helped her up. "We don't want any broken bones."

"How far are we going?"

"As far away from those clowns who set the cabin on fire as we can." Though he had his phone, there was no service here.

They were on their own.

Navy SEAL training had included a wilderness survival course. The biggest takeaway was the Rule of Three. You could survive three minutes without oxygen. You could survive three hours without shelter in extremely harsh conditions. You could survive three days without water. You could survive three weeks without food.

Right now, it was the shelter component they had to address. They needed to get out of the snow that was falling with no sign of stopping. Wet clothes would send their body temperatures plummeting plus steal the remainder of their rapidly depleting energy. They had been tramping through the snow for close to two hours, and though he could keep going, he didn't know that Kylie had that kind of stamina.

He looked about and spotted a clearing big enough for what he had in mind. "Come on," he said. "We're going to build a lean-to."

Finding poles came first. Using his knife, Josh stripped the poles of their branches and set them aside. He and Kylie then set about inter-twining the branches together.

It was painstaking work, especially in the cold, to weave branches in and out. Fingers awkward in gloves, they managed to weave a covering of sorts. When it was large enough, they attached it to the poles with the lengths of rope he'd brought with him. The tarp in his pack would do nicely for ground cover. In less severe weather, he'd have used it for overhead protection, but he feared it wouldn't hold up in the heavy fall of snow, and they needed some-thing to keep the coldness of the ground from seeping into them.

"Our room awaits," he said, gesturing to the primitive shelter.

"It's perfect." Kylie sank to the tarp-covered ground. "I didn't know how tired I was until we stopped running."

Before he could respond, an explosion lit the air, sparks raining down like a Fourth of July fireworks celebration. Ordinarily, fire in the mountains raced over the land with terrifying speed, but it couldn't get a start in the snow.

"What was that?" she asked.

"At a guess, I'd say the men who set the cabin

on fire just blew up our truck." So much for his plan to circle back and retrieve it.

The expression in Kylie's eyes said she'd had the same thought and understood the implications of being stranded with no vehicle.

"Get what rest you can," he said. "Tomorrow, we move. We have to work our way back to some kind of civilization."

He didn't add that their circumstances were more than grim. They had a few power bars, a couple of bottles of water and only the clothes they were wearing. If they hadn't had to flee from the cabin so abruptly, they could have better stocked their bags with supplies he'd brought from home. As it was, they were at the mercy of the elements.

About to shut down his flashlight to save the battery, he saw the blood on his pants, remembering how he had snagged his pants on a nail while he was getting into the tunnel. The incident came into focus as he recalled the sting of the pain when he'd landed on his knee in the tunnel. He hadn't paid much attention to it at the time—he'd been too busy escaping before succumbing to the heat and smoke—but the nail must have pierced the flesh.

"What is it?" Kylie asked.

"Nothing. Just a cut."

While she held the flashlight, he searched for the first aid kit he kept in his duffel bag. It wasn't big, but it held the basics. After making a slit in his jeans, he tended the wound the best he could.

It wasn't a cut after all but a puncture and deeper than he was comfortable with. Puncture wounds could turn nasty if not treated immediately. When he had finished cleaning it, he put liquid stitches on the wound to hold the skin together and bandaged the wound. That should take care of it.

He hoped.

Kylie made a trip behind a copse of trees. What she wouldn't give for a roll of toilet paper.

After taking care of business, she did her best to clean her hands in the freshly fallen snow. That would have to do.

She returned to the camp and lay down on the tarp. Though she willed herself to sleep, the rest she so sorely needed refused to come. Her body had finally stopped shivering, but her mind spun in a thousand directions. What were the lieutenant governor and the mobster meeting about? It had to be something big; otherwise, they wouldn't have gone to such lengths to get the flash card.

When no answer came, she set it aside to wonder how much time she and Josh had before the men trying to kill them realized they weren't inside the cabin and started out after them.

Could they afford taking the time to rest? She was about to ask him, when he said, "It's going to take some time for the fire to stop burning in the cabin and the men to get inside. Then it'll take more time for them to realize that there aren't any bodies. Eventually, they'll find the trap door and follow the tunnel until they come to the opening."

"And after that?"

"They'll be on our tails. We'll have to hustle come morning, but we needed to get out of the storm for the night."

"How did you know what I was thinking?" she asked. The idea that he knew what she was thinking was unsettling, reminding her of their past. He'd often been able to anticipate her feelings and concerns and knew just how to respond. The irony was that she had no idea how to respond now.

"Because I was thinking the same thing.

We're okay to rest for a few hours. We're going to need it.

"In the Teams, we learned to sleep when we can because we never know when we'll get the next opportunity."

"Smart."

"Yeah. I know your mind's racing, but let it slow down."

The low timbre of his voice soothed her sprinting thoughts until she was able to shut off her worry.

To her surprise, the next time her eyes drifted shut, they stayed that way. She surrendered to the rest she desperately needed… Until a startling sound had her waking and bolting upright.

Chapter Six

The sound of a truck engine, a low sputter growing into a throaty growl, was unmistakable. Josh berated himself for not getting up earlier. His leg had kept him awake for much of the night. When he had finally given in to exhaustion, he'd slept fitfully. He'd planned to have him and Kylie on their way far earlier. Now the bad guys were closing in.

"Grab your stuff," he said. "We're getting out of here."

His leg was bleeding badly, but there was no time to treat it.

"Your leg—"

"It'll be fine."

The engine stopped, signaling that the truck couldn't penetrate the woods any farther.

In a perfect world, they'd have erased all signs of their presence, but their world was far from perfect. Thrashing noises as their pursuers tromped through snow told him that even now they were headed his and Kylie's way. From the sounds of it, there were at least two, possibly three.

There was no time to dismantle the lean-to, including repacking the tarp. Having to leave it and the rope behind was a blow. He and Kylie barely had time to grab their bags before the men were upon them.

A throbbing ache had settled in his leg. He ignored it and, grabbing Kylie's hand with his left, pointed with his right. "See that stand of pines? That's our goal."

She sent a disbelieving look his way. "That's a good hundred yards away, and you're hurt—"

"Forget about that. We have to move and *move now*."

Uncaring about the noise they made, they ran. They could make it, he told himself. Kylie had run track in high school, and he was in tip-top physical condition. Or, he had been before injuring his leg. He couldn't worry over it now.

The human body was equipped with automatic survival mechanisms, one of the most important being the release of adrenaline. At the first sign of threat, the body released the chemical before parts of the brain even registered the danger.

Adrenaline levels spiked as the body prepared for one of two choices. Fight or flight.

Right now, his body readied itself for flight. His energy surged, telling him he could do this.

The frigid mountain air seared his lungs, but he didn't stop.

He couldn't.

Frost had covered everything with a quiet glow that looked almost ethereal. Kylie wanted to revel in the beauty that only nature could provide but knew that they didn't have the luxury of that.

Gunshots chased them.

They had to keep moving. When bullets sprayed the air around them, Josh threw her to the ground and covered her body with his own. His large frame felt invincible, but no matter how strong he was, he was no match for a bullet.

Something was off with Josh. Last night, he had dismissed the injury to his leg, and she'd gone along with it. This morning, though, the wound was bleeding again. Moreover, his face had an unhealthy sheen to it. She'd seen that before in her line of work—it was fever. Fever had its own flush.

She knew he wouldn't appreciate her asking about it, especially when they were running for their lives, but the first opportunity she had, she'd get the truth out of him. She doubted he'd bring it up, stubborn as he was. That was something that hadn't changed about him.

When they reached the pine trees, they took long breaths, and she waited for him to say something. They had to come up with some kind of plan if they were to evade the men who were after them.

The only problem was that they had only what they carried with them. Scratch that. Of course that wasn't the *only* problem. The weather was worsening, and even though the snow had stopped, the temperature had dropped.

The cold, coupled with extreme exertion, spelled trouble. They were burning up calories at an alarming rate and had only the most meager of rations with no way to replenish them, but they dared not stop to eat.

Josh stumbled. His labored breathing told her that he needed rest.

He slumped a bit, and she looked more

closely, noting that the dark crimson stain on his pants leg had spread.

The wound he'd dismissed had bled enough to soak through the leg of his pants. She'd known it was bad, but how had she not known just how truly bad it was? As if things could get any worse. She nearly started crying but held back the tears. The last thing Josh needed was her going to pieces.

"Why didn't you say something?" she asked.

He gave a lopsided smile. "We couldn't stop. Not then."

"Fool." But her hands were gentle as she helped him to the ground. She'd have given her right arm for some kind of cover. A blanket. The tarp they'd had to leave behind. Something.

"Don't worry," he said. "It's so cold that it won't bleed much."

She pointed to the leg of his pants. "You call this not bleeding much?" It was all she could do not to rail at him.

"We had to keep going," Josh said. "We have to keep moving now. They're almost on us."

"When were you going to tell me how bad your leg was?" she persisted.

"It's not important."

She shot him an impatient look. "Of course it's important. How do you expect to run when you're bleeding like that?"

"The only thing that matters right now is keeping ahead of whoever is after us. I can't afford to pamper my leg." The annoyance in his voice told her to back off.

He pulled a compass from his pocket. "We need to keep heading south."

And then what? But staying one step ahead of the men after them didn't leave time for questions.

Only running.

Josh knew he was in a bad way. His breathing was growing shallower by the minute. His leg ached abominably. He felt Kylie glance at him more and more often. She understood the danger of infection just as he did.

"We've got this," she said.

"Yeah. We do."

It was too bad neither one of them had been able to put any confidence in their voices.

He stumbled over a branch, and she propped him up. He was too big to use her as a crutch. Though she was tall, she was slender.

He turned to the Lord. *We need Your help.*

Please give me the strength to keep going. Though he uttered the words silently, he knew the Lord had heard them.

When you think you can't take another step, try for half a step. But keep moving. His drill instructor's words resounded in his mind when the desire to give up crept in and discouragement sat heavily on his shoulders.

You're a SEAL, he told himself. It was time he started acting like one.

"What's wrong?" he asked when Kylie held up a hand motioning for silence.

"There's movement ahead," she said. "I don't know how long we can remain going in this direction."

"So they found us." He didn't waste energy on worry. "It had to happen eventually."

"Yeah." Kylie swiped at her hair, drawing his attention to the scratches and abrasions that covered her already scarred palms.

"If we don't move and stay beneath the bushes—" she gestured to some undergrowth nearby "—maybe they'll move on."

He heard the desperate hope that filled her words. He hadn't heard any dogs and gave thanks to that. While he and Kylie might fool the men with their makeshift hiding place, they wouldn't be able to evade search dogs who could sniff out the faintest odor.

"If we stay hidden, there's a good possibility that they'll search a different area." His words were whispered, scarcely moving the air. They quickly took cover.

When a rustle of snow-covered ground came, and then another, this time closer, he put a finger to his lips.

Their pursuers were probably conducting a grid search. If they marked off this area, he and Kylie could breathe easy for a couple of hours. That would end when the men returned to check the area again.

The sounds grew fainter as their pursuers moved farther away.

"You're really calm," she noted.

"It's not the first time I've had to hide from the bad guys." He and his SEAL team had frequently played hide-and-seek with marauding groups of terrorists in the Stand. They'd become adept at hiding in the craggy rocks that had dotted the Afghanistan landscape, resting during the day when the heat was treacherous and moving at night when the temperature had cooled.

Worry had drawn lines on Kylie's forehead and in the small space between her brows. He longed to erase it, but there was no way around the fact that they were in a bad fix. He wouldn't get far if he tried to move; worse, he was getting weaker with every passing minute. But if they didn't move, they would be discovered.

He leaned toward her. "I need you to do something for me."

"Anything."

"I need you to get out of here before the men find us. Go and get help." Unspoken were the words *Save yourself.*

The mutinous look on her face told him what she thought of that. "No."

"It's the only way." He took her hand and cradled it in his own. "I can't make it."

"I won't leave you. Either we go together or we don't go at all."

He kept his exasperation out of his voice as he asked, "What do you think will happen to you if we stay where we are?"

Tears streamed down her face. "I don't care."

He was powerless against her tears, and he knew it. "Okay. Suppose we both stay. How are we going to get out of here? I can't walk."

"You'll lean on me."

He let out a humorless laugh. "You can't carry me."

"I won't. I'll just be your crutch."

The idea of using Kylie as a crutch stuck in his craw. The events of late had made her fragile, both physically and emotionally. And he didn't want to slow her down when she was in very real danger.

A navy SEAL, ex or not, didn't lean on a woman, but that was exactly what he'd have to do.

After the men tracking them had cleared the area they were hiding in and had checked it off in their grid, Kylie and Josh ventured out. With him propped on her shoulder, she took an experimental step. And nearly crumpled under his weight. Okay. This was going to be harder than she'd thought.

She refused to give in and braced her shoulder under his arm for a second step. When she straightened, she felt her knees buckle. Though Josh carried not an ounce of fat on his body, he was a big man, probably outweighing her by a hundred pounds or more. She stiffened her knees and took a step forward.

"You could give a mule lessons in stubbornness."

"You comparing yourself to a mule?" She was trying to lighten the mood. They'd need every advantage they could have if they were to survive this, and a sliver of humor was all she had.

"Yeah. I guess I am."

"It fits."

"This isn't going to work," he said after a few minutes and pushed away from her.

"It has to. Now put your arm around my shoulders and let's try this again." This time, she knew what to expect and lifted with her legs.

They took a step forward. Another.

"We're getting it," she said after she felt they'd developed a rhythm of sorts. "We're getting it."

"But how long can you keep it up?"

She'd already asked herself the same question. Though she was in good physical condition, she couldn't support Josh indefinitely. Frustration and worry turned her voice tart. "As long as I need to," she said and gave him a fierce glare. "I'm not leaving you, so quit your whining and pick up the pace. Don't SEALs have some kind of thing about never giving up?"

"Something like that."

With Josh leaning heavily on her, their pace was slow, made even slower because of the treacherously slick ground. She watched every footstep, at the same time keeping an eye on Josh, making sure that he didn't slide.

His closeness caused her breathing to quicken and her heart to race.

She had never stopped caring about Josh, having carried his image in her heart ever since they'd parted. Though their circumstances were dire, his nearness infused her with sweet longing. How could she be entertaining such feelings when their lives were at stake? Yet she couldn't deny them. They had taken root and were growing stronger with every passing moment.

Get your mind in the game, girl. Her and Josh's lives depended upon her.

If this had been a movie, she would have waited anxiously to see how it unfolded. If it had been a book, she would have been turning the pages to get to the end. But it wasn't a movie. Nor was it a book.

It was her life. And, suddenly, the adventures she saw enacted in movies and described in books weren't exciting at all. She and Josh were being chased by bad guys with one goal: to get the flash card and then to kill them.

Her mind was as weary as her body, her thoughts jumbled into a tangled mess.

She and Josh picked their way over the ice-covered ground. She stumbled over a particularly uneven place but managed to right herself before she took Josh down with her. That would have been disastrous since she didn't know if she could get him back up. She didn't even know if she could get herself back up.

She should have concentrated on weight-lifting during her workouts at the gym. The thought caused a small chuckle to escape her lips.

"What's so funny?" he asked.

"Just thinking that I should have done more weight training." She hoped he'd laugh along with her.

He didn't.

"You're wearing yourself out," he said after another twenty minutes had passed. "You can't keep carrying me." She heard the scowl in his voice.

"I'm hardly carrying you." She kept her

voice low even though the men had moved far enough away that they couldn't hear her and Josh. Though she couldn't say for certain, she thought they'd moved to the west.

Josh was doing everything he could not to lean on her any more than possible, but she was taking more and more of his weight. "But a rest sounds good right about now."

They found a boulder to sit on, and Josh eased himself down, allowing his injured leg to stretch out in front of him.

Her breath was coming in short pants that told their own story. She'd done her best to hide her exhaustion, but she knew she wasn't fooling him. She saw the concerned looks he darted her way when he thought she wasn't looking.

She undid her bag and brought out half of the remaining trail mix. They ate sparingly, knowing that it and a couple of power bars would have to last them until the next day. If their ordeal lasted more than that, they were in real trouble. After a small sip of water each, she repacked their things.

"We'd better get going," she said.

"No. *You'd* better get going." He held up a hand when she would have protested. "I've thought it through. You can't keep going like this."

"Who says I can't?" She did her best to infuse her voice with strength, but she wasn't fooling him. She could see it in his rock-hard gaze. "So what do we do?" she asked in a quieter voice.

"I spotted a place in the rocks. Over there." He pointed to a hollow in the ground about twenty yards in front of them. "I'll stay there. You go and get help. You'll move a lot faster without me. You can make it. Get to town and bring back help. That's the only way we'll survive."

"You can't stay here by yourself." If the men hunting them found him, he wouldn't be able to defend himself.

"We don't have a choice."

"There's always a choice." With that, she stood, scanned the surroundings and found what she was looking for. She came back with two sturdy branches.

"You have your knife on you?"

He gave her a what-do-you-think look and pulled it from the sheath on his left ankle.

"Get busy and start taking the twigs off these branches." She didn't give him the opportunity to protest but started collecting smaller branches to use at the corners. "We're making a litter."

"Unless you plan on carrying two sets of

poles at a time, it'll be a travois." He gave a small smile that told her he was joking.

She knew that. Right now, her brain was so splintered with worry that she could scarcely think. She knew that he was trying to take her mind off their situation with some humor.

Appreciating it, she made a face. "Okay, since you're so smart, what's the plural of travois?"

"You've got me there."

She wanted to tell him that everything would be okay, that they'd find their way out of this and have a story to tell their grandchildren.

That pulled her up short. *Grandchildren?* She and Josh were light years away from having a relationship, much less anything more permanent. That was aside from the reality that they might not make it out of here at all.

She couldn't afford the risk if she let down her walls for Josh. Parting from him eleven years ago had torn her heart into shreds. She wasn't ready to face that. Not again.

Obviously, her mind wasn't firing on all cylinders.

"What makes you think you can drag a travois over the ground any easier than carrying me?"

"I was hardly carrying you," she said. "I let

you lean on me. But I think this will be better. Let me worry about pulling it."

Building a travois would require time and effort. Dragging it might leave a trail and even make sounds that could alert their attackers.

Mentally she cataloged the reasons why it didn't make sense and then balanced them with why staying together was the right call. Josh knew the way to Silveridge, the nearest town, approximately eight miles away. Having him with her made more sense than trying to find it on her own.

In the end, none of that mattered. She couldn't leave him. Period. She wouldn't abandon him.

"Take off your jacket," she told Josh.

He didn't waste time arguing with her, only did what she said. She did the same, then set about tearing the sleeves from their shirts. Removing even a layer of clothes in the extreme cold was dicey, but she needed the material if she was going to make a travois. In the end, she decided she didn't have a choice.

It was a rough-and-ready job, but it gave her what she needed. She used the sleeves bolstered with pine boughs to weave in and out to make the bed of the travois and tied them to the poles. It wasn't the sturdiest, but it would have to do.

When she put her jacket back on, she noticed the difference in warmth immediately. Even the thin material of her shirt's sleeves was better protection than nothing beneath her jacket. It couldn't be helped.

Between the two of them, they were able to fashion a decent enough travois.

She had one more chore to do, one she'd been putting off because she was afraid of what she'd find.

"Lie down," she ordered. "I need to look at your leg."

Once again he did as she instructed, but his scowl told her that he didn't like it.

Blood had soaked through the bandages. She needed to staunch its flow and then apply a fresh bandage. A check of their supplies showed that they were down to only a few bandages.

She removed the old bandage and tried not to wince at the angry red wound. As quickly and efficiently as she could, she applied a new bandage and hoped Josh hadn't caught her gasp of dismay.

Though he hadn't said anything during the

procedure, she understood that he knew just how bad his leg was.

"All ready," she said with as much cheer as she could summon.

She picked up the poles of the travois and gave an experimental tug. Okay. This was going to be harder than she had anticipated, but she could do it. She didn't have a choice. Somewhere she would find the strength to pull Josh to town.

After only a half hour into the trek, her shoulders burned as though a white-hot poker had been held to the flesh. Her arms weren't much better.

How could she keep going? Yet she couldn't stop. She had to get Josh to a hospital. His life depended upon it.

She paused for a moment, only a moment, but the relief was so tremendous that she stretched it into another. And another.

You can do this. The voice in her mind warred with the reality of her throbbing arms and shoulders. Her thigh muscles ached nearly as badly, as she'd used her legs to bear a good deal of the weight. Her breath whistled sharply from her overworked lungs while every muscle screamed in agony.

All it took was putting one foot in front of the other and then doing it again and again. What was with her? She'd been tired before. But she'd never pulled a travois with a two-hundred-pound man on it before.

Her breath was in rags, and her lungs stung as if they'd been filled with battery acid. Her vision blurred as a result. She blinked to clear it, to no avail.

She stopped to let the burning subside and found that her eyesight had cleared. A momentary blip, she assured herself. She'd make it to the next copse of trees and take a break.

A short break was all that she needed. Of course it was. Time for her muscles to relax, for her resolve to shift into gear once more.

"Kylie?"

So much for her hope that Josh would sleep through her pause.

"Problem?" he asked.

She wanted to laugh at the irony of the question. "No problem. Just getting my bearings."

"Keep heading s-south."

Grateful that she knew which direction was south, she nodded, forgetting he couldn't see her. "Will do."

His voice was slurred, she noted. Pain, certainly, but it was the worsening of the infection she feared the most. If the infection got into his bloodstream, things were going to get worse. Infinitely worse. With herculean effort, she pushed that from her mind.

For now, she had one goal: to make it to the next stand of trees. From there, she would make it to the one after that and then the one after that. Small goals added up to big achievements. She'd read that somewhere.

With that in her mind, she put one foot in front of the other and resumed trudging over the rough ground.

Do. Not. Give. Up.

The four words became her mantra. She matched her steps to them as they played in her mind. Make it to that bush. Make it to that pile of rocks. Make it to the next snowdrift. Just... make it. The self-imposed challenges kept her going until she no longer needed them; she only needed to keep lifting her feet and setting them down again.

You are stronger than you think. When she'd returned home from Afghanistan, she'd seen a therapist to deal with everything she'd undergone. The physical torture had been bad enough, but losing Ryan, her almost-fiancé, had been the worst.

She would never forget holding him as he bled out, begging him not to die and knowing that he was already gone. If he'd lived, if they'd returned to the States and gotten married as he'd wanted, where would she be now?

Not here. That was certain.

Was it guilt that she'd never given him the answer that he'd wanted that had caused the pain in her hands to continue? That was the therapist's diagnosis. Kylie had dismissed it, but it continued to niggle at her.

Had it taken seeing Josh injured and in pain for her to put the pieces together?

If so, what did that mean for her? For Josh?

The questions would have to wait. For right now, she had her hands full trying to save their lives.

If she'd believed in prayer, she'd have prayed. As it was, she could only hope she could do this. Hope was a paltry substitute for prayer, but it would have to do.

Chapter Seven

The first mile went okay. Sure, it was hard, but she was doing it. Sometime between the second and third mile, she started feeling the strain. Before the end of the third mile, she was limp with exhaustion and pain.

When she took another step, she wanted to weep, but tears weren't going to help so she gritted her teeth and took another step. And another.

They hadn't encountered their pursuers since they cleared the grid where she and Josh had been hiding. Were the men close by, ready to pounce at any moment?

Muscles burned across her shoulders, down her arms. Her back no longer screamed; it was the quiet agony that was somehow worse than the shrieking pain. Her mouth felt coated with sand, which made no sense as they were in the middle of a snow-covered wilderness. She tried to work up some saliva to allow her to swallow and get rid of the sand, but her lips and tongue were so dry that she couldn't even summon a drop or two of spit.

The coppery scent of blood was fresh in her nostrils. That made no sense either, and then she knew what it was. Her hands. The blisters she'd noticed earlier had probably popped.

Great. Just great.

Everything about her hurt, and now her hands were bleeding. The blood hadn't seeped through her gloves yet, but she could feel its moistness between her fingers. She did her best to ignore it. She had bigger things to worry about.

She ignored her hands, just as she ignored the fiery sensation in her shoulders and arms. She only wished she could ignore the fear that was somehow worse than any physical pain.

And then there was the cold. Exacerbated by their wet clothes, it had worked its way into their bodies with merciless persistence. With their nearly empty bellies, they had little energy. What strength they had was spent in fighting the cold.

So intent on her thoughts was she that she

missed a fallen log and dragged the travois directly over it.

Josh's grunt caused her to set down the poles and hurry to him. "I'm sorry."

"Don't be," he said.

She knew he was angry, not at her but at himself. She wanted to erase the self-blame that filled his eyes, but she understood him well enough to know he wouldn't welcome comforting words, so she kept her mouth shut.

What was there to say? She couldn't tell him that things would get better. And she couldn't alert Josh to her concerns. He'd insist that she stop, that she leave him and make her way to town. The truth was, their circumstances were so bleak that even if she'd been able to rally the words, they would have stuck to her tongue.

Aside from that, she wouldn't fool Josh. He knew the score. She only wished the numbers would tip in their favor.

"Kylie. Stop."

The words came out more harshly than Josh had intended. Shouting at her was the last thing he wanted to do, but he had to get her attention.

He couldn't bear the thought of her pulling

the travois another step. How she'd lasted this long, he didn't know. Though he couldn't see her, he could all but feel the strain on her body as she put one foot in front of the other with dogged determination.

She hadn't uttered a word of complaint. He wished he could summon the same resilience and unswerving resolve she showed, refusing to give up even when any rational individual would declare it was the right thing—the only thing—to do.

She kept going. Whether she didn't hear him or just didn't pay attention, he didn't know.

Physically, he felt better, having rested while Kylie pulled him. That, in turn, intensified his sense of guilt.

Her steps were becoming increasingly slow until they were more of a shuffle, her feet barely moving, only dragging over the ground in a sideways movement.

He tried again, this time gentling his voice. "Kylie, stop. Please." He breathed out a silent prayer that she would listen this time.

"Can't stop," she called over her shoulder. Unspoken were the words that if she stopped, she'd never be able to start again.

He understood.

He also understood that she was killing herself with the effort. The feisty girl he'd known had grown into a woman filled with grit who didn't let up, no matter what. He appreciated that quality; at the same time, he didn't want her to collapse because she was pushing herself too hard.

Because of him. Because he'd been careless enough to cut his leg on a nail.

Guilt sluiced over him in relentless waves that were as hard to bear as the growing pain in his leg. It didn't help that his brain felt fuzzy, his thinking foggy. "You're falling-down tired." Why did it sound like an accusation? He didn't mean it that way. Or maybe he did. He didn't know anymore. "You can't keep going," he added with as much patience as he could muster.

Her selflessness in pulling him on the travois and her determination not to give up only made him admire her more, stirring up old feelings. He tried to tell himself that they were only leftovers from the past, but that was a lie.

His feelings belonged to the here and now. Even while on the run and after a night spent roughing it, she was the most beautiful woman he'd ever seen. He wanted to share all that—

and more—with her, but it wasn't the time or the place.

"Who says?" The umbrage in her voice would have caused him to smile another time. But not now. Not when she sounded like she was ready to keel over.

"At least take a rest."

"Can't."

The single syllable was more of a groan than a word. If he'd been able, he would have stood and forcibly taken the poles of the travois from her. From the jut of her chin, he knew he'd have a fight on his hands. Kylie had always been stubborn. It was that stubbornness that had kept her going, but even that couldn't defeat the sheer weariness she had to be feeling.

"Please," he said. "For me."

She paused, and he prayed that she was considering it.

He'd prayed more in the last thirty-six hours than he ever had. He knew God heard those prayers. It was no small blessing that the men hadn't caught up to them yet, but the obstacles hadn't let up. If anything, they'd grown. Now he was dealing with a heavy dose of guilt that only grew heavier with every step Kylie took. Not for the world would he have wanted her to be injured rather than himself, but he wished with all of his heart that it was he who was pulling the travois.

"Okay." The two syllables were a blend of reluctance and relief. "For a little while."

When she lowered the travois to the ground, he wanted to cheer. He'd gotten her to let go of the poles. Now all he had to do was keep her from picking them up again. She winced, and he twisted his head enough to witness the extreme care she took in removing her hands from the poles. What was going on?

And then he got it. Her hands were probably pocked with blisters from gripping the poles.

"Let me see your hands."

"They're fine."

"Take off your gloves."

"What if I don't want to?"

It was worse than he'd feared if she was so reluctant to remove her gloves.

He was angry. Angry at the men who were after them. Angry at Kylie. But mostly he was angry at himself. If he hadn't been so careless to cut his leg on a nail, they wouldn't be in this fix.

"I'm sorry," he muttered.

What did he do now? He could handle pain

for himself, but knowing Kylie was in pain tore him apart.

He gentled his voice and tried again. "Kylie, please, take off your gloves. Let me see."

It wasn't a request but an order, however softly it was uttered. Normally, her hackles would have gone up at being issued such an edict, but she was so exhausted that she couldn't summon the energy to offer even a token protest.

Slowly, painfully, she removed one glove and then the other. Even those small movements hurt. Though the gloves had protected her hands for a while, the leather had worn through. Rubbed raw, with huge blisters forming on her palms, her hands were a mess. A few of the blisters had already popped and were now oozing pus and blood.

Just great. Josh wasn't the only one in danger of infection.

There was no way she could hide the damage from him. "I haven't had my manicure today."

He didn't laugh, and she feared that the joke sounded as feeble to him as it did to her. Too bad. It was all she had. Reluctantly, she held out her hands, palms down.

Gently, he turned them over and growled. "Why didn't you say anything?"

"Because I knew what your reaction would be. It's not a big deal," she added. "They'll heal." In enough time. Right now, she feared infection might develop in the open wounds.

"Give me the first aid kit."

They'd used much of the supplies tending his leg; all that was left were alcohol cleansing pads and a few bandages. With infinite tenderness, he cleaned her palms.

The antiseptic stung, but she didn't flinch. When he wrapped her palms in gauze and then placed bandages over them, she steeled herself.

"We better look for a place we can bed down for the night," he said. "We aren't going any farther."

"You're really good at giving orders."

"Glad I'm good for something."

The bitterness in his voice was her undoing. "I've done everything I can. I don't know what else to do." She was beyond exhausted. Her arms and shoulders ached abominably. And her hands...

"Sorry," he said. "You've been a trouper."

Though she'd told herself they should keep moving while it was still light out, she knew that neither she nor Josh were up to it. His breathing was short, labored, a testament to the pain he must be enduring.

Her own breathing wasn't much better. So much for her workouts at the gym.

It didn't help that another dust-up of snow was blurring the landscape. She started looking for a place they could take shelter. They both needed to get out of the snow and find a place where they could dry off and rest for a few hours. Just as deadly as their pursuers was the dropping temperature.

Her eyes passed over what looked like an indentation in a cliff, when something about it caused her to take a second look. It was a cave.

After checking it out to make sure an animal hadn't taken refuge there, she pulled in the travois. When she tried to help Josh out, he pushed her away. "Leave me," he said. "I'm too heavy for you to lift. I'll be comfortable enough here."

She undid the ties holding him in place, and he stretched. "You were amazing out there."

She didn't feel amazing. She felt like she was letting him down and letting herself down, too. Somehow, she'd grown to care for him again. Her heart gave a decided bump at the admission.

How had she allowed that to happen? When

she'd gone to him for help, she'd warned herself against developing feelings for him. Fear for herself had sent her to him. Now it was fear for him, which was far stronger.

She pulled out two energy bars, then set hers aside, intending to give it to Josh. He needed it more than she did. When she judged the time right, she handed it to him.

"No," he said. "You're the one who's doing all the work. You should have both portions."

In the end, they both ate their own share. Though the energy bar tasted more like sawdust than actual food, she felt her energy picking up at having something in her stomach. She broke it off in small pieces, trying to stretch it out.

"Pretty rotten, isn't it?" he asked.

"Yeah. That's why I'm pretending it's a good old-fashioned candy bar loaded with real chocolate and sugar and nuts."

They finished the snack, and she found herself digging into the foil wrapping for any missed crumbs. She stuck the wrapper in her pack and wished she had a dozen more of the bars, bad tasting as they were.

Her belly no longer growled in hunger. Instead, there was a dull pain as though its walls were rubbing against each other, sloshed by stomach acids. The sensation brought back memories from the camp, where the guards had used starvation to keep the prisoners weak and unable to fight back.

"You're beautiful," Josh said unexpectedly.

Irritation brewed with pleasure to surge through her. The last thing she needed was Josh telling her that she was beautiful, not when she was feeling distinctly unbeautiful, not when she was wondering how she was going to go on.

"My hair is matted. I'm filthy. And I'm starting to stink. Then you go and say something like that."

Her voice rose with every word. She wanted to punch him. At the same time, she wanted to wrap her arms around him, hold him close and kiss him. She didn't think about her PTSD. She didn't think about the killers who were following them and could catch up with them at any moment.

"You'll always be beautiful to me."

She hadn't cried when her shoulders had burned pulling the travois. She hadn't cried when the blisters covering her hands had burst. But she cried now. Her shoulders shook with sobs that wouldn't stop.

Finally, the sobs subsided to give way to sniffles. When her hands started to ache, something they frequently did when she was feeling vulnerable, she rubbed them. She noted Josh's gaze in her direction, a question in his eyes.

"Want to tell me now how you got those scars?" he asked.

"It's an ugly story."

He only waited.

"The prison commandant wanted me to go on camera and denounce what the NGOs and our government were doing to help girls learn to read. I refused. So he cut my hands. Over and over."

She'd gotten the telling out without crying. That was progress, wasn't it? She hadn't been able to do that with the therapist.

Josh took her hands in his and gently caressed them, his fingers kneading the damaged flesh and bringing blessed relief. Such was his tenderness that the unwanted tears threatened to make an appearance again. "Thank you for telling me. It couldn't have been easy."

Feelings for him swirled through her mind, working their way to her heart. Hadn't she already lectured herself about falling for him again?

She pushed that away and focused on the now. "No. It wasn't." But she was glad she had told him. His hands felt so good on hers that she didn't yank them away from his grasp as she might have. His touch brought back so many memories, the sweet memories of youth. At the same time, though, it stirred up new feelings, those of a woman. The woman she was today.

She looked at him and recalled the man she'd once loved and lost. She wanted to chalk up her emotions to the reaction of the danger they faced, but she knew that wasn't the truth. The truth was she was learning to care about the man far more than she'd ever cared about the boy.

Even with pain etching hard lines in his face, he was the most appealing man she'd ever known. His dark eyes, fringed by lashes most women would kill for, radiated an innate goodness that would never be dimmed.

He should have looked vulnerable now, but she could detect no vulnerability in him, only frustration that his body could not do what he wanted it to. Relying on someone else had always been anathema to him.

Some years back, she'd been on assignment in Germany. There, she'd visited a museum specializing in medieval art and had come across an oil painting of a soldier readying for battle, the leashed strength clearly visible in the set of his jaw and the bunched muscles of his chest and arms.

It had reminded her so much of Josh that she'd carried the image with her for years afterward.

"Penny for your thoughts," Josh said.

The quip brought her up short. She couldn't tell him what she was really thinking, so she brought their talk back to their escape.

"A penny would be a gross overpayment." She didn't follow up for several minutes, then asked, "What are we going to do?" Absurd question. He didn't have answers any more than she did.

"We rest now," he said. "It'll be dark soon enough. Tomorrow morning, you're going to hike the rest of the way to town. When you get there, you're going to have your hands seen to and tell somebody where I am. It'll work out. You'll see." His voice was fading.

The weakness of it prompted her to remove her own coat and lay it over him. With only a shirt to protect her body from the cold, she shivered violently. In her worry for Josh, though, the shivering seemed of minor importance.

He was silent after that. His rough breathing

told her he had fallen into an uneasy sleep. Despite what he'd said, she knew there was a very slim possibility of him surviving this. He was willing to sacrifice himself in order to give her the opportunity to live.

Though she no longer believed in prayer, she was tempted to beg the Lord for His help. Josh was right. She couldn't keep pulling the travois, but what choice did she have? Leaving him behind wasn't an option.

They had little in the way of supplies, especially food. She knew Josh would insist she take it with her so as to keep up her strength.

Was there a way out of this that didn't require Josh sacrificing himself?

What was it he had told her about answers to prayers? Something about the Lord answering prayers in His own way, in His own time.

The trouble was, time was running out for Josh. Time was running out for both of them.

She put a hand to his forehead, more concerned than ever when she found it hot to the touch. He was definitely feverish, and she had nothing to give him.

She listened. And listened some more. All she heard was the sough of the wind and the beat of her own heart. She lay on the hard ground and imagined herself nestled in a blanket in front of a roaring fire. *You survived six months in a prison camp*, she reminded herself. If she could endure that, she could do this. No problem.

At one time, she'd been a fervent believer in the Lord and His goodness. It was that faith that had sustained her when her parents had divorced and left her at age eighteen on her own. It was that faith that had spurred her to go to school and get her degree in journalism while working two jobs. It was that faith that had given her the courage to travel all over the world to capture images of the damage wreaked by hurricanes, tsunamis and war.

When she hadn't been able to attend church on her travels, she'd worshipped on her own, always giving thanks to the Creator.

After enduring the harshness in the prison camp and witnessing the inhumanity the guards had subjected the prisoners to—men and women and children alike—she had felt that faith, the one constant in her life, slip away until it had finally died altogether. Starvation, beatings and continual humiliations had whittled the faith from her until all that remained was a memory of the belief she'd once held so dear.

There'd be no relief in faith. Not for her. Not anymore.

She feared there'd be no relief from any quarter at all.

Chapter Eight

Josh groaned softly. Cold and pain had awakened him after only a few hours of sleep.

He hated the circumstances they found themselves in. He hated the cold. He hated the pain that was radiating in ever-increasing circles in his leg. Mostly, he hated his own helplessness.

He knew Kylie was hurting. He could barely bring himself to look at her, to see the lines of pain etched on her beautiful face, now covered with dirt and grit. Guilt and self-loathing were a cruel mix that lashed him with stinging stripes.

He had failed her badly. He had failed himself. *Quit feeling sorry for yourself.*

Too bad the words were easier said than done.

He thought of the SERE course he'd undergone before he had completed SEAL training and claimed his Trident: Survival. Evasion. Resistance. Escape.

Thanks to Kylie, they had both survived and evaded, but for how long could they keep it up? At the moment, capture seemed imminent, and though both would do their best to resist, they had precious little reserves to call upon.

Face it. He couldn't crawl his way out of a paper bag right now.

"Don't," she said, startling him. He'd thought she was still asleep.

"Don't what?"

"Don't beat yourself up over what's happened. It wasn't your fault. None of it."

He'd been feeling sorry for himself, not a good look on anyone, especially not a navy SEAL.

He wanted to think further about their investigation but didn't have the energy. *Think about something else.*

"Tell me more about your time in Afghanistan," he said.

She was quiet for so long that he feared she wasn't going to answer. "Why do you want to know?"

"Because I care about you and want to understand what happened."

"Now isn't the time."

"Are you sure? Maybe it's exactly the right

time." What he didn't say was that they might not have another time.

Her expression said that she understood too well. "Maybe you're right."

When she finally started, the words came out in a frenzied rush, as though she had to get them out before she retreated into silence once more. "I accompanied an NGO that was working to establish a school for girls. And though I wasn't part of the NGO, I believed in their cause and wanted to show what was being done to help the girls receive an education."

Her smile came and went. "They were so eager to learn. They were like sponges, soaking up anything the teachers could give them. One of the workers wrote to his parents and asked if they could gather up books and send them. When a box of books arrived, the girls started to cry. They were that happy. A shipment of gold would not have been more welcome. One girl—she was only fourteen—she and I took a liking to each other. Her name was Nadime."

She raised her head to look at him. "Are you sure you want to hear this?"

He had a feeling he knew where this was going and wanted to tell her no, he'd changed his mind, but he forced himself to nod.

"The NGO workers and the village men had built a school. I was taking pictures that I sent back home. The girls were fascinated with the pictures and wanted to see everything."

He braced himself when pain filled her expression.

"When the soldiers came, I didn't understand what was happening. Not at first. And then the shooting started." Her voice turned husky, as though her breath were caught in her throat, strangling her. "They killed all the villagers, except for the girls. They were going to be traded. They saved the NGO workers to be used as bargaining chips."

"And you?"

"And me." She took a long breath. When she continued, her voice was flat, as though every feeling had been sucked from it and from her. "They made us walk, for what seemed like days. The only food we were allowed was a cup of water and a little bit of rice at the end of the day. When we reached some kind of camp, they separated the men from the women.

"What they did..." He heard the grief in her voice, grief mixed with a good dose of fury. He understood. When grief couldn't contain all the horrors, fury took over. Oddly, the fury was easier to handle. Grief was another matter. It burrowed itself deep into the soul and heart.

"It's okay. You don't have to say it."

"The girls were traded with another group. The last time I saw Nadime, she was crying for her mother. I tried to reach her and was beaten for my efforts." Another long breath. "We were kept there for six months, until US forces came and rescued us. I heard that the girls were returned to their village, but all their parents had been killed. I think they were sent to a refugee camp." She closed her eyes, as though to blank out the dark memories.

His gut clenched, and his anger went on simmer as he imagined what Kylie had endured. No wonder she'd come out of the experience with PTSD. More than wanting to give into his anger, however, he ached inside at what she'd suffered.

He pictured her anguish at knowing that the girls she'd tried to protect were sent to a refugee camp. Much of the supplies sent to camps were confiscated by corrupt officials charged with distributing food, water, medical supplies and other necessities before they ever reached the people. They were sold on the black market. Worse than the corruption, though, was the violence, and even molestation, that went on with depressing regularity.

With all his being, Josh wished he'd been part of the rescue team. His hands fisted as he thought of what the commandant and guards of the prison camp where she'd been held had inflicted upon innocent civilians. Would he mete out the same treatment to them that they had shown Kylie and the others who had been starved and beaten all because they were trying to help girls whose only crime was wanting to learn to read? He wanted to think that he would show mercy, but he honestly didn't know.

"You're the most amazing woman I've ever known." The realization that old feelings were rekindling caused the breath to pinch tight in his chest. The woman she'd become was even stronger than the one he'd known eleven years ago.

"Hardly." She gave a dismissive gesture. "But I survived. And that's what we're going to do here. Survive." She uttered the last word so fiercely that he believed her. Almost.

"Thank you for telling me."

She dipped her head. "I haven't shared all of that with anyone, not even my therapist."

"Why not?"

"I don't know." Her expression turned thoughtful. "Maybe I just didn't want to say the words out loud."

That wasn't uncommon.

He wanted to tell Kylie that she needed to talk about all that had happened, but she didn't need him to tell her what to do. She just needed him to listen.

He longed to hold her, to comfort her, to do anything he could to wipe away the painful images. Did he dare to risk his heart if he were to take her in his arms and offer her comfort? He needed to protect her; at the same time, though, he needed to protect himself.

And so he did the only thing he could. He prayed.

Kylie was relieved when Josh closed his eyes again. The uneven rumble of his breathing told her he'd given in to sleep once more.

She didn't know how close the men chasing them were. They had probably holed up for the night, just as she and Josh had. Had they found a cave, as well? Or had they camped in the open?

Come daylight, they'd be on the hunt again. She and Josh couldn't outrace them. Nor could they outfight them.

She drifted. Or dreamed. She wasn't sure. Pictures unfolded in her mind, a slow-motion movie complete with captions. No, not captions... Instructions.

Startled by the vivid dream, she woke panicked, looked around and saw that Josh was where she'd left him.

Only the sound of his tortured breathing stirred the darkness.

The dream nagged at her. It had contained a niggle of an idea of how to save Josh and herself, but whatever it was had vanished. Could she recreate it? No. All she had left was the wisp of a memory.

She started with the facts.

Josh was unable to walk.

She was unable to pull him in the travois any farther.

The cold was worsening.

They had little food.

If they were to save themselves, it was up to her.

Ideas noodled around in her mind.

And then she had it. As each picture unfolded to reveal the next, she knew what she had to do. Rather than leaving Josh on his own and making the trip to town by herself, putting both of them at greater risk, she'd turn the tables. She'd go after the men chasing them.

She pushed the idea around in her mind. She didn't have many options. Did it make sense to go after the men herself? If she left Josh alone in the cave while she found her way to town, he'd be helpless. He was growing weaker by the moment. And what guarantee did she have that she'd make it to town?

After a mental tussle, she decided that it made sense. Though their pursuers hadn't found her and Josh yet, it was only a matter of time before they did. Better to go on the hunt and find them first. Surprise was a powerful element in taking down the enemy.

Granted, it was only a figment of a plan, but it could work. All she had to do was take out two or more bad guys and force them to help her get Josh to town. No problem.

A grin that was more of a grimace tugged at her mouth. She could do this. She would do this. And she felt her energy return. More, she had her spunk back. It had been MIA for so long that she'd feared she'd never be able to count on herself again. Now she was ready to take the fight to the enemy.

Years ago, she'd had to face down several

gang members in her quest to dig up a story. They'd done their best to intimidate her, but she'd stuck to her guns and gotten what she wanted.

What was the expression she'd heard from one of the SEALs who'd rescued her and the others in the prison camp? Oh, yes. *Ready, guns loaded and safeties off.* Could she imitate that SEAL, to ready herself, have her gun loaded and the safety off? The metaphor was close enough to the reality of the situation to have her lips press together in resolve.

She went through their meager supplies. A check of the pack revealed an extra pair of socks. She filled the socks with hefty rocks she found scattered around the cave, then tied them at the ends and gave one an experimental swing.

The rocks provided enough heft to give a good wallop. She would just have to get in the right position to give a good swing and make sure she hit her opponent where it would do the most good.

Not much. But she could work with it.

A mental tally of their weapons momentarily deflated her enthusiasm. They had two guns between them. Fortunately, she was skilled in both weapons; however, the men after them were no doubt armed to the teeth with handguns and rifles. She couldn't leave Josh defenseless and would leave one weapon with him along with his knife. Though she lacked a man's strength, she had some first-rate moves courtesy of her martial arts training.

She set her teeth. "You can do this," she said quietly to herself. A scripture from Matthew that she'd memorized long ago came to mind. *With people this is impossible, but with God all things are possible.*

With that, she tidied her thoughts and did her best to sleep. She'd need all the energy and strength she could summon if she was to go up against two or more armed men.

She was going hunting.

Chapter Nine

Josh jerked awake, dismayed to find that he'd drifted into some kind of semiconsciousness without being aware of it. It took a moment for him to get his bearings, to realize that he was not on the outskirts of Kandahar fighting terrorists. He was in the Rocky Mountains battling homegrown killers who were every bit as dangerous.

Was this how it was to end? With him slipping in and out of reality until he finally gave way to the infection that was even now coursing through him?

When he'd been deployed, he and his buddies had occasionally engaged in dark speculations about the bullet that might take the life of any one of them. There were no certainties in combat. A bullet, he understood. But to be taken out by infection from a rusty nail wasn't how he'd pictured going out.

The maudlin trail of his thoughts scared him, and he did his best to force them from his mind. He was drifting now, his mind blank of thought. He was both cold and hot, a strange paradox that confused him.

He tried to look around, but pinpricks of white blurred his vision.

Josh blinked. Another blink and his vision cleared.

Cold found its way into him, dug its claws deep and refused to let go. His body tried to shiver, but he found it couldn't. He lacked the energy to work up one good shiver. In other circumstances, he was certain he would have found that funny. In these, it wasn't funny at all.

Pain blossomed through him, radiating from his lower thigh, and even though he couldn't shiver, he could feel the pain just fine.

Josh heard Kylie make a trip outside and then return. She tossed back and forth as though her mind refused to settle. He understood. As exhausted as she had to be, she appeared unable to allow sleep to claim her.

Involuntarily, he let out a moan.

Kylie was by his side in an instant. "How are you?"

"Sore." He moved his head experimentally.

"But better. I think." That was a lie. If anything, he was worse. He prayed the dim light concealed the sweat that had gathered above his lip and across his forehead. "What's on your mind?"

"I'm trying to work through something."

"Tell me."

With growing alarm, Josh listened to the plan Kylie outlined.

"No." He managed to refrain from shouting. "No way are you going after those men by yourself." He knew she must be feeling desperate to even suggest such a foolhardy idea. He didn't blame her; he was feeling pretty desperate himself.

"Do you have a better plan?" she asked in an even tone.

He didn't, but that wasn't the point. He wouldn't let her walk into the enemy camp. She couldn't take out two or more men. Not by herself. Even a trained operative like him might have trouble taking down heavily armed men.

Patience strained thin, he sent a hard look her way and then realized she wouldn't be able to see it. "They probably won't kill you, but they'll play with you. Make you hurt and hurt plenty before they take you to McCrane. Is that what you want?"

He immediately regretted his words. From what she'd told him about her time in the prison camp, she knew all about men "playing" with those they'd captured.

On the other hand, she might not make it as far as getting to McCrane. The men might just kill her on-site. Either scenario sent chills rattling through him.

She raised her chin, the movement catching his gaze even though he couldn't make out her expression. "I'm doing this. With or without your help." She paused. "But I'd rather do it with you on my side."

He barked out a mirthless laugh. "What am I going to do? I can't even walk."

She made a noise that told him exactly what she thought of that. "You're going to tell me how to track them and then how to take them out. And I'm going to do exactly as you say. I'll bring them back here, and they'll help me get you to town."

"What'll we use for a vehicle?"

"Their truck."

Her plan wasn't just bad. It was terrible. How was she going to take out two or more men on her own? It didn't matter how trained she was in self-defense, she couldn't do it.

He wasn't ready to give in. He had to make her see that what she was planning was a suicide mission. As dire as their circumstances were, at least they were still alive. All he had to do was convince her to give up her foolhardy plan and to take off toward town.

He looked for a flaw in her plan. "I thought you said you wouldn't leave me," he pointed out.

"I'm not leaving you on your own." Her tone was one of infinite patience. "At least not for long," she amended. "Only long enough to take out the men and force them to help us."

Josh held his tongue and finally accepted that he wouldn't talk her out of this. And, as she pointed out, what other choice did they have if she refused to leave him here? "If you're going to do this, you need to know some things."

She leaned in. "Tell me."

"Let's start with tracking." He held up his fingers, forgetting again that she couldn't see him. "Look for what doesn't belong. Anything. A scrap of paper. A tin can. Even a bent branch. No matter how careful they are, people leave something of themselves behind.

"And smell. Don't forget smell. Everyone starts to stink in the forest. That's nature's way of protecting them from predators like bears or mountain lions."

She made a face. "Don't remind me."

"I'm serious," he said. "You'll probably smell our trackers before you see them."

"Won't they smell me coming?"

"They aren't expecting you. Unlike animals, most people don't see or smell what they don't expect."

"What else should I look for?"

"Abandoned campfires. Depressions in the ground where someone was sleeping. Like I said, anything that doesn't belong."

"You know a lot about tracking."

"It's a lot of what I did when I was deployed. The landscape's different here, but the same rules apply. If you're really going to do this—"

"I am."

"Then don't try to take them out all together. You need to separate them. We know there are at least two of them. What we don't know is if there are any more. That'll complicate things."

Could he stand by and let her do this? And then he was reminded that he didn't have a choice in the matter.

Prayers swirled through his mind, quiet pleadings with the Lord for Kylie's protection. Prayer had become a constant companion while he was deployed; that hadn't changed when he'd returned and started work for the US Marshals and then S&J.

Eleven years ago, he hadn't been enough to keep her. Now, he feared he wasn't enough to keep her safe.

Kylie wanted to speed up time. Waiting to put her plan in action was taking a toll on her nerves. The adrenaline rush she'd experienced when she'd come up with the idea had settled to a low simmer. She wanted that rush. Needed that rush.

If she didn't leave soon, she feared she'd lose the momentum that had been pumping through her veins when the plan had first come to her. Who was she to think she could pull off such a plan? Sure, she'd had self-defense training, but she wasn't a pro. Not by any means.

Josh must be secretly laughing at her.

"Right along now, you're wondering if you can do it, aren't you?" Josh asked.

"Something like that." Oh, how she hated to admit it. Hated to acknowledge that she had a boatload of doubts, along with an equal number of fears, that hadn't occurred to her when she'd first conceived of the plan.

"Did you ever doubt yourself when you were in the SEALs?" she asked.

"Not before we executed a plan, no. It was only after it was over that I thought I ought to have my head examined and wondered how my team and I managed to get out alive. There was this one time..." He stopped, shook his head.

She looked at him in amazement. "I'm having a hard time believing that you were ever afraid."

"Believe it. SEALs have giant egos, but in the end, we're just human, like everyone else. It's natural to have doubts, but you can do this."

"You didn't think so earlier," she pointed out.

"I had some doubts," he admitted, "but I hear the resolve in your voice. You're determined. That counts for a lot."

Warmth washed through her at the words. "Thanks. I needed to hear that." If he believed she could pull this off, then she knew she could.

"Don't thank me."

For six months after returning to the States, she'd seen a therapist. She'd wept, cried and finally demanded to know why she wasn't getting back to her normal self.

"You went through a terrible ordeal," the therapist had reminded her. "You can't just snap your fingers and make those memories disappear. Give yourself time to recover, to grieve over the friends you lost.

"You're stronger than you think," he had said during their last session. "Never forget that."

The words had remained with her, a source of comfort and a reminder that she had not only endured the ordeal, she had survived.

She called upon that now as she helped Josh move farther into the cave in case their pursuers got past her.

"You don't have to do this," he said. "We'll find another way."

There wasn't another way, and they both knew it.

She wanted to tell him that she had never stopped caring about him, but she kept the words to herself. Another time, another place. Maybe. For now, she had to focus on finding the men intent on killing them and then forcing them to help her get Josh to help.

Mentally, she prepared herself. She wouldn't kill them. Not unless absolutely necessary, but she would if it meant saving Josh's life and her own. If her time in the prison camp had taught her anything, it was that squeamishness had no part in survival.

Those who had managed to stay alive after enduring the brutal treatment their captors had inflicted upon them hadn't done so by turning away from what had to be done. They had done what was necessary, just as she would do now.

"Like I said," Josh continued, "do your best to separate them. I'm figuring there are two, maybe three, men on our trail. Take them out one at a time."

"What if I can't?"

"Watch. Bide your time, then be prepared to strike when the time is right. You'll know."

She listened.

"Take care of yourself," he said. "I haven't lost a client yet."

"Is that what I am? A client?"

He looked uncomfortable. "Friend."

Friend sounded right. So why did she want more? With more effort than it should have taken, she pushed that from her mind.

"It's time," she said.

Fear rushed through her at what she was planning. Overriding the fear, though, was a cold determination. The will to survive. No one would take that from her. No one could.

With that, she prepared for war.

Chapter Ten

Josh despised being left behind. He'd have rather taken a bullet than send Kylie off on her own. No soldier, no real soldier, rested easy if he was forced to sit by and watch as others fought his battles.

His gaze followed Kylie as she climbed out of the cave, her bag hampering her movements. How she'd managed to get him in there in the first place was still a mystery. She must have used every ounce of strength she had to pull the travois through the small opening.

He hadn't let on how bad off he was. There was no sense in worrying her more than she was already.

His leg no longer hurt. That was good. Right?

But he was burning up. Not good.

If he had been physically able, he would have stopped Kylie from going on this mission. The

irony of it wasn't lost on him. If he'd been physically able, they wouldn't be in the situation in
the first place.

He'd wanted to tell her before she left that
he was gut-busting proud of her, but all he'd
managed to get out was a grunt. Did she understand how much he admired her and yet
how afraid he was for her? The warring emotions tore through him, a tornado of respect and
frustration, love and anger. The anger was self-
directed, that he couldn't do anything to stop
her and didn't see any other way out for them.

If she'd agreed to head out on her own, she
might have made it to town. If she didn't come
back from her self-imposed mission, he would
never forgive himself.

In the quiet, where the only sound was that
of his labored breathing, he prayed. Prayed for
Kylie. Prayed for himself.

Senses on high alert, he listened with his
whole body. Was that a rustle in the bushes?
Had the men gotten by her and were even now
planning their attack on him?

Had they taken her captive? If so, what were
they doing with her? To her? Worrying held its
own kind of terror. What if she was even now
being interrogated? What if...

Images crowded his mind, and he did his best to dispel them. Entertaining gruesome pictures wouldn't help.

But he couldn't stop the questions racing through his mind. How could he have allowed the woman he had never stopped loving to track potential killers *on her own*? He'd dated sporadically over the last eleven years, but none of the women had ever touched his heart. They had been pleasant enough companions, but that was all. There'd been no connection with them. Finally, much to his mother's chagrin, he'd given up dating altogether.

If he was honest, he'd have admitted years ago that there had never been anyone for him but Kylie. Never had been, never would be.

The tears she'd shed earlier had sliced his heart into tiny pieces. Not for the first time, he wondered how people could treat their fellow human beings in ways that defied description. He thought he'd seen the worst the world had to offer and knew he had only been fooling himself. Pain and cruelty knew no bounds.

That Kylie had survived what she'd endured spoke volumes about her strength and courage. That she had come out on the other side, ready to take on new enemies and fight for what was right, only added to the weight of the remark-able woman that she was.

She was remarkable. Why hadn't he told her that before she'd left, encouraged her? She'd needed that more than she had the few things he'd been able to tell her about taking down the men pursuing them. Was it because he was ashamed that he couldn't go with her?

The answer came swiftly. Yes.

She was strong, fit and able, but she was still a woman pitted against two or more killers. He had given her what advice he could in tracking and capturing her quarry. But was it enough? She'd had nothing to eat in over twelve hours and precious little rest.

If she managed to track the men, if there were only two men rather than three, if she was able to separate them and if she could take them out... There were too many *ifs*. He was burning up again. *Ifs* were a part of his work, but Kylie shouldn't have to face them, not alone. His vision clouded. *Ifs* got people killed. *Ifs*...

The darkness took him before he finished the thought.

Kylie knew Josh had tried to hide how sick he was, but she'd seen the unhealthy color in his face, had smelled the foul sweat that came from fever. She had to do this. What was the motto? Failure was not an option.

If she wasn't able to get him to a doctor soon...

Following his tips, she tracked the men in less than an hour. Finding them wasn't difficult. They'd taken no precautions in covering their tracks, clearly not concerned that the hunted would turn hunter.

That part had been relatively easy. Now came the hard part.

They'd spent some time building a snow wall to protect them from the worst of the wind. She had to give them props for that, but they'd flubbed every other rule of wilderness tracking, including building a fire that gave away their location from a good distance. She didn't blame them for wanting the warmth, but the scent of woodsmoke was as good as a neon sign signaling their location.

She counted three men. Okay, that wasn't exactly good news, but she refused to let it throw her. With Josh's words fresh in her mind, she speculated on how to separate the men and cull one from the other two.

How to separate them? When she saw one

man leave the campfire and head into the thicker woods, she had her answer.

Distract him when he was returning from answering nature's call. She fingered the chain at her neck, a gift from Josh shortly before they parted eleven years ago. She'd kept it as a reminder of that long-ago summer. Now she held on to it for a lingering moment.

For courage.

For strength.

For victory.

Okay. She could do this.

When she heard him making his way back to the camp, she nestled at the side of a tree and gave a faint moan. From her vantage point, she could see his hesitation as he retraced his steps after taking care of business.

Another moan on her part, more plaintive this time.

"Who's out there?" he called. "Bert? Vinnie?"

She let a third moan answer for her.

"Bert, if that's you playing with me, I'm gonna—" His threat went unfinished as he thrashed through the snow-covered ground with no regard for the racket he was making.

She smiled to herself. He was angry now.

Angry and careless. A dangerous combination for him, but a plus for her.

When he was close enough, she made her move and leaped from her hiding place. When he came close, she swung the rock-filled sock at the back of his head. He dropped with a thud. Exhilaration coursed through her. She'd done it. One down, two to go.

The man's partners didn't show up. Had they heard him fall? Or were they just playing it safe? She tied him up with a zip tie she'd gotten from Josh.

She took one of his gloves and stuffed it in his mouth. It wouldn't do to let him cry out to his compatriots. Finally, she removed his boots and bound his ankles with another zip tie. The boots she tossed to the side.

Carrying him was out of the question, so she rolled him into the underbrush to conceal him and then did her best to cover their tracks in the snow.

She didn't deceive herself into believing it would be as easy to take out the other two men. When this one didn't return within a reasonable time, they'd be on their guard and would start looking, not just for their buddy but for whoever had taken him out.

Preparation was key, and she started with making certain her weapon was secured in her waistband.

The other men hadn't grown alarmed yet. She'd give them a few more minutes before they started searching. She edged closer to their camp and listened.

"Where's Bob?" one man asked. "It shouldn't take him this long."

"Don't know. Maybe he got lost." The other man, the smaller of the two, snickered.

"How far did he have to go?" The question was clearly rhetorical. She listened as the bigger man, whose face resembled a hunk of unpolished granite, appeared to give orders. "Why didn't you keep an eye on him?" he asked, irritation plain in his words. "You know he's a loose cannon."

The smaller man grumbled, "Since when did I become his babysitter?"

"I didn't say that." Annoyance coated every syllable.

Clearly the men were growing on each other's nerves. Could she use that to her advantage?

"Go check on him," the big man said. "If he's gotten himself lost, we need to find him. We can't afford to have him stumbling around and giving away our location."

"Why don't you go look for him?"

"Look, Vinnie. I'm the boss of this outfit. You do what I say when I say it."

The one named Vinnie raised his fist, then slowly dropped it. "Someday you'll push me too far, Bert."

She approached from the south and came up behind the smaller of the two men. Better to take him on first.

As silently as possible, she closed the distance between them and, when she was less than a foot away, pulled her gun and held it to Vinnie's back. "Drop your weapon and kick it away."

A sharp hiss of breath told her that she'd succeeded in taking him by surprise. He did as she'd instructed, kicking his gun into some nearby bushes.

"Now you," she said to the other man as he approached. "Take out your weapon and kick it away."

Bert glanced at Vinnie, held at gunpoint, and begrudgingly did as she said.

With both men disarmed, she thought of her next move.

"Get over there by your partner," she ordered Bert.

It was safer to have the two men close together rather than spread out. Bert did as he was told, but he had his own surprise and pulled a second weapon from the back of his waistband. "Now you drop *your* weapon," he told her.

The two of them faced off. If she dropped her gun, he would probably kill her. She was reminded of old Westerns where the good guy squared off from the bad one.

"I'm figuring you ain't as good with a gun as I am," Bert said, "and I can fire off a bullet faster than you can blink."

He was right, of course.

"I won't kill you. That's not what we were paid to do. Killing costs extra."

With little choice, Kylie dropped her weapon.

"Tie her up," Bert ordered Vinnie. "And while you're at it, stuff something in her mouth."

After retrieving his gun, Vinnie started to do as ordered, then abruptly stopped and pointed it at Bert. "You do it. I'm tired of taking orders from you."

Bert looked stunned at this show of rebellion and reached to grab the weapon from the

other man. In the scuffle, Bert dropped his
own weapon. While the two men wrestled for
Vinnie's gun, it went off. Vinnie dropped to
the ground. The slack look on his face and the
spreading crimson stain on his chest told their
own story.

Kylie couldn't afford to feel any regret. She
snatched up her weapon and aimed it at Bert
before he could train a gun on her. She needed
only one man to pull the travois.

Not a sign of remorse crossed Bert's face at
the other man's death.

Still holding the gun on him, she pulled a zip
tie from her pocket and handed the restraint to
him. "Tie this around your wrists. Make sure
you pull it tight. Once we get back to where
I left my friend, you're going to help me take
him to your truck."

He sneered. "You gonna make me?"

"Try me."

He did as she ordered, but the look in his eyes
promised that this wasn't over. With Bert in the
lead, a gun to his back, and her giving directions, they started back to where she'd left Josh.

When Bert suddenly spun and lashed out
with his leg, she was ready. She sidestepped
his kick, then cuffed him at the side of the

head with her cupped palm. She'd picked up the move in her Krav Maga training, a good one if you wanted to get a foe's attention but not knock him out completely.

He staggered a bit but remained standing.

"You try that again and I'll use this—" she gestured with her weapon "—rather than my hand. Got it?"

"Got it." He glared at her, meanness glittering in his eyes.

If she hadn't been so intent on getting back to where she'd left Josh, she might have been concerned by the naked hatred she read in his gaze. As it was, though, he was no more than an annoyance. She had more important things on her mind than worrying about a man who was clearly a bully.

They made their way back to where she'd left Josh. By the time they reached the cave, dawn had come and gone, but there was no breathtaking sunrise to lift her spirits. There was only a dirty smear of light that reflected her mood.

She forced Bert into the cave. "Look who I found," she said to Josh.

A half smile found its way across his face. "You did it."

"Thanks to your tips." As she looked at him

more carefully, she saw that it wasn't really a smile at all, but a twist of his lips that couldn't hide the pain. It only added to her urgency to get him to a hospital.

"Bert here volunteered to help us get you to his truck."

When Josh raised his brow at the word *volunteered*, she smiled, hoping to cheer him up a little at the humor in it. "Well, maybe he didn't exactly volunteer. And then he's loaning us the truck to drive to town. What's more, he insisted we have these." She poured out the candy and jerky. Concerned Josh wasn't strong enough to manage on his own, she unwrapped the snacks and held up a chocolate bar to his lips while keeping her gun trained on Bert. She was gratified when Josh took a couple of bites.

"Try some jerky," she said and handed him a piece of the dried meat. He needed the protein.

Josh took a bite of jerky before putting it down as though it took too much effort to eat. His lack of appetite was almost as concerning as the sickly color of his face. Had it only been yesterday that they were desperate for food?

Kylie had been riding an adrenaline high, but the rush she'd experienced only a short while ago when she'd captured the men had rapidly vanished upon realizing that Josh was too weak to even eat.

She considered tying Bert's wrists to the poles but rejected the idea. He needed to be able to lift the poles and maneuver them.

With some difficulty, they got Josh, still lying on the travois, out of the cave. She winced with every twist and turn, knowing that each jolt sent daggers of pain through him.

"You can't make me pull this thing," Bert growled once they'd cleared the cave.

She trained her gun on him.

"Oh, I think I can. But if you refuse, you'll be doing it with a bullet in you."

"You'd shoot me? I don't think so." He sounded smugly sure of himself.

She didn't hesitate and shot him in the upper arm, making sure she only grazed the fleshy part. She didn't want to disable him; she still needed him.

A howl ripped from the man's lips. "You shot me!" The disbelief in his voice should have been satisfying, but she was too worried over Josh to appreciate it.

"I warned you. Now pick up your feet and get moving. Remember that I'm right behind you. If you stop, if you complain, if you do anything I don't like, I'll shoot you again." She meant it. She didn't have time for anything other than getting Josh the help he needed.

"You'll pay for this," Bert said.

"I was hoping you'd say that. It gives me a reason to shoot your other arm if you do anything I don't tell you to."

He muttered under his breath. Fortunately for him, she couldn't make out what it was.

The first leg of the journey went smoothly enough until Bert started to lag and she had to motivate him by aiming her gun at his other arm. She didn't blame him. He had nothing to look forward to now but serious jail time.

They made an awkward procession, but it worked. Bert issued more threats, but there was no real heat behind them. He knew he was beaten. By the time they reached the truck, he was panting heavily. The truck had been parked away from the men's camp where the trees were thinner.

"Help him in the truck," she said.

Bert undid the straps holding Josh to the travois and lifted him into the passenger seat.

"Fasten the seat belt around him," she instructed.

With another spate of muttering, Bert did as ordered.

Once Josh was settled, she considered what to do with Bert. She didn't want to leave him un-guarded, but she couldn't take him with her and Josh. Even bound, he might be able to over-power her while she was driving.

She fastened a zip tie around Bert's wrists, then motioned to him to sit down. She knelt beside him and removed his boots.

He wouldn't be going far. Not in this cold and not without shoes.

"You can't leave me here," he whined.

"Watch me." She gathered up his boots and carried them to the truck.

Josh roused a bit. "You're something else," he said when she got behind the wheel.

"I'm practical." She slanted him a worried look. "How are you feeling?"

"Better now." He barely got the words out before lapsing into unconsciousness again.

She told herself she'd done a good job. She'd captured the men after her and Josh. More im-portantly, she had transportation to get him to the hospital, but none of that mattered if she lost him.

Another look at his drawn face had her con-cern for him deepening. His skin was the color of old-fashioned school paste.

The sooner she got him to the hospital, the better. She started the engine and pulled away, noting the murderous look on Bert's face as she passed. She and Josh rode in silence. That was okay with her. If they talked, she might not be able to keep her worry to herself.

When they reached a main road, she noted that snow had been pushed to the side by repeated traffic. Despite that, slick spots still dotted the surface. As the clouds obscured the sun and the temperature dropped, she had to slow down, afraid she'd hit a spot of black ice.

Another glance at Josh told her that he was fading. He slumped further in the seat until only the seat belt was holding him in place.

"Josh?"

He didn't respond.

Time was running out.

The road had narrowed to a stingy two lanes. In addition, the snow had started up again. She wondered if she should be grateful for its steady fall that kept her attention on the road and prevented her attention from drifting to Josh.

She pressed down on the accelerator.

Hurry.

Chapter Eleven

Kylie struggled to focus. Worry, edged with a large dose of leftover adrenaline courtesy of taking down the trio of men, charged her senses.

Josh hadn't spoken since they'd started on their way. She wanted to believe he was only sleeping, but this wasn't a healthy kind of sleep. He appeared to have slipped into unconsciousness. His breathing was shallow, punctuated with a shuddering cough.

Unexpectedly, she found herself thinking of the words of a childhood prayer, something she hadn't done in a very long time.

She drove as fast as she reasonably could, but the grayish light and patches of black ice forced her to slow her speed. Sliding off the road wouldn't help.

She followed signs with a large *H*, indicating the hospital. When she drove to the emergency entrance, she honked, waiting for help. She took

off her glove and put her hand to Josh's forehead. His skin was clammy to the touch, and his
face, usually deeply tanned, was a putrid green.

"Hold on just a little longer," she whispered.

"He cut his leg on a nail," she told the two
orderlies who transferred him from the truck to
a gurney and wheeled him into the ER. "I'm
pretty sure infection has set in." She was running along beside them, fully intending to stay
with him, even knowing that was impossible.

"Let us see to him," one snapped when she
attempted to barge her way through double
doors that prohibited entrance to anyone but
hospital employees.

"The best thing you can do is stay out of the
way," the other said with more compassion.

She slumped against the wall.

While Josh was being examined, her hands
were seen to by an ER doctor who gave a low
whistle. "What did you do to them?"

Unwilling to go into the whole story, she
only shook her head and waited while he treated
them. Though she longed to find a place where
she could clean up, she couldn't leave without
news of Josh's condition. Doing her best to ignore the looks people directed at her, she staked
out a place in the waiting room. The smell of

disinfectant stung her nostrils, but it was the fear oozing from the people anxiously await-ing news about loved ones that overpowered everything.

She understood. Too well.

Fear had its own odor, one that seeped into the pores. She needed a shower in the worst way, but even that wouldn't wash away the stink that clung to her.

She supposed she should call the authori-ties and tell them of the men she'd left in the woods. They were probably freezing. Though they didn't deserve any consideration, she didn't want to have their deaths on her conscience. After getting the state police on a hospital phone, she explained that she and her friend had been attacked in the woods and managed to get away. She then gave the location of the men and promised she'd make herself available for a statement the next day.

When a nurse walked into the waiting room, everyone stood, Kylie included. The nurse found the appropriate people and delivered news about a patient. Kylie approached him and asked about Josh.

"Your friend's in surgery. Go home," he advised. "When we learn something, we'll let you know."

"I can't leave. Not until I know he's going to be all right."

Eyes warm with sympathy, he said, "You look like you're about to fall over. Your friend isn't the only one who needs some rest."

She supposed she did look the worse for wear.

"Like I said, go home. You can't do anything for your friend here. Do we have your contact information?"

Kylie started to mumble an answer and realized she didn't know what to say. What would the nurse say if she told him that she couldn't go home because she was afraid it was being watched and that she'd ditched her phone because she was being chased by men intent on killing her? Beyond that, she didn't have enough money on her to rent a motel room, even a cheap one.

The nurse gave Kylie a sympathetic look. "We have a couple of rooms here for family members with no place to go. I think there's one empty if you'd like me to arrange it for you."

"Th-that would be won-wonderful." In her gratitude, Kylie tripped over her words.

A shower and shampoo later, and donned in pink scrubs that the nurse had brought her, Kylie lay down on the narrow cot, intending to close her eyes for only a few minutes. When she awoke, the room was dark. How long had she slept?

Was Josh any better?

Feeling more than a little self-conscious in the scrubs, she found out what room he was in. After explaining to the floor nurse that she was the one who had brought Josh in, she was given grudging permission to see him, but for only two minutes.

He looked pale in the lights of the room that had been dimmed for the night.

When the doctor she'd spoken with earlier appeared, he gave Kylie a stern look, then smiled slightly. "Your friend is doing remarkably well. His vitals are normal. Everything looks good." He looked over her scrubs, and his smile broadened. "I can see that one of our nurses set you up."

She nodded.

"You got him here just in time," the doctor said, his voice grave once more. "A few more hours and it would have been too late to stop the infection. He might have lost the leg." He glanced at her bandaged hands. "I'm glad to see you got those attended to."

She scarcely heard him. "Please tell me that Josh is going to be okay."

"He'll be fine. Given some rest and time, he'll be good as new."

She could only imagine how the idea of rest and time was going to go over with him. They'd deal with that when it happened. Right now, it was enough to know that he was being cared for.

In the meantime, she had to keep him safe.

The truck she'd taken would be easily identifiable, and that meant it could be traced. Once McCrane and Winslaw discovered that their men were behind bars, they'd hire more to come after her and Josh.

They weren't safe and wouldn't be safe as long as she had the flash card in her possession. And when she handed it off to the right person? What then?

She feared they'd never be safe again.

Josh dreamed.

Only the dreams were more the stuff of nightmares.

He and Kylie being pursued through the wilderness by men intent on killing him and abducting her. The crippling pain in his leg. Fear for Kylie as she set off on her own to take out the hostiles.

He shook off the remnants of the nightmare and focused on the present.

A day and a half had passed since he'd been admitted to the hospital. He was feeling better today and anxious to talk, but what did you say to the person who saved your life despite him doing everything he could to discourage her?

A smile touched his lips as he recalled how she'd forced one of their pursuers to carry him on the travois to their truck and then left him there in the wilderness. His smile did a belly flop when he thought of how he'd let her down.

She was stubborn and strong and tough and, above all, loyal. She hadn't given up on getting him to the hospital. Since he'd been in the hospital, they hadn't done much talking. He'd slept for much of the time while she'd sat by his bed, a fierce protector.

Guilt piled on his shoulders along with a dawning awareness that he and Kylie weren't safe here. When McCrane didn't hear back from his men, he'd start looking. If the men had been taken into custody and any one of them had asked for a lawyer, word would have made it back to the boss.

All it would take was for just one of the men to have told McCrane's lawyer that Josh was badly injured and needed medical care to have teams scouring the hospitals, looking for him and Kylie.

McCrane and Winslaw wouldn't give up searching for them. One thing he'd learned during his work was that bad guys were all the same. Their nationalities, their skin color, their ideologies might be different, but at the core, they all wanted one thing: to control others.

He and Kylie needed protection.

He pressed a call button. When a nurse arrived, he told her that he needed a phone.

Within a few minutes, he was talking with his S&J associate Luca Brady.

Josh outlined the situation as he would a sitrep.

The ex-ranger's response to the situation report was equally terse. "Be there at 1300."

Kylie didn't like the look of the men who had just entered the waiting room. Nor did she like the expression in their eyes, one of cold resolve. Though she didn't recognize them as any of the men who had chased her and Josh, they had the same look about them: tough and mean.

She slipped behind a large plant and listened when they talked with the receptionist at the front desk, worry ribboning through her. When she heard them ask about a "friend" who might have been brought into the hospital with a leg injury, she hurried to Josh's room.

She knew the hospital wouldn't give out information about patients, but she also knew that men like that wouldn't let that small obstacle stop them.

"We have to get out of here," she said upon walking into Josh's room, and then told him about the men she'd seen in the waiting room.

"I called Luca. He'll be here in ten minutes."

She feared they didn't have two minutes, much less ten.

When she saw the two men walking purposefully down the hallway, she knew she and Josh were in trouble. Their guns had been taken when she'd checked Josh into the hospital. She looked wildly about the room, looking for anything she could use as a weapon.

A stainless steel bedpan. A bottle of cotton swabs. A pitcher of water.

Think.

Her gaze landed on a small locker where she assumed Josh's belongings were stored. Though the pants had probably been thrown away, maybe his belt had been kept. She found the belt and wrapped it around her fist, making certain that the buckle was facing outward.

When the first man entered the room, she was ready and plowed her fist into his jaw with all her might. He grunted in pain as the metal buckle bit into his skin.

She didn't let up and kept grinding the buckle into his face until he flung her away. She landed on the linoleum floor but sprang up immediately, ready to do battle again.

Josh ripped the IV from his arm, took the pole and slammed it into the gut of the second guy. In his weakened state, however, he lacked strength, and his opponent grabbed the pole from him and threw it to the ground.

Just when Kylie was ready to jump on him, a third man barged in. She was about to use the bedpan on him when he caught her wrist. "Hold on. I'm on your side."

Luca. Now that she wasn't in the midst of battle, she recognized him. Luca threw his weight behind a punch that had Josh's attacker dropping to the ground. He tied up both men using zip ties.

By this time, bystanders had gathered in the hallway.

"Looks like the SEALs needed the Rangers to pull their fat out of the fire," he said.

Josh snorted. "Get us out of here."

Kylie was worried for Josh. He wasn't well enough to leave the hospital, but what choice did they have? "How are we getting out of here?" she asked.

"Find us a wheelchair," Luca said.

She left the room, ignoring the group that was dissipating outside the door, found a wheelchair and took it back to the room.

Josh climbed into the chair. "Let's roll."

Once they got outside and into the vehicle, Luca drove west of town, taking them to a small bungalow.

Its unassuming appearance caused Kylie to wonder if it was safe.

"Don't let its looks fool you. It's fortified on the inside and the outside," Luca said, apparently guessing at her thoughts. "No one's getting in there unless they have an RPG. You'll be safe enough here. What's more, it isn't on the books."

"Did you get the boss's okay?" Josh asked.

Luca gave a quick nod. "You know Gideon. He'd do anything for his people. By the way, that guy you tangled with at the gas station didn't give up anything. Far as I can tell, he didn't have anything to give up."

"Tell Gideon thanks for me."

"Call me if you need something." Luca turned to Kylie. "See that he gets some rest."

Kylie nodded. "Thank you. For everything."

"Josh is one of ours," Luca said simply. He handed her two sets of keys. "Two of our guys parked a couple of trucks in the garage."

Kylie had more reason than ever to appreciate Luca when she saw the sacks of clothes plus burner phones for her and Josh. She couldn't wait to shed the hospital scrubs and get into some real clothes.

Josh took a sack of clothes and disappeared into one of the bedrooms.

"Luca came through for us again," he said when he reemerged a few minutes later in jeans and a flannel shirt. He slipped one of the guns his friend had left into his waistband. "He's as good as they come. He saved my team more than once when we were deployed in the Stand at the same time as his Ranger unit."

She knew that those who had served in the Middle East often referred to Afghanistan as the Stand.

"It's a good thing he's on our side," Josh added. "Once, he held off six tangos while another buddy and I got our wounded from a courtyard where they'd taken fire. He refused to give up, even when it seemed we wouldn't make it. He ended up taking two bullets that day."

"Then I'm doubly glad he's on our side." She gave Josh a critical study. "You're looking better."

"I'm sorry. Sorry for not believing in you. And I'm sorry to have caused that." He gestured to her bandaged hands.

"They'll heal. The important thing is that you're going to be all right."

"The doctor said I'd be good as new."

To her mortification, tears appeared in her eyes. She'd been afraid—so afraid—that Josh would die, all because of her. She didn't think she could have lived with it. For the first time in days, she felt like they might be okay.

Did he know how she felt about him? She longed to tell him, but they were still in the midst of a very real danger, one that wouldn't let up until they figured out what the bad guys were up to and brought them to justice. But what if he didn't accept her feelings for what they were... Would he dismiss them as gratitude on her part?

"It's okay," she said, swiping at her cheeks as the tears fell. "I'm just glad you're going to be all right." She studied him another moment, the man who'd nearly lost his life to keep her safe, and before she knew what she was doing, she leaned in and pressed her lips to his.

Feeling after feeling poured through her as she kissed him. Wrapped up in the sensations, she let her mouth linger there for longer than she'd planned.

Then, acutely aware of what she'd done, she pulled back. A sharp pang washed through her at the loss of contact. What had she been thinking?

"This isn't smart," she said. "We have things to do."

"No." His soft voice sounded flat. "It isn't."

She nodded. This was what she wanted, wasn't it? For him to agree with her? Then why did she wish with all her heart that he hadn't?

Josh wanted to prolong the kiss.

He wanted to take their relationship back to

where it had been eleven years ago. No, that wasn't true. Then, he'd been scarcely out of his teens without any idea of what real love was, and Kylie had been only eighteen.

They were grown now, their feelings those of adults. They had each seen much, perhaps too much, of the world, and knew what they wanted and what they didn't. His feelings were those of a man who loved a beautiful, strong woman. How could he not? Kylie was everything he'd ever dreamed of, so much so that he wondered if he could ever be worthy of her.

But Kylie was vulnerable, and he was loath to take advantage of her. She had been right when she'd said it—this thing between them, whatever it was—wasn't smart, not when their enemies were circling them, but he was tired of playing it smart. He wanted to keep on holding her, to absorb the scent of her, to feel her softness.

"You ought to get some sleep," Kylie said. "You're still recovering." Her voice was gentle. She lifted her hand, as if to stroke his cheek, but abruptly dropped it at her side.

He resisted the impulse to take her fingers in his and focused on the practical. "Eat first, then rest." SEAL Rule Number One: eat when you can because you don't know when you'll get another opportunity. "I don't know if I said thank you for saving my life."

"You told me." She smiled. "More than once."

"You could have left. No one would have blamed you." It was important that he get that out.

Her brow furrowed. "Is that what you think of me? That I'd leave you?"

"No. Of course not." He shook his head. "I was just pointing out that you were a hero back there in the mountains."

"I believe the word is *heroine*," she said lightly.

He smiled. "Take the compliment. I'll get started on lunch."

"Why don't I put together some food and you sit down?"

He didn't argue. He knew he had pushed it today and was now dragging. His body was protesting in exhaustion.

"Thanks. We both need food and rest. Tomorrow, we're going after the people who're trying to kill us."

Kylie moved close, caught his gaze. "We're safe."

"Yes." But he saw the question in her eyes. For how long?

Chapter Twelve

During the night, Kylie thought of what to do with the SD card. She and Josh needed to find a place to stash it. Going to the police with a story about the lieutenant governor and a mob boss conspiring together would probably get them laughed out of the station house. All they had was a picture.

"We need to get that card somewhere safe," Josh said that morning, echoing her thoughts. "What if I give it to Luca to take to S&J? They'll keep it safe."

"If all of S&J are like Luca and Matt, then count me in." She chewed on her lip.

"What is it?" he asked.

"I want to visit my former editor. She knows more about what's going on in Denver than anyone I can think of. Maybe she'll have some ideas about how McCrane and Winslaw are connected."

"Who is she?"

"I told you about her. Bernice Kyllensgaard. I was one of her staffers for seven years." Kylie smiled at the thought of her take-no-prisoners editor. She had been on staff at the newspaper until after she was released from the prison camp and had decided to go freelance.

"Kyllensgaard. Scandinavian?"

"That's right. With some German mixed in."

Josh nodded. He called Luca, explained that they needed something safeguarded and asked if he'd pick it up. The former ranger agreed and arrived within the hour.

"I'm gonna owe you big-time when this is all over," Josh said and clapped his friend on the back.

"Don't think I won't remind you of it," Luca said and then took off.

After a quick breakfast, Josh and Kylie drove one of the trucks provided by S&J to the office of Denver's biggest newspaper. The paper had once occupied a huge building that had bustled with activity. The current one was barely two stories high, a sad comedown compared to the block-long, six-story establishment that had once housed the paper.

Kylie understood that print media was a dinosaur compared to online sources of information, but it was still an eye-opener to see what had become of one of the most respected papers in the state.

When they were shown to the editor's office, Kylie introduced Josh to Bernice, then explained why they were there.

Bernice's eyes wore a troubled look by the time Kylie had finished.

"You can see what we're up against," Kylie said.

Her former boss's mouth was a grim line. "What are you two doing to keep yourselves safe?"

"We're going after McCrane and Winslaw," Josh answered. "It's time we turned the tables, and the hunted become the hunters."

"Do you have any ideas of how we can get the goods on them?" Kylie asked. She knew her friend was tapped into the movers and the shakers of the city. Bernice was fond of saying that if she didn't know something, it wasn't worth knowing.

Bernice tapped a finger to her chin. "There's a rumor going around that McCrane has a girlfriend over on the east side of the city. You might start with her."

"He's married," Kylie said and then felt like a fool for stating the obvious.

Bernice shot her a don't-be-naive look. "So he's married. What's your point?"

"Do you have a name and an address for this woman?" Josh asked.

The older woman nodded. "Let me make some calls and get back to you."

Kylie gave her the number of her burner phone.

"You two take care of yourselves," Bernice said and leaned forward to kiss Kylie's cheek.

Kylie gave her a warm embrace. "Thank you. For everything."

"Your friend seems to have a lot of connections," Josh said when they were outside.

"She's been in the business a long time." Kylie's stomach chose that moment to growl. "We'd better feed me before I get hangry."

"Hangry pretty well describes me, too."

They picked up burgers and fries at a fast-food place and then pulled into a deserted park to eat in the car.

"Genuine American burgers and fries were one of the things I missed most when I was deployed," Josh said after polishing off one burger and starting on another. "We could get them in some countries, but we were whistling in the wind in others when it came to finding a good old-fashioned burger and fries."

"I know what you mean. There's enough fat and grease in this bag to clog our arteries for a year."

"Good." And though his eyes were still worried, the darkness in them had lifted. "Happens I like clogged arteries."

She smiled. "So do I."

After the time in the mountains when hunger had constantly gnawed at her stomach, she wanted to down the burger in two bites, but she took her time, savoring every morsel. "This is the best hamburger I've ever had," she said with lip-smacking appreciation.

He grinned. "When you're right, you're right."

Just as they were polishing off the last of the fries, Bernice called.

"The girlfriend's name is Gemma Hardin." When Bernice gave the address, Kylie motioned for Josh to write it down. "Thanks, Bernice. You've been a big help."

"Take care."

The lighthearted conversation of moments ago died as she started the ignition and they got on their way. The knowledge that killers were after them and they had a job to do tended to take the fun right out of the day.

Kylie drove to what had once been a rundown area that had resembled a war zone. Last she'd passed through here, small cookie-cutter houses lined the streets, plastic toys lay in the yards and rusted cars sat on blocks. Drug buys and gang fights had been commonplace. A few old-timers and those who couldn't afford to move away had remained, refusing to leave their decades-old homes.

Now, gentrification was taking place, turning what had been a haven for street people and addicts into an upscale place of boutiques, coffee shops and high-rent apartment buildings that had the advantage of being within walking distance of a number of services.

"The neighborhood has really come up in the world," Kylie said. Though she approved of the improvements, she couldn't help worrying over the older residents who could no longer afford the expensive area but had nowhere else to go. What happened to them?

The trouble with gentrification was that it made life unaffordable for a neighborhood's original residents. The city fathers had promised to find a solution, but that had largely been forgotten as the tax base grew and people rushed in to claim the trendy refurbished lofts, homes and condos.

"It's pretty enough," Josh agreed. "But I can't help wondering where the gangs and drug buys have moved to."

She nodded. Gang activity and the drug business wouldn't stop; they were only shunted off to a new place. She checked the address he'd written down and pointed to one of the new multiuse buildings.

"There."

They found a parking space not too far away and walked to the pretty building that boasted a bistro, hair salon and other businesses on the ground floor. They took the elevator to the floor where Hardin's apartment was listed.

"You won't find her," a lady who appeared to have just returned from grocery shopping said, juggling her bags while reaching for her keys. "Gemma moved out a couple of weeks ago."

"Would you know where she went?" Kylie asked.

"No. We weren't close. Knew each other enough to say hi, but that was about it." The lady tucked her tongue between her teeth, a considering expression on her face. "But you might check with her veterinarian. She had a cat she loved to distraction. I remember her saying once that she would need to board it while she got settled in a new place."

"Do you happen to know the name of the vet?" Josh asked.

"No. But she said it wasn't far from here." The woman shrugged. "Sorry. That's all I can tell you."

"Thank you," Kylie said. "You've been a big help."

She and Josh returned to their car and searched vet offices in the area. They found one only six blocks away.

Just as she turned the ignition, a gray sedan drove by, windows open.

Josh reacted first. "Get down!"

Gunfire cracked the truck window, two bullets imbedding themselves in the upholstery. Fortunately, neither she nor Josh were hit, but glass shards from the driver's side window rained down on her.

Still shaking, she stayed hunched over.

Josh reached for her hand and closed his fingers around hers. "You okay?"

She didn't answer immediately, still trying to process what had just happened. "I'm fine." But when she touched her face, her fingers came away bloody. "I don't know about you, but I'm tired of being somebody's target."

There was a look of ferocity in his eyes. "We're going to change that."

Josh hovered as an EMT treated the cuts on Kylie's face and neck and wished it had been him who had been sitting in the driver's seat. He had sustained a few cuts, but she had taken the brunt of it.

His lungs constricted to the point of pain that she'd been put in danger yet again.

"You were fortunate that none of those cuts went deeper," the young woman said. "It could have been a lot worse."

The police drilled both him and Kylie about what had happened. Josh did his best to hold back his impatience.

No, they didn't know who took the shot at them.

Yes, they saw the car, a gray sedan.

No, they didn't get the plates as they were too busy ducking bullets and trying not to get killed.

Yes, they'd make themselves available for further questions if necessary. Not for the first time, he questioned his resistance in telling the police about McCrane and Winslaw's involvement, but it came back to the matter of proof.

One photo didn't prove that the lieutenant governor and the mobster were involved in any kind of nefarious scheme, much less that they had orchestrated the attacks on Kylie and himself.

If the police were compromised, he and Kylie couldn't go to them too early without hard evidence of what was happening. And why. They needed something that was too big for dirty cops to sweep under the rug.

He knew that McCrane and Winslaw were guilty, but convincing the police was another matter.

The last thing he wanted was to draw attention to himself and Kylie. Better to stay under the radar until they found the proof they needed.

By the time they were finished, both he and Kylie were more determined than ever to find McCrane. That started with finding his girlfriend, which started at the vet's office.

They walked into the office and found it packed with anxious pet parents waiting to have their dog or cat and even a bull python seen by the doctor. Fortunately, no one was waiting at the front desk, so Josh headed there and explained to the receptionist that they were trying to find out if Gemma Hardin had boarded her cat there and, if so, could he get her contact information.

"I'm sorry, we can't give out that information," the twentysomething girl said in the voice of someone who was trying to sound professional but was probably a very new hire.

"Thanks anyway," Josh said, and taking Kylie's elbow, they walked outside. "I've got a friend at S&J who can find any information we want."

Thirty minutes later, they had a current location on McCrane's girlfriend.

They found Gemma in a small rented house on the west side of the city. The neighborhood looked like it had seen better days, with houses in need of paint, and trash stirred by the wind, dancing in the street.

After trying the doorbell and getting no response, Josh rapped sharply on the door. The curtains at the front window fluttered before the door was cautiously opened.

Gemma Hardin kept the chain on the door as she stared out at Josh and Kylie. Both her eyes were circled by faint bruises that looked to be a couple of weeks old.

"Who are you?" she asked in a voice that was

probably meant to sound aggressive but came across as scared. "And what do you want?"

"Someone who wants to see George Mc-Crane put away," Josh said. "From the look of you, you may be wanting the same thing."

Self-consciously, she touched her right eye and then her left. "This? This was my fault."

"Did McCrane tell you that?" Kylie asked softly. "Did he tell you that he had to hit you because you did something wrong?"

"No. I fell. That's all." The uneasiness in Gemma's gaze gave the lie to her words.

"Are you sure?" Kylie asked. "You don't look it. And that bruise looks like it was made by a man's fist." Kylie kept her distance to avoid scaring the woman off, but she didn't break Gemma's gaze as she said, "You deserve better. You don't have to be any man's punching bag."

"What business is it of yours?" the other woman demanded.

Kylie didn't have to search for the answer. "It's every woman's business when she sees another woman who's been beaten."

Josh tucked his hands in his pockets. "Can we come in? Get out of the cold."

Gemma looked uncertain. "I guess so." But she made no move to unchain the door.

"Is McCrane the reason you left your apartment and moved out here?" Kylie asked. "There's no shame in being afraid. Especially not of a man like that."

Gemma looked like she wanted to answer, was even about to answer, when a shot rang out. Gemma's face went slack as the bullet bored into the side of her head. Another struck her in the chest.

Josh sprang into action. "Help me pull her inside," he said.

When she didn't move, he started to bark out the order and then saw her face. She was in shock. He should have realized. The sight of someone being gunned down could well trigger a PTSD episode.

He kicked the door aside with enough force to snap the chain lock and pulled Gemma's body into the house, at the same time motioning for Kylie to stay low. He slammed the door shut before feeling for a pulse. He found none.

"She's gone."

More shots sounded, peppering the front door and piercing the air with cracks much like those of fireworks. If he was correct, there were at least two different kinds of weapons being fired. That meant two shooters. Maybe more. He and Kylie were seriously outgunned. This wasn't gunfire from ordinary handguns. The rapid fire reminded him of battles overseas where machine guns were employed.

"We're in big trouble," Kylie said. She seemed to be coming round.

"Tell me something I don't know."

He regretted his sarcasm, but he was worried over how they'd get out of this. They couldn't compete with the rapid-fire shots thrown their way. The only way out was to take the men out and to do it quickly. McCrane seemed to have an unlimited number of men at his disposal.

"Call 911," Josh said. "Tell them that there are multiple shooters. And tell them to hurry."

Josh crouched low by a window, opened it enough that he could return fire. He kept the shooters busy, but they had far greater firepower than he did. What happened when they advanced? He and Kylie couldn't just sit here.

He and the shooters traded shots, but it was getting them nowhere. He handed Kylie his backup piece. "Can you keep them busy?"

"Where are you going?"

"I want to circle around behind them and take them by surprise."

She looked like she wanted to object but only nodded.

He let himself out by a rear door and, keeping low, did a wide loop around where he'd roughly placed the shooters. If his calculations were correct, he should come upon them from the back.

With Kylie returning fire, they wouldn't know that he had slipped away.

The rev of a motorcycle engine told him that one man had taken off. If possible, he wanted to take the remaining man alive. He found the shooter where he'd guessed and crept up behind him. Something must have alerted the man, for he spun and turned his weapon on Josh. Josh didn't give him time to use it. Instead, he kicked it from the man's hands.

He could have shot the man right there, but he wanted to take him alive and question him. He and Kylie needed answers before they went to the authorities.

The two men fought for control. His opponent was on the small side, but he had a wiry strength to him and managed to hold his own against Josh's larger frame.

"You're a big 'un," the man said. "I'll give you that. Too bad your fighting doesn't live up to your size."

Josh didn't bother replying. He'd learned over the years that there were two kinds of fighters: those who talked a good fight and those who remained silent and then put your lights out.

When Josh lashed out with his good leg, catching the other man behind the knee, the man fell but not without taking Josh with him by grabbing his arm and dragging him down to the ground. Ordinarily, he'd have been able to withstand the other man's tactic, but his injured leg was still not up to full strength.

They wrestled there on the snow-covered ground. For every blow Josh delivered, his opponent matched it with one of his own. Though he wanted to take the man alive, it might not be possible. While he was deployed, he'd killed more of the enemy than he wanted to count. Wartime had its own rules. What of now, though? The question plagued him with relentless persistence.

In the end, he accepted that he might well have to kill again if he were to protect the woman he loved. He didn't have time to ponder over that. Just when he thought he had bested the man, the shooter slipped from Josh's grasp and took off running.

Josh started after him, but his opponent's lead plus his own weakened leg left him hopelessly outpaced. With the man went the only lead they had.

Something on the ground caught his attention, and he bent to pick up a gray-colored mechanism. When he recognized what it was, things shifted into place. Like how their pursuers' semiautomatics had the firepower of a machine gun.

He hurried back to the house and saw that Kylie had placed a blanket over Gemma Hardin.

She grabbed him and hugged him hard. "You're all right. I didn't..." She gulped back a sob and then, obviously aware of what she'd done, pulled back. "I thought you'd been shot. Maybe even killed." Her shuddering breath told its own story of her worry.

"I'm okay." Unnecessarily, he added, "They got away."

"It doesn't matter." Her voice shook ever so slightly. Was it concern for him?

He wanted to ponder the idea, but now wasn't the time. He put it away. For now.

"You're all right. That's all that matters."

Her voice had steadied. He wanted to tell her just what her words meant to him, to let her know that he felt the same about her, but he couldn't find the words. They'd each been through an ordeal in the mountains only to survive and find that it wasn't over. If anything, the targets on their backs had grown larger. She knew that as well as he did and didn't need to hear it. So he kept quiet. There'd be a day when he'd tell her what he felt. But not now.

Instead, he held the polymer device out for Kylie to study.

"What is it?" she asked.

"A Glock switch. It turns an ordinary handgun into a mini machine gun." A spark of satisfaction streaked through him at the discovery of what this was all about, but the satisfaction was short-lived as he realized what trafficking in Glock switches meant.

Kylie's expression flashed from excitement to alarmed comprehension. "That's why it felt like we were in a war zone."

"Exactly. A weapon that's been modified with one of these bad boys can have a rate of fire of 1200 rpm."

She held out a hand, and he gave it to her. "It looks like it's plastic, but it doesn't feel like it."

"It's a polymer compound, probably made on a 3D printer."

"So anyone with a 3D printer could make one." The dawning horror in her voice echoed his own feelings. Turning out Glock switches would be chillingly easy. Gang warfare would turn into battlefields if these got out, not to mention what would happen if warring countries got their hands on them. Even a small militia could rule the battlefield with Glock switches turning ordinary weapons into machine guns.

"They weren't using these when we came out of the vet's office."

"No. This kind of firepower would be bound to attract the police. The shooters followed us here and then opened up on us. A dozen of these could turn a street shooting into a massacre," he said. "Multiply that by a hundred. Or a thousand." It wouldn't take much to produce the switches in terms of time or money. Making them on a 3D printer would be ridiculously easy.

Kylie visibly shuddered. "We'd have a war zone right here in middle America."

"That's right."

"Is this what it's all been about?" she asked. "Covering up a Glock switch operation?"

"There may be more yet. It could be a full-out weapons operation, selling them here and overseas.

"We agreed that Winslaw was mega-rich," Josh continued, "but there's money. And then there's *money*. Winslaw has never made any secret that he's ambitious. There are rumors he's after the governor's seat. From there, he could ride it all the way to Washington. That kind of ambition takes money. Lots and lots of money."

"But to sell weapons? If it ever got out..." She stopped, a stunned look crossing her face.

"Now you're getting it. He can't afford for this to get out. Neither of them can. That's why they want the card. That's why they're willing to kill for it."

"Why did those men take off then?"

"I don't know." He and Kylie couldn't afford to be questioned by the police again. Twice in one day was too much of a coincidence.

He grabbed her hand. "C'mon. We're getting out of here before the police show up."

Spent both emotionally and physically, they headed back to the safe house. They both needed rest. They'd just had a major break in the case, a cause for celebration, but the discovery of the Glock switch painted a grim picture.

Chapter Thirteen

A morgue didn't care how cold it was outside. It was still colder inside the sterile room with its equally sterile appointments. Josh had been in far too many of them. An occupational hazard.

An overhead fluorescent light cast the room into shadows, giving an eerie impression. Cinder-block walls and shelves of stainless steel trays with stainless steel instruments only added to the air of gloom. The overall effect was one of cold efficiency.

And death.

A day had passed since Gemma Hardin had been gunned down. Josh had wanted to be at the autopsy, and though he'd discouraged Kylie from coming, she'd insisted on accompanying him.

The medical examiner was there, meticulously washing instruments at a sink, then drying them on a precisely folded white towel. She didn't look up until she had finished her task. When she did, her face was unsmiling.

Josh had known Doris Dunnaway for several years. She was in her normal uniform of scrubs, white lab coat and Crocs. The no-nonsense doctor didn't mince words; nor did she pretty them up when reporting facts. Ordinarily, civilians weren't allowed in the morgue, but Doris had made an exception for him. She was friendly with a number of S&J operatives, who often came from various law enforcement backgrounds.

"A hollow point," she said. "Dumdums. We won't be able to match it to any other bullets. It destroyed itself along with any brain matter and anything else it came into contact with."

Josh understood the jargon. Dumdums were a particularly nasty kind of bullet, meant to obliterate their target.

Whoever shot Gemma knew what he was doing.

His attention shifted to Kylie, who was making small mewls of distress while trying valiantly to hide them. He had visited enough morgues that the odor of death no longer bothered him as it once had. Not so Kylie, who looked distinctly green.

He'd attended other autopsies. Too many. It never got easier. If anything, it only got harder, especially when it was that of a young woman who should have had her whole life ahead of her.

The ME pulled a small tin of eucalyptus-scented salve from her pocket and handed it to Kylie. "Put a little of this under your nose. It'll help."

She did as suggested and smiled weakly. "Thanks."

"Anything else you can tell us about Ms. Hardin, Doc?" Josh asked.

"She was nine weeks pregnant." At this, the doctor's voice became pinched, as though the words were hard to get out.

Josh gave a low whistle.

"I can identify the fetus's paternity if I have something to match it to," she continued, voice back to its usual brisk tone. "Give me something—a hair, a coffee cup—anything belonging to the father."

Josh knew her well enough to realize that her cold manner did not mean she didn't care. It allowed her to view the results of the unspeakable acts people committed against each other without losing her professionalism and her ability to do her job. One day, he'd found her weeping after finishing an autopsy upon a six-year-old child killed in a drive-by shooting. He'd never mentioned it to her, knowing she would have been mortified upon learning he'd seen her that way.

He nodded. "Understood."

After a few more minutes, he hustled Kylie out of there. He should never have brought her, but she'd insisted. Aside from that, he didn't want to leave her alone. Their enemies were closing in.

"Pregnant," she said once they were outside. She shivered, and he knew it was not only from the cold. "Gemma must have been terrified. She knew that McCrane couldn't let that get out. No wonder she went into hiding. And we brought her killers right to her door.

"I really want this guy," she finished fiercely. "More than ever now. But first I want a shower to wash off the smell of death."

He understood. He also knew that the stink of death didn't wash away, but he didn't tell her that. They returned to the safe house, where they showered and changed clothes.

An hour later, he said, "Let's make some coffee."

Kylie nodded. "Okay."

He brewed a pot for the two of them, and they settled down at a table with a laptop, one the safe house was equipped with.

He sensed her impatience as he scrolled through several years of newspapers.

"What're you looking for?"

"Here." He pointed to an article from several years back about the closing of a plastics manufacturing factory. Further reading showed that the facility was owned by Winslaw. Things started to click into place.

"Winslaw owned a plastics factory. When plastic got a dirty reputation, the factory went under, but it wouldn't take much to retrofit it to make Glock switches."

Kylie bent over his shoulder to read from an article in the business section of the paper. "'Twenty-thousand-square-foot factory closed with over five hundred workers laid off.' I think we ought to pay a visit."

"I think you're right."

Kylie felt the familiar exhilaration of tracking down a hot lead.

The idea that Winslaw and McCrane were selling Glock switches and weapons on the black market was a terrifying one. Anyone with enough money, including terrorists like those who had kidnapped her, could buy the goods and equip their own private army.

It wouldn't take a lot to manufacture the Glock switches, but they would sell for astronomical amounts of money.

"Winslaw and McCrane could already be selling the switches," Josh said. "That means big money coming in."

Follow the money was a cliché, but it had been proven true over and over. "Where does all the money go?" she wondered aloud. "It has to show up somewhere. They can't just hide that kind of money. Not with all the regulations in place."

Something nagged at the back of her mind, something about another of Winslaw's business ventures. Then she had it. She recalled reading about him recently buying a strip mall. Such a purchase seemed out of his purview until she remembered that it held a laundromat and a dry cleaner's. "They're laundering it. Literally. Laundromats make great places to funnel money." She told Josh about the strip mall, which also contained a nail salon, a gaming arcade and a couple of low-end restaurants.

"All quick turnover businesses," Josh said in a

musing tone. "All good places to exchange dirty money for clean. The money's almost impossible to trace. By the time the authorities catch on, the dirty money has disappeared and all that is left are legitimate businesses turning a small but steady profit."

"Why haven't the feds caught on before? An operation this big is bound to have attracted notice."

"I'm sure it has. Could be they don't have sufficient proof. Or they were bought off." His pause told her that he was reluctant to finish what he'd been about to say. "Or killed off."

She let that last sink in but didn't react. "You sound like you know what you're talking about."

"I've been fighting bad guys most of my adult life. The plot doesn't change, only the characters and the scenery." The weariness in his voice told her that he had seen too much of the world's evil.

"We still don't have proof that they're behind all of this," she said. "All we have are some guesses."

"Educated guesses," he reminded her.

"That and five dollars will get you a cup of coffee."

"You're out of touch," he said, grinning. "Coffee is over six dollars now."

The factory was located in a formerly robust industrial area. Now it, along with other businesses, had been abandoned. Plywood replaced what had probably been giant maws in the walls, once occupied by windows. Gang graffiti marred the cinder blocks. It was a depressing sight.

Josh drove around back to park. No sense in advertising their presence.

"What do we expect to find here?" she asked. There was no sign of any activity, legal or illegal. Her excitement took a nosedive. Had they been wrong in thinking that Glock switches were being manufactured here?

"I don't know," Josh admitted.

The place looked like the abandoned factory it was purported to be with one exception: the doors were bolted with brand-new heavy-duty locks. "Why spend the money on new locks for an abandoned building?" she asked. Her senses came alive. Maybe they were on the right track after all.

"Maybe because it's not abandoned," he said.

They circled the building and found that part of the plywood covering a window had been ripped away. Josh pried the rest of it off. He lifted her up and swung her over the window ledge, then followed.

Kylie blinked in the dim light. At first glance, the building appeared empty, but then she saw rows of machinery stacked in a far corner. It didn't appear that production had started. Yet. Pallets held thick sheets of plastic. The same color as the Glock switch.

Had it been a prototype, a first of more to come?

She did a rough calculation of how many Glock switches could be made from the amount of plastic and the resulting mayhem. The loss of life was incalculable.

"Looks like they're getting ready to go operational soon," she said.

Josh put a finger to his lips and pointed to the front of the building. The click of metal against metal told her that someone was opening the front doors.

She looked to the window, but he shook his head. No time.

They hid behind a pile of what looked like discarded machinery.

"The boss isn't gonna like that you used the

switch on the lady journalist and that guy," they heard a man say.

"Doesn't matter," another responded. "They'll be dead soon enough."

A coarse laugh ensued. "When you're right, you're right." The first man made a hissing noise. "That window," he said. "It was boarded up earlier, wasn't it?"

"Yeah. Come to think of it, it was."

A pause. "We know you're here," the guy called out. "Might as well show yourselves."

She heard the men's footsteps echo across the space as they began searching. It was only a matter of time before they discovered Kylie and Josh's hiding place.

"Well, lookie who I found here," the first man said, stumbling upon them. His partner joined him.

Josh and Kylie stood. "Get out of here," he said. When Josh motioned for her to move behind him, she refused and stepped out so that she faced the two men.

"I told you to get out of here," Josh repeated.

"I don't take orders from you," Kylie retorted. "They're two of them. You need me."

She took the measure of the man who had

appeared to single her out. The other man faced off with Josh.

"One thing you can say about McCrane and Winslaw is that they have friends in low places," she said to nobody in particular.

The men cackled out rough-sounding laughs.

"We could shoot you right now," the smaller man said.

"You could," she agreed, "but then you'll never get what's on my camera. That's what you want, isn't it? I don't imagine your boss will be very happy with you."

He appeared to think about it. "I could break every bone in your body."

"Could you? You look to me like someone who's all hat and no cattle."

A scowl replaced his smirk. The time for wordplay was over. Her man came in hard and fast. She sidestepped, gratified when his own momentum carried him to the ground.

"You like playing, little girl?" the man asked upon picking himself up.

"I like winning."

He swept out his leg and tried to trip her, but she danced out of the way. So far he'd only been testing her. Now would come the real fight.

Josh would have his hands full with his man;

she couldn't depend upon him to come to her aid. This was her fight.

When the thug reached for her this time, he found his target. So large were his hands that the expanse between his thumb and little finger completely circled her neck. He could crush her windpipe if she didn't escape his grasp within the next few seconds.

She brought her knee up and aimed for his groin. *Nailed it.*

Immediately, he released her. The agony she read in his gaze told her she'd gotten in a good blow, but would it be enough to get him to back off?

She had her answer in a second when he advanced once more, grabbed her hair and slammed her head into the wall. The man probably outweighed her by eighty or more pounds. He'd obviously been combat trained. When he threw a punch at her neck, she dodged and took it on her shoulder instead. Pain sang down her arm all the way to her fingers.

She couldn't let it stop her. Her life depended on it, as well as Josh's—she had to keep this man from joining the attack on him.

If she could only hold out until Josh finished off his opponent. She dared not look his way, not wanting to distract him. Plus, she needed to fix all of her attention on the man who looked like he was only getting started on her.

She twisted her leg around his ankle and yanked forward. When he fell, she fell with him, but she was prepared and rolled away as soon as they hit the ground. She didn't stay down.

He wanted to play rough? Well, so could she. She was on him, delivering blows, one after another. Some he managed to dodge, others he took. She smelled blood. His and hers.

For a half a moment, her vision grayed from where he'd slammed her head against the wall. Pain throbbed through the side of her head, and she kept consciousness through sheer will.

Shake it off.

Fury screamed through her, and she jammed her fingers into his eyes. He yowled. She followed up with a fist to the underside of his chin.

He staggered back. When his phone suddenly chirped with the notification of a text, he pulled it out and glanced at it. "We gotta go," he told his partner. The man speared her with a hate-filled glare. "Another time, sweetheart."

"You okay?" Josh asked her after the men hurried out.

The side of her head still rang from the nasty blow she'd taken.

"Kylie." The alarm in his voice had her squaring her shoulders.

"I'm fine."

"Must have been something important to have them tearing out of here," he said.

"Like McCrane calling them to another job. I can't say I'm disappointed. My guy was about to mop the floor with me."

"Don't sell yourself short. You were a real tiger." He paused. "You could have taken off, but you held your own and then some."

At his words, a surge of pride swept through her, and she pumped her fist in the air.

Her flash of victory dissipated, and she expelled a breath slowly. "Is this ever going to be over?"

"It will be. We just have to hang on."

She wished she believed that.

Kylie's words stayed with him as he drove. She had been right when she'd voiced aloud her fear that the goon who'd attacked her would have been mopping the floor with her in another minute.

He couldn't keep putting her in jeopardy, but how was he to keep her safe?

"Let me take you away," he said. "Put you somewhere safe. I'll come back and deal with McCrane and Winslaw." Even as he said the words, he knew she wouldn't agree.

But he had to try.

"You know that's not going to work," she said, shaking her head. "They won't give up until they have what they want. It's not just the SD card. They want me, and they want me dead."

"Don't you trust me? I said I'd take care of them."

"I trust you more than anyone I know." Her sigh tore at his heart. She sounded infinitely weary. At the same time, there was hard resolve in her eyes.

One of the things he most admired about her was her indomitable spirit. She wasn't going to give this up. No matter what.

"You've done more for me than I had a right to ask. And I wouldn't blame you if you wanted out. But I'm sticking around," she said. "I won't run. I can't. If I do, I'll never be able to trust myself again." She heaved out a breath, as though the words had cost her the last of her remaining energy.

"You aren't responsible for bringing down a

crime syndicate or a corrupt politician. Write the story, take the pictures, but let the professionals handle it." The words were right, but he heard the pleading in them. The last thing he felt like right now was a professional. His feelings for Kylie had mixed him up until he didn't recognize himself.

"Someone has to stand up and say 'enough.'"

"It doesn't have to be you."

"Why not?" she challenged.

She had him there. "Because..."

"Because why?"

He couldn't tell her. Didn't have the words. The truth was that he was falling for her all over again. Or maybe he'd never stopped loving her. And didn't think he'd survive if she was hurt. Or worse.

Kylie clasped her hands in her lap. "I'm not going anywhere."

He'd known that, but he'd had to try. His only option now was to protect her at all costs.

Chapter Fourteen

Back at the S&J safe house, Kylie fixed supper. It was simple fare, a can of chili and a cornbread mix she'd taken from the pantry. She and Josh ate heartily and then cleaned up together.

"You're being awfully quiet," she said.

"Lots to think about."

"Want to share?"

"Maybe later. I'm still trying to get it straight in my mind. When I do, I'll let you know."

He bent to put dirty dishes in the dishwasher. When he straightened, he stood as rigid as the soldier he'd been. It did her heart good to see it. Despite not knowing what they would do next, despite still having targets on their backs, despite everything, she smiled.

Knowing Josh hadn't suffered any permanent effects from the infection was all that mattered. The rest of the stuff, they'd take one day at a time. Even though her body was ready to collapse, her brain wouldn't shut down. Questions buzzed through her mind.

Apparently, his mind was equally occupied. "Who knew we were going to see Gemma Hardin?"

Kylie had asked herself the same question.

"Bernice," she answered reluctantly. "But it's not a big stretch to think that we might be looking for Gemma. Anyone who knew Mc-Crane was keeping a girlfriend on the side could have guessed that would be our next move. We could have been followed from the paper."

"But not just anyone gave us the address where we were shot at."

She could see what he was angling at but... "Bernice wouldn't set us up. Why would she?" Kylie refused to believe that her friend would set her up to be killed. Bernice had given Kylie her first real break in the business. It had been Bernice who had encouraged her to take her work overseas and tell the stories that no one else was telling. It had been Bernice who had helped pitch Kylie to other editors when she'd decided to go freelance.

Josh held up a hand, presumably to ward off any more defense of Bernice. "I don't know. What I do know, though, is that she's the one who told us that McCrane had a girlfriend, and she's the one who gave us that address."

Kylie knew Josh was only trying to talk through the possibilities, but that didn't mean she had to like it.

"Bernice gave us Gemma's old address, not the new one," she said.

"That's right," Josh said, "and we were shot at while we were at that address, if you remember."

"And at the new address," Kylie felt bound to point out. "Bernice didn't know anything about that. She couldn't have set us up there."

"You're right. But we could have been followed from Gemma's old place to her new one."

"Bernice believed in me when no one else did," she said. "She gave me my first job. I don't believe she tried to have us killed. I *won't*. We can settle this. We'll go see her tomorrow."

He was shaking his head before she'd even finished speaking. "If I'm wrong, we'll only offend her. And if I'm right, we'll give away the fact that we're onto her."

Kylie nodded, but she didn't like it. She didn't like it at all.

Though they made small talk for a short

while, the argument had put a rift between them, sending a chill through the air.

Giving them both space, she headed to one of the bedrooms. She got ready for bed and wished she knew what to do. Not for the first time, the impulse to pray returned. How tempting it was to fold her hands and pour out her heart to the Lord, asking Him to help her and Josh find the answers they needed. If she did so, however, how did she reconcile what she'd experienced in Afghanistan?

Or could she?

Her earlier belief in God had been naive, even simplistic. That belief had sustained her through most of her adult life, but she understood now it wasn't enough. Her faith had needed to grow, to stretch.

She couldn't pretend that the Lord hadn't known what was happening. Nor could she tuck the whole thing away and pretend that she hadn't witnessed such inhumanity. If she did, she would be denying the sacrifice the NGO workers had made and the courage of the villagers. And Ryan's memory.

None of this was helping, and she pushed the questions along with the images they evoked to the back of her mind. Right now, she and Josh had a mystery to solve.

Still, the question persisted in her mind of who else knew they would be at Gemma Hardin's old address at that time. Could this all be a coincidence? It was possible, but she felt it wasn't likely.

Bernice might have talked to someone and inadvertently let it slip. An innocent mistake. Or someone at S&J, someone who knew Josh and Kylie were using the safe house, could have sold them out.

That didn't feel right either. And she found herself thinking thoughts she didn't like.

Come morning, neither mentioned the disagreement of last night. They tiptoed around each other, verbally and physically. Tension filled the air, making Josh know they had to do something different.

They needed a lead. It was doubtful that Winslaw and McCrane would return to the factory. So where did he and Kylie go from here?

"What do you usually do when you come across a puzzle you can't solve?" Josh asked.

"Start taking it apart. Piece by piece."

"That's what we do here. We start taking it apart. Piece by piece. And then we'll put it back together so that the pieces are in the right place."

"Thanks for being on my side." The words were so soft that he had to strain to hear them.

"There's nowhere else I'd rather be."

The words were out before he could think better of them. Still, he didn't want to take them back. Sharing the last few days with Kylie had made him think of eleven years ago. They had both changed, but his feelings for her hadn't. If anything, they'd grown stronger.

She was no longer a young girl and he a boy only a few years older. They'd stretched themselves and been tried in ways neither had foreseen.

"You look like you're a thousand miles away," she said.

He shook his head. More like eleven years away. She was even prettier now than she was then, but it wasn't only her beauty that pulled him. It was her integrity, her determination to do the right thing even if it put her in jeopardy, that drew him to her.

It was his job to make certain that it didn't cost her life.

★ ★ ★

"Can you do a search of all of Winslaw's appearances and activities in the last…let's say… six months?" Josh asked. "I want to get an idea of where he's been, who he's been seeing, anything you can find."

"No problem." Kylie booted up the laptop and started. A first pass didn't reveal anything interesting. The lieutenant governor had visited two veterans who had just celebrated their ninety-ninth birthdays. Nothing there. Then there was a visit to the children's hospital and another to a ribbon-cutting ceremony for a new civic center.

She did another pass, deeper this time. Still nothing. What was she missing? She tried different combinations of words and still couldn't make any connections to McCrane.

She looked up. "Nothing so far, but it isn't going to be anything that shows up right off. Something small, maybe. Something you might not think much of unless you were looking closely."

"If it's that small, how are we going to see it?" he asked.

"Oh, it will stand out once we see it, and we'll wonder why we didn't click on it right away. Once we see it, we won't be able to unsee it."

More research. And still no results. What was she missing? The question taunted her.

Then she saw it. There was a second trip made to the nursing home in which Winslaw had visited several elderly men. That was a goodwill publicity move. There couldn't be anything there... But further reading showed that the LG had made several more trips to the facility. Two faces recurred regularly in photos.

Two men, both ninety-nine according to the article, smiled at the lieutenant governor in one photo. He had wedged himself in between them, with a big birthday cake taking center stage. Other elderly residents in suit jackets crowded the stage around him.

She studied the deeply lined faces of the two men. Given their permission, they'd make wonderful studies for portraits, and she made a mental note to visit the care facility when this was all over.

While one man's eyes wore a vague expression, the other had a piercing gaze that looked like he had seen much of the world and hadn't forgotten a thing.

Her gaze remained riveted on the picture

until she grew impatient with herself. But could a ninety-nine-year-old man be involved with what was going on?

"You see something," Josh said. "What is it?"

She pointed to the story on the screen. "I'm not sure. But I keep coming back to it."

She read the story to him. "Winslaw might not be the brightest bulb in the chandelier, but he doesn't waste his time on things that don't matter. So why is he making return visits to this particular place?" And why were there two recurring faces? The photos showed Winslaw with several different men, always clustered together in groups, over the course of his visits. But she'd spotted the same two men in several of the pictures. If it hadn't been for the one man's piercing gaze that had captured her attention, she might not have noticed.

She did a little more digging and came up with the names of the men. Lyle Thompson and Omar Redken.

A deeper search revealed that Redken had been involved in organized crime in the fifties.

"Wow," Josh said, reading over her shoulder. "Looks like he did it all."

The article described how Redken had run

Colorado's crime family with an iron fist, only being taken down on tax evasion charges.

"Like Al Capone," she murmured.

"Just like. Redken served twelve years in prison," he read further.

Something scratched at the corner of her memory, something she should remember, but it slipped away. The scratching sensation told her that it was important. But what? She had a feeling that if she could pinpoint it, they might be able to put together more pieces of the puzzle.

"It's time for another road trip," Josh said.

Familiar excitement zinged through her at the thought of tracking down a lead. "When we get to the nursing home, let me take point," she said.

"You can't go."

"What do you mean I can't go?"

"It's too risky." She was about to protest when he continued, "If I'm caught, I can talk my way out of it, or call for backup. If they get you, there's nothing they won't do to get those photos, and after that they'd have no use for you. We need to keep you safe—if we keep you safe, we keep the story safe until you can get it out to the right people."

Emotion clogged her throat. She knew he was trying to protect her, but maybe he had a point. "Do one thing for me," she asked.

"What's that?"

"Be careful. And come back." *To me*, she nearly added but stopped herself in time.

When had she stopped thinking of Josh as her protector and started thinking of him as the man she wanted to return to her?

Chapter Fifteen

Josh understood Kylie didn't like being left behind. If the positions had been reversed, he'd have felt the same way, but he couldn't risk her being identified.

The care facility was upscale, posh even, the appointments quietly elegant, the staff courteous and helpful.

When he was shown to a table in the dining room where he was told Mr. Redken sat, he noted the domed plate covers, fine silverware and fresh flowers. It appeared the residents lived the good life.

"Mr. Redken, I'm Jake Greene, a graduate student doing my dissertation on organized crime," he said. "I was hoping you would give me your impressions."

Redken looked up and stuck out his hand. "Omar Redken." His gaze moved over Josh, seeming to miss little. "Little long in the tooth to be a student, aren't you?"

When undercover, Josh had always found it best to stick to the truth as much as possible. He had anticipated that and gave a rueful shrug. "I did a stint in the military. When I came back, I wanted to go in a different direction. Got my master's in political science and am now working on my dissertation in organized crime."

The elderly man subjected him to another long study, then gestured for an attendant to pull up a chair. "Sit if you have a mind to listen to an old man relive his past."

Redken asked Josh a series of questions, then nodded when he answered as though satisfied. "Colorado in the fifties was wide open for organized crime. Those were the days."

Josh sat back and listened as Redken talked at length about his life as one of the major players in Denver's wild and woolly days.

"We did it all," Redken said. There was no boasting in the words, only a statement of fact.

"I was one of the best," he concluded after telling story after story of bank robberies, embezzlement, money laundering, you name it. "Never was caught for any of that. It was tax evasion that took me down. Did my time. Now

I'm enjoying my 'retirement.'" He winked at the last.

Josh wanted to bring up Winslaw, but he didn't want to push the old man and steered the conversation to family. "Does your family come see you often?"

Redken smiled proudly. "I have a grandson who is making his own mark in the state. He's in state government."

Winslaw...that was the connection. Josh tried to appear casual. "Oh?"

The man nodded. "His father, my son, was born on the wrong side of the blanket, as we used to say. He took his mother's name. They both stayed out of the rackets, I'm proud to say.

"He likes to hear stories about the old days. He asks a lot of questions, always listens to the answers like he's really interested. I was something back then. Me and my boys ran the city, most of the state. We played rough, sure, but we had a code. We never hurt women or children, not like the scum who run things today. There's no honor in what they do. No honor at all."

Josh wondered if he knew his grandson was running with people like McCrane—making weapons that would indeed hurt women and children.

"You're fortunate to have a grandson who visits."

"That I am. Some of the folks here have no one who comes to see them. They pretend they don't mind, but you can tell that they do. My grandson didn't always come to visit, but lately he's been real attentive."

A shadow moved into Redken's eyes.

"Is something wrong?" Josh asked.

"He and I didn't part on the best of terms the last time he was here."

"What happened?"

"I told him I was changing my will. I'm leaving my money to this place, a scholarship if you will, to help people who can't afford a decent place to live once they can't live on their own."

In spite of the older man's background, Josh was impressed with Redken's generosity. "That's very decent of you."

"I'm not going to be around much longer. No sense in pretending that I am. I want my money to do some good after I'm gone."

"And your grandson didn't like the idea?" Josh could only imagine Winslaw's reaction.

Redken gave a wry smile. "You could say that. He said that I was stealing from him. As if spending my own money is stealing." The smile was replaced by a look of disgust. "It's not like he and his wife aren't rolling in money as it is. My lawyer's coming tomorrow with the new will. As soon as I sign it, my grandson won't be able to pester me about it anymore."

Josh and Redken continued the conversation until the older man had finished his meal and announced that he was tired. An attendant pushed his wheelchair to his room.

Josh left, eager to share with Kylie what he'd learned, but when he returned to the safe house, it was to find it empty with a note on the table. *Had an errand to run. Be back soon.*

She was all right. He repeated the words until they were burned into his brain, but he still couldn't shake the uneasiness that fell over him like a dark cloud.

Kylie couldn't sit idle. Not when Josh was out tracking down the most promising lead they'd had so far. She had to do something. She'd decided to visit Bernice and lay to rest any doubts about her friend.

Grateful that Luca had left two vehicles for her and Josh, she'd started the remaining truck and set out for the newspaper office. Now she sat in the parked vehicle outside of it. She got out of the truck and entered the building.

"Kylie, I didn't expect to see you today," Bernice said upon greeting her, "but I'm glad you stopped by."

"A lot has happened since I last saw you." Kylie recounted finding Gemma only to have her shot in front of her eyes and then related the incident at the factory.

Upon hearing of the latest events, Bernice shook her head. "You and your friend sure attract trouble. I'm just glad you're all right."

Kylie smiled. "Me, too." They talked about where her career was headed and future jobs. Everything was normal, and she was glad to put aside her doubts about a woman who had been nothing but good to her.

Her gaze drifted to a degree hanging on the wall behind the desk. Bernice Redken Kyllensgaard.

"Redken," she said aloud. "I remember you telling me that your maiden name was Redken." She had forgotten that until she'd seen the neatly printed name on the document.

Looking puzzled, Bernice nodded. "That's right."

"Any relation to Omar Redken?"

Bernice's body language shifted, and with it, the room filled with a subtle tension that hadn't been there only moments ago. "What do you know about Omar?"

"So you *are* related to him."

"He's my grandfather. Though I can never seem to find the time to see him these days," Bernice said lightly. She smiled but it seemed forced.

"I just heard his name recently." A coincidence. That's all it was, but she recalled years ago her mentor herself saying that there was no such thing as coincidence.

"Where did you hear it?"

Kylie realized she'd gone too far. "I just ran across it somewhere." She made a show of checking her phone for the time. "I'd better get going."

"Stay," Bernice said. Her tone had hardened. "I want to know where you came across the Redken name."

Her friend's words were like a weight in her chest. Kylie tried for nonchalance and stood. "I really don't remember."

"Not so fast." Bernice pulled a gun from her top drawer. "You're too nosy for your own good. That's always been your problem. Too eager to find answers without thinking through where those answers might lead you."

Kylie stared at the woman she'd called friend for seven years. Panic coursed through her. "I don't know what you're talking about."

Bernice eyed her shrewdly. "Oh, I think you do."

Kylie's mind raced, and she knew it was too late to backtrack. So she gave up pretending she didn't understand the significance of the connection. "How could you be involved with Winslaw and McCrane? They're both lowlifes who don't care how many people they kill with their jacked-up weapons."

Bernice laughed coldly. "Money. What else? You think a photojournalist's pay is bad. Trying being an editor. Especially when print media is folding up faster than you can unfold a newspaper.

"There was a time when print journalism was a respected field. Now it's a joke. Online stories appear before we can get a paper out." She flung her arm to indicate the building. "Did you notice that there's scarcely anyone working here? And those who do are all down on the production floor.

"Besides, I decided I was tired of working my butt off for next to nothing. Granville Winslaw is my cousin. When he asked me to throw in my lot with him and McCrane, I went for it. Granville's running for governor next term and needs media backing, even if it is only a washed-up newspaper. He knows I have connections."

"You and Winslaw are cousins," Kylie said, wrapping her mind around all that Bernice had just told her.

"You could say that I'm part of the family business. It doesn't hurt that the business has made us all very, very rich with more to come." She smiled menacingly.

"What happened to you?" Kylie asked in equal parts horror and incredulity.

"I got a large dose of reality. That's what happened. I always knew my family was founded on crime—there was a time when I tried to carve my own path, one of integrity. But look where that got me." She gestured with her free hand. "I'm coming up on retirement and don't intend to eat cat food because I can't afford anything else."

"You call murder getting a dose of reality?" Kylie shook her head, pleading with her eyes. "If you go to the authorities now, I'll go with you. Put in a good word for you. If you turn state's evidence, you may get off with a lighter sentence."

"You always were a Goody Two-shoes. As for your offer, thanks but no thanks. I have no intention of spending time behind bars."

"What are you going to do?"

"I'm going to hand you over to my partners." She motioned with the weapon. "Sit down and stay down. Or I'll take care of you myself."

"You mean kill me."

Bernice shrugged. "If that's what it comes to."

Kylie did as her one-time friend ordered. She needed to play it smart and stay alive.

She looked at the woman she no longer recognized, a woman she'd admired and respected for years, and wondered how she could have been so wrong. "You'd do this? Turn me over to the men who want to kill me? We were friends. Doesn't that mean anything?"

"Not as much as the money I'm going to make once we put the switches into production. I'll be richer than I ever dreamed." She paused, and a whisper of remorse crossed Bernice's face. "Look, Kylie, you're a good photojournalist, and I'm sorry you got caught up in this, but there's nothing I can do."

"You can let me go."

Bernice barked out an unladylike laugh.

"Have you heard what McCrane does to people who cross him?"

Kylie knew the man was ruthless.

"If I want to save my own hide, I don't have a choice. After that, it's out of my hands."

Kylie tried to stay calm. "And you think that excuses you?"

Bernice shifted the gun from one hand to the other. "Who's to say? Besides, I've grown accustomed to the good life. How do you think I live the way I do? Do you think my salary covers the BMW and my clothes, the trips abroad?" She made a scoffing motion. "Think again. I couldn't afford a two-story walk-up on what the paper pays me."

Kylie had occasionally wondered how her editor managed to live as she did, but she'd chalked it up to family money—it turned out she'd been partially right.

"Has it all been an act?" Kylie asked. "You helping me with my career? Giving me breaks to get ahead?"

"No." Now Bernice's voice softened. "You reminded me of someone. Someone from a long time ago. She was a little naive but determined to do the right thing, just like you."

"Yourself?"

"Yes. Why the surprised look? I used to have ethics. I was a crusader when I started out in this business. Determined to show the world for what it was and then change it." She looked weary for a moment. "But then I got my eyes opened. The hard way. One of my stories was about the deputy district attorney. He was dirty as they come, and I was going to expose him." She stopped again.

"What happened?" Kylie asked.

"My editor pulled me aside and said that if I kept after that story, I'd alienate not only city hall but every other player in town. I had a choice to make. My career or my self-respect. I chose my career."

So, Bernice had started on this crooked path a long time ago. No wonder she'd agreed to Winslaw's offer. "You always told me to go after the story, no matter whose feathers I might ruffle."

"Maybe I wanted to relive my glory days through you." Bernice waved the gun at Kylie. "Now sit down and shut up before I forget that I liked you once."

Realizing that Josh would have no way to know she'd been here, Kylie tore off the gold chain she was never without and threw it to the ground, kicking it under the desk. Maybe he'd find it. Bernice pulled a roll of packing tape from her desk drawer.

Quickly and efficiently, the older woman bound Kylie's arms and legs to the chair. "McCrane will be here any minute, and then I won't have to look at your eyes so filled with righteous indignation."

"You don't mind that they're going to kill me?"

Bernice lifted a shoulder in a negligent shrug. "Why should I mind? Like I said, I gave up my ethics a long time ago."

Though Bernice had admitted to her guilt, Kylie was still struggling to take it in. How had she been so unaware of the woman's perfidy? Easy. She'd seen what she'd wanted to see.

She'd never thought of herself as naive. Somehow, though, she'd missed the clues about her longtime friend.

She had to try to make the woman see reason. "You would murder me to make a few dollars?"

"A few dollars?" Bernice's laugh grated against Kylie's nerves. "Try a few million dollars. Maybe even more. We're sitting on a gold mine."

"You always valued the truth above all else."

Kylie hitched her chin to a plaque above Bernice's desk and read, "'Facts do not cease to exist because they are ignored.'" The Aldous Huxley quote hung there, a silent indictment of what the editor had become.

For a moment, a whiff of regret moved into Bernice's eyes. "That was only so much nonsense. Money and power write their own truth." She sighed. "I'm sorry it came to this. If only you'd kept your nose out of it, everything would have been fine."

Kylie understood there would be no going back from this. Bernice had drawn her line in the sand. "I'm sorry. Sorry for you."

At that moment, McCrane showed up and, with the ease of familiarity, went to a large globe, pressed a button to reveal a small but well-stocked bar, and poured himself a drink.

Kylie had been in the office numerous times over the years but had never known the globe was anything but what it looked like.

"You're a hard person to kill, Ms. Robertson," McCrane said.

"Thank you."

He raised a brow. "It wasn't meant as a compliment."

"Nevertheless, I took it as one."

The sparring was over.

She wanted to fight, to show him, to show all of them, that she wouldn't be taken so easily, but she was bound to the chair, gift wrapped like a present with a bow on top. "I'm not alone."

"I'm counting on that. The ex-SEAL will come charging to your rescue. We'll take him out, as well."

Being used to lure Josh here sent a fiery bolt of acid spilling through her stomach. She should have held her tongue.

Winslaw showed up fifteen minutes later, one of his henchmen at his side. She recognized him as one of the men from the warehouse.

Though it was warm in the room, Winslaw didn't remove his gloves.

"What are you doing here?" Bernice asked.

"Just paying my cousin a visit while I take care of some business." When the lieutenant governor pulled a weapon, Kylie braced herself, but he didn't turn it on her. Instead, he used it on Bernice.

There was a pop, and Kylie couldn't help crying out at seeing Bernice gunned down that way. She wondered that somebody didn't hear the shot and come running, then realized that the shot was muffled. In her fear, she'd missed the suppressor upon first seeing the weapon.

"Good," McCrane said. "We were going to have to get rid of her anyway. She was getting greedy, always wanting more money."

"I can't say that I blame my cousin," the LG said. "It seems that it runs in the family."

McCrane looked annoyed. "What are you talking about?"

Winslaw bent to remove the gun from Bernice's hand. "You know that I studied accounting in school," he said. "One thing I learned is that a pile of money split three ways is a lot less than if that same money stays in one neat pile." Calmly, he put his weapon in McCrane's hand, fired it again, and then picked up Bernice's .38, making the whole thing look like a shoot-out. He didn't rush but took his time as though he was merely moving a pile of papers from one spot to another rather than planning on killing a second person in a matter of minutes.

The mobster didn't look worried, only annoyed. "What are you doing now? Stay focused. We need to move her body."

"Oh, I don't think that'll be necessary," Winslaw said.

"We can't just leave her here."

"Can't we? It'll be perfect. It will appear that you and she killed each other."

Understanding finally dawned in McCrane's eyes, and his expression grew alarmed. "You can't kill me. We're partners."

"Yeah? You were always the one giving orders, thinking you were so much smarter than me. Did you think I didn't overhear you and Bernie making jokes about me, about how ignorant I was? Well, who's the ignorant one now? And don't bother calling for your men. They're working for me now. Turns out they can be bought if the price is right."

McCrane's eyes widened. "Wait. You're wrong. I never called you—"

The mobster tried to run, but it was too late. Winslaw shot him in the back.

He then placed a decorative pillow against the gun's muzzle, held the gun in Bernice's hand and pressed the trigger, shooting the mobster once more. Seeing Kylie's horror, he only smiled. "The police will assume they shot each other."

"What about me? Are you going to shoot me, too?"

"No. You're not getting off that easy."

Kylie couldn't keep back the tears that gathered in her eyes. Whatever else Bernice had been, she hadn't deserved that.

"Isn't that sweet?" Winslaw mocked. "Too bad it's not going to help. I have to give you credit for staying one step ahead of us, but that's over. If you weren't afraid before, you should be now." The menace in his eyes underscored his words.

Kylie kept her expression impassive. Showing fear wouldn't help. Not with the man who stood over her, a pistol in his hand, gazing at her with contempt.

He ripped off her bindings and, at the last minute, grabbed the pillow he'd used to silence the shot. The man didn't miss a beat. He then hustled her out of the back door of the building but not before assigning the man with him to guard the office.

"A man will probably show up looking for her," he said, pointing at Kylie. "You know what to do with him."

Before shoving her in a car, he tied her hands behind her back with the length of tape he'd taken with him. "You couldn't leave it alone, could you?" he mused aloud. "Just had to find out what was going on. Now you know. Too bad you won't be able to write a story about it. Who knows? It might have earned you a Pulitzer."

She ignored that. Josh would come for her. But would it be in time? She couldn't depend upon being rescued. She had to save herself.

No. That wasn't right. The Lord was with her. He had always been with her, but she'd been too blind, too stubborn, too prideful to see it.

Could He forgive her?

Her heart knew He would. She only wished she hadn't waited so long to understand that He'd never left her.

Chapter Sixteen

Irritation with Kylie took a hard turn to worry when she wasn't back within an hour. Josh slammed his fist into his palm. The note she'd left told him nothing.

Where had she gone? She hadn't said anything about going somewhere this morning when he'd left. He knew they hadn't left things in a good place between them, but he'd planned on talking through things when he got back.

Didn't she realize she was still in danger?

Then he had it. Yesterday, she'd said that she wanted to go see her mentor. She planned to prove to him and to herself that Bernice wasn't dirty.

Could she really have been so foolish as to confront her friend and ask outright if she was involved in the whole nasty business of weapons trafficking?

Why didn't she wait?

He had only to look at himself to find the answer. He'd practically dared her to prove that her friend wasn't involved. To Kylie, that was as good as a challenge, and she'd never been one to back down from a challenge.

Okay. Take it easy. Could be that she'd gone there just to talk, but he knew better.

What if she'd confronted her editor and the woman had turned on Kylie? It stood to reason that she'd have a backup plan in case anyone ever caught on to her.

When he reached the newspaper office, he was confronted by a burly man who had *hired gun* written all over him. Beneath the bruises and swollen eye, Josh recognized the man as one who had tried to take him and Kylie out in the warehouse.

"Boss said how you'd probably be showing up and that I was to take care of you," the man said. "I've been wanting a rematch with you. We'll see who's the better man."

Josh didn't have time to fool with the thug. "Let's see you do it."

"I could just shoot you, but I want to have some fun with you first." He ran an appraising look over Josh.

The man came at him, fists flying. Though

his technique lacked style, he had plenty of muscle behind his punches.

Josh was ready, refusing to allow the injury to his leg to slow him down. He had two rules when it came to fights. Finish them. And finish them fast. He planted his foot, shot out a fist and served a solid blow to his opponent's nose, smashing it. While the man swiped at the blood pouring down his face, Josh rotated on his other foot and delivered a roundhouse kick to his solar plexus that sent him sprawling.

His opponent grabbed Josh's ankle, pulling him to the floor. Pain screamed through his bad leg, but he ignored it. The two men grappled for dominance until Josh pressed his thumbs against a sensitive spot on the man's neck, rendering him unconscious. He bound his wrists with plastic cuffs and pushed him out of the way.

Inside the office, he found two bodies. The relief that poured through him that neither belonged to Kylie was tempered by questions over whether she'd been there in the first place and where she was now and who had taken her.

A glint of gold caught his eye. He stooped to pick up a thin chain. Kylie's. That answered the question of if she'd been there. He pocketed the chain and prayed he'd be able to give it to her.

He examined the bodies and saw that it was a clumsy setup to make it appear that Bernice and McCrane had killed each other. The police and ME's office would find the truth. He called the police and gave a terse explanation, but despite the order to wait where he was, he took off. He didn't have time to wait around for the authorities to sort things out. He needed to find Kylie.

It didn't take a lot of brain power to know that Winslaw was behind it.

Where would he take Kylie? And then he had the answer. The plastics factory.

"Where are you taking me?" Kylie asked.

"Wouldn't you like to know?"

As Winslaw drove out of town, she recognized the scenery. They were on the way to the plastics factory.

"McCrane and Bernie always thought they were smarter than me," he said. She'd never heard anyone refer to Bernice as Bernie. "I guess I showed them."

The man's arrogance was more than galling, but maybe she could use that against him. Ego was a powerful motivator, especially for someone like Winslaw who used power and cruelty to bring his enemies down.

"How did you and McCrane get involved?"

"McCrane knew I wanted to run for governor and that I needed money. He knew I owned a strip mall as well as the factory and said we could help each other. I didn't want to climb in bed with a mobster, but he kept pushing. Finally, he did some digging and discovered that Omar Redken is my grandfather. My father never took his old man's name. Never had anything to do with him. I thought the connection was dead and buried. Until McCrane."

"People wouldn't hold it against you. You weren't even born when your grandfather was sent to jail."

"Don't you get it? Dirt sticks. If word got out that I had a mobster in my family tree, I'd be dead politically. McCrane has a way of making people fall into line. Then, when he told me about the Glock switch operation, I changed my tune. Even with a small operation, we've been raking in money hand over fist. Thanks to you, I have to find a new location, but I'll find a new place to set up shop."

"You beat McCrane at his own game."

"I let him think what everyone else does—that I'm not good for anything but playing the fool. Why do you think I was content to do just that? People are careless around fools. They think they don't pay attention to what is being said. I've picked up more juicy tidbits about colleagues and their wives by just staying quiet with a vacuous expression on my face than I ever would by spying on them.

"As for McCrane, all I had to do was bide my time. He thought he was using me, but I was using him. Just like I used the governor."

He smiled indulgently at Kylie. "People think I'm a yes-man, a gofer, but I'm ten times—twenty times—the man the governor is. He does what he's good at—making speeches and kissing babies. The rest, he leaves to me. The arrangement suits us both."

She was impressed by his willingness to play the buffoon. The man had fooled everyone. The governor, his staff, the public. Even Mc-Crane.

"It's too bad you stumbled on our little secret. You're a smart lady, but you were too smart for your own good. That never works out well."

"You're plenty smart, all right," Kylie said.

"It's just too bad that you chose to work for the wrong side."

Winslaw stretched his mouth in an ugly smirk. "The wrong side, as you put it, is the power side."

"I don't see it that way."

"No? Like I said, too bad. You could have gone places. Bernie told me about you, said you were one of the smartest people she'd ever met. She also said that you were incorruptible."

Winslaw must have been closer to her than Kylie had thought.

"I'm sorry. For Bernice. And for you. You could have made a difference in the world. A good difference."

"Oh, I'm going to make a difference, all right. You'll be hearing about it for years to come." Playfully, he tapped his temple as though to remind himself of something. "Oh, that's right. You won't be around. What a shame."

She rolled her eyes. "Are you going to murder me just like you did Bernice and McCrane?"

He laughed. "You've got spunk. I'll give you that. Too bad it's not going to save you. Pretty soon, I'll have enough money to give me the power to turn this country around and take it back to what it used to be. The governor is stepping down. People will look to me for leadership."

"You're sick."

He backhanded her.

Her face throbbed, and she did her best to ignore it. When she was able to speak again, she said, "You won't win. People will see you for what you are and be disgusted by it. The trouble with people like you is that they become so good at lying, they start to believe their own lies."

He looked like he wanted to hit her again. "You don't know what you're talking about. The people will rise up and need a leader. A strong leader who will pull them out of the mess that our country is in." His voice grew with every word until he was shouting, but he seemed unaware of it.

"It will be me that they turn to. *Me.* Do you understand?" Spittle gathered at the corners of his mouth. At the same time, his face turned more and more florid, and she wondered if he was having a stroke. She remained quiet as he pulled into the parking lot at the factory.

He stopped the car and pulled her from it. After marching her into the building, he tied her to a chair with a length of rope. Immediately, she noted that the machinery and supplies had been removed. Obviously, Winslaw had been planning this.

"I hated to get rid of everything, but the insurance settlement will come in handy. I'll start over. Bigger and better."

Insurance? "What are you going to do?"

"You'll see."

With that, he strode away from her toward the exit, pouring a can of gasoline over the floor as he went.

"You're going to torch your own factory?" Terror raced through her at the idea of being trapped inside the building as it went up in flames.

"Thanks to you and your boyfriend, it's been compromised. Good thing it's insured. I'll end up with a boatload of cash and be able to set up operations somewhere else."

"You try collecting on the insurance money, and they'll know it was you." She had to keep him talking.

"I made a point of reporting vagrants holing up in the factory, setting fires to keep warm. As for you, it isn't much of a stretch to think that you returned to snoop around some more."

"Nobody's going to believe this was an accident. The police will see the ropes and the chair."

"You know as well as I do that the ropes and chair will be burned in the fire. I won't say it's been nice knowing you. So cliché. I have some other loose ends to tie up, so you'll forgive me if I take off."

With that, he struck a match then dropped it before he exited the building. The gas he'd poured on the floor ignited immediately.

Even knowing it was hopeless, Kylie fought against the cruel bite of the rope. Fear washed through her as the heat of the flames grew stronger. The idea of being burned alive gave new energy to her struggles against the rope, but nothing was going to break it. With the acceptance that she was going to die, regret settled in her heart. She wished she had told Josh that she loved him, that she had never stopped loving him. It was too late for that; just as she feared it was too late for her.

A prayer tumbled from her lips.

It didn't seem strange to be praying. Sometime in the nightmare of staying alive in the mountains, her faith had returned. How had she ever gotten along without it?

She was grateful she'd made her peace with the Lord. She'd spent so much time being angry with Him, even when she'd known better and had actively rejected Him and His teachings in the last year. But beneath it all, the belief that had sustained her through so much of her life was still alive. Still breathing.

"Forgive me, Lord, for having been so stubborn. You did everything You could to help me see the truth, and I was too foolish to look. Whatever happens, I know You love me."

Smoke began to fill the room. She prayed it would take her before the flames, flames that were even now eating their way through the room. It was only a matter of minutes before they reached her.

Josh smelled the smoke as soon as he arrived at the factory. He'd been right. Winslaw had brought her here. He punched in 911, gave a terse description, then hung up. There was no time.

Fear such as he'd never known sent a frenzied path down his spine at the idea of Kylie burning alive. He had to get to her. Every prayer he'd ever uttered raced through his mind as he pled for Kylie's life.

"Please, Lord, keep her safe until I can get to her."

He pushed open the door, an acrid odor filling the air. He shielded his eyes and nose the best he could. The old building was going up with alarming speed.

Within him, an angry beast stirred and stretched out the claws of a predator. He'd protect her. No matter what. Even if it meant sacrificing his own life to do so. He loved her.

Had he waited too long to tell her? *Lord, please watch over Kylie until I can get to her.* Had the Lord heard his prayer? He didn't know.

The warehouse was huge. How did he go about finding her? "Kylie? Kylie! Where are you?"

Flames jumped from place to place, playing hopscotch. When one passageway was blocked, he turned to another, only to find it blocked, as well. He stayed low, all the while shouting her name. Smoke hoarsened his voice, reducing it to a grunt, but he refused to quit.

Something caught his attention, a sound different from the crackle of the flames. He paused, listened. Had he imagined it? No.

A faint voice reached him. "Josh? Stay back."

"Kylie!"

"Go back. I'm surrounded by flames."

"Not happening." He followed her voice, fighting his way through the conflagration, and then saw her bound to the chair. He stopped, struggling to breathe and to absorb the terrifying scene.

"Hold on," he shouted over the crack of fire and the hiss of smoke. "I'm coming."

Getting to Kylie meant walking through fire. He would have done that and more if it meant saving the life of the woman he loved. His heart stopped at the sight of her, helpless and afraid. Panic flared in her eyes while her mouth trembled as the fire drew ever closer.

Winslaw would pay for this. He would pay dearly.

The grim promise fueling his determination, Josh fought the ropes that bound her, even as a flame singed his arm. Seeing that he was getting nowhere with the knots, he kicked the chair legs, breaking them, then lifted her into his arms, despite her hands and legs still tied to the chair. His injured leg buckled for a moment, and he wasted valuable seconds straightening it.

Now he had to reverse his steps, this time carrying her. He hunched over and did his best to shield her from the worst of the blaze.

If ever he needed the Lord's protection, it was now. A prayer on his lips, he forged ahead. "Hang on," he shouted and ran through the wall of fire.

It took only seconds to make it to the other side of the blaze, but those seconds were the longest of his life. He ignored the intensity of the heat. He ignored the hiss of the smoke. He ignored the roar of the flames.

He ignored everything but saving Kylie.

Sparks landed on his arm, igniting the sleeve of his jacket. With both arms around Kylie, he wasn't able to put out the flames and did his best to protect her from them. Pain speared through him, but he scarcely noticed.

Outside, he carried her away from the factory and lowered her to the ground. After putting out the flames on his sleeve, he ran his hands over her. Nothing appeared to be broken. When she got to her feet, he steadied her as she swayed. "Are you okay?" he asked.

"Never mind about me. Your arm." Her eyes filled with tears.

"It'll heal." He brushed his lips over hers. "I thought I'd lost you. I thought I'd lost you." His voice broke.

She wasn't given the opportunity to respond when the scream of sirens screeched through the frigid air.

"The EMTs are here," he said and was glad to note that his voice had steadied.

They were both checked out and treated for smoke inhalation. The burn on his arm was wrapped in gauze.

It wasn't the first time he'd endured burns. While deployed in the Stand, he'd pulled a buddy out of a burning building, his hands and arms suffering second-and third-degree burns. The burns had healed, though he still bore the scars. These wounds would heal, as well.

"Are you sure you don't want to go to the hospital?" Kylie asked.

"I'll be fine." He was a lot more interested in finding Winslaw than he was in seeing a doctor. "Do you know where Winslaw went?"

"He said something about tying up a loose end."

Loose end? Kyllensgaard and McCrane were dead. Who did that leave? And then it came to him. The LG's grandfather. The change of will. He had to do it today or it would be too late.

Josh grabbed her arm and urged her to the truck.

"Where are we going?" she asked.

"To prevent another murder."

They found Winslaw in his grandfather's room, his hands gripping a pillow, holding it over the elderly man's face. Redken appeared to be asleep.

"It's over, Winslaw," Josh said. "You're done."

Surprise flickered in his eyes before he said, "You've got nothing on me."

"Really?" Josh motioned Kylie in so that Winslaw could see her.

"Why won't you die?" he shouted in furious disbelief upon seeing her. In the same instant, he pulled a gun from his waistband.

Before Josh could react, help came from an unexpected source. Redken sliced a hand across Winslaw's wrist, causing him to drop the gun.

Kylie snatched up the gun and pointed it at the lieutenant governor.

"You made war on a woman?" his grandfather wheezed. "Have I taught you nothing? And then you try to kill me? I should have known it was only my money you were interested in."

Kylie stared Winslaw down. "Now it's your turn to be afraid."

Chapter Seventeen

It was time. Time to tell Josh of her feelings for him, feelings that had only intensified over the last hour after he'd saved her from the fire.

They could have both died in the warehouse inferno, and she refused to allow another minute to go by without telling him that she loved him. Life was too fragile to waste time wondering what might have been.

But she wasn't given the opportunity.

She had the satisfaction of seeing Winslaw being led away in cuffs, protesting at the top of his voice, and then she and Josh were whisked away to make statements to the authorities where they were split up to give testimony. The feds, in the form of the ATF, were brought in and statements had to be made all over again. The Alcohol, Tobacco, Firearms and Explosives people grilled them until Kylie was falling-down tired.

"Tell us why you didn't go to the authorities when you first found out about McCrane and Winslaw," an agent directed.

"As I said *earlier*," she said with heavy emphasis, "we didn't have any proof. Think about it. Would you have believed us if we'd gone to you with a picture of the two men together and nothing else?"

The agent had the grace to blush. "Probably not."

The questions continued until both the local police and federal agency were satisfied. Exhausted, she and Josh stumbled out of the precinct. She needed a shower in the worst way followed by sleep.

"Shall I take you home?" he asked.

She shook her head. "Let's go back to the safe house."

Though she could have gone to her condo, she couldn't stomach the idea of facing the mess she would encounter there. But that wasn't the real reason she suggested they return to the safe house. She wanted more time with Josh. The future was by no means settled.

The following morning, they packed up their belongings. She looked about the S&J safe house and found herself reluctant to leave. Though they'd been there for only a short while, it had felt like home in a way her condo never had. Because she had shared it with Josh. A little hum danced in her throat at the thought.

"What now?" Josh asked.

"I have a story to write." She paused. "And you?"

"I need to go back to work. My vacation is over."

"Some vacation." How did she thank him for what he'd done for her? Would he be insulted if she offered to pay him?

"Thank you. You saved my life."

He nodded. "I think we're pretty well even given that you saved my life, too."

She wanted to say so much more that her jaw ached from keeping it inside. Did she have the courage to tell him what was in her heart? The moment was snatched from her when his phone rang.

His gaze never leaving hers, he answered the call. "Gideon. Yeah, I was just heading into work now. I'll be there in forty-five minutes." He closed the phone. "My boss."

"Oh." She was hoping they'd have more time before they had to return to their lives. More time to find out the answer to the question *Who might we become together?* "I guess you'd better go."

"I'll see you home first."

Whatever she'd been about to say would keep. The ride to his place, where she would pick up her car, was quiet, each wrapped up in their own thoughts.

"I'll see you later," Josh said upon letting her out.

"Later."

She didn't want to leave him with things left unsaid between them. Reluctantly, she got out of the car and went into her condo. She had to set about getting her life back on track. The mindless chores of cleaning the condo and doing laundry gave her time to think. Perhaps she and Josh could have a future together.

A frisson of pleasure zinged through her at the thought.

By the time she had put the condo to rights and had outlined a story that would no doubt rock not just the state capital but the entire state and much of the Southwest, she was well and truly tired.

She reflected on all that had happened in the last days. With the photo and the prototype of the Glock switch as evidence, there was even more proof of what McCrane and Winslaw had been up to.

So when she went to bed it was with the expectation of sleeping soundly. And she did, until her dreams took her back to the prison camp, then inexplicably placed her in the burning building. Cries from mothers and children segued into the crackle and hiss of fire and smoke.

"No! No!"

She reached for a weapon, anything with which to defend herself. Grasping wildly, she grabbed the first thing her hand encountered.

A scream awakened her. She looked about to see where it had come from, only to realize that it was her own. Disoriented, drenched in sweat, she sat up in bed and found herself gripping a lamp, ready to wield it like a weapon.

She remained sitting, shaking uncontrollably. When the worst of it was over, she tried standing. Her knees buckled, but she stiffened them and took a step. The act of forcing one foot in front of the other took her back to the time in the mountains when she had struggled dragging the travois. She had gotten through that; she would get through this, as well.

She'd learned from experience that there was

no point in trying to go back to sleep and went through a ritual she'd developed. First prayer. Ever since she'd invited the Lord back into her life, she'd made prayer a priority.

Hot chocolate, because even though she was covered in sweat, she also had the chills. A warm shower, to wash away the sweat. The familiar routine calmed, soothed. And, finally, work.

She needed the work, the doing. She booted up her laptop and worked on an article, all the while doing her best to put this latest episode out of her mind, but it wouldn't stay in the tidy box where she assigned it. It snuck back, creeping into her thoughts in such an insidious manner that she finally let it have its way.

Deal with it now. Get it over with. She wrapped her arms around herself and rocked back and forth. When the tears came, she let them have their way.

Why now? Everything was going well. What if it rendered her unable to write as it had in previous instances when she'd fallen behind in meeting her deadlines?

But that wasn't the worst of it.

There'd be no future with Josh. There'd be no future with anyone.

★ ★ ★

Josh knew there were things left unsaid between him and Kylie. He'd longed to tell her of his feelings, but Gideon's call had postponed that. Maybe it was just as well. They both needed a little normalcy before they delved into whatever there was between them.

The assignment he'd been given was a one-day protection detail, escorting a teenage media star to her hotel, followed by shopping and then a luncheon being held in her honor, all the while shielding her from the paparazzi. Her regular bodyguard, who would normally have been on the job, had suffered a brief bout of food poisoning and had been in the hospital overnight. By midnight, he was back on duty.

Josh had never been so relieved to end an assignment. Going shopping and attending luncheons weren't in his wheelhouse. He returned home and slept in his own bed for the first time in over a week. Not surprisingly, he slept soundly.

The following morning, he drove to Kylie's condo. Was it too soon to tell her of his feelings? Did she need more time? The last thing he wanted to do was frighten her by coming on too hard, too fast. She'd proved herself time and again in the mountains and afterward, but he knew that she still didn't believe in herself as he did.

He rang the doorbell, waited impatiently.

Worry danced through him the moment he saw her face. It looked ravaged, as though she'd been seriously sick. What had happened?

And then he knew. A PTSD episode. The signs were all there. The skin drawn tautly over her cheekbones. The shaking hands. The smile that wasn't a smile at all.

He reached for her, but she neatly sidestepped his embrace. He followed her inside.

"You had another episode." It wasn't a guess but a statement of fact.

She nodded.

"Let me help you. You don't have to do it alone."

"I can handle it. Go now, please." She held the door open, clearly indicating that he should leave.

He ignored that and closed the door behind him. "Can you tell me about it?"

She took a seat on the sofa and, with a heavy air of resignation, gave the gist of the attack.

He nodded, absorbing what she said, all the while wondering how he could help her defeat the terrors that had taken hold of her.

"You don't have to be alone." Had he already said that? "I'll stay. We'll deal with it together. Just like we did in the mountains."

She shook her head even as he said the words. "I do better on my own. I have a routine. Besides, you have work."

He sliced through the air to dismiss the idea that he'd put work before her. No job was more important than Kylie.

Tears ran in tiny rivulets down her cheeks. He longed to wipe them away but didn't dare.

"I can't be with you, Josh. If you're honest with yourself, you'll see that I'm right and that it won't work. I'm too broken."

It tore his heart into slivers of pain to hear the words. "You shouldn't be alone." And he realized his error immediately.

Her head came up. "Who are you to tell me what I should or shouldn't do?"

"I'm sorry. That came out wrong."

"Go. Please, just go."

It wasn't in his nature to give up. He wanted to rail against the trauma that had her in its grip. He could fight that, but he couldn't fight her.

This wasn't over. He'd make her see that they belonged together. But it wouldn't be today.

★ ★ ★

Kylie sat back, startled when she noted that she'd been working for five hours straight. Satisfied with her work, she saved it, then turned off the computer.

In the last week, Winslaw had been arrested for murder, conspiracy to commit murder, weapons trafficking and a host of other felonies. In addition, he was facing RICO charges. If he was convicted, the Racketeer Influenced and Corrupt Organizations charges alone would keep him in prison for decades. That, plus the murder charges, would see to it that he didn't see the outside of a prison for the rest of his life.

It seemed like an eternity since she'd seen Josh. A dozen times, she'd been tempted to go to him, to tell him that she loved him with all of her heart and always would. And a dozen times, she'd rejected the impulse.

She was broken. Her experiences in the prison camp had irrevocably damaged her. How did she tell him that she couldn't let anyone, not even him, get close to her?

She'd once thought she was strong, but that belief had been shattered by the PTSD, which had her questioning everything she'd once believed about herself. She'd pushed herself to finish three articles in record time, afraid if she slowed down even slightly, the PTSD would lay claim to her again. She'd shop them around to various news magazines and pray they'd be picked up.

A tiny movement caught her attention as a spider wove a small web in the corner of the kitchen. She watched the progress, noting how the creature took its time. It didn't push itself. No, it simply kept at the task, patient and meticulous.

Her therapist had tasked her to be aware of occasions when she was impatient with herself and to find new and more healthy ways of dealing with life's challenges. When the doorbell rang, she looked at her sweats and wished she'd taken time earlier to change her clothes and brush her hair out from its straggly ponytail.

Josh stood there, tall, strong and unswerving. He was everything she'd ever wanted. "Can I come in?"

She stepped back, gestured him inside.

"I couldn't stay away any longer," he said and drew her to him.

Awareness spiked when he skimmed her cheek with the back of his hand.

She couldn't pull away, especially not when

his voice turned soft and his touch was as gentle as thistledown.

"You told me once you were a survivor. You survived the prison camp. You survived being chased by killers in the mountains. You survived the fire. Are you telling me now that you're going to let one puny episode of PTSD defeat you?"

She pulled back. Puny? Is that what he thought? "You don't know anything about it."

"Then tell me."

"If you'd been with me during that episode, I could have hurt you, knocked you unconscious. Maybe worse." She shuddered, thinking of what could have happened.

"I've done my own share of surviving. I was out in those mountains with you, if you remember." He slanted her a look inexplicably filled with humor. "Do you think someone who weighs a buck five is going to take me out?"

The question was asked lightly, but she heard the challenge in the words.

Josh was that rare combination, a man both strong and vulnerable, hard when needed but tender in the right places. Right now, it was the vulnerable and tender parts that called to her in ways she was only beginning to understand.

Eleven years ago, she'd been a young girl, more in love with the idea of being in love than she was with a man. Today, she was a woman who recognized the difference.

Impulsively, she pressed her cheek to his, the barest caress.

He held her in place when she started to pull away. "Stay," he said, his voice so filled with pleading and hope that she was nearly brought to tears. "Just stay."

The knowledge that he was as moved as she was strengthened her. It also scared her.

She wanted a future with him, a home, a family. Could she handle that, knowing a PTSD episode could launch a sneak attack at any moment?

"Leaving you was the hardest thing I ever did," he said. "I never forgot you, never stopped loving you."

"Nor I you."

"I love you. I always have. I always will." With infinite gentleness, he kissed her, a kiss filled with sweet promise.

She didn't resist and returned the kiss. "And I love you. You fill me up. You make me want more. To *be* more."

"You are everything I've ever wanted," he

said. "I don't deserve you, but I'll do my best to be the man you deserve." She heard it in his voice, the fierceness and the love.

Frissons of warmth raced down her spine. "We have the next fifty or sixty years to work on it."

"You're pretty smart for a lady in sweats and a ponytail."

There would be a tomorrow for them. And all the tomorrows after that. She was exactly where she wanted to be.

Forever.

★ ★ ★ ★ ★

brand new stories each month

Romantic Suspense

Danger. Passion. Drama.

MILLS & BOON

Keep reading for an excerpt of a new title
from the Intrigue series,
BIG SKY DECEPTION by B.J. Daniels

Chapter One

Clay Wheaton flinched as he heard the heavy tread of footfalls ascending the fire escape stairs of the old Fortune Creek Hotel. His visitor moved slowly, purposefully, the climb to the fourth and top floor sounding like a death march.

His killer was coming.

He had no idea who he would come face-to-face with when he opened the door in a few minutes. But this had been a long time coming. Though it wasn't something a man looked forward to even at his advanced age.

He glanced over at Rowdy lying lifeless on the bed where he'd left him earlier. The sight of his lifelong companion nearly broke his heart. He rose and went to him, his hand moving almost of its own accord to slip into the back under the Western outfit for the controls.

Instantly, Rowdy came to life. His animated eyes flew open, his head turned, his mouth gaping as he looked around. "We could make a run for it," Rowdy said in the cowboy voice it had taken years to perfect. "It wouldn't be the first time we've had to vamoose. You do the running part. I'll do the singing part."

The dummy broke into an old Western classic and quickly stopped. "Or maybe not," Clay said as the lumbering footfalls ended at the top of the stairs and the exit door creaked open.

"Sorry, my old friend," Clay said in his own voice. "You need to go into your case. You don't want to see this."

"No," Rowdy cried. "We go down together like an old horse who can't quite make it home in a blizzard with his faithful rider. This can't be the end of the trail for us."

The footsteps stopped outside his hotel room door, followed swiftly by a single knock. "Sorry," Clay whispered, his voice breaking as he removed his hand, folded the dummy in half and lowered him gently into the special case with Rowdy's name and brand on it.

Rowdy the Rodeo Cowboy. The two of them had traveled the world, singing and joking, and sharing years and years together. Rowdy had become his best friend, his entire life after leaving too many burning bridges behind them. "Sorry, old friend," he whispered unable to look into Rowdy's carved wooden face, the paint faded, but the eyes still bright and lifelike. He closed the case with trembling fingers.

This knock was much louder. He heard the door handle rattle. He'd been running for years, but now his reckoning was at hand. He pushed the case under the bed, straightened the bed cover over it and went to open the door.

Behind him he would have sworn he heard Rowdy moving in his case as if trying to get out, as if trying to save him. Old hotels and the noises they made? Or just his imagination?

Too late for regrets, he opened the door to his killer.

"MOLLY LOCKHART?" The voice on the phone was male, ringing with authority.

"Yes?" she said distractedly as she pulled her keyboard toward her, unconsciously lining it up with the edge of her desk as she continued to type. She had a report due before the meeting today at Henson and Powers, the financial institution where she worked as an analyst. She wouldn't have taken the call, but her assistant had said the caller was a lawman, the matter urgent, and had put it through.

"My name's Sheriff Brandt Parker from Fortune Creek, Montana. I found your name as the person to call. Do you know Clay Wheaton?"

Her fingers froze over the keys. "I'm sorry, what did you say? Just the last part please." She really didn't have time for this—whatever it was.

"Your name was found in the man's hotel room as the person to call."

"The person to call about what?"

The sheriff cleared his throat. "Do you know Clay Wheaton?"

"Yes." She said it with just enough vacillation that she heard the lawman cough. "He's my...father."

"Oh, I'm so sorry. I'm afraid I have bad news. Mr. Wheaton is dead." Another pause, then, "He's been murdered."

"Murdered?" she repeated. She'd known that she'd be getting a call one day that he had died. Given her father's age it was inevitable. He was close to sixty-five. But *murdered*? She couldn't imagine why anyone would want to murder him unless they'd seen his act.

"I hate to give you this kind of news over the phone," the sheriff said. "Is there someone there with you?"

"I'm fine, Sheriff," she said, realizing it was true. Her father had made his choice years ago when he'd left her and her mother to travel the world with—quite literally—a dummy. There was only one thing she wanted to know. "Where is Rowdy?"

The lawman sounded taken aback. "I beg your pardon?"

"My father's dummy. You do know Clay Wheaton is... was a ventriloquist, right?"

"Yes, his dummy. It wasn't found in his hotel room. I'm afraid it's missing."

"Missing?" She sighed heavily. "What did you say your name was again?"

"Sheriff Brandt Parker."

"And you are where?"

"Fortune Creek, Montana. I'm going to need to know who else I should notify."

"There is no one else. Just find Rowdy. I'm on my way there."

BRANDT HUNG UP and looked at the dispatcher. The sixty-something Helen Graves was looking at him, one eyebrow tilted at the ceiling in question. "Okay," he said. "That was the strangest reaction I've ever had when telling someone that their father's been murdered."

"Maybe she's in shock."

"I don't think so. She wants me to find the dummy—not the killer—but the *dummy*."

"Why?"

"I have no idea, but she's on her way here. I'll try the other number Clay Wheaton left." The deceased had left only two names and numbers on hotel stationery atop the bureau next to his bed with a note that said, *In case of emergency*. He put through the call, which turned out to be an insurance agency. "I'm calling for Georgia Eden."

"I'll connect you to the claims department."

"Georgia Eden," a young woman answered cheerfully with a slight southern accent.

Brandt introduced himself. "I'm calling on behalf of Clay Wheaton."

"What does he want now?" she asked impatiently.

"Are you a relative of his?"

"Good heavens, no. He's my client. What is this about? You said you're a sheriff? Is he in some kind of trouble?"

"He was murdered."

"Murdered?" He heard her sit up in her squeaky chair, her tone suddenly worried. "Where's Rowdy?"

What was it with this dummy? "I...don't know."

"Rowdy would have been with him. Clay never let him out of his sight. He took Rowdy everywhere with him. I doubt he went to the toilet without him. Are you telling me Rowdy is missing?"

Brandt ran a hand down over his face. He had to ask. "What is it with this dummy?"

"I beg your pardon?"

"I thought you might be more interested in your client's murder than his...doll."

Her words came out like thrown bricks. "That...*doll* as you call it, is insured for a very large amount of money."

"You're kidding."

"I would not kid about something like that since I'm the one who wrote the policy," Georgia said. "Where are you calling from?" He told her. "This could cost me more than my job if Rowdy isn't found. I'll be on the next plane."

"We don't have an airport," he said quickly.

She groaned. "Where is Fortune Creek, Montana?"

"In the middle of nowhere, actually at the end of a road in the mountains at the most northwest corner of the state," he said. "The closest airport is Kalispell. You'd have to rent a car from there."

"Great."

"If there is anything else I can do—"

"Just find that dummy."

"You mean that doll."

"Yes," she said sarcastically. "Find Rowdy, *please*. Otherwise...I'm dead."

Brandt hung up, shaking his head as he stood and reached for his Stetson. "Helen, if anyone comes looking for me, I'll be over at the hotel looking for a ventriloquist's dummy." She frowned in confusion. "Apparently, that's all anyone cares about. Meanwhile, I have a murder to solve."

As he headed out the door for the walk across the street to the hotel, he couldn't help being disturbed by the reactions he'd gotten to Clay Wheaton's death. He thought about the note the dead man had left and the only two numbers on it.

Had he suspected he might be murdered? Or traveling alone—except for his dummy—had he always left such a note just in case? After all, at sixty-two, he was no spring chicken, his grandmother would have said.

Whatever the victim's thinking, how was it that both women had cared more about the dummy than the man behind it?

Maybe worse, both women were headed this way.

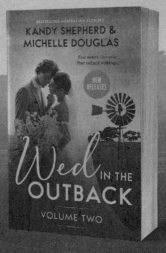

Subscribe and fall in love with a Mills & Boon series today!

You'll be among the first to read stories delivered to your door monthly and enjoy great savings.

WE SIMPLY LOVE ROMANCE